PASSION'S TORMENT

Travis reached up, tracing his fingertips down the side of her face, his touch so light that Kate wasn't even certain he was making contact with her flesh at all.

"You feel it too, don't you?" His voice was husky.

She turned her back on him, her arms hugging her sides. This man had the power to bewitch her, to hurt her. She had to stay away from him.

But he made it so hard . . . so hard. His hands slid over the curve of her shoulders and down her arms, coming to rest just above her elbows. She did not pull away. Her head lolled back, pillowed by the hard muscles of his chest. Arching her neck sideways, she allowed him full access to the slender column of her throat.

Damn, she couldn't let him. She couldn't. But as her mind pleaded for sensibility, her body revelled in the sweet insanity of his mouth nuzzling her ear. She twisted to face him. Her hands moved of their own accord, tracking the sculpted muscles of his back. He pulled her closer; she could hardly breathe, but didn't care. She wished he would hold her tighter still. Oh, God, she had to stop this . . . had to . . .

She shifted her hands to his chest, her palms tingling against the surging beat of his heart. It was wrong, all wrong. Travis Hawke could not be the man who came so gently to her bed that long ago night. Travis Hawke was a man who seemed to have no gentleness in him, a man whose gun was an extension of his right hand. His motive wasn't love, it was a job, or worse. And in him she sensed secrets that could destroy them both . . .

CAPTIVATING ROMANCE FROM ZEBRA

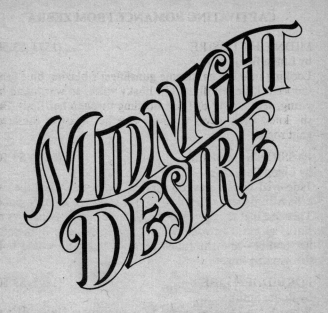

MIDNIGHT DESIRE

BY LINDA BENJAMIN

ZEBRA BOOKS
KENSINGTON PUBLISHING CORP.

ZEBRA BOOKS

are published by

Kensington Publishing Corp.
475 Park Avenue South
New York, NY 10016

First printing: April 1985

Printed in the United States of America

for Max Collins,
and his fascinating
POINT-OF-VIEW

and for the Mississippi Valley Writers Conference held annually in June in Rock Island, Illinois, proving that no matter how much you know, you can always learn more

Chapter One

1867

Kate McCullough jabbed a needle through the embroidery hoop on her lap, wincing when the needle jabbed her thigh as well. She studied her handiwork sourly, deciding the spray of violets more closely resembled a bouquet of squashed grapes. Mrs. Russell would not be pleased.

But then Kate was far from pleased herself. Her brown eyes reflected the battle she was waging with her notable temper. The battle was lost when she tried to heave away the hopeless crosspatch of cloth, only to find it securely stitched to her skirts. With a grumble of disgust she snipped the hoop free and rose to stalk across the small parlor.

How much longer would she have to put up with this maddeningly boring nonsense anyway? Even after six months she could scarcely believe her beloved father had given her up to this prison of needlework and tea parties. Not that Mrs. Russell's Finishing School was exactly a penitentiary. It was just that when compared to the rolling prairies and endless blue sky of the Kansas plains, the exclusive Boston boarding school seemed suddenly to have sprouted bars and moats.

The dimming twilight signalled the coming night in her stylishly furnished dungeon. Kate considered leaving the room shrouded in gloom to match her mood, but Mrs. Russell would be dropping by any moment now to check on the progress of her sampler. Kate lit the lamp, not certain she could put into words why she would rather sit in darkness.

Darkness to take her back to moonglow nights and woodsmoke, lowing oxen and mournful coyotes, darkness to take her home. Mrs. Russell meant well, but the woman hadn't the remotest idea how Kate could miss a place as uncivilized as Leavenworth, Kansas, a burgeoning jumping off point for travellers heading west now that the War Between the States had ended.

"Because it's my home," she sighed aloud. The only home she had ever known.

She had been too young to remember any of it, but she could well imagine her bear of a father, his red beard flowing, packing his young family's few worldly possessions into the back of a Conestoga wagon and heading west twenty-two years ago. With his lovely wife, Bonnie, and their infant daughter at his side, he had left Boston behind for good. How often had her father regaled her with the tale while they sat together around a crackling campfire?

"The family thought I left my mind back on the moors in Scotland," Bryce McCullough would boom, his sandpaper voice ripe with indignation, "how else would I dare take my dear ones to such a heathen land?" He'd hug her close, the scent of his trail-stained buckskins mingling with her own.

"And how could I not?" he demanded, his blue eyes piercing her brown ones. "How could I not take my own flesh and blood with me on the greatest journey a man could know."

8

But on the path to their new life, cholera had intruded on her father's lovingly nurtured dream. Bonnie McCullough died near a nameless creek in southern Ohio. Six weeks later a barely alive Bryce McCullough staggered into the encampment of a drifter named Dusty Lafferty, his wagon, everything he owned lost to the ravages of a flood-swollen Mississippi.

"You were squallin' to drown the thunder of God Himself," Bryce would laugh. "Tucked under my arm like you were, Dusty mistook you for a bagged fox." Dusty, who had become Uncle Dusty, a crotchety plainsman, who would die for her if she but asked.

"And the way you turned out, he wasn't too far off."

Kate giggled. "I'd rather be the fox than the chicken any day."

Scotsman and drifter had become fast friends, trying their hand at "anything the good Lord would allow — and," Bryce chuckled, "some things He didn't allow, when we were hopin' He had his back turned." Then twelve years ago the two men pooled the meager savings of a lifetime to gamble on the booming business of freight hauling, supplying new western settlements with whatever they needed to grow and prosper. McCullough Freight Company had grown and prospered as well. And Kate had been a real part of that success, traversing the spirit-sapping alkali trails right alongside her father and Dusty. God, how she missed those days!

Now here in Mrs. Russell's parlor she could only grimace ruefully, as she settled her hands on her hips to encounter yet another example of what half a year in this place had done to her. Fancy cakes and puddings combined with enforced inactivity had rounded her once wiry figure well past what she considered acceptable. Yet Mrs. Russell would accede to none of her pleas to allow her to either eat less or work outdoors more.

"A lady, Miss McCullough," the stiff-backed headmistress intoned, "does not chop wood, nor ride bareback across the grounds with her hair unpinned. Nor does a lady, when served a portion of Mrs. Dowdle's apple-plum torte respond with 'What is this mule fodder anyway?' "

Just thinking of the trainload of admonishments Kate had endured since her arrival in Boston sent a wave of rebellion through her formerly slender body. With a flurry of motion she whisked away the pins that imprisoned her russet hair in a plaited corona about her head. She combed her fingers through the braid, then tousled the freed locks like a spirited mare let loose of her tether.

"That's more like it," she told the four walls. Crossing to the ornately carved, gilt-edged mirror that dominated the windowless room she had to wonder why Mrs. Russell even bothered. Surely, the face that stared back at her from the oval looking glass was much too hard angled to ever be considered attractive, even with the softness of added weight. She decided the freckles didn't help any either. And her hair missed any chance of being exotically dark thanks to the fiery highlights reminiscent of the Scot around whom her world had so long revolved.

"I wish you could see for yourself, Pa," she said, wrinkling her nose at the image. "It isn't doing a mule's whiskers worth of good to have me in this danged school. No man with two eyes would want what he sees anyway, no matter how much you try to turn me into a some kind of dainty dumpling."

For long seconds self-pity vied with a fierce belief in her own self-worth, hammered into her since the cradle by her benignly arrogant father, belief tenuously

10

held and easily lost when the subject shifted to confidence in herself as a woman. Confidence shaken six years ago by a dashing young teamster named Billy Langley, then shattered utterly short months later by a nameless, faceless stranger in a San Francisco hotel room. She sighed heavily, surprised that the pain of remembrance could be as sharp and deep now as when it was new.

"I tell ya, Bryce," Billy Langley had grumbled, striding into her father's freight office, "you gotta do something about that daughter of yours." He slapped his hat down on his boss's desk, unaware that Kate had followed him from the barn, and was now standing just outside her father's open office door.

She was sixteen and flush certain that she was in love for the first time in her life. Billy was nineteen, handsome, and he hadn't made fun of her clothes when he'd hired on as an outrider two weeks before. In fact, when her father had introduced them, Billy had actually doffed his hat, grinned and said, "I'm pleased to make your acquaintance, Miss Kate McCullough."

He'd been more than pleased a few minutes ago in the barn. He told her he loved her! Kate's blood tingled just to think of it. The way he held her, kissed her, touched her . . . If Dusty hadn't come in when he did . . .

She blushed, recalling how she'd had to scramble to button her shirt. She'd never seen Dusty so angry. Billy had seemed almost frightened, yet strangely angry as well. While she had tried to explain to Dusty what happened, Billy had all but run from the barn.

"Afraid of losing his job," the grizzled freight hauler growled.

But Kate wouldn't listen. She ran after Billy, terrified that he would be upset with her.

Her heart climbed into her throat. Her eyes stung

11

with the effort it took not to shed the tears that ached to spill down her cheeks, as she listened to Billy Langley's true opinion of the boss's daughter.

"I been doin' my best to be a gentleman about this, Bryce," Billy was saying, his tone of voice suggesting that Kate had been anything but a lady. "But it can't go on like this any more. Kate's puttin' a helluva damper on my love life. Women won't come near me. She follows me around like a moon-eyed puppy, throwing herself at me."

What was he saying? He was the one who had approached her, told her he couldn't stop thinking about her, told her he thought she was pretty, told her so many wonderful things. The words he said now obliterated all those that had gone before.

"I know she's your kid, boss, and I don't mean no harm, but hell, even you gotta admit Kate ain't exactly no regular woman." When Bryce's eyes narrowed ominously, Billy hurried on, "Of course, that's not to say she ain't real nice. Maybe even purty if you put some meat on her bones. But lots o' girls her age are already married. And I think Kate's beginnin' to notice that kind of thing." He swallowed and cleared his throat noisily, obviously recognizing that he was on fragile ground with Bryce McCullough. But for the first time Kate perceived an odd cunning in the man. As Dusty had said, Billy wanted his job.

How better to keep it than to suggest desperation in poor, plain Kate? She could almost feel her father's sympathy rising for his lonely, unpretty daughter. Sympathy rooted in guilt, because Billy only put into words what her father had already long believed. If Bryce McCullough had a blind spot about Kate, it was his irrational concern that her looks had grown to favor his over her mother's.

She wanted to scream at them both to shut up. But

she couldn't speak, she couldn't move. She could only listen, as they shredded the tiny, budding confidence she had in herself as a woman.

"Kate's not your gentle little lady, Bryce," Billy said, seeming to gain some small measure of courage by the fact that he was still standing. "Kate don't *act* female. And she don't always smell female either, hangin' around the livestock like she does and wearin' them godawful buckskins. Lord knows, I've never even seen her in a dress. Hell, Bryce, a man just might be set to wonderin' if she really is a woman under all that dirt. She sure don't have no woman's figure, if you get my meanin'."

Kate's cheeks burned as she remembered his hands on her breasts. Obviously he had found her lacking.

She supposed it was to her father's credit that he had heard Billy out before he came around his mammoth oak desk to slam a meaty fist into the young man's handsome face. But for Kate the humiliation had not yet ended.

"I won't have no spineless laddie-buck pointin' out any faults in my Kate," Bryce grated, towering over the sprawled Langley, who was gingerly testing his jaw for re-aligned teeth. "I know she's no prize fer looks, but she's got the spirit of a she-bear and the heart of a mountain lion, and as long as you're workin' for me, Billy Langley, you'll put up with her sparkin' after ya." He straightened, scratching his beard thoughtfully. "In fact, you be nice to her, and I'll make it worth an extra ten dollars a month in your wages. Just make damned sure you keep your hands—."

Her strangled cry gave away her presence to the two men. Awkwardly, her father tried to explain, to apologize. But it was too late. Even her own father believed a man would have to be paid to be in her company.

"You know yer looks don't matter to a decent man,

Kate," he'd said. "A decent man'll look past the trappings to the woman beneath. Someday, somewhere, I'm sure there's a man for you. You don't need the likes of good-lookin' whelps like Billy Langley."

Good lookin' whelps like Billy Langley. Oh, if only you knew, Pa, she thought, as she crossed the parlor to sit on the brocade love seat. She had promised herself that day in his office that no man would ever make a fool of her again. Yet even the promise had not stopped what happened in San Francisco.

Abruptly she banished the troublesome thoughts. They were skirting dangerously close to that most bittersweet memory — a night of dreams that had become a nightmare.

She concentrated instead on the sudden unease that gripped her as she thought of her father. Though the room was warm, she shivered. How she wished he could be here with her now, this moment, to tell her everything was all right. Just as he always had whenever she was frightened or lonely as a little girl, growing up without companions of her own sex, her own age.

He had fussed at times over the lack of feminine influence in her life, but Kate had never felt the loss. Her father, for all his faults, had been all she needed or wanted in her life. Never had he seemed disappointed with the person she had become, though there had been times when he'd blatantly tried to steer her toward more womanly pursuits, like the ladies' sewing circles of Leavenworth.

And there was always Lydia. Lydia Cornell, an attractive middle-aged widow who'd run out of money, but not out of luck five years ago in Leavenworth. Her father had found her in a local saloon, making a pathetic attempt at applying for a job.

"It'd like to broke your heart, Kate, seein' a proud

14

woman like that having to lower herself just to put food on the table."

"I can imagine," Kate gritted, watching Lydia make herself at home in Kate's bedroom.

"I've always said we could use a housekeeper," he told Kate. But Kate was not so naive as her father supposed. A blind man couldn't have missed the way her father looked at Lydia. Besides, the house they had lived in at the time could be cared for with a broom and a featherduster. It was only after Lydia's arrival that her father decided they needed the mammoth two-story Yardley mansion, which had recently come available for sale.

Still he had never forced her to do things she didn't want to do. That was why she had been so incredulous when he had come to her seven months ago and decreed, literally decreed, that she was going east to Mrs. Russell's. It was not like him to be so high-handed with her.

He had not even sent her away during the War Between the States, allowing her to ride trail with the wagons as always, in spite of the constant threat of attack by rebel guerrillas. When the war ended two years ago, he'd given no hint that the business wouldn't continue as it had since the day it was founded—with Kate as a full and equal partner to Bryce McCullough and Dusty Lafferty.

She extracted a letter from her dress pocket, hoping to find solace in something that had been in her father's hand. She smiled at his bold scrawl, the words attesting to the affection they often found difficult to put into words when face to face. Bryce McCullough was weakening. In spite of the distance between them, Kate's influence was as strong as ever over the bull-headed Scot. She wanted to go home, and at last, in this latest missive he seemed about ready to concede

15

defeat and allow her to do just that.

She studied the letter as though the intense scrutiny would somehow allow her to read more than the words penned there. Nowhere had Bryce McCullough responded to her repeated inquiries about how the business was faring without her. She had been teasing, of course. But it wasn't like her father not to mention the other pride and joy in his life, McCullough Freight Company, one of the largest, most lucrative freight hauling outfits west of the Mississippi.

"What aren't you telling me, Pa?" she wondered. "There's something wrong, I know it."

In fact, Kate hadn't been able to shake the feeling that something was amiss the day Bryce announced that he was sending her east. She had tried without success to get him to talk about it, even to accusing him of attempting to turn her into a lady so that she could at last land the husband who had so far eluded her.

It wasn't fair to jab him with the memory of how he had hurt her that day with Billy Langley. But if he was sending her east to groom her for husband-hunting, she wanted to know about it. She was not blind to the fact that it was beginning to worry him just a little, as her birthdays came and went, that no man had ever paid her court.

Kate grimaced. That was because her father didn't know just how vigorous she had become in discouraging suitors — a fact that had come to have nothing to do with Billy Langley, and everything to do with a mysterious stranger in San Francisco.

"Stop it, Kate McCullough!" she snapped. "You've done quite enough thinking about him lately. It's done. He was there, and he was gone."

Yet the feeling stayed with her, never completely disappearing — a longing so intense it frightened her.

She paced the floor, unwilling to give in to it. Almost desperately she forced her mind elsewhere. To Mrs. Russell. Where could the woman be? If she was coming, she certainly would have been here by now. Something must have detained her. At least Kate would be spared a lecture on her stitching until morning. Blowing out the lantern, she left the parlor and headed up the stairs to her bedroom.

As one of the older students at the school, she had been allowed the privilege of a room to herself. She smiled ruefully. She was not altogether convinced the gesture stemmed from Mrs. Russell's benevolence. The headmistress did not want Kate giving the younger girls pointers on how to spit tobacco.

Inside her bedroom, Kate closed the door and walked to the open window. She gazed down on the well-manicured grounds below, scarcely noticing the gentle breeze that sifted through the gossamer curtains. The windows had been open that night in San Francisco.

She hugged her arms tight against her body, giving in to the odd melancholy that ruled her night tonight. Where was he? What was he doing? Did he ever think of her? Was he even still alive?

Long minutes passed before she at last decided to go to bed, even knowing that she was too restless to sleep. Burrowing into the sheets, she focused on the fingers of moonlight dancing across the floor.

She had to go home — and soon. On the trail, hauling freight with barely a minute not filled with harsh physical labor, she had thought about him only occasionally. Now in these endless days of cooking and sewing, it was only occasionally that she did not think of him.

Tonight was proving no exception.

She closed her eyes, giving herself up once again to

17

the wonder of that long ago night.

The bed was soft, featherticked, attesting to the luxury of one of San Francisco's finest hotels. Kate ran her hand along the clean white sheets, not bothering to suppress a yawn. This would be one of the few times in her seventeen years that she wouldn't miss sleeping under the stars. The bed looked positively wonderful after four months on the trail, most of the last two spent eating alkali dust on the water-scarce route from Salt Lake City to the Humboldt.

Now the last of the shipment had been delivered, the drivers paid off, and it would be at least another day before her father and Dusty decided it was time to head back to Leavenworth. Scrunching down between the sheets, she thought about the two men in one of the rooms down the hall. They'd invited her to come drinking with them, but for once she had declined.

She was loathe to admit it, but lately she had grown annoyed at being included in some of their more bawdy pursuits, as though she were no different from any of their other hard living drivers. Yet she would have fought to the death if they had tried to exclude her, simply because she was a woman. She freely acknowledged that wanting it both ways made little sense, but it didn't stop the contradictory feelings.

Billy Langley's cruel assessment of her as a woman had had more of an impact on her than she dared admit. And even though her father had eventually fired him, it had not lessened the pain of his words. Billy hadn't been able to resist a parting shot. "I doubt there's a man in the world willing to scrape through those buckskins to get at what's underneath, Kate. A man don't want a woman who can outrope and outshoot him." He'd laughed. "Or even outcuss him. A man wants a lady."

18

A lady. Kate sighed in the darkness. She couldn't pretend to be something she was not. Surely there was a man somewhere who would find her desirable just as she was. And if there wasn't? Damn, she admonished herself sharply, then to hell with the arrogant bastards!

Why couldn't they just be pleasant company like Jim Collier, Leavenworth's sheriff? He took her to dinner, to plays—always the gentleman, giving her the chance to show the snobs of Leavenworth society that she wasn't a total disaster. With Jim she could almost feel comfortable in her role as a lady. Of course, that was largely because she had no vested emotional interest. She and Jim were only friends. The one time he had asked to kiss her good-night, she had declined and he had not pressed her. Just being asked was enough to give her ego a boost.

"It's nice to know a young lady who doesn't indulge in carnal feelings," Jim said, raising the back of her hand to his lips. Kate congratulated herself for keeping a demure smile plastered on her face. Not indulge in carnal feelings? Only because she hadn't found anyone to indulge in them with, she thought ruefully.

She'd managed to free her hand from his grasp without seeming too obvious. If only Jim could have kindled the same spark in her that Billy had. But the only real spark he'd ever kindled had been anger. That had been the one time he hadn't taken her to a play or to dinner, but for a ride outside of Leavenworth. Kate grimaced, remembering that spooky cave he'd taken her to. He'd loved the dark maze, but it had given Kate the willies. She'd demanded to be taken home, and they'd never visited the cave again.

Kate shifted restlessly on the bed. Even her father had encouraged her relationship with Jim. "I'm not gettin' any younger, Katie. A man wants grandchildren."

19

"Oh, Papa, please," she grimaced. "Not with Jim Collier. He's just fine when I play the lady, but he turns positively green when I put on my buckskins. I swear he about had apoplexy when I hit the spittoon in Barton's Cafe."

"What am I going to do with you?"

She giggled. "Buy me a drink?"

Her father had laughed, but now in the darkness of her San Francisco hotel room Kate could find nothing amusing about how she was perceived by the opposite sex. "If they don't like me the way I am they can just take a flyin' . . .

She rolled over, dragging the sheet over her head. No more thinking about that kind of nonsense. For now she would just have to content herself with dreaming of the perfect man, a man who would find her to be the perfect woman. She closed her eyes, drifting to sleep almost at once.

It was there. Something. But she was so sleepy. A dream? Yes, a dream. She was still in her hotel room, but she was no longer alone.

"Pretty coy," came the husky male voice. "Already in the bed."

"Mmmmm," she murmured. It was going to be a very nice dream. She hoped she didn't wake up before she saw his face.

He padded across the room to the edge of her bed, moonlight and shadows flitting over him. She couldn't catch even a glimpse of his features. But it was a strong face, handsome—she was certain of it. She would dream of nothing less.

She bit her lip as she felt his weight displace part of the mattress. He was sitting next to her. Her own body shifted languorously. This was all so wondrously realistic.

He leaned close and she breathed in the clean,

musky smell of him. But she didn't miss the faint trace of whiskey as well. Yet he wasn't drunk. There was nothing clumsy or awkward in his movements. He knew perfectly well what he was doing.

His hands glided across the sheet, pausing to span her waist. "A bit scrawny," he pronounced, but there was no meanness in his voice.

Kate frowned. This was her dream. She wasn't going to let him say things like that any more. He was going to find her perfect. Just as she was going to find him. Smiling, she reached up her hand. She would be bold with this man of her dreams. She followed the curve of his jaw, feathering across a trace of whiskers.

"You didn't shave today."

His lips curved against her palm. "I'll remember to do that next time."

A strange sadness touched her. There would be no next time. No, she wouldn't think that. If she wanted him back, she would just have the dream again.

Her heart skipped a beat as she heard his boots thud to the floor. This was so real, so real.

"Kiss me," she whispered.

"My pleasure."

His mouth closed over hers, and she was awed by the emotions that roiled to life within her. Her blood pounded, her whole body alive to his touch. When his tongue teased her lips, her instincts drove her to respond in kind. The kiss deepened, leaving her breathless when at last he pulled away.

"An eager one," he said, apparently able to see her well enough in the darkness that he could tuck a stray wisp of her hair behind her ear. "I like my women eager."

She caught the false note in that husky voice, as though he were reciting words that had no meaning. He was saying what he thought she wanted to hear.

This was sex to him, plain and simple.

Well, it wasn't going to stay that way. She'd had enough of that with Billy. This man was going to care about her. She stroked his hair. She was going to care about him.

"You're good," he said.

"Thank you," she said, because she didn't know what else to say.

"What's your name?"

"Ka . . . Katherine." Never in her life had she called herself by her given name.

"That's pretty. Like you."

More lies. He couldn't see her well enough to tell her face from the back end of a donkey. She didn't want lies. "What . . . what's your name?"

"Doesn't matter. Don't talk. Just let me. Let me."

His hands moved across her, tugging at the silk ribbons that fastened her nightrail. He shoved the material aside, circling his fingers around her breasts.

She arched upward instinctively, the breath leaving her body in low, throaty moans. Her breasts swelled to fill his hands, then suddenly it was his mouth that suckled at the coral crests.

He was rushing now, moving quickly, too quickly. She wanted to savor the night. "There's no hurry," she said softly, tangling her fingers in his hair.

He paused and she felt his eyes on her. "You don't have any other . . . ah, appointments tonight?"

"Appointments?" She was confused. Where would he think she was going this time of night? "I . . . I only want to be with you."

"You play the game well." He lay down beside her. "If you're giving me the whole night, I won't argue."

Shyly, Kate trailed her hand along his arm, the tautly muscled bicep straining against the material of his shirt. "I want to touch all of you." The words were

22

out, though she couldn't believe she'd said them.

"Undress me," he rasped.

With trembling fingers she reached for the buttons of his shirt. "It's getting cold," she said, her boldness waning a little. "I'll shut the windows."

"No!" His hand snapped at her wrist like a trap on a bear. "I . . . I like fresh air."

His heart hammered against her palm. "Then I'll leave them open," she said, her voice gentle, though puzzled. "Are you all right?"

"Fine."

He was not fine. He was not fine at all. He was afraid. And in him she sensed his contempt for his own fear—perceiving it as weakness. But what was he afraid of?

"Undress me," he repeated, seeking she knew to divert her attention away from his strange behavior. There was little use asking him. He would tell her nothing.

With shaking fingers she undid the buttons of his shirt, skating her hands beneath the cotton to explore his hair-roughened chest. Biting her lip, she drew her hands lower, skirting past the stretched taut denim at his crotch.

He sucked in his breath. "Damn, get on with it. I want it now."

"We have all night, remember? This is my dream."

"It's my money."

Money? What was he talking about? But she felt too good to allow the intrusion of a discordant note—even when he clinked down several coins on the nightstand. "That should cover it." Surely she should be outraged, but there was a strange lethargy in her limbs. She couldn't even mind that her own dream had labelled her a lady of the evening.

"Why would a man with such magic in his hands

need to pay . . ."

"I'm a stranger in town."

Another lie. "Are you married?"

"No."

Again she sensed pain in his answer. "Please, can't you tell me your name."

"What would my name matter? You don't know me."

"I want to."

"No. No one can. Not again. It hurts too much." He stopped. He'd said more than he wanted to. In the moonlit darkness his body came over hers. "Lie still. Don't talk. Just let me touch you. Let me . . ."

His mouth charted a path between her breasts to her navel and down. When he reached her woman's folds, her eyes flew open. "No, please," she gasped, "what are you do— . . ." But he was persistent and unbelievably gentle. Her back arched, her mind seeming to separate from her body as she gave herself over to a world of shattering delight.

When she was again aware of her surroundings, he was nuzzling her neck, murmuring "Thank you."

He was thanking *her*? How could such feelings exist in her own body without her even suspecting their existence until tonight? "Am I . . . did I . . . please you?"

He kissed her throat. "You doubt it?"

"I . . . I've had a complaint or two," she said shakily, thinking of Billy Langley.

"Not from me."

Unconsciously she stroked his back, her nails tracing lazy circles on the smooth flesh. She paused, frowning, when she encountered a three-inch long, half-inch wide ridge that marred the perfection.

"A souvenir from a fall I took when I was a boy."

She felt him tense and knew there was more to the

24

memory than just the physical injury. But she did not want to risk making him angry. She'd never felt more content in her life than she did right now in the arms of this stranger.

"You've made this a special night for me," he said, and she could tell by the odd wistfulness in his voice that he was not a man who had had many special moments in his life. Nor was he a man to be so open with his feelings. It was the darkness, the anonymity that allowed him to be so with her. "You're going to make it even more special for me now."

"You make it sound as though this night has to last you for a long time."

"It does."

"You're going somewhere?"

"The war."

Her heart pounded. She didn't want to think of him dodging bullets somewhere far away from her. "You're a soldier then?"

"Not yet."

"But this is California. You don't have to join. The war is two years old. Why now?"

"I never wanted to die before."

His voice was matter-of-fact, but the words chilled her.

"You're cold," he said.

"Frightened."

"Of me?"

"*For* you."

"Why?"

"I don't want you to die."

"If you knew, maybe you wouldn't say . . ." He stiffened abruptly. "Damn, stop asking me questions!"

He settled his body atop hers, his movements rougher, more hurried. He was angry, but she suspected his temper was a defense against deeper emo-

25

tions he had never shared with anyone.

"This is my dream," she said. "Tell me what hurts and I'll make it better."

"Why do you keep calling this a dream? I'm no one's dream."

"You're mine."

"Damn! I pay you. We have sex. That's all." But his arms surrounded her, and there was more in the embrace than lust. No matter what he said, his body told her differently. And then he was saying it, speaking from his heart for perhaps the first time in his life. "Love me, Katherine. Love me. One night in my life I need someone to love me."

The despair in his voice brought tears to her eyes. And in that instant she knew it was a woman who had hurt him. Kate took advantage of the darkness, seeking to give him what he seemed so desperately to need.

"I do love you," she said, and in a very real way, at the moment, she did.

He staked his arms on either side of her, readying himself. Her legs opened, her body eager to know him, love him fully. He was her dream. And he needed her, wanted her, as much as she wanted him.

He drove himself inside her, hard and deep. The pain was quick, quickly past, but it brought with it the sudden horrifying realization that she was not asleep, not dreaming. Dear God, there was a man in her bed and he had just . . .

"Who are you?" she cried, struggling to free herself. But she didn't have to push him away, he was already rolling off her.

"A virgin whore?" he hissed. "What the hell is going on?"

"I'm no whore," she stammered, still not quite certain what had just happened, and how much she herself had contributed to its happening.

He was sitting up, yanking on his pants. The fury was emanating from him in waves. He had sought a night of loving, no matter how misbegotten, and he'd found only more pain and confusion. "A woman in the saloon downstairs sent me up here," he said, trying as hard as she to make sense of this night. "Room 515."

Kate trembled, reaching a hand out to touch his still naked back, assuring herself of what she already knew. This was most certainly no dream. "This is room 516," she said softly.

"Sweet Savior! Why didn't you say something? Why did you let . . . how old are you?"

"Seventeen."

He swore again. "Do you often let men into your bed at three in the morning, Katherine?"

"I thought I was . . . dreaming."

He slammed into his boots. "You dream of being raped?"

"Not raped . . ."

"I came here for one night, because I haven't had a woman since . . ." He stopped. "Damn you."

Kate's temper niggled at her. "Damn *me*? You come in here. I'm sound asleep. You take off my clothes. You . . ."

"I'm sorry."

Her planned tirade ended in mid-sentence. He really was sorry. "It wasn't all your fault."

He stood abruptly and swept up the money he had laid on the nightstand. Without looking at her, he dropped it on the bed. "Take it. You earned it."

Kate went rigid with shame and humiliation. She had wanted to help ease his conscience, because she sensed some deep awful hurt in him, but now . . . now. Why had he ended it this way?

Without another word, without her ever having seen his face, he left the room.

You earned it. In the darkness of her room in Mrs. Russell's Finishing School Kate reached over to the reticule on her night table. She opened it, emptying the five twenty-dollar gold pieces into her palm. "Someday I'm going to find you," she said softly, "and I'm going to throw these right in your face."

In spite of herself she remembered the anguish in his voice, but remembered equally as well how it had changed to gun-metal coldness. So many times she'd relived that night, altering its ending. He had stayed, made love to her, then gone off to join the war, not because he wanted to die, but because he believed in a just cause.

And always she believed she would find him again. That if she ever saw him, somehow she would recognize him. And he would have been looking for her, because he'd never been able to forget that night either.

She threw back her blankets and climbed out of bed, crossing over to the mirror. Her reflection mocked her. At least he couldn't call her scrawny any more. She sighed. Would she never rid herself of her obsession for that man? That night?

Pointing a finger at her reflection, her voice harsh to suppress the hurt that fired her words, she vowed, "No man's ever going to hurt you again, Kate McCullough. You hear me? If and when you find a man, it'll be you doing the using, not him. And God help him if he tries to make it otherwise."

She moved back over to her bed, but was still too restless to sleep. As before, she experienced a strange sense of foreboding, and it centered not only around her nameless, faceless lover, but around her father as well. Something was terribly wrong. More than ever she wanted to be home.

Not waiting for her emotions to settle to a less volatile level, she marched over to her rolltop desk. It was time she stopped asking her father if she could come home. It was time she told him she was coming.

As for her mysterious lover, her heart told her what logic so easily denied. Somehow, some way they would meet again. And he would answer for that night, answer for the five gold coins, answer for the cruelty of his parting words. Because though she fought it with everything in her, she had not lied when she said the words: She loved him.

Chapter Two

Kate's hand shook as she penned her father's name on the linen stationery. What was the matter with her? It was more than thinking about San Francisco. Her breath caught at the sound of the knock on the door.

"Come in, Mrs. Russell," she called out, knowing it would be no one else at this late hour.

The headmistress stepped into the room and gently closed the door. Kate studied her in the dim light of the lantern, disturbed all the more by the woman's silence. Mrs. Russell had never been one to be at a loss for words, especially not with Kate. From the first moment Kate had stepped off the stage and Mrs. Russell had ordered her to rid herself of her tobacco, the woman had single-handedly taken on the task of reshaping Kate's character, whether Kate wanted it reshaped or not.

From Mrs. Russell Kate had learned to cook more than beans and grits, had agonized over sewing more than hides together, and had learned to excise the colorful words of the teamsters from her everyday speech. But now Mrs. Russell stood quietly in the closed doorway and Kate's feeling of unease clawed at her like a living thing.

"Is something wrong?" she ventured at last, when the woman continued her maddening silence.

"Oh, Katherine," the woman began, then stopped.

"Mrs. Russell, please, what is it?"

"I don't know . . . I just don't know how to tell you . . . Oh, Katherine . . ."

"Just say it right out," Kate said, her voice shaking. Somehow she already knew. She just knew. The woman's words only confirmed what Kate's heart begged to deny.

"It's . . . it's your father, dear. I'm afraid I've received some dreadful news."

"No." She knew, but she didn't want to know.

"There was some sort of accident. I'm so sorry." The woman pressed a letter into Kate's hands. "If there's anything at all I can do . . ."

"No. I mean . . . please, if you could . . . if you could just leave me alone."

"I don't think I should . . ."

"No, Mrs. Russell, it's all right."

The woman nodded. "But if you need anything, anything at all, you call me, you hear?" She turned and left the room.

Kate forced her legs to move. She stepped over to the lamp. Her hands shook as she read the words. It was from Dusty. Dusty, who had taught her how to harness her first yoke of oxen. Dusty, who had saved her father's life so long ago and become an adopted uncle to a boisterous tomboy who refused to believe girls couldn't do anything boys could do. Dear, sweet Dusty. The letter was as simple and direct as the man himself.

Dear Kate,

I wish I could tell ya myself, instead of doin' it like this. But I got no choice, girl. Your pa's been

31

kilt. They're saying it was an accident with the team on the road. Come home before Blanchard takes over the whole shebang. I miss Bryce like the devil. God love ya.

Your Uncle Dusty

Blanchard. Kate stiffened. Frank Blanchard had arrived in Leavenworth to start up a freight outfit shortly before she left for school. Was Blanchard after her father's company now that he was dead?

Dead. Bryce McCullough dead. She stared at the date in the top left corner of the note. Dear God, it had been written two weeks ago. Her father had been dead for two weeks, and she hadn't even known. Dead.

She would never again hear his gravelly voice tell her he loved her. Never thrill to the way his bullwhip could flick a fly off a bull's ear without touching the animal. Never see his blue eyes shine with pride, knowing he'd never missed having a son. Never . . .

Kate McCullough did something she seldom did in her life. She cried.

No amount of persuasion from Mrs. Russell could get Kate to change her mind. The next day she was aboard a train, heading home. The clicking of the rails beneath the cars helped numb her mind to the pain of her father's death. Days and nights blended together, until two weeks had passed and Kate could again think of Bryce McCullough without feeling a searing blaze of emptiness and loss.

Standing in the Columbia, Missouri, stage depot only exacerbated her suspicions of what she would find when she arrived home. The stage line had recently been bought outright. The new owner's name was emblazoned in golden letters across the door of the Concord Coach — Frank Blanchard. Her fists clenched unconsciously. The man was wasting no time. Still there was nothing she could do about it here. She wanted to get to Leavenworth as quickly as possible.

She had just paid for her fare at the ticket agent's cage when she felt the prickling sensation of a pair of eyes boring into her back. Three bone-jarring days in a stage from St. Louis had left her in no mood for any kind of harassment, no matter what her watcher's motives might be. She shot a venomous look behind her, surprised and not a little embarrassed to find no one there.

"You're just getting jittery so close to home, Kate," she told herself. More and more the need to know the truth of her father's death tore at her. If Frank Blanchard had anything to do with Bryce McCullough's death, he would pay hell.

Outside on the boardwalk, she revelled in the sights and sounds so similar to home — the comings and goings of loaded freight wagons, the bawling of oxen, the braying of mules. How good it would feel to be in Kansas again.

Fidgeting with the waistline of her dress, she debated glumly whether or not she would survive the final two days of her journey. Her added weight had not allowed her the comfort of her buckskins. At least the dress seemed less snug than it had at the trip's outset. If only she didn't have to put up with the godawful stays . . .

To take her mind off her irksome attire, she stepped over to the Concord's driver, who was hitching up his matched team of six sleek Kentucky trotters. The horses stamped and snorted impatiently, as if eager for the run to begin.

"They're beautiful," she said.

33

The driver looked up from the doubletree, a scowl deepening the weathered lines of his face. "Just keep your distance, missy."

"Will we be leaving for Leavenworth on time?"

"Five minutes."

Kate patted the flank of the right side lead bay.

"Watch out there," the driver growled. "Barney can be a mite skittish."

The words weren't out of the man's mouth when the horse reared, knocking Kate sideways. The hostler cursed, shouting at the animal, trying vainly to shove past the wheelhorse to get to Kate. But in the same instant Kate regained her feet, leaping toward the shying gelding, whose actions now threatened to send the whole team—stagecoach and all—bolting away. In a flash of motion she was on his neck like a tick on a hound's ear, forcing the gelding to lower his head as she gripped his mane and hung on.

The horse reared again, tossing his head. Kate felt herself being lifted off the ground, skirts billowing, legs flying. Instinct drove her to grab for the bridle. With one hand she clung to the leather, with the other she ran her fingers along the horse's muzzle, all the while speaking soothing nonsense.

This time when the gelding tossed his head, her feet did not leave the ground. She continued to talk to him, stroke him, until finally the animal settled, his nervousness muting to a lingering playfulness as he nuzzled his head along her side.

The driver let out a long, low whistle, coming around the traces to stand beside her. "I'll be damned. I never seen nothin' like that in my life. I thought the stage was headed halfway to Leavenworth without me." He stuck out a hand. "Name's Jeb Kerns."

Kate shook the hand, feeling positively exhilarated. "Actually, I wish I could do it again." Her joy was tem-

34

pered somewhat when the grizzled driver did not release her hand, instead turning it over in his own.

"Maybe you could ride up top with me, huh,
missy?"

Kate knew it was considered an honor to ride with
the driver instead of being cooped up inside the stage,
but the way he was looking at her suddenly made her
skin crawl. As graciously as she could manage she retrieved her hand and gave him a thin smile. "I don't
really want to be sandwiched in between you and the
guard."

"Ain't no guard this trip," Kerns said, licking his
lips.

Kate backed away from him. "That's a little unu-
sual, isn't it?"

"Nothin' of value. Company decided to save the
money."

So Frank Blanchard was a penny-pincher, too, Kate
thought, but said nothing. It was foolhardy to run a
stage without a shotgun messenger but she was too
anxious to be home to make an issue of it.

She welcomed the gawking stares of the small crowd
that had formed. Anything was better than letting
Kerns get any more ideas. Besides, it was as though
the tiny adventure had revived her, stirred her, awak-
ened her from a six month lethargy, a hibernation of
spirit in which she'd used self-pity as a shield to keep
from looking too far inside herself lest she not like
what she found. It was time to stop concerning herself
with what others might think of her and concern herself only with what she thought of herself.

The driver's continuing litany of praise brought her
out of her reverie. "Damn, you sure know how to handle a horse, miss," he said. "I still don't believe what
my eyes tell me I saw. You sure you won't ride up top
with me?"

"It's not really so amazing," she said. "I've been around horses all my life."

"In Leavenworth?"

She nodded. "My father and I run a freight . . ." She stopped, sobering. "Perhaps you knew him — Bryce McCullough."

She could have sworn she saw a flicker of recognition in his squinted gaze, but then he turned, putting an abrupt end to his peculiar flirtation. "Five minutes on the nose, missy. You're late, I don't wait."

Kate was left to puzzle over the man's strange behavior. Even though the early morning temperature promised a scorcher of a day ahead, she felt the gooseflesh rise on her arms. What was she going home to? She remembered Dusty's letter. *They're saying it was an accident with the team on the road.*

Why did she know already that her father's death was no accident? She was more than familiar with the dangers of freight hauling. The elements, Indians, stampedes — each had shown Kate the stark reality of death at a tender age. But she knew with a gutwrenching certainty that Bryce McCullough had fallen victim to no natural disaster. Her father had been murdered.

The chilling knowledge tore through her at the same time she again experienced the very real sensation of someone studying her covertly. Furious, she whirled, but saw no one. Only her fellow passengers getting ready to board the stage. She had to get a grip on herself. She was coming positively undone.

Then she noticed him. Standing alone near the rear boot of the stage. He didn't appear to be looking at her. Nor did she remember seeing him inside the depot when she purchased her ticket. Still, there was something almost too nonchalant about his stance. Gritting her teeth, she marched over to him.

36

"If you have something to say to me, mister," she snapped, "then say it. I don't appreciate . . ."

The words snagged in her throat as he tilted his black broad-brimmed hat away from his forehead. A thunderbolt would have had less effect on her. She was staring at the most devastatingly handsome male face she had ever seen in her life. Features sculpted by an artist's hand—eyes, nose, mouth, chin—each separate part of his face glorified the whole. Surely, the Greeks had had gods no more beautiful than this.

His face was all the more devastating because in her dreams she had given such a face to the man who had become her obsession—her San Francisco lover. To stand here with this stranger and even for an instant imagine . . . No, she had to put a stop to such fanciful notions.

But she couldn't stop herself from wishing that she had not been so exhausted at the hotel last night. That she had taken the clerk up on his kind offer to have a bath drawn for her. And then she hated herself for the thought, and hated this man for making her think it.

She balled her fists at her sides. *It didn't matter what he thought of her. It mattered only what she thought of herself!*

Her father was dead. How could she even consider her appearance as having any importance right now? How dare this no doubt arrogant jackass make her aware of how dowdy and drab she looked anyway? She couldn't even stop her mouth from falling open as she continued to gape at him.

"That's a good way to catch flies," he drawled, and she was irrationally annoyed that his voice was as deep and rich and warm as his eyes. Annoyed, too, that the sound of it made her remember yet again another time, another place, another man. She was being a fool. It was only because she had told herself over and over that she would one day meet her unknown lover,

37

that this man had unsettled her so.

His eyes—blue, dark as midnight—seemed capable of arresting even the act of breathing. It must have been so, because her next breath was long and shuddering, as if she'd forgotten to breathe for some time.

"Why . . . why have you been watching me?" she demanded, wishing to heaven she could control the uncharacteristic quiver in her voice.

"Have I been?" His mouth curved into a lazy smile, daring her to prove it, his even white teeth accenting the sun-darkened flesh of his face. He raised his hat perfunctorily, as if he had only just now thought that it was something he should do in her presence, but he did not remove it. He merely adjusted it to a more comfortable position atop the tousled black locks that skimmed the collar of his shirt.

"Just stay away from me!" she hissed, her heart hammering. So like him. Too much like him. She had to get away from this man before she made a complete idiot of herself.

"Hard for me to stay away from a pretty lady. Besides, I never could resist a woman who had a way with horseflesh."

She shot him what she hoped was a quelling look as she waited for the smirking laughter that would follow his words. But none came. Nor did his gaze waver. She found herself growing oddly warm after the earlier chill that had swept through her when she thought about her father's death.

For all the anger she had felt, still felt, for she was certain it was this man who had been staring at her, it was Kate who turned away, though she was loathe to give him the satisfaction. Obviously he was playing some sort of game with her. Whatever his motive—be it meanness, or simply his way of alleviating the boredom of the trail, she was not going to fall prey to his

38

male charm—charm, she suspected, he had in abundance. Though it occurred to her suddenly that he very rarely put it to use.

"Just leave me alone," she said, hurrying over to the door of the stagecoach.

"Can't do it," he shrugged, following. He yanked the door open and offered her a hand up.

Kate gave him an acid look and climbed into the stage unaided, horrified to watch him vault in behind her. No, no, no, her mind screamed as he settled himself and his saddlebags on the seat opposite her.

"It's two days to Leavenworth, Kate. I'll wager we're going to be great friends by the time we get there." He stuck out a hand. "The name's Travis. Travis Hawke."

She glared at the hand, but did not touch it, then deliberately shifted her gaze to stare out the window. Out of the corner of one eye, she saw the hand drop back to a tightly muscled thigh. She longed to see the expression in those blue eyes now, but nothing would make her turn to look.

Two more passengers boarded, a man and a woman who giggled and cooed at one another, then scrunched down next to Kate. She felt her head start to pound. She was shoulder to shoulder with the woman.

"You don't suppose you could move to the other side, could you, dear?" the woman asked, her voice high-pitched and maple sweet. "We're newlyweds, Hank and I."

"My condolences," Kate gritted before she could stop the words, quickly amending them to a stammered congratulations.

The snort of amusement from across the stage ended any thought she might have had of complying with the woman's request. The blast furnace temperature of the cramped quarters combined with the increasing aggravation of her corset set her teeth on

39

edge. It was all she could do to keep from scrambling up the side of the coach and taking the driver up on his leering invitation to ride with him.

When she dared a glance at the dark-haired stranger, she had to bite back the epithet that rose in her throat. He was lounging sideways, seeming to deliberately flaunt the roominess of his side of the coach.

The temperature, or was it her temper, rose perceptibly just watching the insufferable bastard.

Grimly, she slapped the canvas curtains into place. At least she would be spared some of the dust . . .

In one motion he jerked the curtains from their anchors above the door and tossed them to the floor.

She clamped her jaw shut on the string of epithets that rose to her lips. It had been there for only the briefest instant in those blue eyes. But she had seen it. No. She shook her head. That was ridiculous. It couldn't have been fear.

"You've just made this a damned dusty ride," she said, studying him intently now.

He seemed not to notice, lounging back as he had before. "I like to see where I'm going."

She decided to spare his life only because the driver at last cracked his whip and shouted "Yo!", sending the stage lurching forward. In minutes fine eddies of Missouri dirt swirled through the windows.

It was the perfect final touch — a carpet of grime settling over Kate's sweat-drenched, cramped, corseted body. She closed her eyes, mentally girding herself for the longest two days of her life.

They were a mile out of town when it hit her. Travis Hawke had addressed her by name.

Chapter Three

Kate studied Hawke with a new intensity, grateful that his eyes were closed and he seemed to be dozing. Damn the wretch anyway! That he could sleep in this stifling heat.

She searched her memory, seeking desperately to place him outside of her dreams. In her mind's eye, she changed his appearance—added a beard, a mustache, even dressed him in a fancy suit to take the place of the dark levis and gray homespun shirt he wore. She put him in buckskins, in bearskins. In each transformation, he remained infuriatingly handsome, but in none of the guises could Kate ever recall having met this man who had known her name, when she had not known his.

And yet . . . and yet.

No. She must be wary. She was assigning traits to this Hawke she had given to her phantom lover. In her dreams since that San Francisco night she had kissed a man who looked like Hawke, surrendered herself to a man who looked like Hawke, making the man Hawke himself infinitely more dangerous to her.

Though she assured herself she studied him only to decide whether or not she knew him, she found her

41

eyes traversing parts of him that could not possibly aid her recognition. He had perched himself diagonally across from her in the corner of the bench seat, his legs, bent slightly at the knee to accommodate their length, angled toward her. She felt the color rise in her cheeks as she pictured the tautly muscled flesh beneath the denim.

Shifting her gaze, she noted shirtsleeves turned back to the elbow, dark hair stippling tanned forearms. The shirt was open at the throat, foreshadowing the beginnings of a sleek, broad chest. His thumbs snagged the waistband of his levis just below a flat belly, fingers lazily interlocked just above . . . She gasped, averting her eyes at once, aghast at her appalling behavior.

"It's really something, isn't it?" the woman next to Kate inquired.

"I beg your pardon?" Kate squeaked, jerking her head guiltily toward her too-close seatmate. Her breathing returned to normal only when Kate realized the woman was referring to the Missouri countryside. She mumbled her concurrence, even while she swore an end to her scandalous survey of Mr. Travis Hawke.

"Yes, I'm finding Missouri to be quite beautiful," the young woman went on, side-tracking long enough to introduce herself as Laney Nolan. Her husband snoozed noisily at her side, his head pillowed by her shoulder.

"Uh huh," Kate agreed, scarcely aware of what Laney was saying. "Beautiful." Why was she looking at Hawke's face when she said that? And what was it about his face that changed when she said it? Then it struck her. Just barely perceptible, but it was there. The corner of one side of that generous mouth was ticked upward as though he were trying very hard not to smile.

No. The man's eyes were shut! How could he see

her, how could . . . Dear heaven, had he been awake all along? Had he been amused by her scrutiny from the first?

"I've never been west of the Mississippi before," Laney said, oblivious to Kate's distress. "Harold and I are from Virginia, but we had nothing left after the war. So we decided to start over again in California."

Kate nodded perfunctorily now and then, whenever Laney paused in her discourse on the history of her family. But what she really wanted to do was kick Travis Hawke right in the . . .

"Just how long have you lived in the west, Kate?"

The thinly disguised irritation in Laney's voice got through to Kate, when the question had not. She wondered wearily how many times the woman had repeated the query without receiving a response germane to the question. She vowed to be more attentive. If nothing else, it would take her mind off the increasingly galling Hawke.

She did her best to sound animated as she told Laney about growing up the daughter of a free-living freight hauler.

"You've battled Indians?" the newlywed gasped.

"And befriended Indians as well," Kate said, finishing up her tale of supplying settlements from Leavenworth to San Francisco these past twelve years. Though obsessed with curiosity about Hawke's reaction to her unconventional life, she would not look at him. Not now. She chalked up her reticence to embarrassment, unwilling to admit she feared he had judged her as Billy Langley had so many years ago, and that he too had found her lacking as a woman. Unwilling further to admit that the hurt would somehow be even greater, if he did. That the hurt would approach what she felt that long ago night in San Francisco.

She was enormously grateful when the driver chose

43

that moment to pull the team to a halt for nooning. She couldn't have borne another moment in that closed-in compartment. The oppressive heat of midday was suddenly nothing compared to the oppressive heat of Hawke's nearness. Why this was so, she couldn't have said. He'd said nothing, done nothing, since they'd left Columbia, yet she had been acutely aware of his presence every bone-jolting mile of their journey.

It was more than the fact that he seemed to know her. It was Travis Hawke himself. Travis Hawke, the man. Though she easily labeled him a drifter, she perceived a sense of purpose about him that was downright unsettling. A purpose that had something to do with her.

She shook her head, annoyed once again that her imagination was getting the upper hand, simply because she found the man's looks marginally passable. Well, her lips thinned ruefully, more than marginally. Still, he was undoubtedly so conceited she should consider it miraculous that he was even able to squeeze his head into the stagecoach. He'd probably left a broken heart in every town he'd ever visited.

She dared another glance at him. He might be worth a broken heart at that. To feel those strong arms around her, feel his mouth on her mouth, feel his hands . . . It had been so long, so long. She wanted to believe she could recapture the magic of that night with another man, that she didn't have to spend her life looking for someone she might never see again, who might not even be alive.

Stop it! she fumed inwardly. *Just stop it!* When the driver jerked open the coach door, she clambered out without a backward glance.

"I would have helped you down," came the husky voice behind her.

She stiffened, but did not turn around. She could

well imagine those blue eyes laughing at her, now that he could no longer feign sleep. But she was not about to give him the satisfaction. She was hot, dusty, tired and achingly uncomfortable. And no man was worth risking a broken heart.

"I trust you enjoyed the sights, Kate," he said, striding over to her.

Her cheeks burned. She would not look at him.

"Smile, Kate," he said. "I told you we were going to be great friends, remember?"

She remembered only too well. *A broken heart in every town.* She had to get away. "*Friends* do not pretend to be asleep, and then eavesdrop on conversations!"

"What would you have had me do? Hang my head out the window?"

"You could have hung your whole body out the window for all I care." Blast the man! Why did she allow him to continually push her to the edge of her temper?

If she expected her outburst to spark a response in kind, she was sorely disappointed. He only smiled. This time it did reach his eyes.

Great friends. It seemed suddenly more a targeted objective to him, than a casual wish. What could her friendship possibly mean to Travis Hawke?

"If I was eavesdropping, I apologize," he said. "It was just that I was so thoroughly caught up in your adventures as a bullwhacker."

The glint in his eyes bespoke teasing and a genuine amusement, something she sensed was as foreign to Travis Hawke as greenery after a plague of locusts. Still all Kate could see or remember was Billy Langley's cruel, condemning pronouncements that she didn't look, act or smell female. And now she transferred those judgments to Hawke. Somehow, some way he was making fun of her. And she was damned if she was going to stand here and wait for him to deliver the final blow to her pride.

For the first time since the sheltering anonymity of San Francisco, Kate had allowed a man to nudge the defensive barriers that had kept her safe for so many years. In spite of her grandiose assertions of not being hurt, not being used — she was all too aware of the vulnerability Hawke stirred in her by conjuring the image of her dream lover. And the awareness terrified her. Because for months she'd been telling herself she wanted a man to help her forget that very lover. No, she dare not want Travis Hawke. The price, she suspected, would be much higher than she was willing to pay.

She twisted her hands in front of her. "Just leave me alone, Mr. Hawke. Please."

The driver had built a fire and was making coffee, but she ignored it. Unbidden tears rimming her eyes, she marched toward a winding stand of oak and cottonwood. To get her mind off Hawke, she would concentrate on something far more mundane. It was time she freed herself from the pinching, binding, infuriating prison of her stays.

She crunched along a deer trail for several yards, not pausing until she left the stage and her fellow passengers well out of sight. Just being alone soothed her, the sheltering coolness of the trees revived her. She was delighted to discover a burbling brook, barely a foot across, snaking its way through the carpet of green. Kneeling beside it, she dipped cupped hands into the tumbling water, holding the sweet wetness against her face for long minutes.

She scooped up several more handfuls and drank deeply, not minding in the least the water that dripped down her arms and onto her dress. She had to resist the impulse to plop herself bodily into the small stream. The only other dress she could wear was packed away in her valise in the rear boot of the stage, and she was not going to give up her hard-found solitude even for the short time it would take her to retrieve it. Too, she was not yet ready for another encounter with Hawke.

Sitting back on her heels, she unfastened the hooks on the front of her dress, then yanked her arms out of the sleeves. She slipped it off her shoulders, allowing it to hang freely from her waist. Her chemise gapped open slightly, exposing a firm swell of pale breast, its coral tip puckering against the chill of the water that had dampened sections of the thin garment. She paid it no mind, concentrating solely on being rid of the stays that bound her from her hips to the underside of her breasts.

Awkwardly she reached behind her and began to tug at the lace string that had held her lungs captive far too long. She grumbled angrily when it did not pull free at once. She had needed the help of the maid at the hotel this morning to imprison herself. Now Kate wished fervently she had asked Laney Nolan to come along to aid in her escape.

She jerked harder, then cursed in earnest when the mistied bow snagged into a knot. Scrambling to her feet, she twisted her body in every conceivable direction, seeking vainly to find a better angle from which to attack the snarled thread. She was not going back to the stagecoach wearing the odious thing, even if she had to shred it with her bare hands.

"Can I help?"

She whirled, her arms instinctively crossing in front of her barely covered breasts. "How dare you?" she sputtered, glaring furiously into the unreadable countenance of Travis Hawke. "How dare you spy on me again!"

He displayed not the slightest hint of embarrassment

47

at discovering her in her state of dishabille, as though it had been no accident. Or as though he had been watching her for some time.

"I wasn't spying," he demurred, his eyes roving across her bare shoulders, seemingly capable of looking straight through arms to her quivering breasts beneath. "I heard all of the cursing and swearing and thought maybe you'd been besieged by a band of renegades. After all, I've never heard words like that coming from the mouth of a . . ."

"Don't say it!" she spat. "Don't you dare call me a lady!"

His eyes widened. "I'd hardly consider it a curse."

She turned her back on him, unable to cope with the jumble of emotions that roiled through her. He was barely four feet away. The long, lean length of him warmed her as if he were the flame of an approaching forest fire. She had been in this man's arms! He had made love to her countless times. But it was only in her dreams. She tried to stop it. But the transference was done. She was making Travis Hawke and her mystery lover one and the same.

She knew she should shove herself back into her dress at once, but she couldn't force her arms to move.

Damn him to hell anyway! What did he want from her? Surely, he was all too aware of how shamelessly attracted to him she was, as much as her mind begged to deny it. Did he find her interest amusing?

She trembled. Perhaps he had perceived her interest and followed her from the stage to alleviate the tedium of the trail in a far more primitive fashion than simply spying on her.

"I'm not going to hurt you, Kate."

How was it he could read her mind? And how was it that she still could not bring herself to ask how he knew her name? Deciding her only safeguard against

48

this man who had such an unnerving effect on her, was to pretend no effect at all, she gritted her teeth and said, "As long as you're here, you might as well make yourself useful. Get me out of this thing."

She held herself still as he crunched through the underbrush to stand behind her. When he bent to examine the knot, she could feel the heat of his breath on the nape of her neck. Suddenly lightheaded, it was all she could do to keep her knees from buckling.

"You've got yourself quite a mess here," he said, trying to work the recalcitrant lacing. The back of his hand grazed her upper arm.

Kate shivered, then prayed he didn't notice.

After several minutes of futile manipulation, he muttered, "I think I'll have to use my knife."

"Please do," Kate said. Anything to end the feel of his hands on her body, no matter how cursory and dispassionate he was being. "I'll never wear this damned thing again as long as I live anyway."

He chuckled. "I don't know why you ladies wear 'em in the first place. If you'd just sew the dress a little larger . . ."

She stiffened. The last thing she needed from Travis Hawke was a reference to her plentiful figure. "Just cut the blasted lace and get out of here!"

Hawke slipped the knife from the sheath on his belt and deftly sliced through the knot.

Kate sighed with heartfelt relief, allowing the offensive garment to fall free of her body. She couldn't resist running her hands along her emancipated sides.

"From the looks of things back here," Hawke murmured, "you didn't need the infernal thing anyway."

She felt the blush begin on her shoulders and spread outward and down to encompass her entire being. Snatching up the front of her dress, she jerked her arms into the sleeves. But she was shaking too much,

49

her fingers fumbling too badly to fasten the hooks that would join the bodice together. She clutched the material in front of her.

His hands settled on her shoulders, his thumbs kneading the tightly bunched muscles in the back of her neck. "Don't be afraid of me, Kate." His voice, so husky, so warm, sent a river of fire spilling across her flesh.

She did not resist when he shifted his hands to turn her to face him. She lifted her head to study his eyes, near blue-black now, piercing, questioning. Billy Langley had looked at her like that once. And so, she imagined, had her one time lover. It was there in every taut line of his body. He wanted to kiss her.

Wasn't this precisely what she wanted? To appease her reawakened physical needs? To end her obsession with a nameless, faceless stranger who had one night stumbled into her life, then vanished? And with a man as compelling as Travis Hawke, it would be the stuff of her fantasies. Then why did everything in her beg for her to turn and run. To not dare risk comparing Hawke with the dream.

Because she knew, knew by the look in those midnight eyes — Travis Hawke was not a man to settle for appeasing physical needs. At least not with a woman as woefully inexperienced as herself.

Pride warred with desire. He couldn't know how truly naive she was. She couldn't give him that kind of power. She'd been with a man only once, and that had ended badly. She was all too certain he'd already guessed how much she wanted to feel those well-muscled arms of his surround her, feel the pressure of his lips against her own. This from a man about whom she knew only one thing — his name.

No, this couldn't happen. She was foolish to think he would settle for a kiss. His motives were not her motives. She was adventurous to be sure, but she was also desperately lonely in the aftermath of her father's death. Her heart was on dangerous ground. She was a woman terrified to acknowledge that the stirring needs that pressed her were not entirely physical, but were rooted in a very real need to love and be loved.

Travis Hawke was a man responding to the call of his sex, availing himself of a woman who was proving herself all too willing. She was setting herself up for the one thing she had vowed would never be her fate again—to be used by a man.

She had to think. She had to stop him. Stop him from doing what her heart pleaded for him to do. To make her feel loved for herself alone—no matter how brief the illusion.

But his thumbs were tracing feathery circles at the base of her throat, and her neck arched back of its own accord. She would stop him. Yes, she would stop him. But first she would force herself to use him just a little, use him as she was certain he intended to use her.

Her lips parted as his mouth came crushing down on hers.

Chapter Four

Travis Hawke watched Kate McCullough stalk away from him to disappear into the stand of oak and cottonwood that lined the roadside. He had thought the noon stop-over would be the perfect opportunity for them to talk. But he was finding Kate a most frustrating person with whom to have a conversation. He swore softly.

"Great job so far, Hawke," he grumbled, trying to decide whether or not to follow her. Currying Kate McCullough's favor was instrumental to the success of his plans in Leavenworth. Yet so far her best opinion of him seemed likely to run to tar and feathers.

"She don't like you much."

Hawke turned to study the stage driver for a long minute before he answered. "When did that become your business?"

"Bryce McCullough's whelp. Didn't recognize her at first with a dress on. She never seen me, but I seen her once in Leavenworth. She's headin' into a whole pack o' trouble. Maybe I think it's my Christian duty to look out for her."

Hawke said nothing.

"You from these parts?" the driver prodded.

"That your business, too?"

"Not too friendly."

Hawke didn't blink. "Not too."

The man stuck out a hand. "The name's Kerns, Jeb Kerns."

Hawke ignored the hand, unwillingly remembering that Kate had done the same to him. With Kate, though, he had found the incident amusing. There was no humor in him now.

The driver wiped his hand down his shirtfront, as though the gesture could somehow wipe away Hawke's insult. "Listen, mister," he said, "you'd best watch yourself. I know who sent for you. And I know why."

Hawke knelt beside the saddlebags he had retrieved from the stagecoach. From one of them he extracted a .45 Colt and a gunbelt. With a deliberate motion he sighted down the black barrel, though he kept the weapon pointed at the dirt. "Kerns," he said, "you'd better not know anything at all."

Kerns stared at the gun, then at Hawke. "You don't scare me none." His voice betrayed the lie. "I been waitin' for this chance to talk to you." He glanced behind him, apparently assuring himself that the Nolans, who were sharing a cup of coffee beside the fire, remained out of earshot. He looked again at Hawke. "You're the one, ain't ya? The gunfighter Frank Blanchard sent for."

Hawke cocked the pistol and spun the cylinder. Kerns stepped back a pace.

"You must not like living, Kerns," Hawke said, straightening. "Or you would've learned a long time ago when to keep your mouth shut." With lightning swiftness he grabbed the stage driver by the shirtfront and yanked him over to the rear boot of the coach. Out of the corner of one eye, he too checked the Nolans. They were intent on each other. They did not look up.

He shoved his gun in Kerns's face. "Tell me what you know and why you know it, or you're a dead man."

"Please, mister," Kerns said, his eyes wide with the knowledge that he had pushed the wrong man too far, "I didn't mean no harm. Honest."

"What do you know about Blanchard? And what do you know about me?"

"I read the letter," Kerns croaked.

"What letter?" Hawke jabbed the gun barrel against the tip of the man's nose.

"The one Blanchard sent to Ed Reno." Kerns was shaking from head to foot, but Hawke did not back off.

"You read Blanchard's mail?"

"He got me curious, that's all." Kerns was babbling now. "He got me real curious about that letter. He gave it to me special about a month ago, instead of just puttin' it in my mail pouch. So when I was drivin' the stage that day, I read it. He was askin' Ed Reno to send up some gunhand no one would know in Leavenworth. It was just after Bryce McCullough got himself killed." Kerns swallowed convulsively. "When I seen the letter was addressed to Reno, I knew Frank was lookin' for a gunfighter. Reno's killed more men than Quantrill and for less reason."

Hawke uncocked the gun, shoving it into the holster on his hip. "So I take it you were planning on having Frank pay a little money to keep quiet about all this newfound knowledge of yours?"

Kerns shook his head violently. "I'd never do nothin' so stupid as that, honest, mister."

Hawke grimaced. That was exactly what the man had planned to do. Only now he realized he may have gotten in over his head. The man continued to ratttle on nervously.

"When I seen it was McCullough's she-cat you were

54

eyein' up and down in Columbia, well, like I said, I just knowed who you was."

"When we get to Leavenworth, Kerns, you keep riding. I don't want to see your face again."

"But . . . but Frank would wonder why I up and left."

"If you stay," Hawke said, "Frank won't have to wonder why you're dead."

Kerns nodded weakly, but he wasn't finished pushing his luck. "I'll go. Just tell me somethin'. Are you gonna gun Dusty Lafferty? Or just sweet talk McCullough's brat into selling Frank the company?"

"You've got a real way of courtin' a bullet, Kerns. Keep it up and I'll introduce you."

"Frank must be payin' you a helluva lot, mister. You're cold as a lizard's belly. Anybody can see it. 'Cept Kate. You ain't let her see it, have ya? You're all smiles with her."

Hawke shifted his weight to the balls of his feet.

"Does he figure gettin' a man into her bedroll can help him steal the old man's company? Likely she don't get too many takers. Never seen a woman act less female."

Hawke slammed a fist into the man's jaw, sending him sprawling butt-first in the dirt. "You talk too much, Kerns," he gritted. "Blanchard's a fool to have a man like you on the payroll. When you leave Leavenworth, don't stop 'til you hit the Pacific."

He strode toward the trees, pausing long enough to slant a glance back toward Kerns who had yet to pick himself off the ground. His voice was as cold as mountain rain. "One word to Kate McCullough about this conversation," he raised a finger for emphasis, "one word, and you won't have to worry about Leavenworth—because I'll kill you before we ever get there."

As if to stress his contempt for the man, Hawke did not look back again. He entered the copse of trees near the same spot where Kate had disappeared ten minutes before.

He scowled as he walked. He was a man used to danger, but unknown variables like Jeb Kerns often made the risks outweigh the rewards. If Kerns knew what had brought him here, it meant someone else might know too. He gave himself a mental shrug. It was a chance he would have to take. Blanchard made any risk acceptable.

Side-stepping a thorny shrub, he considered the problem of upgrading Kate McCullough's evaluation of him. It was vital that she trust him. He smiled bitterly. In one-on-one encounters with women, he'd rarely been found wanting. It was a fact he acknowledged with more matter-of-factness than arrogance. Women liked the way he looked. He hadn't done anything to earn looking this way, but he wasn't above using whatever advantage he could, especially now when the stakes were so high. What Kate would think of him afterwards made no difference. What anyone thought of him made no difference.

He stopped, tugging at the low hanging branch of a sapling. When had the callousness become as much a part of him as the gun weighting his thigh?

He did not want to hurt Kate McCullough, though he accepted the fact that the time would come when he had no choice. He would do what he had to do. She was the innocent forced into a deadly game she had had no part in creating. And in spite of her blustering bravado, he sensed a fragility about Kate that put the lie to her posturing. Too many times today she hadn't been able to meet his eyes. She was afraid, though he couldn't yet guess of what.

Obviously it wasn't horses. He shook his head. He

still couldn't believe that stunt she'd pulled with the shying gelding at the stage depot in Columbia. Kate McCullough was a baffling mix of contradictions — well able to take care of herself against twelve hundred pounds of horseflesh, yet easily flustered when the attention focused on her became too personal.

He scratched his chin thoughtfully, remembering her scrutiny on the stage. He supposed he'd embarrassed the hell out of her, but it had been all he could do not to smile. She had pronounced him beautiful, her brown eyes softening, her lips parting just a little. She couldn't possibly know the picture she'd presented at that moment. She couldn't know that it was she who had become beautiful.

Grimacing, he snapped off the twig in his hand. That was all he needed, a personal interest in Kate. If she ever found out who he was, what he was, worse — what he was doing here . . .

Yet the personal interest was there. He'd felt it the first minute he'd laid eyes on her in the stage depot. He'd known who she was because it was his job to know. But he hadn't known that the bullwhacking daughter of a freight hauler was going to rouse not only his professional curiosity, but his male curiosity as well.

He was considering the dangers of that interest for both of them when he saw her. She was standing next to a small stream, so intent on cursing and swearing at someone or something that she remained unaware of his deliberately noisy approach. His eyes widened as he sized up her state of dress, or rather undress. His jaw tightened unconsciously. She'd better be cursing some*thing*. If some*one* was near her and she was dressed like that . . .

He drew nearer, his lips curving wryly. She was not under attack after all, at least not by anything human.

57

He suppressed a chuckle as he watched her battle the apparent snag in her corset lacing. He'd known her scarcely four hours, talked to her hardly at all, yet he knew what he was seeing right now was Kate McCullough being unabashedly herself.

For long minutes he stood there, amazed at the quickening of his pulse. When she twisted her body trying to get at the knot, he didn't miss the firm swell of pale breast peeking out from her loosened chemise. He tried to ignore the tightening in his loins, but he could not ignore the reality of her effect on him. He was drawn to this woman. He couldn't be, shouldn't be, but he was. Kate, who stirred a memory he'd locked away years ago.

He wanted to feel her beneath him, naked and needing, feel himself buried inside her. He was achingly, annoyingly aroused—lust churning in his guts as it had not for a long time. In fact, he acknowledged with no particular interest, it had been a long time since he had experienced any emotion at all about anything at all.

Yet the danger Kate McCullough could present to his purpose in Leavenworth was slammed home with each step he took, his pulse rate rising as the distance between them closed. Damn, he wasn't some cuckolded fool to fall under the spell of a woman. Not again. Stepping to within a few feet of her, he cleared his throat, praying suddenly that she would be angry enough to spare them both the complication of becoming more than *great friends*. "Can I help?"

She did not disappoint him. She whirled, furious. But even as she berated him for daring to intimate she was a lady, he did not miss the light in the depths of those coffee eyes. Damn, she was feeling it, too. It appeared neither one of them was going to be sensible about this. Drawing his knife, he freed her from her corset, then found it impossible to resist the bared flesh of her shoulders.

"Don't be afraid of me, Kate," he rasped, kneading the tension from the back of her neck. Her skin was satin smooth and warm, so warm. He turned her to face him.

Her lips parted slightly, her eyes wide and pleading. She was asking, but he doubted she was even aware she was asking. Damn, how he wanted to kiss her, hold her, take her, right now.

It seemed like forever since he'd felt this way. He'd thought whatever gentleness there was in him was lost, buried long ago. Buried with Anne. His jaw hardened, a fierce bitterness surging through him. No, he wouldn't think of Anne. Not now. Now it was Kate. Sweet, vulnerable Kate with her warm brown eyes— trusting and not trusting. Afraid.

Afraid of him? he wondered, caressing her cheek with his fingertips. Did she suspect . . . ? No, it wasn't that kind of fear. He could see it now. Subtle, shy, only thinly veiled. He glided his palm downward until it rested along the side of her throat. She wasn't afraid of him, she was afraid of what he was doing to her. Damn, he was more than a little afraid of what was happening himself.

He took his lips to her mouth, relishing the softness, the sweetness he found there. His arms curled around her, surrounding her, crushing her to him. He wanted her. It was insanity, but still he wanted her.

The kiss deepened. His tongue teased her, cajoled her, coaxed her to give him what he'd never in his lifetime had. Give him solace, give him peace.

His hands trailed downward along her ribs, then up, his thumbs coming to rest beneath her breasts. He savored the feel of her thudding heart, her shallowed breathing. She was waiting, waiting . . .

He tugged open the unhooked front of her dress, sliding a hand over her chemise, encompassing the lush swell beneath. His groan met her whimper, the thickening in his groin demanding to be appeased.

"Oh, God, Kate," he groaned. "Let me. Here. Now. Please, let me."

It was too much to ask of her. Too much to ask of a woman who would one day hate his guts. The most damning part of all was that it was lie. A lie for him. A lie for her.

His conscience nudged him then. What was left of it — after the war, after Anne, after so many things. His conscience — condemning, because he dared use her — use her for Blanchard, use her for himself.

Kate, who reached him, when he'd sworn nothing and no one ever would again. Kate, who stood to lose the most — from Frank Blanchard and from Travis Hawke.

He thought of the lie, even as he dared hold her, kiss her, touch her. The lie.

Frank Blanchard had indeed sent for a hired gun. A hired gun to finish what he'd started with Kate Mc-Cullough's father. A hired gun to gain Kate's trust. A hired gun to kill her.

A hired gun named Travis Hawke.

Chapter Five

Kate trembled, her body thrilling to Hawke's bold embrace. When his hand closed over her chemise covered breast, she arched forward instinctively, encouraging the sweet intimacy. Her soft whimper became a moan as she felt her nipple grow hard against the heat of his palm.

"Let me, Kate," he rasped, his breath hot against her ear. "Let me. I'll make it good for both of us." With the tips of his fingers he trailed circles around the taut bud, even as his lips slid across her cheek to once again lay claim to her mouth.

In the suffocating tedium of boarding school she had immersed herself in her San Francisco fantasy, imagining herself in the arms of her passionate, handsome stranger. And now Travis Hawke was here, and he was real, and the wonder of it was almost too much to bear. Too much, because even though Hawke resembled her lover, she knew nothing of the man inside the magnificent body. Hawke was as much a stranger as the man in her hotel room had been. She couldn't make the same mistake twice.

The same? Billy Langley had kissed her and it had wakened her to the newness of passion. Jim Collier had kissed her and wakened nothing. Her dream lover had left her achingly unfulfilled—craving him. Now with Hawke—the feel of him, the scent, the taste . . . the same? It couldn't be, couldn't be . . .

She tugged at his shirt, imprisoned in the waistband of his pants. If he had the scar . . . Her hand fell away. She didn't want to know. What if he was? What if he wasn't?

The prickly stubble of his beard abraded her tender flesh, a sensation she found curiously exciting. She pressed herself against him, revelling in the hot moist breath fanning her cheek, the wet, probing tongue dancing with her own.

A cool breeze sifted through her hair, as his hand eased aside the flimsy material of her chemise to find and sear the naked flesh beneath. The motions were much the same. And the feelings, dear God, the feelings, how she had forgotten the awesome power of them. She was surrendering, giving herself to this man about whom she knew nothing.

She tried to think, tried to stop herself from succumbing to this madness, but Hawke gave no quarter. He wanted her, the proof of his desire hot and hard beneath the denim that brushed her thigh. The feel of him frightened her, even as it exhilarated her. He wanted her! This man of her dreams was alive and aroused here in her arms.

"We can't do this," she rasped. "Please, it's insane. I don't even know . . ."

"You don't have to know anything, except that I want you. And you want me." He lifted her chin between his thumb and forefinger. "Say it. Say the words, Kate. Tell me you want me."

She sought desperately to deny it, to force the words past her lips, but they wouldn't come. Even had she said them, she knew he would have seen through the lie. She did want him. God help her, she did. She'd already made love to him a hundred times in her dreams. Now that he was here, real, she couldn't deny what her heart had longed for since that night in San Francisco.

"Say it," he said again, his voice hoarse. "I want to hear you say it."

"I want you," she said. "Yes, damn you, I want you." Her heart pounded, her knees refusing her legs' plea for support. How had she allowed this to come so far? She'd come to the stream to rid herself of her godawful corset and now suddenly a man, a live flesh and blood man, was holding her, touching her, caressing her, loosing emotions in her over which she was finding she had no control.

It was painfully obvious that Travis Hawke had mistaken her for some practiced woman of the world, just as the other . . .

What would happen when he discovered the truth, that she was merely a frightened woman with only the bawdy gossip of trail-rough teamsters and one night of serendipitous magic to guide her path?

She dared not let him guess just how inexperienced she was. She had to convince him she knew what she was doing. Had to convince him because she wanted no end to what he was doing to her. Without stopping to consider the outrageous boldness of her actions her hand snaked downward, closing over the front of his trousers, molding itself to the rock-hard evidence of his passion. His low, throaty groan thrilled her, encouraged her to be bolder still. With her free hand she tugged at the buttons of his fly, praying he kept his eyes closed so that he did not see what she so fiercely felt—the scarlet blush suffusing her face.

"God, Kate," he groaned, tangling his fingers in her russet hair, "I need this. I need it now."

She allowed him to guide her down to the carpet of soft green, inhaling the pungent scent of the grasses wreathing her head. She bit back a sigh as his mouth left hers to blaze a trail of fire along her neck to the valley between her breasts. Her hands fell away from their task at the opening of his trousers, her mind too drugged by the surging tide of her own passion to continue to do anything but feel what Travis Hawke was doing to her body.

"Oh, please, please," she whimpered, her words giving way to gasps as his mouth closed over a coral tipped breast. Her body writhed, her hips arching upward of their own accord, answering the ancient call of her sex. Each tiny part of her was kindling to his flame. She burned for him, unable, unwilling to question the ultimate cost of this moment of madness.

She had a name to the face and body that had haunted her for five years. She had a name and it was Travis Hawke. He couldn't be the same man, but somehow he was able to evoke the same wonder in her body. She could no more turn away from him now than she could turn away from herself. Whatever fate had brought him to her, she intended to use it, use him. And afterward, she would have no illusions. The same fate that brought him to her would take him away again. But for this tiny breath of time she wouldn't think or consider or reason, she would only feel—feel like a woman loved by a man.

That he didn't love her, that she didn't love him made no intrusion on her fantasy. She had wished this, dreamed this, wanted this far too long. She couldn't let the real world interfere now.

She arched upward, as he continued to suckle her breast. "Love me," she murmured, threading her fingers through the sweat dampened thickness of his hair. "Right here, right now, I want you to love me."

She wished the words back at once, when his mouth broke contact with her flesh. He raised himself up, staking his arms on either side of her, his eyes boring into hers. "Love?" The word was strangled and for the briefest instant she was aware of a searing agony in the depths of those midnight eyes. Then just as abruptly the pain disappeared, to be replaced by a look of such studied indifference that she knew it was forced. "What we're doing has nothing to do with love, Kate."

He destroyed the illusion, shattered the fantasy. She bit her lower lip, hoping to stay the tears of shame that burned behind her eyes. Mortified, she pulled the sides of her chemise together in front of her.

"I didn't mean it that way," she snapped, hoping the defensive tone of her voice was noticeable only to herself. "It's just something I say when I . . . when . . . I . . . do this."

He swore, the words crude, jabbing her like a physical pain. He shoved himself off her, sitting next to her with one arm perched on an upraised knee. "I'm sorry," he gritted. "I'm no one to be passing judgment. God knows, I didn't have you pegged as a virgin . . ."

She struggled to rise, keeping her head averted, lest he see the tears she had not been able to hold at bay. No, she was no virgin. Thanks to another stranger in another place. He had used her that night to assuage some unspeakable pain in his life. But what was Hawke's excuse? Or her own?

"You're so like him," she whispered, not realizing until she saw his startled gaze that she had spoken aloud. She breathed a heartfelt sigh when he asked no questions.

Wrestling with her chemise, she worked the fastenings by feel, her vision blurred, her heart aching. Five years of imagining crumbled in an instant. What a fool she'd been. She'd sworn not to be used, yet be-

65

cause Hawke reminded her so exactly of her dream lover, she had let down her guard. A tear struck the back of her hand. It would not happen again.

Praying he was not looking at her, she swiped at her tears, then straightened, mentally girding herself to turn and face him. He would not have the satisfaction of thinking he had somehow hurt her. But she couldn't suppress a horrified gasp when she heard a voice calling out from somewhere nearby.

"Yo, Hawke! You there?"

The stage driver! Her hand flew to her mouth. If he found Hawke here with her . . .

She turned, ready to beg him not to say anything. But all she saw was his retreating back, as he hurried away from her on a line to intercept the advancing driver. He was hunched low, skirting bushes and trees, keeping his ear cocked toward Kerns. Kate hugged the bark of an ancient oak, peering around the trunk, keeping Hawke in sight, but making certain Kerns did not see her. Fresh tears stained her cheeks. She did not have to beg Hawke not to say anything. He was apparently so shamed at the thought of being caught in her company that he was doing everything he could to make certain that didn't happen.

She closed her eyes. Most men liked to brag of their conquests. But no doubt Hawke found her too plain to be worthy of boasting. She couldn't dwell on the dismal thought too long. Kerns was rapidly approaching her position. Scrunching behind the tree, she held her breath. She hadn't finished re-fastening her dress. Her lips felt swollen from Hawke's savage possession. If Kerns found her like this, the worst would only be too obvious.

From what sounded like nearly a quarter mile off, she heard Hawke shout, "I'm over here, Kerns! What do you want?"

66

Kerns was nearly upon her, when Hawke's voice halted him. She didn't miss Kerns's snort of disgust. "The stage is leavin'! Where the hell you been?"

The driver's heavy footfalls started again, only now they were moving away from her. She heaved a shuddering sigh. With trembling fingers she finished dressing. She cringed at Kerns's next words.

"Dallying with that little miss out here, were ya?" he cackled. "Does she have a woman's body after all?"

The snap of twigs and the rustle of brush announced Hawke's retracing his steps. She guessed both men were barely fifty yards away from her now. Almost against her will, she found herself straining to hear Hawke's reply to Kerns's leering question.

"I'm alone, Kerns. I was just stretching my legs."

She sagged against the tree, blowing out a long breath, then was instantly annoyed that she would feel any sort of gratitude to the arrogant bastard. No doubt he was just saving his own conceited image. He wouldn't want it tarnished by . . .

Stop it! she fumed inwardly. She'd had more than enough self-pity to last a lifetime these past months, yet it had become such a habit, the response was all but automatic. Grimacing, she determined to rid herself of the noisome trait.

Only after she'd heard the two men walk away did she stand and head back to the stage herself. As she walked, she considered the sudden notion that Hawke's desertion of her may not have been entirely self-serving after all. Could he have left her to keep Kerns from blundering into them — not to save *his* reputation, but *hers*?

She stooped to pluck a spray of mistflowers, stroking her fingers over the feathery blue petals. She forced herself to relive the last minute of her impassioned encounter with Hawke. He had been more than willing to finish what he'd started, until she had foolishly mentioned the word *love*. She hadn't meant it literally, but the damage had been immediate and irrevocable. The look in his eyes — even in her memory — had the power to arrest her breathing. Haunted. Agonized.

"Who was she, Travis Hawke?" Kate asked aloud. "Who was she that even the thought of her can cut you to the heart?"

She hated the comparisons she kept making to that long ago night, yet she knew they were inevitable. Now she wished she had felt for the scar. But what if he was the same man? He obviously didn't know it. Was she going to confront him, as she had so often promised herself? Ask how things had been going these past five years?

And what if he wasn't? The memory of that night would haunt her forever. Who was he? Where was he?

Not knowing had its advantages. She doubted Hawke would welcome meeting an indiscretion from his past.

Damn! She didn't care what he would welcome. She had to know. One way or another, she had to.

She stepped out of the glade to see Kerns dumping the remains of the noon coffee onto the cookfire. The flames hissed and sputtered out. He must have felt her gaze on him, because he looked up suddenly, his beady eyes regarding her with an odd intensity.

"Been wonderin' how long you was plannin' on keepin' the rest of us waitin'," he said. "I got a schedule to keep. Of course," he paused meaningfully, "if'n you got a good reason to stay in them woods, I could make an exception."

"I apologize if I've made you late," Kate said stiffly, then stepped past the driver to the coach. The Nolans were already inside, studying her reproachfully. She straightened, prepared to meet Hawke's equally annoyed countenance, though his reason would scarcely be her tardiness. But when she swung her gaze to the opposite side of the coach, it was to discover that Hawke was not aboard. Frowning, she glanced around the camp. She hadn't seen him since she'd returned, so she'd simply assumed he was inside.

"I'll give you a hand up, missy," Kerns said, coming up behind her. "Though, o' course, you're still welcome up in the driver's boot with me at any time."

The suggestive glint in his eyes made her want to vomit. When he dared touch her elbow, she jerked away. "I can manage on my own, thank you."

She climbed aboard, settling herself in the seat that had been Hawke's on the first leg of their journey. When the driver secured the door shut behind her, it was all she could do to keep the question from leaping from her throat. *Where was he?* But she wouldn't give the foul-minded Kerns the satisfaction. Nor, she assured herself, did she care for the thought of what Hawke himself could construe of her interest in his whereabouts.

She suppressed a grateful smile when Laney Nolan solved her dilemma for her. "Aren't we going to wait for Mr. Hawke?" the young newlywed asked as Kerns prepared to hoist himself up to his diver's perch.

"Nope," came the curt reply.

"But we can't just leave him . . ."

"Ain't leavin' him. He left us."

"What are you talking about?" Kate demanded, a nameless anxiety touching her. "He didn't leave. He was just . . ." She stopped. "I mean, where would he go? He wouldn't be left afoot in the middle of nowhere."

"Said to drive on without him. I didn't ask no questions. None of my business." With that Kerns climbed into the driver's seat, effectively ending the conversation.

"Why would he do such a crazy thing, Kate?" Laney asked, apparently assuming that Kate's superior knowledge of western ways would offer some insight into Travis Hawke's request that he be left behind on a Missouri roadside a dozen miles from anywhere.

But Kate could only wonder herself. Why? Why would he do this? He'd told her nothing about staying behind when they were alone together by the stream. She almost laughed out loud. Hadn't told her his plans? The man hadn't told her anything at all. They'd been about to share their bodies, not their lives.

"Kate, what is it?" Laney demanded. "Are you all right?"

Kate looked into the girl's stricken face. Her voice was shaky, but she managed to choke out, "I'm fine."

"You look terrible."

"I'll be fine. It's just . . . just the heat. It wears you down after awhile."

"If you can't get used to it, I hate to think about Harold and me," Laney laughed, obviously accepting the weather as the reason for Kate's pallor. She patted Harold on the knee, as he smiled at her adoringly.

Kate shifted her gaze to the landscape. It was that kind of look the man of her fantasies had often given her in the throes of their make-believe passion. The look she now admitted she had longed to see in Travis Hawke's eyes when she asked him to make love to her in the woods.

Not only had her request instantly put him away from her, it had actually opened some deep and awful wound from his past. Had she inadvertently hurt him so badly that he couldn't even abide sitting in the coach with her for the remaining day and a half of their journey to Leavenworth? Would her last memory of those midnight eyes forever be the agony she'd

70

brought to them?

Try as she might she couldn't shake off thinking about him, a man she might never in her life see again. She had to know, somehow she had to know if he was the one. Even when Kerns shouted "Yo!" and the stage lurched forward, she found herself scanning the roadside, hoping he would appear at the last instant and call for the stage to halt.

But it didn't happen and Kate laid her head back on the upholstered seat fighting off the strange despair that took hold of her. Her fantasy mingled with reality—the memory of a hot, searing tongue, exploring hands; and yet unknown delights. And now he was gone. Just as her dream lover was gone.

She would forget Hawke. She must. She was heading toward Leavenworth, toward home. Toward home forever changed because her father was dead. And on that reality no fantasy could intrude. If it took her the rest of her days, she would find out who murdered her father and why.

The stage had travelled barely a quarter mile down the road when the first bullet ripped through the door.

Chapter Six

Kate dove for the floor of the compartment, grabbing at the terrified Nolans, forcing them to do the same. A second bullet gouged a hole in the coach's interior bare inches above her head.

"Dear God, what's happening?" Laney cried.

"Holdup!" Kate grimaced, shoving the girl's head back down when she attempted to peer out the window. "Keep low. It's our best chance." Above the din of gunfire she listened for the crack of the whip, Kerns's shout, the feel of the horses lunging forward into a hard run, but it didn't happen. What was the matter with the man? Had he been shot? As she thought it, she felt the motion of the stage slow, then stop.

She caught the sound of an approaching horseman and wished to hell her own gun wasn't packed away in her valise. If she'd been wearing her buckskins . . . Her jaw clenched. There was no help for it now. She would just have to hope the gunman didn't cross the line from robbery to murder.

Her anger rose perceptibly when she heard Kerns's anxious shout. "Take it easy, mister. Don't shoot!" Damn the man. He hadn't even attempted to make a run for it, nor had he fired a single shot in their

72

defense.

"Just keep them hands up and you'll live to see the sun set," came the terse command.

"Will he kill us?" Laney squeaked.

"Not if we do what he says," Kate said, keeping her voice calm for the girl's sake. She decided to dare a glance out the window. What she saw sent her heart into her throat. A lone man with a gunny sack over his head sat astride a dun gelding, holding Kerns at bay with a rifle. Not that the driver was making any threatening motions. His hands were raised and he seemed more than content to take orders from the outlaw.

"You in the coach," the gunman called out, "get out here now. And no tricks." He dismounted the dun, letting it dance nervously away. His voice seemed unnaturally low and guttural, as though he were attempting to disguise it. Would someone recognize his normal voice?

The thought struck her like a thunderbolt. Hawke. The outlaw was of a similar build, the knee-length yellow slicker he wore effectively hiding his clothes. No, that was absurd. Why would he? But then where was Hawke? He couldn't possibly have gotten far enough away from the coach not to have heard the gunshots. Damn, he was armed, he could have come to their aid. Why hadn't he?

She forced her attention to Laney, who was sobbing openly now. Her husband made a vain attempt to comfort her, but he was shaking so badly himself he could barely speak.

"I said get the hell out of that coach!" the gunman growled. "Or I'll just start puttin' bullets in it."

Kate shoved open the door. "That won't be necessary," she snapped. "Though if you decided to put a few bullets in your head, I doubt anybody would stop you."

73

"Watch your mouth," the man said, still masking his voice.

"Got no money this trip," Kerns put in. "Company didn't even bother to send along a guard."

"Now isn't that convenient," Kate growled, drilling Kerns with a look.

"Not after money," the outlaw said, and Kate knew his eyes rested squarely on her. She shivered, as though someone had just carved her name on a tombstone. The man levelled the gun in her direction. "Which one of you ladies is Kate McCullough?"

No one spoke. Kate could feel the blood draining from her face. What did this man want with her? And why did she know it had something to do with her father's death? It struck her then that the man knew full well who she was. That he was just toying with her, or keeping the fact that he knew her from those who would be left alive as witnesses.

"Why . . . why do you want to know which one of us is Kate?" Laney asked in a shaky voice.

Under the mask Kate knew the man was smiling. "I'm going to kill her."

Laney made a small noise in her throat, but otherwise said nothing. Kate felt a stinging in her eyes. The woman was young and to Kate a bit silly, but she had just put herself in a class with the bravest people she had ever known.

"If you don't tell me," the gunman said, "I'll just have to kill both of you ladies."

He levelled the rifle at Laney Nolan's head.

"Don't," Kate said softly, "I'm Kate McCullough." She took a step toward him. "But then you already knew that, didn't you?"

The man said nothing.

She stood very still as he shifted the gun to her chest. If she'd tried to move, she would have fainted. A

74

fact that made her furious. She didn't take her eyes from the bore of the rifle. In the space of the next minute she would be dead. Dead.

Incongruously, each second seemed to expand outward, to become a precious entity unto itself. Images, scenes, whole segments of her life swirled, beckoned, as though demanding a final acknowledgement. But the moment her mind settled on was not a trail-dusted ride on muleback with her father, or the dawn rainbow that followed a flashflood one spring on the Platte, nor even that bittersweet night in San Francisco. Instead she saw, felt, tasted as clearly as the moment it happened the sweet velvet texture of Travis Hawke's mouth on her own.

Hawke. Had he heard the shots and ignored them? Had he himself been waylaid by the outlaw? Or— No. Hawke couldn't kiss her like that and then . . .

The outlaw raised the rifle to her face, his thumb on the hammer, ready to draw it back. Laney Nolan screamed. Kate closed her eyes. *Please, God, don't let me die thinking it's* . . .

The shot echoed and re-echoed.

Kate's knees buckled. She sank to the ground, vaguely aware of how surprised she was that she could still hear Laney screaming. Her eyelids were lead weights, yet somehow she forced them open. As though detached from herself she watched the gunman's arm go slack, the rifle clatter to the ground, his body weave, stagger back, then seem to collapse in upon itself as he fell heavily to the hard-packed earth. She stared at the stain seeping from the man's chest, forming a grotesque red mud on the roadway. His fingers twitched, then stilled, a strange gurgling sounded in his throat, then nothing.

Her own breathing grew shallow, her body impossibly heavy to lift. She wanted to go to the dead outlaw, pull away the mask, but she couldn't move. She wasn't even certain she was still alive.

Only vaguely aware of Laney's shrill cry, she scarcely felt the brush of Harold's body, as the man pitched into the dirt beside her in a dead faint.

It was the crunch of boots on the road that got through to her. She looked up, feeling a rush of relief so profound she had to bite her lip to keep from crying out.

"That was some shootin'!" the stage driver hooted. "Like to never knowed what hit 'im."

Hawke's eyes never left Kate's. She couldn't even blink, so stunned was she to see him. It was then that the harsh reality slammed home at just how certain she had been that the outlaw, the man who wanted her dead, was Travis Hawke. She forced her gaze to the rifle in his right hand, carried as naturally as a physician carried a medical bag. Nothing in his stride, the set of his jaw or those midnight eyes told her anything of what he was thinking. He had just killed a man, yet to look at him was to see neither regret nor satisfaction.

Her eyes followed him as he paused beside the outlaw. Stooping down, he gripped the gunny sack covering the outlaw's face. She wanted to turn away, but found it impossible. He jerked off the sack.

"Know him?" he asked.

She could only nod weakly, feeling a wave of incredulity mixed with nausea washing over her. "His . . . his name was Billy Langley." He looked different than she remembered. A jagged scar marred the left side of his once handsome face. Kate had seen wounds like that from the war. A bayonet? A sword? "He worked for my father once. A teamster. My . . . my father fired him. He . . . there were reasons. But to kill me . . . why?"

She watched as Hawke wrapped Billy's body in a

blanket, then dragged it back to the rear boot of the stage. What in God's name was she going home to? First her father's death, and now she hadn't even arrived home and an attempt had been made on her life by a man who had once kissed her and called her pretty.

"Please, help me with Harold!" Laney's plaintive voice interrupted Kate's roiling thoughts.

She knelt beside the girl. "He'll be all right. It was just all the excitement."

"You think he's a coward, don't you?"

"I think we all react to things in different ways," Kate said gently. "Harold didn't pass out until *after* the danger was over. And he didn't point me out to Billy Langley either."

Laney gave Kate a shaky smile. "Thank you."

"No," Kate said, "thank *you*."

"If you folks are done tellin' each other how brave ya are," Kerns grumbled, "I've got a schedule to keep."

"Don't think your superiors aren't going to know the disgraceful way you handled this whole thing, Kerns," Kate said, as Hawke and the stage driver lifted the unconscious Nolan into the stagecoach. "You didn't do a damn thing to get away from that yahoo. In fact, it was you who told the shotgun messenger to stay behind in Columbia."

"Am I supposed to be scairt o' your threats, missy?" Kerns hefted himself into the driver's box. "Frank Blanchard don't tell his drivers to die for their stage."

"But Blanchard doesn't give a hoot if his passengers die, is that what you're saying?"

"Why don't you just ask him for yerself?"

"I'll be asking Frank Blanchard a helluva lot more than that," Kate said.

"Missy," Kerns said, spitting out a wad of tobacco that just missed the hem of her dress, "you be sure and let me know when you're gonna let ol' Frank have it. I wanna be there."

Kate ground her teeth together to keep from loosing the expletives that sprang to her throat. The beady-eyed little snake wasn't worth the effort.

She climbed into the coach, yanking the door shut behind her. Laney was settled on the opposite seat, gently cradling Harold against her.

"Do you know why that man would try to kill you, Kate?" the girl asked.

"I have no idea," Kate said, leaning back on the upholstered seat. "But I most certainly intend to find out. Billy was a man who would do just about anything for money."

"I would suggest you stay the hell out of it," a hard voice grated.

She glared at Hawke, who hoisted himself into the coach and plopped himself down beside her. "I don't recall asking for your opinion." By now her temper was frayed beyond endurance. She had to clamp her jaw shut to keep from taking all of her fury out on Hawke. Hawke himself hadn't exactly put himself on her good side, in spite of the fact that she now owed him her life. For that matter how had he managed to so conveniently absent himself from the coach at just the precise time she would need to have her life saved anyway?

Laney evidently had no problems with his timing. "Thank God you were able to dispatch that highwayman, Mr. Hawke," she said, the all but fawning admiration in her voice galling Kate all the more.

"I saw him sneaking around in the rocks when I got back to camp," Hawke told her, though Kate had the distinct impression he was speaking not for La-

78

ney's benefit, but hers. "I decided to see what he was up to."

"What if he'd been up to absolutely nothing," Kate said. "Then you would have been sitting here in the middle of nowhere."

"There'd be another stage along in a couple of hours," he said, seeming not in the least to mind her continued irritation. In fact, he was almost amused. And again it occurred to her that Travis Hawke was not a man to be amused by much of anything. There was a coldness about him, an aloofness she sensed was second nature.

The look in his eyes when she'd spoken the word "love" suggested that events in his life had put the hardness in him. That given a choice, he might wish it otherwise. But she couldn't think about that now. There were other things to consider.

"You know," she said, "Langley could have shot me three times before you shot him." It was time to see just how far Travis Hawke would go to stay in her good graces. "Any particular reason you waited so long?"

"Kate," Laney interrupted, her tone chastising. "How can you say such a thing. Mr. Hawke . . ."

"*Mister* Hawke can answer for himself," Kate said, looking him square in the eye, while Laney went back to ministering to her husband.

"Perhaps I should have waited a minute *longer*," he said quietly.

That did it. "You spy on me in the woods, accost me bodily, then disappear. Then when I'm about to have my face shot off, you conveniently reappear just in time to save me. How do I know your aim wasn't off? Perhaps you shot your accomplice instead of your intended victim."

She was trembling and she couldn't stop it, nor

79

could she stop him when he pulled her against him. In spite of the heat, she felt the gooseflesh rise on her arms. She hated the feeling of weakness that swept through her. She was not used to being dependent on anyone or anything. And she did not like being indebted to Travis Hawke, most especially for saving her life.

Even so she did not pull away, allowing him to hold her for long minutes. "I'm sorry it was so close, Kate," he said at last. "I couldn't get a clear shot at him from the rocks. I had to climb down a way and by then he had the gun on you. I just took my best shot."

She took a deep breath. "I . . . uh . . . I guess I should say thanks."

He snorted. "That's a hard word for you, isn't it?"

"No more than telling the truth is for you."

"What's that supposed to mean?"

She had felt his arms tense ever so slightly, though his voice had betrayed nothing more than a mild curiosity. It would seem in spite of her reality-clouding fantasy about a man who looked like Hawke, her instincts were still on target. Travis Hawke was a practiced liar. And so had her lover been in San Francisco. No. She was just being fanciful again.

"It means what I said. Oh, not that you lie straight out or anything." She tilted her head to study those midnight eyes. "But there's a world of things you aren't telling me, Hawke. And it's the not telling that makes me wonder just what kind of a polecat you really are."

"Are you always so free with your compliments?"

"I try not to play games with people. If I think it, I say it."

"That can be dangerous."

"I can handle dangerous."

"Like you handled Billy Langley?"

"I'm still alive, aren't I?"

"Damn — you are one helluva . . ."

"Helluva what?"

"I don't know. I never met anyone like you before."

"Haven't you?"

His eyes narrowed uncertainly, and in that instant she was convinced that even if he was the man in San Francisco, he was unaware that she was the woman. "Maybe you're the one who should be wary, Mr. Hawke."

"Are you dangerous, Kate?"

Her hand skimmed the opening of his shirt, the fantasy flaring to life. "What do you think?"

His pulse quickened. Son-of-a-bitch, when had he lost control of this whole mess? He was not going to care about this woman. That wasn't why he'd agreed to come to Kansas. He'd learned his lesson about caring long ago. He'd forgotten it for awhile with Anne, but then, oh God, how she had rammed it home for good. Kate's hand slid under his shirt to toy with his nipple. "Ah, Kate," he said softly, "for me I think you're going to be damned dangerous."

He kissed the top of her hair, shifting his position and hers to pull her fully onto his lap.

"What are you doing?" Kate gasped, glancing at Laney to see that the young woman had averted her eyes in utter embarrassment.

"Better to have her see you on my lap, than have her see what your straying hands have wrought in a certain part of my anatomy, woman."

Kate gasped again, as he moved his hips against her rump. Even their combined layers of clothing could not disguise the rigid flesh of his sex.

"I'm sorry I broke off our little meeting in the woods," he said, his voice hard against her ear to be

81

certain Laney could not hear.

Her trembling now was no longer the aftershock of almost dying. No, this was different, very different indeed.

"I remember how soft your skin is," he rasped, his lips trailing over her earlobe, his breath charting a path of heat through her entire being. "I remember your breast in my mouth, Kate. I remember the nipple hard against my tongue."

"Damn you," she whispered. "Don't do this."

"I thought you were immune to dangerous things." His hand glided upward along her body to settle under her breast. "I want you, Kate."

"Why?" She almost sobbed the word.

"Don't question it, Kate. Just want me back."

Her head lolled against him. "I do. It's insane, but I do."

He nipped at her ear. "When we get to Leavenworth . . ."

Her eyes closed. Right here in the stagecoach would have been reasonable enough to her passion-drugged mind. "Yes," she whispered. "Yes."

"If you knew how insane this really was," he said hoarsely. "If you really knew . . . damn . . ."

"Knew what?"

"Nothing . . . never mind."

"Hawke," she said, then hesitated, deciding finally to plunge ahead. "Hawke, how did you know my name?"

"I asked."

"Asked who?" Her heart quickened, and it no longer had anything to do with his nearness. She wasn't going to like his answer.

"The ticket agent at the Columbia station."

The tenseness was back. He was lying. Her unease escalated. "What do you really want, Hawke?"

82

"You."

Another lie. "What do you want, Hawke?"

"All right, I want a job."

"I beg your pardon?"

"I've done some freighting. Done just about everything at one time or another. And I want to hire on with your outfit. I heard about your father's death and figured you would be the one to talk to."

"You bastard!" she hissed, shoving away from him in one violent motion, no longer concerned with what Laney Nolan or anyone else heard or saw. "A job? All of this over a job . . . You couldn't just ask." It was Billy Langley all over again. Her fury was so great it was all she could do to keep herself from striking him. "You'll have no job with me, Mr. Hawke. Ever!"

"Damnit, Kate, I know what you're thinking. But what happened in the woods has nothing to do with my wanting a job."

She couldn't judge truth from lie this time, perhaps because she was no longer touching him, but more likely, she admitted despairingly, because she was again judging him against a phantom met by chance years ago. A job. He wanted a job. That was all it had been. No matter what he said. He wasn't the man in her fantasy. Her own foolish dreams had put him there.

Used her. The words ripped at her fragile self-image. Travis Hawke had held her, touched her, kissed her because he wanted to work for her.

"I'm certain my father hired all the men we needed earlier this spring," she said, as stiffly as she could manage. "We have no need of your services."

He started to say something, but apparently thought better of it. She sat in her corner of the rocking stagecoach, seeking desperately to assess her

83

feelings about this man.

Part of what she felt right now was hate — true and awful in its intensity. She hated him for taking advantage of her, yet still she wanted him, because try as she might she could not let go of the fantasy of loving him for five years. His kiss, his touch exacerbated her aching need to know if a night with Hawke could end her obsession with that night in San Francisco.

No, the bastard would never work for her. But she knew with a fierce, quivering certainty that she would one day have Travis Hawke in her bed.

Chapter Seven

It wasn't right that Leavenworth should look the same. Kate studied the ribbon of buildings along the waterfront from her vantage point on the Perkins Ferry. She stood beside the left front wheel of the stage, stepping into the occasional sprays of water that slapped onto the flat vessel from the swift-flowering Missouri. She could see past the levee to some of the buildings on Shawnee Street, Delaware, Cherokee, and beyond. Others she just knew would still be there. The churches, the schools, the businesses, the jail, the post office—everything that made Leavenworth the prosperous community it had become. Nothing had changed. Even though she'd not been home for seven months. Even though her father was dead.

The wheels of the stage had been blocked to prevent rolling, so Kerns had kept the team in harness. He was standing next to the right side lead horse, keeping the fussing and stamping to a minimum on the ten minute crossing.

The ferryman walked the length of the raft, up and back, on the starboard side, opposite Kate, using his twelve foot pole to both guide and propel the small craft on its short journey.

Kate smiled slightly as she noticed the Nolans huddled inside the stage. Harold had turned green after his first ten seconds on the choppy water.

"Decided to yield to the inevitable and give me that job, Kate?" The soft drawl stiffened her spine.

She whirled, fury sparking through her. He was lounging against the rear wheel, his back resting against the iron rim. His dark eyes mocked her, challenged her. Damn his hide anyway! She had gone out of her way to avoid him during the final day of their journey, even to riding in the driver's boot with Kerns. Her attitude had been anything but subtle, and she had hoped the man had taken the hint. Obviously, he was still determined to make things difficult for both of them.

"You are not going to work for me, Travis Hawke," she gritted. "Ever. I suggest you get that through that excessively thick skull of yours and just stay the hell away from me."

His strides were long and sure across the wet, grit covered surface of the raft-like ferry. "Can't stay away, Kate," he said, stopping so close to her that she was obliged to tilt her head back to look him in the eye. "Guess it must be the way you have with words. You really know how to turn a man's head."

She bit back the retort that rose to her lips, refusing to be baited into a duel of insults. All she needed, she cautioned herself, was a little patience. In another five minutes the ferry would be docked. She would not re-board the stage, but walk the two blocks to her father's freight office, effectively ridding herself of Hawke.

"I'm not going anywhere, Kate," he said, confounding her further by seeming to be able to read her mind.

"Why are you doing this? I told you, I have no job for you."

He reached up, tracing his fingertips down the side of her face, his touch so light that she wasn't even certain he was making contact with her flesh at all. Yet where the cool water had done nothing to alleviate the midday heat, the feel of him so close suddenly made her shiver.

"You feel it too, don't you?" His voice was husky.

She wanted to slap away his hand, but she couldn't force her arms to move. "I feel nothing."

"Now who's the liar, Kate?" He dipped his head toward her, his mouth stopping just inches from her own. "You feel it. I feel it. And it's not going to go away until we do something about it."

"I haven't the faintest idea what you're talking about." She turned her back on him, her arms hugging her sides. This man was a threat, a real, viable threat to much more than her fantasy. In spite of her growing obsession to compare him to the other, her more rational nature screamed at her to stay away from him.

But he made it so hard . . . so hard. His hands slid over the curve of her shoulders and down her arms, coming to rest just above her elbows. She did not pull away. Her head lolled back, pillowed by the hard muscles of his chest, the rocking motion of the ferry adding to her sensual pleasure. Arching her neck sideways, she allowed him full access to the slender column of her throat.

Damn, she couldn't let him. She couldn't. But as her mind pleaded for sensibility, her body revelled in the sweet insanity of his mouth nuzzling her ear. She twisted to face him. Her hands moved of their own accord, tracking the corded muscles of his back. He pulled her closer, her body crushed against his. She could barely breathe, but didn't care. She wished he would hold her tighter still. Oh, God, she had to stop this . . . had to . . .

She shifted her hands to his chest, her palms tingling against the surging heat of his heart. He was so like him, so like him. But it was wrong, all wrong. Travis Hawke could not be the man who came so gently to her bed that long ago night. Travis Hawke was a man who seemed to have no gentleness in him, a man whose gun was an extension of his right hand. His motive wasn't love, it was a job, or worse. And in him she sensed secrets that could destroy them both. Mustering her will, she pushed against him.

"Please," she whispered. "This makes no sense. I don't know you. I don't want to know you."

"You know I want you." Those midnight eyes seared her.

"That doesn't make any sense either. There are plenty of willing women . . ."

A corner of his mouth curved sardonically. "Tell me you're not willing, Kate."

"Damn you!" Why was it she could almost believe he knew about San Francisco, was using it to torment her. But that was impossible. She'd never told another living soul about that night. No, if she had to swim to shore, she was going to get away from Travis Hawke.

Angrily, she shoved away from him. At the same instant a freak wave caught the ferry aft. The small vessel lurched violently. To keep from falling, she grabbed frantically for the rear wheel of the stage, looping her arm through the spokes and hanging on.

But Hawke was off balance. She watched, horrified, as the bucking motion of the raft catapulted him backwards. Instinctively, she reached for him, her fingers closing on air as he was thrown against the rope railing. The rail post cracked, gave way. Kate screamed at the sickening sound of his head slamming against the side of the raft as he disappeared into the swirling water.

In an instant she was on her knees, crawling toward the edge of the raft. "Hawke!" She screamed his name, terrified when all she saw was the rippling brown water. Scrambling to her feet, she tore off her clothes down to her chemise and bloomers.

The ferryman was at her side. "The current's tricky here, lady!" he shouted. "You ain't goin' in!"

Kate jerked away from him and leaped feet first into the Missouri. In the muddy water she could see nothing. Her eyes burned from trying. She broke the surface, then dove again. Nothing.

"Get the hell out of the water!" a voice shouted.

"You're gonna drown!" came another.

She heard the shouts from the raft, recognizing that the Nolans had joined with the ferryman and Kerns to exhort her from the water. But she ignored them all. She had to find Hawke. He hadn't breathed for half a minute.

Half-sobbing she slapped the empty surface. The whirling eddies mocked her. She swam too close to the side of the raft. Harold Nolan made a grab for her. "You've got to get out of there, Kate!"

She pushed away. "Not 'til I find him!"

"He's dead," Kerns spat. "Been too long."

Kate took a deep breath and ducked under the rushing water once again. She used the raft to anchor herself, clinging to its underside, not moving. Always she knew when Hawke was near her. Always. She allowed no other thoughts to intrude. Hawke. Only Hawke.

She dove swiftly to her left, finding a tangle of submerged branches from an uprooted tree, so common in the Missouri. Gripping the soggy, rotting wood she moved her hands along the twisted maze.

Her lungs were screaming for air when she found him. The branches were all around him, shifting, moving, as though seeking to keep their prize like

89

some sort of malevolent beast from the depths of a sea-farer's nightmare. Groping blindly, she locked her arms under his shoulders and heaved upward. He didn't move. More than a minute had passed.

Surrounded by water, her lungs were on fire. Her every survival instinct demanded that she surface and dive again. But she dared not risk trying to find him a second time. She jerked harder. Nothing.

Jamming her hand through the darkness, she followed his body downward to find his leg snarled in the fork of a tree limb. Desperate, terrified, she clawed at it.

Oh, God, don't let him be dead! Don't let him be dead!

She jerked his foot free, grabbed his shirt collar and drove upward with a last, mighty kick. Her lungs dragged in air and water both as she broke the surface. Sputtering, choking she lunged toward the raft.

A half dozen hands grabbed at her, but she fought them off. Only after they had dragged Hawke from the water did she allow them to pull her aboard as well.

She was on her hands and knees beside him, forcing air into her oxygen-starved body in great heaving gulps. But her eyes were locked on Hawke. He was on his back—limp, motionless. Fighting an uncharacteristic hysteria, she crawled over to him. The Nolans, the ferryman, Kerns—all hovered around him, not moving.

"He isn't breathing, miss," Harold said softly. "I'm sorry."

Kate shook her head violently. "He's not dead. He's not!"

Unmindful of her immodest attire, made more so because she was soaking wet, she straddled Hawke's hips. Somewhere in her memory the image was there. Her father dragging a teamster from the flood-swollen Platte. The man was blue, seemingly lifeless, but her father had flopped him on his stomach, turned his head to one side, pushed . . .

She scrambled off Hawke, heaving him over onto his stomach. Again she straddled his hips, shutting out the image of the blue-tinged lips, lips that had . . . She pressed her hands against his lower back and pushed upward hard. "Breath." The command had become a prayer.

Her eyes focused on the corded muscles, unwilling to believe they would never again ripple with life beneath her fingers. Her hands continued automatically, her vision blurring. "Breathe."

Through a haze of tears she saw the trail of red along the back of his head. The wound bled freely, blood seeping downward to pool on the deck.

"It's useless, dear." Harold Nolan tried to pull her away. His hand gripped her arm, urging her to her feet.

"No!" She shook him off.

Laney joined him. "Kate, he's dead."

She glared at them both. "He isn't! Don't say that." His body remained motionless beneath her.

The blood. The motion of the raft hid it from her. But it must be there. The blood. Flowing freely. Because his heart was still beating. He was alive! Damn, he was alive.

She pushed harder, turning his head from side to side, pulling upward on his sides, desperate to try anything to make him breathe. The ferry bumped against the dock.

"Throw 'im back in," Kerns said. "Feed 'im to the fish. He's done for, girl. Can't you see that?"

Kerns dragged her off Hawke. She kicked and scratched at him. "Leave me alone. He's alive. Leave me alone."

Kerns did not release her, instead bringing his hand

91

up to grab a fistful of her breast. Rage sparking through her, she delivered a left hook to his jaw. He shoved her back. Her momentum sent her sprawling, landing hard on Hawke's back.

He grunted, coughed, water choking out of his mouth. Kate was on her knees holding his head, helping him. She barely noticed the ferryman keeping Kerns away from her. Her whole world at this moment was Travis Hawke.

"Lie still," she murmured, threading her fingers through his wet hair. "Please, lie still."

She made no conscious decision, but while he lay there, his chest heaving, she began to tug at the back of his shirt. Her heart hammering, she pulled the tail free of the waistband of his pants.

"Lie still," she repeated, her voice shaking as badly as her hand. She would know. In a breath's time she would know.

He arched his back, struggling to sit up. "What . . . what the hell happened?"

"Please . . ." Was the word a plea for him to remain still, or a prayer that . . .

She lifted the shirt up, but she didn't look. She didn't have to, because her hand brushed across the ridge of flesh. A half inch wide, three inches long. The scar. If she hadn't been kneeling, she would have collapsed.

Travis Hawke—the stranger who had come to her bed in San Francisco.

Chapter Eight

Kate tried vainly to keep Hawke lying down, but even in his weakened state, he managed to struggle to a sitting position.

"What happened?" he repeated, his dark eyes glazed and confused.

"I'll tell you what happened, Mr. Hawke," Laney Nolan said, stooping down beside him. "Kate jumped into that horrid water and saved you from drowning. I've never seen anything like it! Why, we all thought you were dead for certain."

Kate shifted uncomfortably at the odd scrutiny she was now receiving from those midnight eyes.

"You pulled me out?"

She nodded, wishing to heaven he would stop looking at her like that. She still had to think through what she had just found out about him.

"I guess that makes us even then."

She forced her tone to be light. "You're not much on thank yous either, I see."

He smiled, and she was ridiculously warmed by the sight of it. Just minutes ago he had almost died. Gingerly, he touched the back of his head, but his gaze had settled on her disgraceful attire. It was much too late for modesty—and she would have been reluctant to hide herself from him in any event. Her nipples puckered shamelessly in the wet, crisp air.

Unconsciously her finger touched one of them, as she continued to meet Hawke's now searing gaze. Her breathing grew more shallow. She would have taken a step toward him, but Laney bustled up beside her carrying her discarded dress. Kate did not protest when the woman yanked it over her head. Disconcerted, she even stood still while Laney got everything fastened.

And then she didn't have to move, because Hawke was moving toward her. His fingers shifted her bedraggled locks away from her face, and she knew that her eyes had betrayed her, that she was looking at this man with such intense longing that he would have to be the world's most stupid dolt not to see it. And Travis Hawke was not stupid.

He cupped her chin in his palm. "Thank you."

Her arms swept around his middle, as she crushed herself against him, pressing her cheek against the wet hairs of his chest. She clung to him for a long minute, because it was the only way she could prevent him from seeing her tears.

Her heart had known who he was the instant she had laid eyes on him, but her common sense had refused to accept it. It was too preposterous. She had wanted it, dreamed of it for so long, now that it had happened, she was terrified.

She longed to tell him, yet knew it would be the mistake of her life if she did. She had to get away from him to decide what to do. Amazingly, it was Jeb Kerns who provided the perfect opportunity to do just that.

" 'Spose it's a good thing you're still alive, eh, Hawke?" the stage driver called from the dock, where he had already seen to the unloading of the stage. "Put Blanchard in a real pickle to have to find somebody else."

Very slowly, Kate backed away from Hawke. She plastered a look of total disinterest on her face, even as her gaze shifted between the two men. Kerns looked almighty pleased with himself. Hawke was furious, though trying hard not to show it.

"You'd better be on your way to that ocean we talked about, Kerns," Hawke said.

Her every instinct screamed at her to demand an explanation for the cryptic exchange. But she fought them down. Instead, she just gave Hawke what she hoped was a concerned look and said, "Someone really should see to that gash on your head."

His brows furrowed. He had evidently thought she would be the one seeing to it. But her nerves were at the breaking point. Nearly tripping in her eagerness to be away from him, she hurried down the ferry's gangplank. She breathed a soul-felt sigh of relief when Hawke did not follow. He was probably trying to come up with a lie she would believe about himself and Blanchard.

Hawke and Blanchard. How were they tied together? And if they weren't how had he so obviously known that she would not be pleased to learn of a connection between the two men? He'd been ready to take Kerns apart for his ill-advised sarcasm. Damn, he was up to something. And it was more than a job.

"Come on now, missy," Kerns said, reaching toward her, "you can ride up top with me again."

She stepped around him. "Have you ever seen a pig fly, Kerns?"

"No, can't say as I have."

"When you do, that's when I'll ride with you again." She left him standing there, gap-jawed, and continued her walk up Shawnee Street. She was still trying to shake off the effects of almost losing Hawke.

She halted abruptly. Losing him? As though he were hers to lose? He had made love to her once, when he didn't know who she was. He still didn't. And now he was somehow linked to Frank Blanchard, the man she believed connected to her father's death.

What in God's name had she come home to?

She turned quickly, looking toward the ferry. Hawke was standing where she'd left him. Laney was fussing next to him, trying to tie a strip of cloth around his head. But Hawke was not cooperating. He was staring at Kate. Just as she'd known he was.

"I'll be around to see you about that job, Kate," he called.

Her jaw clenched. Oh, he would, would he? Let him come. Just let him. He would find out what it was like to deal with her on her home ground. She continued her march up the street, ignoring the rude comments about her thoroughly disreputable appearance. What'd people expect her to look like when she'd just taken a dive into a river?

Damn. What was she going to do about Hawke? He wanted a job. She had to admit she liked the idea of having him near her. But if he worked for her, it was inevitable that he would one day find out about San Francisco. He seemed attracted to her now, but it could just be part of the game he was playing to get a job. What would happen when the game was over?

She straightened. Why was she concerning herself with what *his* reaction was going to be? What about her own? She still had five twenty-dollar gold pieces to fling in his arrogant face!

The sound of Jeb Kerns's vile laughter rose above the sound of thundering hooves. Kate leaped onto the boardwalk a hair's breadth ahead of the careening stagecoach.

"I told ya to ride, missy!" he shouted as he swept

96

past.

Kate let fly with several choice phrases that would have sent Mrs. Russell spinning into a dead faint, but she made no attempt to brush off the added layer of grime.

"Welcome home," she told herself grimly. The feeling of foreboding that had been with her since before her father's death was back full force, but she was determined to fight it off. Somehow she would put her life back together. McCullough Freight was hers now. She would make her father proud.

Her step picked up, a smile touching her lips. The first thing she would do after she got settled was climb into her buckskins. Then she would personally burn every dress Mrs. Russell had forced on her in Boston.

She watched Kerns jerk the stage to a halt at the northeast corner of Shawnee and Main in front of the four story brick structure called the Planters Hotel. The Nolans climbed down and went inside. Kate kept walking, kept watching. But Hawke did not emerge from the stage. She stopped. The squish of boots on the dirt behind her told her more than she wanted to know. She was about to turn around and give him a piece of her mind, when a familiar, much loved voice caught her attention.

"Katie! Is it really you?"

She let out a shriek of pure joy. "Dusty!"

A grin split the face of the grizzled, gray-bearded man standing on the south side of the street. His bow-legged strides lengthened, but he didn't have to hurry. She was already flying up the street to meet him. Arms outstretched she threw herself body-long against him.

"Oh, Dusty, Dusty," she half-sobbed, not realizing until this moment just how much she had missed this man, her home, everything.

He held her tight in a huge bear hug, assuring her

wordlessly that he felt the same.

"Ah, Katie, it's so good to see ya, girl," he said at last. His hands shifted to grip hers, as he took a step back, holding her at arms' length. "Let me look at ya." His mouth fell open. "My God, what happened? You look like you battled the Platte in the spring floods and lost."

"I went for a swim. We'll talk about it later, okay?" She listened, but could no longer detect Hawke's waterlogged footfalls. Nothing would make her turn around and look.

"Tell me whenever you like, lass," Dusty was saying. "I'm just happy to have you home. Just look at how you've filled out."

"Don't remind me."

He laughed. "Ah, Katie gal, what's the matter with ye? Ye always wanted to be a buxom lass and now you are."

"I can't even get into my buckskins!"

He laughed harder. "No wonder you're madder n' a cut bull." He looked her up and down, his eyes warm and teasing. "You look like a full growed woman, Katie gal. Instead of a scrawny wee tomboy."

Now it was Kate's turn to laugh, as she always did at the incongruous way her father's Scottish brogue had found its way into Dusty's frontier palaver. But she was far from convinced her added weight was anything to be grateful for. Her expression sobered as she caught sight of the red block letters dominating the sign above the doorway on the falsefront building to her left. Mc-Cullough Freight Company. She swallowed hard, fighting off the burning sensation behind her eyes. For the briefest instant she had expected her father, red beard and all, to come thundering out of that office, bellowing a heartfelt welcome.

"I miss him, too, lass," Dusty said quietly.

Kate sucked in a deep breath. "Let's go inside. We've got a lot to talk about."

When she opened the door it was like being kicked in the stomach. Everything in the room spoke of her father—from the massive oak desk and its equally impressive oak chair to the bearskin rug skirting the floor around the potbellied stove. She'd been with her father the night the grizzly had attacked him.

"You met your match when you took on my pa," she said, bending down to give the bruin an affectionate pat. She caught Dusty's amused snort and straightened in mock anger. "Now don't you start about me and my bear."

Dusty perched himself on a stool in front of a wall lined with books. She knew what was coming. "You were only four years old when your pa kilt that bear. But you liked to scared us both into the hereafter that night."

She giggled. She had heard the story a hundred times, but never tired of it, because each time in the telling her pa or Dusty would embellish or outright invent some part of the adventure they had left out the time before. She had no recollection of the night herself, but had been regaled so often of her behavior on that momentous occasion that there were times when she actually believed she did remember it.

"I will never accept the fact that I tried to take a literal bear-back ride on that grizzly."

"That bear liked to take your pa's head off savin' your fanny."

She tried to laugh, but it sounded hollow even to her own ears. She was just postponing the inevitable. "I want the truth, Dusty. How did Pa die?"

He looked at the floor. "I told you in my letter."

"No, you didn't," she said gently. "I have a right to know."

"It was just a stupid accident with the . . ."

"I can check around town."

"Damnit, Kate! I won't have you gettin' yourself killed, too. Bryce'd haunt me fer sure. You just stay out of it."

"I'm already in it. The stage was held up a day out of Columbia."

He stood up. "Anybody hurt?"

"The only person who was even threatened was me. It was Billy, Dusty, he wanted to kill me."

The grizzled teamster stomped back and forth across the room. "You shouldn't have come home. You're goin' back to Boston tomorrow."

Kate slammed a hand down on the desk. "The hell I will! The only place I'm goin' is on the trail haulin' freight. And that's only *after* I find out what happened to Pa."

"I told you . . ."

"You told me nothing!" She sank into the huge chair, frustration and pain tearing at her insides. "Damnit, Dusty, I don't want to fight with you."

"I know, Katie."

"Then tell me. About Pa, the company, everything. Including Frank Blanchard."

Dusty let fly with a wad of tobacco juice that hit dead center in the spittoon near the stove. "All right, lass. I never could win an argument with you." He smiled fondly. "You're too danged much like your pa."

He stepped up to the desk, leaning toward her, his palms flat on its hard surface. "The whole thing stinks o' . . ."

The door opened. Kate looked up to see a tall, blond man bedecked in an army lieutenant's uniform stride inside.

"We're closed today," she said. "You'll have to come back another time."

To her surprise the man seemed not in the least put off by her abruptness. He grinned broadly and ambled over to the desk, extending a hand to Dusty. "Lieutenant Wade Parsons," he said, "out of Fort Laramie."

"You here about the shipment?" Dusty asked.

The lieutenant nodded.

"What shipment?" Kate put in. "For the army?"

Parsons's smile grew even more charming as he directed his attention toward her. "You must be Kate McCullough."

"You could tell by my fashionable attire, right?"

He laughed, a bright, cheerful sound Kate found annoyingly infectious. He lifted her hand, brushing the back of it with his lips. "Fashion wears out more apparel than the man."

"I beg your pardon?" She did not pull her hand away.

"William Shakespeare. The bard. The greatest playwright the world has ever known."

"Bill and I never really got too well acquainted."

He laughed again. "I could introduce you sometime. In fact, I could do even better. I fancy myself a bit of a playwright. I could read you some of my work."

She stood up, unconsciously caressing the back of her hand where his lips had lingered. "Like I said, lieutenant, we're closed today."

He brushed a hand through his hair, trying she was certain not to let his exasperation show. "The reports I had about you were not exaggerated," he said ruefully. "But I'm afraid I must insist that we talk, Miss McCullough. That is, if you want the biggest bonus in the history of your freight company."

"Dusty, who is this man? And what is he talking about?"

"You'd likely find out better if you let him get on with what he has to say."

101

Properly chastised, Kate sat on the edge of the desk. "I'm sorry, lieutenant, it's been a long day."

His eyes travelled the length of her, and she wished she had taken the time to repair the damage done by her dip in the Missouri. She fumbled briefly with her hair, then gave it up as hopeless.

"You've just returned from finishing school in Boston, I believe," Parsons said.

"I think I finished the school. Your reports were most certainly thorough." He was amused by her appearance, but it was not mean-spirited, and she found herself warming to his charm. So unlike Hawke. Her mood darkened. Why did she have to think of him? "Why were you checking on me, lieutenant?"

"It's my business to know who'll be shipping one of the most important cargos in the history of the army."

She looked at Dusty quizzically, but he only shrugged. "They've kept us all in the dark on this one, Kate."

The door opened a second time. Kate's mood soured further. Hawke.

"I'm in the middle of a business discussion here," she snapped, unable to control the riot of emotions the man evoked in her. "Get out."

"Is that any way to talk to a man whose life you've just saved?"

"What's this hombre talkin' about, Kate?" Dusty demanded, striding over to bar Hawke's entry into the room. "Got the smell of a johnny reb all over him."

Perfect, Kate thought. Dusty had just taken an instant disliking to Hawke. In her life, she'd never known her adopted uncle to change his mind about anything or anyone. And when Dusty brought up the subject of the war, the cause was lost. He was totally irrational when it came to anyone who had fought for the confederacy.

"Hawke's no southerner," she said, trying very hard not to sound like she was defending him. "Please, Dusty, he saved my life."

"But he said . . ."

"He's the one who killed Billy."

Dusty straightened. "I'm grateful, mister." But there was little gratitude in his voice. "Billy went plum sour in the war. Seen 'im a couple months ago. With them scars on his face the ladies didn't take to him any more. Got them scars from a reb."

Kate couldn't believe Dusty would side with Billy, no matter how indirectly. He would've skinned him alive in the barn that day when she was sixteen. "Billy was going to kill me, Dusty."

"War twisted him. Rebs twisted him."

Damn, she had to get the subject changed. She loved Dusty dearly, but she couldn't condone his blind hatred. McCullough Freight had lost a lot of good men to the likes of Quantrill, to legitimate confederate troops as well. But it had been a war. Those men had been her friends, too.

To his credit, Hawke seemed to take no offense from Dusty's belligerent attitude. "I'm here about that job, Kate."

"I told you. We don't need anyone."

"Hold on, Kate," Dusty interjected. He faced Hawke squarely, none of his hostility gone, but a new intensity in his voice. "You handle men, oxen, mules?"

"Whatever it takes, I can do it."

"Looks like you been doin' a little swimmin', too," Dusty noted, eyeing Hawke's still damp clothes, then looking at Kate's. "You said Kate saved your life?"

"She fished me out the river."

She grew warm under his steady gaze. To make it worse Wade Parsons was doing his share of staring at her as well. Embarrassed, she muttered, "I would've

103

done the same for any drowning mutt."

Something in his eyes changed, made her regret her sarcasm. It was only a hint of something, a vulnerability. But it was there, though she was certain he would have denied it to the death. She found herself feeling strangely protective of him. Damn, she just couldn't make up her mind about this man.

"I . . . I'm sorry," she said, then not wanting him to think she was apologizing for what she said, even though she was, she added, "we don't have a job for you."

"Now that that's settled," Parsons said, "perhaps we can get back to business, Kate."

She nodded, though she was unsettled by the fact that Hawke remained in the office. She only vaguely noticed that Parsons had suddenly chosen to address her by her first name.

Hawke walked over to the window, pretending to take an interest in the street traffic. Determined to ignore him, Kate spoke to Parsons, "If McCullough Freight is to move your merchandise, lieutenant . . ."

"Please, call me Wade."

She detected the slightest tensing in Hawke. Parsons's familiarity had not gone unnoticed. She smiled just a little. "Wade it is. Now, what are we shipping?"

"I can't say just yet, especially not in front of . . ." he looked at Hawke, "outsiders. You understand."

She smiled a little more. He was a handsome devil. And though she could scarcely believe it, he seemed to be flirting with her. With Hawke in the room, his timing couldn't have been better. "When will you tell me?"

"According to the contract your father signed with the quartermaster at Fort Leavenworth, you're to pull out in five days with the cargo. I imagine I'll have told you before then." He stepped closer to her and again lifted her hand to his lips. "Perhaps at dinner?"

"Is that an invitation?"

"It most certainly is, Kate."

"I'd be honored." A muscle in Hawke's jaw jumped. Very deliberately, she put her hand on Parsons's chest. "The shipment's going to Fort Laramie?"

He nodded, snaring her eyes with his own very green ones.

"I . . . I've made the trip several times."

"Not with this cargo."

"You're making me very curious."

"I like my women curious."

She felt her face heat. She knew Hawke's eyes were on her, and though her conscience nudged her, she intended to milk this moment for all it was worth. "Isn't that the most amazing coincidence? I like my men the same way."

Hawke padded over to her, his strides reminiscent of a cougar stalking its prey. "When you decide to give me that job, I'll be across the street at the Planters."

Kate sensed the coiled fury in him. And part of her couldn't help but be pleased by it. He was jealous. Damn his hardcase hide — he was jealous of Wade Parsons.

"Just what job you be wantin'?" Dusty prodded, before Hawke could get out the door.

"Wagonmaster."

The trail-savvy teamster snorted. "Don't want much. What makes you think you can handle teamsters? Ever bossed men before."

Hawke shrugged. "Army."

Dusty cursed. "I knew it. Officer, right?"

"Captain."

Kate digested this new information about Hawke, deciding oddly that he was telling the truth for a change.

"Got that rebel stink to ya."

"I'll be at the Planters Hotel."

"I'd best be going, too," Parsons said, pressing his lips to her hand. "Dinner tonight?"

She nodded, daring a quick glance at Hawke, who had remained standing in the doorway. He was back to being indifferent. Well, she would show him. She gave Parsons the sweetest smile she could manage. "I'll be so looking forward to it."

Parsons stepped back, bowing slightly. "It will be my great pleasure. As the bard said, 'Beauty provoketh thieves sooner than gold.'"

Kate giggled. She wasn't sure she knew what Parsons was talking about, but Hawke had stomped out the door, and that made it wonderful.

"I'll be by for you at six," Parsons said.

Now that Hawke was gone, she found herself wishing she hadn't accepted the invitation. She was dreadfully tired and wanted only to go home and go to bed. But she smiled, "Six will be fine." Lest he get the wrong impression, she quickly added, "We'll discuss the shipment."

"Of course." He settled his hat on his head, again kissed her hand and was gone.

"I don't trust that Hawke feller," Dusty said, the minute Parsons was out of the office. "But we just might have to hire him."

"Why? If you don't trust . . ."

Dusty sat on the stool. "Nobody else is rushin' to get the job."

"We don't have a wagonmaster?"

"We don't have much of anybody. Not since Bryce . . ."

She hunkered down beside him, gripping his gnarled hand. "Tell me how he died, Dusty. Please."

"He was out by hisself, a short run to a mining camp about twenty miles out. He was yoking up Blue

Boy . . ."

Kate remembered the ornery longhorn. Her father often paired him in the lead yoke. He was well trained, just a bit too smart for his own good. Her father treated him like a spoiled pup.

"Nobody seen it. But a couple o' teamsters and Jim Collier come up on it right afterwards."

"Blue Boy . . ."

"Gored Bryce."

Kate felt the blood drain from her face. She sat on the floor. "I can't believe that. Blue Boy was like a damned pet. He wouldn't have . . ."

"Can't prove it, Kate."

She would prove it. She would. "How much is Frank Blanchard involved in this?"

Dusty's face hardened. "That lizard's been movin' in on every freighter in the territory."

"I rode in his stagecoach to get here."

"He's buyin' everybody else out."

"Buying 'em out or driving 'em out?"

"He offered me a pretty penny for this outfit."

"You didn't . . ."

He looked hurt. "Of course I didn't. But it ain't gonna matter. We're broke, Kate. Flat busted."

"We've got wagons, contracts . . . Parsons just said we'd get the biggest bonus of our lives when we get this secret shipment of his to Laramie."

"We've got wagons, but no one to drive them."

"McCullough has the biggest payroll in the state."

"Not any more, Kate."

"Why?"

"Without your pa . . ." He didn't finish.

"But they work for you, too."

He patted her hand. "They're scared. I ain't the leader Bryce was. Too many accidents been happenin' to McCullough shipments lately. Most of the drivers

107

just up and quit."

"Where's the law in all this?"

"In Blanchard's hip-pocket."

"Jim Collier? I don't believe it!" The man cared too much about her and her father to ever do such a thing.

"Jim's not the law any more."

What next? Kate thought bleakly. "I can't believe Jim would quit like that."

"He didn't quit. He got shot."

"Jim's dead?"

"Worse."

"What could be worse than dead?"

"He was shot in the back. He can't walk."

"Dear God . . ." Kate paced the confines of the small room. "Where can I find Blanchard?"

"Don't you go doing anything stupid, girl. Now that you're home, we'll figure something out."

"Where is he?"

"He has a couple of offices around town. Freight office on Sixth and Delaware. Stage office in the Planters House. Stables, just about half the town, seems like."

"You think he killed my pa, don't you, Dusty?"

"Let me take you to the house. You're tired. It's been a long trip. You got to fix yourself up all pretty for your dinner with the lieutenant."

She relented, only because she knew Dusty would never let her find Blanchard on her own. But she would find him.

If Frank Blanchard had had anything at all to do with her father's death, she would not stop until she saw the man at the end of the rope.

"Is Lydia still at the house?" she asked, as Dusty led her out to a carriage he had brought up.

He looked uncomfortable. "She's there."

"Damn."

"Lydia's all right, Kate. It's just . . ."

"What aren't you telling me?"

"You'll find out soon enough. I'll let Lydia tell you. I've done enough to hurt ye lately."

"You've never hurt me, Dusty," she said, giving him a quick hug. "And you never will. I want to thank you for being here for me."

"Go on with ye? Where else would I be for my favorite niece?"

"We're gonna get this company back on its feet. We're gonna make Pa proud. You'll see."

"Sure we will, Kate." But his voice was as defeated as his eyes. There was something he wasn't telling her.

She climbed into a carriage. So many things to worry about—how her father really died, this unexplained dangerous shipment to Ft. Laramie, the company teetering on the edge of bankruptcy. She felt as she had this morning when she had been under the water too long. She was screaming for air, but if she dared breathe, she would die. Yet staying under the water would kill her just as dead.

Her eyes strayed to the Planters House, as Dusty gigged the horse forward. Even thinking of Hawke brought no respite. He was the man she had dreamed of finding again for five years. Yet now that she'd found him, he was connected to the man who may as well have killed her father.

Was Hawke with Blanchard now? Or was he in his room? She bit her lip. He was likely as exhausted from this morning's dip in the river as she was. Was he stretched out on his bed, sleeping? An outrageous thought struck her. Did he sleep in the raw?

She was grateful Dusty was preoccupied with his own thoughts and didn't see her face heat. So many contradictions in Travis Hawke. So many secrets. She'd saved his life today. Two days ago he had saved hers.

They were even. He'd said it himself. Did that free his conscience to do whatever Blanchard asked of him? Or was he merely going to ask Blanchard for a job, just as he had asked her?

So many secrets.

She had to wonder if one day one of them would get her killed.

Chapter Nine

Hawke sighted down the barrel of the Colt .45 and squeezed the trigger. He nodded with grim satisfaction as the hammer snapped sharply against the empty cylinder. He finished cleaning and checking the weapon, then one by one settled six .45 cartridges home. Slipping the gun into its holster, he slung the belt over a bedpost.

He sat down on the bed, his brows arching slightly as he noted the feather-ticked mattress. No cornhusks for Planters House. To his bone-weary body the bed was almost too much of a temptation. He was still feeling the effects of his encounter with the Missouri River this morning. The knot on his head had settled into a dull throb, but what disturbed him more than the physical pain was his reaction to nearly drowning.

He had expected there to be none. He hadn't given a damn about living for a long time. But this morning's brush with death left him shaken and angry. Shaken because he had discovered he wanted very much to live. Angry because this was hardly the time for a resurrected interest in life.

His target was Frank Blanchard; bringing the man down was all that mattered. If it cost him his own life, so be it. That is, until he met Kate McCullough. Somehow she complicated everything. She was turning his emotionless world inside out. And that made him angrier still.

Refusing to dwell on what it was about her that intruded on his carefully constructed indifference, he went over his plan to destroy Blanchard, telling himself one more time that it didn't matter if Kate was caught in the crossfire. He paced the confines of the small room, knowing that he wouldn't have long to wait. He'd left word of his arrival at the desk. The knock came barely fifteen minutes after he'd entered the room.

He opened the door to a smallish, bespectacled clerk, who was clutching a sealed envelope in his right hand. The hand shook noticeably. His rail thin voice matched the quivering of his body. "I . . . I have a message for you, Mr. Hawke."

Hawke took a step forward. The clerk took a step back. Ruefully, Hawke remembered how the man had upset his entire bottle of indigo ink all over his registration book, when he'd handed Hawke a quill pen with which to sign in. He had the distinct impression that if he so much as said "boo," the clerk would be history. Kerns had obviously not kept his mouth shut.

The small man thrust the envelope toward Hawke, his right arm ramrod stiff. When Hawke took the message it was as though the man were released by some unseen hand. He all but sprang down the hall, tripping over an upturned corner of carpet in his eagerness to be anyplace else. Hawke flipped a coin to the spot where the man had stood, then calmly shut the door.

Inside his room he opened the envelope. A stony smile touched his lips. It was started now. There was no turning back.

112

Whatever part of him Kate McCullough had inadvertently reached was gone, buried once again under years of rigid control. Midnight eyes — flinty hard and cold — stared back at him from the ornately carved mirror above the washstand. He shaved quickly, methodically, then changed his clothes. The dark blue broadcloth complimented the pale blue cotton shirt, the black string tie providing the final touch. He wanted to make a good first impression. It would be the first time he ever met Frank Blanchard face-to-face.

He crossed to the bed and gripped the gunbelt, buckling it around his hips. Hefting the .45, he spun the cylinder. There was no need to hurry. However long it took, Frank Blanchard was a dead man.

When she died, Kate hoped they had buckskins in heaven, because she couldn't imagine ever feeling more herself in anything else. She danced around the spacious quarters of her own bedroom, more thoroughly at ease than she had been in a long time.

"Oh, Pa," she whispered in the comforting stillness, "it's so good to be home."

She hadn't had to let out the seams as much as she'd thought in the supple rust-colored pants and jacket. Threading her fingers through the two-inch long fringe that adorned the outer edge of the sleeves, she couldn't suppress the tingle of excitement that coursed through her. Soon she would be where she truly belonged — on the trail hauling freight, regaining McCullough Freight Company's rightful place as the biggest outfit west of the Mississippi.

Her bath had refreshed her, her buckskins exhilarated her. "Too bad I'll have to take them off in an hour," she grumped aloud. Her dinner engagement

113

with Lt. Parsons was becoming more and more an ordeal to be endured, rather than the pleasant interlude it might have been.

One reason. One word. Hawke.

She flopped belly down onto her bed, hugging her pillow against her breasts. "Damn you," she hissed. "I've wanted you back so long, and now that I have you, I don't know what to do about you."

She opened the leather pouch she'd hitched to her belt and slid the five gold coins into her palm. "Some day," she whispered. "Some day."

And then the magic of that night enveloped her. The touch of his hands, his mouth, the aching need in that husky voice — the need to be held, to be loved. He had told her he'd come to a prostitute to slake a night's lust, but the lie had been in every stroke of his fingers, every caress of his hands. He wanted to care about someone, wanted someone to care about him.

Somewhere, somehow he had been badly hurt. A man with his looks would not have to seek his loving in the darkness with a woman who was his only for a price unless the very anonymity of the act was a defense.

"Stop it, Kate!" she snapped. "You make him sound so lost, so noble. Noble! Bah! Why couldn't he just be some lecher out for a night of lust, while his poor wife grew heavy with another of his brats?"

Her lips brushed the pillow. Because he was not. "I want you, Hawke. And I'm going to have you. You had your turn. Now I'll have mine."

She climbed to her feet. Right now, she had to concern herself with business. She remembered Dusty's parting words, when he'd dropped her off at the house. "Blanchard's come too far, too fast. He can't be stopped. Not without men to drive the wagons and the money to pay 'em."

"I'll get the money, and I'll get the men." She'd said it then, and she said it now. She stared out the window of her second floor room to the well-manicured grounds below, awed as she always was by the stateliness of this two-story white brick mansion that would have seemed more at home on a Georgia plantation than it did here in Leavenworth. But her father had insisted on buying it five years ago. Said they had enough money, it was time he put a decent roof over his daughter's head. To Kate the only roof she ever needed was the sky. Her father hadn't bought the house for her, he'd bought it for . . .

She jumped at the sound of a woman's voice directly behind her. "Lydia, don't do that," she said, her voice a shade harsher than she meant it to be.

"I'm sorry, Kate," the woman said. "I thought you heard me come in." As if in her own defense, she added hurriedly, "I knocked." The delicate china tea-cup she held in her right hand chinked nervously against the matching saucer she held in her left.

"It's all right," Kate said. "I was daydreaming, I guess." She studied the dark-haired woman, frowning slightly. She'd supposed it was rude, but she'd only called a quick hello to Lydia when she'd come into the house, then hurried up the steps to her room, eager to get the Missouri muck off her person. Now that she was actually looking at her, Kate was appalled at the dark circles under the woman's wide brown eyes. Doe eyes, her father always called them. Lydia had a way of seeming like a frightened deer, needing protection.

Kate had to admit that even though the woman was past forty, she was still beautiful. But her skin seemed more pale than Kate remembered. In spite of their sometimes antagonistic relationship, Kate found herself assuming the role of protector.

"Have you been feeling all right, Lydia?" she asked,

hoping to make up for her earlier churlishness.

The woman's eyes brimmed with unshed tears. "I'm just happy to see you. Bryce was worried about you."

"He worried about you, Lydia. Pa knew I could take care of myself." She walked over to her bed and started to straighten the coverlet. It was a reflex action, the kind of busyness that seized her whenever she was around Lydia. She'd never felt especially comfortable around the older woman.

"I miss him terribly," Lydia said.

"Do you?" The words were out before Kate could stop them. She flinched at the hurt expression that crossed Lydia's attractive features. "I'm sorry. I didn't mean that."

"It's all right, Kate. I understand." She took a quick sip of her tea.

What made Kate feel worse was that Lydia very likely did understand. Five years ago Lydia Cornell had run out of money in Leavenworth on her way from nowhere to no place in particular. She'd done a pathetic job applying for a job in the Timber Wolf saloon, where her father had stopped for a cold beer. Bryce McCullough had brought her home and Lydia had been their housekeeper ever since.

The woman had taken on the task of teaching Kate some of the finer points of femininity, something Kate suspected she did at Bryce McCullough's urging. But Kate had stood her ground and Lydia soon gave up. She couldn't change Kate, but she had wrought some subtle changes in her father.

"Kate, there's something I have to tell you. Something I meant to . . ."

"Not now, Lydia. I have to go." She really should start getting ready for dinner with Wade. But for no reason she could pinpoint, she just couldn't be in the same room with Lydia for more than five minutes

116

without the older woman getting on her nerves.

Kate bounded downstairs, anxious to be out in the fresh air. She came to a dead standstill when she caught sight of the man in the wheelchair exiting what had been her father's bedroom. Jim Collier. "What in the name of . . ."

"Sorry, Kate," Jim said. "I hoped Lydia had told you about me."

"What are you doing here? In my father's bedroom?"

"I live here."

Kate sank down on the bottom steps. "You do what?"

Lydia rushed down the stairs. "I tried to tell you, Kate. I did." She scurried over to Jim, making certain the blanket that covered his legs was securely in place.

Jim brushed her hand away. "Stop fussing, Lydia." He wheeled over to Kate. "I've missed you."

"Is somebody going to tell me what's going on?"

"I was ambushed about two months ago."

"Dusty told me."

"I couldn't have made it without Lydia." Jim looked stooped and lost in that chair, not at all the tall, imposing lawman who had once asked her to a town barn dance. She had declined the invitation, partly because she had never learned to dance, but mostly because she would have felt woefully out of her element. But Jim had persisted, probably because he felt sorry for her, and had taken her to dinner and several plays over the course of the past three years.

"I'm sorry about what happened to you, Jim," she said quietly, unsettled by the intense look in his gray eyes.

"And I'm real sorry about your pa, Kate. He was a good man."

"What do you know about how he died? Do you believe Blue Boy killed him?"

"I saw the wound, Kate. It was the bull."

"Damn, I just can't believe that."

"Animals can be unpredictable."

"Yeah," Kate muttered, "so can humans." She stood up. "Just what are you doing in my father's bedroom?"

"He couldn't very well take care of himself," Lydia put in. "He doesn't have any family here. I . . . I remembered how Bryce took me in when I really needed someone."

Kate resisted the impulse to tell Lydia this was hardly the same thing. The woman was again fussing with Jim's blanket. It occurred to Kate then that Lydia needed Jim more than Jim needed Lydia. Kate knew little of Lydia's past, but from the few things she'd ever heard, Lydia had never been without a man in her life for very long.

She pulled Lydia into the parlor. "I want to talk to you. Privately."

"Of course, Kate." Lydia pushed nervously at her neatly pinned chignon. Those damned tears were back in her eyes.

Kate turned her back. "How long was my father dead before you moved Jim in here? Was he even buried yet?"

"Kate! For the love of heaven, what do you think I am?"

"You tell me. I come home to find another man occupying my father's bedroom! You tell me."

"He had nowhere else to go."

"I don't buy that." She turned, hands on her hips. "How long?"

The tears trailed down Lydia's pale cheeks. "Bryce was still alive then. He was the one who had Jim brought here."

Kate felt like she was about one inch high. "Damn.

118

I'm sorry, Lydia. My father never mentioned anything about the shooting in his last letter."

Lydia wiped at her tears. "Bryce always liked Jim. I think he hoped that one day you and Jim would . . ."

"That doesn't explain why he wouldn't tell me about his being shot."

"What could you do in Boston? He wouldn't have worried you. Besides Jim wasn't shot in Leavenworth. He was in Lawrence at the time. They waited until they were sure he could survive the trip before they brought him here. That was about a week after your father had written his last letter to you." She reached into her pocket for a hankie and blew her nose. "The next day Bryce left to take some equipment to a mining camp. He never came back."

"I'm sorry, Lydia. Truly."

"It's all right," she sniffled. "Please, I've made dinner. We can celebrate your coming home."

Kate sighed. "I can't. I have a dinner engagement." She hurriedly explained, lest Lydia think she was just making excuses.

"I understand."

"Stop understanding everything I say," Kate said. "Yell at me once in awhile or something. God knows I deserve it."

"I know you've resented me sometimes."

Kate winced, staring at the floor.

"Bryce is dead," Lydia went on quietly. "Nothing can bring him back. But maybe we could try to be, if not friends, well, maybe . . ."

"I'll try, Lydia," Kate said and meant it. "I promise."

"Then maybe you could promise me that if anything's to be done about Bryce's dying, it has to be left to the law."

"I can't do that. You know I can't. Dusty told me our new sheriff is just one of Blanchard's hirelings. I

119

won't get any justice from him."

"Stay out of it, Kate."

"He was my father."

"I loved him too."

Kate studied the older woman, finally seeing what she'd been blind to, deliberately blind to. She hadn't wanted to share her father with anybody. "Damn, Lydia, why didn't you and Pa ever say anything. Why didn't you get married?"

"Your father never asked."

"Because of me?"

Lydia's smile was kind. "Your father and I were very happy."

"You should still be happy. He should still be alive." She hurried out of the parlor and over to her valise, which she had tossed near the door when she came home. She opened it and pulled out a small, black barreled .44 Navy Colt.

"Kate!" Jim snapped. "What are you doing with that thing? Put it down." He pushed his wheelchair toward the door, anticipating her next move.

Kate strapped the gunbelt around her hips, then slipped the gun into the holster.

"You're not going to be seen wearing that thing!" Lydia cried.

"I'm going to talk to Frank Blanchard."

"Kate, don't be a fool!" Jim was livid. "Frank Blanchard is a very dangerous man."

She crossed the room, avoiding his outstretched hand. "A Lieutenant Parsons will be coming by shortly. Tell him I might be just a little late, will you? Frank Blanchard is about to find out that I can be a very dangerous woman."

Chapter Ten

Hawke unconsciously flexed his gun hand as he was escorted into Frank Blanchard's private suite in the Planters Hotel.

The man who escorted him was not the sort Hawke would have pictured as Blanchard's personal body-guard. The six-foot-seven giant probably tipped the scales at well over three hundred pounds. When he spoke, it was with such painfully precise diction, each word an entity unto itself, that it could only have come from a lifetime of slurred speech.

"Mr. Blanchard will be with you shortly," the man pronounced, leaving Hawke alone in the suite's opulent dining room.

Hawke used the time to examine the room's lavish appointments. He would take any clue he could get into the personality of the man he intended one day to kill. Oil paintings, mostly still life, lined the four walls. The furniture was French—Louis XIV, from the eta-gere to the twelve foot dining table. Hugging the floor in front of the marble hearth was the most luxurious Persian carpet Hawke had ever seen.

He was looking at the fireplace when the door opened. "Ah, Mr. Hawke, I'm so glad you could join us." The continental accent could only belong to Blanchard. His heart pumping a surge of adrenaline through him, Hawke turned and faced his nemesis for the first time.

Hawke's first thought was that the man hardly resembled Satan. Light brown hair graying at the temples accented a face remarkably unlined for a man approaching his fiftieth year. Blanchard's handshake was firm, almost hearty, his gray-green eyes openly assessing.

"Please, join me in a drink before dinner." He poured Hawke a bourbon and water. For himself he poured only water. "Nothing stronger than wine for me. Keeps the body in its most prime working order."

Hawke accepted the drink, still trying to mesh this flesh-and-blood Blanchard with the one whose movements he'd been tracking for nearly two years. To any who met him, Frank Blanchard would seem the picture of aristocratic breeding. Until he'd come to Leavenworth seven months ago, he'd spent the previous four years in Europe and South America, acquiring, no doubt, some of the accoutrements in this room. He was a guest much sought after on the world's most elite social calendars — a rich, powerful, supremely self-confident man.

But that was because the lords and ladies did not know the true circumstances of Frank Blanchard's beginnings, nor the consequences of his avocation as a self-styled herbalist. No one knew the true man better than Travis Hawke, though he'd never met him before in his life. But then Hawke had made it his business to know, because Frank Blanchard was the man responsible for the death of Anne Parker Hawke and the death of her unborn child. Hawke's wife. Hawke's child.

"You seem a trifle weary, Mr. Hawke," Blanchard said, "or should I say wary." He chuckled slightly. "The accommodations aren't quite what you're used to, I take it?"

"On the contrary, I'm quite impressed. Perhaps I'll have to ask for more money on this job."

Blanchard laughed heartily. "I knew I hadn't made a mistake in sending for you. I think you'll do nicely for what I have in mind."

"Which is?"

Blanchard shook his head, "Please, not before dinner. It distresses me to discuss business on an empty stomach." The man gestured toward the elaborately set table in the center of the room. "You'll join me, of course?"

The giant walked into the room. "I will take your gun before the meal, Mr. Hawke."

Hawke stiffened. "I don't think so."

"Now, now," Blanchard chided, "don't misunderstand Otis. He's just following my orders. I detest firearms, most especially at the dinner table."

Otis hung his head. "I'm sorry, Mr. Blanchard. I thought I done it right."

"*Did* it right, Otis."

"Yes, Mr. Blanchard."

"It's all right, Otis, Mr. Hawke won't be shooting anyone tonight. Will you, Mr. Hawke?"

"I'd hate to make a promise I might not be able to keep," Hawke said softly. "The night is young."

Blanchard's eyes widened slightly. For the first time he hesitated. He seemed about to change his mind and insist Otis follow through on his request, then he tilted his head back and roared with laughter. "You're a cold one, Hawke," he said, still chuckling. "But then I asked Ed Reno to send me a cold one. One who wouldn't draw the line at killing a woman."

Hawke said nothing, but his mind jumped immediately, unwillingly to Kate. As much as he was loathe to admit it, he was more and more considering ways to take down Blanchard with minimum danger to that increasingly annoying young woman.

A knock on the door sent Otis at once to answer it. Hawke's brow furrowed to see Jeb Kerns being led into the room.

"One of my most loyal employees," Blanchard explained, a wave of his hand indicating that Hawke and Kerns were to seat themselves on opposite sides of the table. Blanchard sat at the table's head, while Otis stood ramrod straight against the wall, eyes straight ahead, seemingly aware of nothing more in the room.

"This is one of life's true pleasures, gentlemen," Blanchard went on, "fine food, fine company." He clapped his hands sharply twice and instantly a young Chinese lad scurried into the room. The boy looked to be no older than fourteen, but he proved to be well up to the task of keeping everything at the dinner table running smoothly.

Blanchard proposed a toast before the first course arrived. Each man raised a glass of red wine, Kerns lifting his only after he had seen Blanchard and Hawke doing so. "To success." The man's eyes had an unnatural glint. Hawke merely nodded and gave the wine a courtesy taste. Kerns gulped down the whole glass.

Hawke managed to stifle a grimace when the first course proved to be birds' nest soup. He hoped consuming half of the gruelish Oriental delicacy would be enough to appease his host.

"I see you have an open mind when it comes to sampling international cuisine, Mr. Hawke," Blanchard said. "You continue to surprise me. Such ecumenism in a gunfighter is most unexpected."

"The element of surprise is just part of my job."

Blanchard's smile disappeared when he looked at Kerns.

The stage driver was completely out of his element. "What is this stuff, boss?" he grumbled. "Tastes like the bottom of my laundry water."

The slightest twitch of a muscle in Blanchard's jaw was all that betrayed his fury, but Hawke noticed it and for the first time could see for himself that Frank Blanchard was capable of projecting one image to the world, while his true self remained coiled, hidden, ready to strike.

"I thought you might enjoy having dinner with Mr. Hawke and myself, Jeb," Blanchard said. "I understand you and Mr. Hawke became quite good friends on your journey to Leavenworth from Columbia. You even had a bit of an adventure at the dock this morning."

Kerns's crude expletive got another reaction from that muscle in Blanchard's jaw.

"We ain't no friends, boss. I was just feelin' him out for ya is all. As fer him fallin' in the river, it was McCullough's she-cat who pulled him out."

"Kate?" Blanchard questioned, looking at Hawke. "She saved your life?"

Hawke shrugged. "I saved hers on the ride in. Makes us even, the way I see it."

"Yes, I heard about the holdup attempt also. Dreadful business, simply dreadful." To Kerns he said, "I don't recall mentioning that checking out Mr. Hawke was part of your job when I hired you, Jeb."

Hawke sensed the danger in this conversation for the grimy stagedriver, when Kerns did not. The man was so arrogant that he truly believed Blanchard had invited him to share his dinner. Blanchard was fishing for something and things would not bode well for Kerns when he landed it.

Hawke needed to make no pretense about the Peking duck. It was delicious. Mouthwatering perfection. Now that Kerns had arrived, he was in no hurry to draw Blanchard into a business discussion anyway. He might as well enjoy the meal.

Afterwards, the young Chinese brought finger bowls and towels. He also brought each man a small plate on which lay a fortune cookie. Hawke finished drying his hands, noticing that Kerns had already wiped the grease from his fingers onto his shirt.

"Now, gentlemen," Blanchard said, "shall we read our fortunes?"

Hawke broke the umber cookie and unrolled the tiny slip of paper. Kerns, watching him, did the same.

"I'll be damned," Kerns guffawed, slapping his knee, "this here paper says I'll be takin' a long trip real soon. Can you imagine? It's like them Chinks knowed I was a stage driver."

"You may bring my special wine now, Chin Li," Blanchard said. "Are you going to tell us what your future holds, Mr. Hawke?"

Hawke read the neatly penned script. "A new job brings unimagined riches." He cursed inwardly when he thought again of Kate, the riches having nothing to do with money.

The boy, who had disappeared into another room, hurried back to the table with a dust-covered brown bottle.

Blanchard gave the boy an imperious wave of the hand, indicating he was to pour. "I've been letting it breathe for precisely one half hour," he said. "Now it will be perfection."

As Hawke held up a clean glass for the boy, he looked at Kerns. "Your fortune is even more accurate than you think, Kerns. Didn't you tell me you were heading west? The Pacific Ocean, I believe."

Kerns nearly choked on the egg roll he was devouring. He reached quickly for the glass Chin Li had just

126

filled, gulping down the wine.

"Jeb, where are your manners," Blanchard chided. "I don't dine with goats." He reached over to open a small packet, which he mixed with his tea. "Rare herbs, Mr. Hawke, more precious than gold. Excellent for the health, if you know which are good, which are deadly."

"And you know?"

"Learned at my grandmother's knee. A vicious old woman who often dispatched enemies at her dinner table."

Hawke had stabbed a stray egg roll with his fork. He gave Blanchard a sidelong glance. "Dare I?"

Blanchard chuckled. "Really, Mr. Hawke, I said granny dispatched *enemies*. You are not an enemy." He paused meaningfully. "Are you, Mr. Hawke?"

"You set an interesting table," Hawke parried, enjoying the verbal duel. He'd come a long way for Blanchard. He was in no hurry.

"Ah, now another toast, gentlemen, please."

"My glass is empty," Kerns complained.

"Chin Li, please see to such an oversight at once." Quickly the boy refilled Kerns's glass.

"To loyalty," Blanchard said, raising his glass.

Hawke sipped the wine. "Excellent."

Blanchard smiled. "You even appreciate fine wine, Mr. Hawke. I am so very impressed."

Kerns rose from his seat, holding his middle, all but doubled over. "Help me, Frank. I don't feel so good."

Blanchard didn't move.

Kerns stumbled forward, knocking over his wine glass, scattering the remains of his meal. "Please, Frank . . ."

His eyes were wild. He was sweating profusely. "My mouth's on fire. I can't . . . I can't . . ." His words slurred. He staggered toward Blanchard. "Please, please, boss . . ."

127

"Loyalty, Jeb, loyalty." Blanchard traced his finger along the rim of his wine glass. "You should never read another man's mail. Most especially mine."

Kerns's eyes went wide with horror. "No! No, Frank, please." He gripped his stomach and pitched forward onto the floor.

"Loyalty, Mr. Hawke," Blanchard said, as Otis moved in automatically to remove Kerns's body, "should never be taken lightly."

"Poison?" Hawke's voice reflected no particular interest.

"The root of the monkshood in a particularly lethal dosage, I'm afraid. Not at all difficult with such an unsophisticated, or should I say barbaric, palate as that of Mr. Kerns."

"It can make getting dinner guests quite a chore though."

Blanchard leaned back in his chair. "I think it's time we got down to business, don't you? Ed Reno assures me you're one of the best there is."

Hawke allowed a slight upturn of one corner of his mouth. "I couldn't say. I don't read Ed Reno's mail."

Blanchard laughed heartily. "Ah, Mr. Hawke, we are going to work well together, you and I."

"If the price is right."

"Money, yes. But you can have power also. I have holdings in every state and territory — railroads, freight, silver mines, gold mines . . ."

"What's a man like you doing in Leavenworth, Kansas? What can McCullough Freight Company mean to you?"

"All in good time, Mr. Hawke. All in good time. You can't expect me to divulge all of my secrets over a glass of wine, now can you?" Blanchard raised his glass. "A toast."

Hawke lifted his glass.

"To a successful mission, Mr. Hawke."

"A successful mission."

Blanchard made a motion with his head and both Otis and Chin Li left the room.

"Dinner was exceptional," Hawke said, and was rewarded by a self-satisfied look in Blanchard's eyes. The man liked to be flattered.

"I do enjoy the finer things in life. What good is all of my money if I don't? But of course, I don't debilitate myself with hard spirits. And I know the secrets of the herbs, Mr. Hawke. I'm going to live to be a hundred, and never be sick a day doing it. Never have been."

"But you don't get everything you want."

"Most perceptive. I would hardly have sent for you if I did." He dabbed at the corners of his mouth with his napkin.

"You want McCullough Freight Company."

"Oh, I want much more than that tiny little freight outfit. It's not the company itself, it's the contracts. Future earning potential, if you will. That wily old Scot had virtually every military and civilian freight contract in the territory."

"And when he wouldn't sell out to you, you had him killed."

"Really, Mr. Hawke. We mustn't get into sordid business details. I've multi-million dollar investments. I could survive quite comfortably without McCullough."

"Then why do you want it?"

Blanchard smiled the smile of the sated cat with a cornered mouse. Not hungry, but ready to kill just for the sport of it. "That, Mr. Hawke, is my business. And my business alone."

"Fair enough. I've already talked to Kate McCullough about a job."

"Your conscience isn't going to bother you now that the little snip has saved your life?"

"I don't have a conscience, Mr. Blanchard. But Kate is not someone I would take lightly." He most certainly hadn't been able to take her lightly, not from the moment they met.

"I want you working for her. I want you heading up her next shipment. Though, of course, you'll be taking orders from me."

"Of course."

Blanchard blazed a look directly at Hawke. "I have one question to which I must have an answer. One day I may well tell you to kill Kate McCullough. Will you do it?"

The door slammed open. Both men turned toward the sound. Hawke swore.

Kate McCullough burst into the room, her .44 pistol levelled at Frank Blanchard's head.

Blanchard made no defensive move, nor did Hawke. Instead he studied her buckskins. "Run out of stays?"

The glare she gave him might have killed a man in frail health. Hawke only grinned, once again enjoying the odd way they had of sparring with one another. "You wouldn't give me a job, remember?"

"So you have to work for a snake?"

"At least I won't starve working for Mr. Blanchard." He took a sip of his wine.

"Now, now, Miss McCullough," Blanchard put in, obviously not nearly so calm as Hawke, "Kerns mentioned the attempted holdup yesterday on my stage line. I was most distressed to hear that you were almost killed."

"Yeah, I'll bet you were," Kate grated. "What upset you was the *almost* part of it. You wanted me dead!"

"Such violent talk from such a pretty little thing."

"Don't you go calling me names, you pig. You killed

130

my father and you're not going to get away with it. Maybe you put a bullet in Jim Collier, too. And maybe you've got the new law in your back pocket, but you don't have me there. And you never will. McCullough Freight is mine! I'm going to run it just like my pa did. And I'm going to run you right out of Leavenworth."

"Not if you persist in letting potential employees like Mr. Hawke get away from you. I'm seriously considering making him wagonmaster of a two-hundred-wagon shipment I've got leaving for Ft. Union next week."

Kate's eyes drilled Hawke. The accusation, the hate. She felt betrayed, but there was no help for that.

"Freight to the moon for all I care, Blanchard. But do it legal and stop interfering with McCullough."

"My offer to buy you out still stands. I can tell by your presumptuous attitude that you haven't checked with your creditors lately. You'll be back on your knees when you do."

"You'll be the Queen of England before that happens."

"Your manners are giving me indigestion young woman. I'm going to have to ask Mr. Hawke to escort you out of here."

She shifted the gun to Hawke. "He can try."

"I really would prefer that you not shed blood in this room. My Persian carpet would be ruined."

Kate picked up Blanchard's wine glass, still half full. She didn't take her eyes from his face as she tipped the glass and its contents onto the exquisite carpet. "Ooops, how careless of me."

For the first time Blanchard made no attempt to mask his rage. He stood up, his face purpling. "You little bitch, I ought to . . ."

"Kill me. Like you killed my father?"

"I did not kill your father. Not that I have to defend

131

myself to you. I heard about his unfortunate accident, and I'm not going to pretend not to be pleased. But if I had killed him I would not be so boorish as to have him gored by a bull. There are other more subtle ways."

"Don't bother, Blanchard. All you're telling me is that you didn't do the job yourself. That you paid one of your lackeys to do it for you. It's the same thing. You're responsible for my father's death."

"Hawke, get this . . . this woman, and I use the word loosely, out of my sight."

Kate shoved the gun into her holster. "I'm leaving. But I'll be back one day with proof, and I'll see you hang."

"I'll see you to the door, *Miss* McCullough," Hawke gritted. He gripped her elbow and propelled her out of the room.

"That was stupid," he hissed in her ear, when they reached the hotel hallway, "very, very stupid. You don't attack a man like Blanchard on his home ground."

"You shut up. You don't tell me what to do. I can see where your ethics are. With whoever pays you the money."

"Isn't that where an employee's loyalty is supposed to be?"

"Not when your conscience says otherwise. But then, I don't suppose you have a conscience, do you, *Mister* Hawke?"

"Whether I do or not isn't any of your business, Kate." He guided her out into the hallway. "Stay away from Blanchard."

"He killed my father!"

"And you have proof of that?"

"I should have pulled the trigger."

"What stopped you?"

"I want Blanchard to hang . . . not me."

132

"That's honest. By the way, I like the way those buckskins fit you."

"We're back to your favorite subject, I see."

"Tell me it's not yours, too," he said, his voice getting that husky tone that turned her legs to butter.

"Why . . . why are you working for . . . why . . ." Oh, God, why couldn't she think of anything but those arms surrounding her, those lips . . .

"You're trembling, Kate." His hand caught her. "You weren't trembling when you held that gun on Blanchard, but you're trembling now. Why?"

"Damn you." The words were a whisper, a plea.

He took his mouth to hers, covering her lips with his own. The sweet honey taste of her sent a shaft of desire ripping through his body. It made no sense, no sense at all, but still he wanted her, wanted her with a need that drove all other thoughts from his mind.

His hand trailed up her waist to her breast, revelling in the way it swelled to his possession. He wanted to take her here, now in the hallway of the hotel; maybe then he could concentrate on his mission, concentrate on Frank Blanchard, for Kate's sake, as well as his own.

The swelling of her breast sparked the swelling in his groin. "You promised me, Kate," he rasped, "you promised me when we got to Leavenworth."

"I should never have said yes. I . . ." His midnight eyes ensnared her as always. Something lurking in their depths, something she doubted he could put into words himself. He was hurting — this Travis Hawke. Something was ripping him apart inside, and she had to fight the urge to pull him close, to hold him, to draw his pain into her own body.

"Come to my room, Kate. Now."

She jerked away, her eyes overbright with tears. Oh, she wanted him, she wanted him so badly. Heaven help her, she was in love with him. He was the dream, the dream of her life—and the sweetest of miracles was that he wanted her back! "Which room?" she asked, her voice shaking. "Which room is yours?"

He leaned close to kiss her again. "Two twelve," he said, his warm breath fanning her cheek.

She swallowed hard. "I'll meet . . ."

She leaped back from Hawke, as Dusty Lafferty came howling up the hallway. "Kate, you haven't done anything crazy yet, have ya, lass?"

Kate gazed at Hawke, her eyes capturing his squarely. "Not yet."

Dusty gripped her arm. "I'm gettin' ye out of here before you do."

Kate allowed Dusty to lead her down the hall, her emotions roiling over what she had been about to do. Hawke made her crazy. Her body ached for him, craved him in a way she never thought possible. She glanced back only once, to see him duck back into Blanchard's room.

The secrets, the pain, the look in his eyes—all wrapped up with Blanchard, with her father, with everything. She knew it, felt it, sensed the danger to herself, but she couldn't stay away from him any more than she could stop breathing.

Two-twelve, his room number. She couldn't. She mustn't. Her heart pounded as she followed Dusty out of the hotel. She would. She had to.

"Sweet young thing," Hawke murmured, as he stepped back into Blanchard's suite.

Blanchard grunted. "One day it will be my very great pleasure to put an end to that little chit's interference once and for all." He raised his glass. "To a successful association, Mr. Hawke."

Hawke finished his wine, then bid Blanchard goodnight. He didn't want to overstay his welcome.

Back in his room he extracted something gold and shiny from his saddlebags. He studied it for a long minute, reading the legend inscribed on it.

Blanchard had brought him here. But what Frank Blanchard didn't know was that he would have come anyway. Ed Reno was merely a pawn in an elaborate plan that had been set in motion two years ago, when he had first discovered Blanchard's involvement in Anne's death. Nothing was going to stop him from killing the man. Not his conscience. Not Kate McCullough. Not even the shining metal in his hand.

He read the legend one more time, then stuffed the badge back into his saddlebags, slapping the flap closed. And just as effectively he closed his mind to what the badge stood for. Closed his mind to who and what he was—Travis Hawke, special agent to Wells Fargo and Company.

His job, his duty may have meant something once. Before Anne. Before Anne met Blanchard. Only one thing meant anything now.

Kate McCullough would not see Frank Blanchard at the end of a rope. Travis Hawke intended to kill him long before the law touched him. And if Kate got in the way, God help her. Hawke would not.

Chapter Eleven

Kate collapsed into her father's oak chair in the Mc-Cullough Freight office, feeling more defeated than she ever had in her life. Three days of going from creditor to creditor had sapped her of her spirit. Dusty was right. McCullough Freight was all but bankrupt. Only the formalities remained to be carried out.

The company still held many lucrative contracts, but no longer had either the money or the manpower to make good on any but the smallest of them.

Her father's accounts were still open at the harness maker, the livery, and the general store. Each store owner had been a friend of the family for years. None pressed her for payment. The banks, however, were another story. They wanted their money. In fact, Amos Jensen at First City Bank had become downright belligerent. But when she had demanded to know the exact figures and conditions of the note, he'd become evasive as well.

"It's done, Katie," Dusty said. "We gave it our best, but it's done."

"No!" She leaped to her feet, pacing angrily back and forth across the small room. "We can't just give up."

"Give up!" Dusty cried. "Katie, I've been holdin' this company together with frayed rope. Me and your pa did all we could."

"Yes, you and Pa," she said. "I thought I was part of this company. Why wasn't I told about any of this? I had a right to know."

"You did, I don't deny it. But Bryce . . . Bryce was your father. He loved ye. He was scared. I never seen Bryce scared. Not scared for himself but scared for you. There were threats. I know Blanchard was behind 'em. But once Bryce slipped up, mentioned somebody named Sinclair. When I asked him, he denied it. He was jumpier than a stallion about to be gelded."

"That's why I was suddenly shuttled off to become a lady!"

"Aye."

Kate stood up and walked over to the small multipaned window that faced Shawnee Street. She wiped at the dust on a wood divider. "I thought Pa wasn't happy with the way I turned out. That he was worried about my landing some husband."

Dusty's spurs jangled as he tromped across the wood floor. He touched her shoulder. She turned to face him. "Katie, you can't believe your pa was disappointed in ye? Such a thing just ain't possible."

"Then why Mrs. Russell's? Why not just send me to San Francisco to gather up some freighting contracts?"

"He didn't want ye doin' nothin' for the business. Nothin'."

"But, damnit, that's what I mean. It's my business, too."

"Aye, I won't fault you on that. I fought him on it, but he wouldn't talk to me. My own partner and he wouldn't talk to me."

Kate sensed the hurt that had caused this man second most dear in her life. "Pa must have thought it

137

would be dangerous for you, too."

"Musta thought I was gettin' old."

"Dusty, don't say that."

"In the war me, you, and Bryce run freight for the union, sometimes behind rebel lines. Don't tell me that wasn't dangerous."

"It was a war."

"I don't see the difference."

"Maybe I do," Kate said thoughtfully. "In the war we had to fight the confederates, but no one was personally trying to kill Kate McCullough and Dusty Lafferty. Pa may have found somebody who was."

"Maybe," Dusty grudgingly allowed. "But maybe I coulda helped him."

"I could have helped him too. If I'd been here. Instead he has me doing needlepoint and making pastries at some stupid school. Do you know they wouldn't even let me ride bareback? Or swear. Or anything."

She could tell Dusty tried hard to look aghast. "Not let you swear? My god, Katie, how did ye ever survive it?"

"My father wanted me to get a man, didn't he? Didn't he? But he didn't think I was good enough as I was. I had to be lady-ed up before any man would come near me."

"Bosh, Kate! Your father kept a tight rein on the buckos, never *let* 'em near you. Any man could see it in ye. The promise. And how that promise has filled out. Your pa would be bustin' his buttons."

She folded her arms in front of her. "What are you talking about. I've turned into a dad-gummed mush ball."

"You've turned into a woman full growed Kate, and a damned pretty one I'd wager, ifn' you ever bothered to gussy yourself up."

"I did all the gussying I could stand the other night

138

for Lieutenant Parsons." She ruefully recalled the dinner. He'd spent the night quoting Shakespeare, while she poked at her steak and thought about Hawke. At least Wade seemed too stuck on himself to notice that she had not been thoroughly enamored with him. "He wouldn't even tell me what the shipment is going to be. Said it would be best if the Fort Leavenworth quartermaster filled us in the night before we're ready to leave. Finding out the big secret was the only reason I agreed to have dinner with him!"

"Was it? Or did you want to make that Hawke jealous?"

"Most certainly not!"

"This is Uncle Dusty you're talking to, Kate. Never seen you look at a man like you looked at Hawke. Not even Billy."

She redirected her gaze out the window. "I couldn't care less what Travis Hawke thinks. But I do care what Pa thought. If he figured I was all right, why'd he offer to pay Billy for courtin' me?" The hurt of that day had been so great that she had never mentioned it to anyone since, not even Dusty, to whom she often thought she could talk about anything.

"Bryce was sorry about that every day of his life. He never meant for you to hear, but he was feelin' bad because he tried so hard to keep the men away from ya. He figured if he paid one of 'em, he would have the upper hand. That way he wouldn't have to worry about Billy . . . forcin' himself on you." Dusty's craggy face reddened.

"He wanted to pay Billy to keep him *out* of my bed?"

Dusty nodded, staring at the floor.

She sighed. She knew her father had meant well, but he had succeeded only in making his daughter believe herself totally undesirable.

"So are you going to tell me if there's somethin' to

this Hawke and you?"

There was something to him all right, Kate conceded to herself, but she had no idea yet what it would eventually mean. She thought of his room number again. Two-twelve. Had he lain awake for her the other night? She shook her head violently. She had to think of something, anything, other than Travis Hawke.

She grabbed up several of the papers she had strewn across her father's mammoth desk. "The way I read these figures, if we can get the Fort Laramie contract through we can make up most of our losses. Even turn a profit."

Dusty grudgingly accepted her change of subject. "Big risk. Big money."

"That's what we need right now. To get a tough one through. Make people believe in McCullough Freight again."

"We have the wagons, the livestock, but no drivers. I told ye that."

"We'll offer 'em double the standard wage."

"They wouldn't do it if you offered 'em triple. They're scared. Scared drivers don't do anybody any good. They woulda died for Bryce, but Bryce is gone." He slapped a hand on the desk in frustration. "They like me well enough, but they know I'm not Bryce."

"I'm Bryce's daughter."

"They won't work for a woman, Kate."

"Hell, none of 'em even think of me as a woman thanks to Pa!" She shook her head in exasperation. She was damned on both sides. There was no escaping it. Finally, she put words to the thought prodding the back of her mind. "Would they work for someone else? A man they could accept as wagonmaster?"

"The right man, maybe."

Her mind was waging a war. She could well picture a man as compelling as Hawke bringing back the

140

teamsters. But she was damned if she was going to ask him. He was likely already on Blanchard's payroll. No, she couldn't lower herself. Not after she'd sworn the man would never work for her.

She straightened, catching sight of banker Amos Jensen. He was headed toward the office and his gait suggested he was bringing anything but good news.

The mustachioed bank president shoved open the door and stepped inside, not bothering to doff his high-topped hat to Kate. He cleared his throat. "You stormed out of the office so abruptly this morning, Miss McCullough, that you didn't allow me to finish telling you about the note."

"I stormed out of your office, Mr. Jensen," Kate said, "because you refused to tell me anything about my note."

"Your father's note," he corrected imperiously.

"My note," she said. "My father is dead. I will honor his debts and mine."

"That's very noble of you. But I doubt anyone could make good on this particular note. It's due in less than three months."

"What are you talking about? None of the other bank notes are due before the end of the season."

"I'm afraid this note is a little different. Your father was a bit desperate when he acquired it. He needed the money to finance a big train to the Humboldt."

"Just spit it out, Mr. Jensen."

"You know I admired your father."

"But admiration doesn't put money in your pocket."

"I don't think I deserve that."

"And I don't deserve what you're doing to me."

"This is purely business. Your father would have understood this. I have no choice. In seventy-five days you'll be required to come up with one hundred thousand dollars."

Kate sagged into the chair. The drive to Ft. Laramie would net the money. But under three months there and back? It would be close. Damned close. Maybe too close. "I can't get that kind of money that quickly, and you know it."

"Then the noteholder will have no choice but to foreclose on McCullough Freight."

"The noteholder? You mean the bank, you carpetbagging son-of-a- . . ."

"Kate," Dusty warned. "No sense gettin' him any more riled than he already is."

Jensen brushed some imaginary lint from his jacket. "It so happens that the note holder is *not* the bank."

"What are you talking about? My father borrowed the money from First City Bank and I have the papers to prove it! So don't try and pull any . . ."

"The bank sold the note."

"Sold it? To whom?" But she already knew. His words only confirmed the grim truth.

"Frank Blanchard." She mouthed the name along with Jensen.

"I wonder how you sleep at night, you low-lying maggot," she grated. "Get out."

For long minutes after Jensen had gone, she sat in her father's chair trying to accept the defeat that had just been handed to her.

"I'm sorry, Kate," Dusty said. "We gave it a helluva run, didn't we?"

"And we aren't done yet!" she said, slamming back the chair and climbing to her feet. "Not by a long shot. We'll make that Laramie shipment, and we'll get Blanchard's money back here on time."

Dusty looked uncertain. "Damn, you're cuttin' it awful close to the vein, Kate."

"What choice do we have?"

"And you're talkin' like we got a crew to drive the

cargo."

"We'll have it. We'll have it all."

"You're gonna hire that reb, ain't ye?"

"We don't know he was a reb."

"*I* know it."

"He's the man for the job, Dusty."

"I know that, too. Go on with ye. Get him, if you can."

She gave him a swift kiss. "I love you."

"You'd better."

Swallowing her pride, Kate marched across the street to the Planters Hotel. Her stomach was churning. She was terrified. She was going up to his room, but not for the reason she had told him earlier. This was not the time to fulfill her fantasy. She had a shipment to get through, her father's company to save. But what if he tried to force her to go through with that foolish promise?

No, surely he was a man of some honor. She thought of him with Blanchard and wondered.

Using every ounce of her courage, she knocked on the door to room two-twelve and waited, then knocked again.

Nothing.

She fought an unreasonable anger that he hadn't just been sitting around, waiting for her. How dare he? Didn't he know how difficult this was for her? Did he have to make it harder by forcing her to track him down? And where would he be? Dear heaven, what if he'd checked out?

She all but flew down the stairs to the lobby. "Travis Hawke," she said to the bespectacled clerk, taken aback by the sudden whitening of the man's face. "Come on, Walter, where the hell can I find Travis Hawke? He's registered to room two-twelve."

"I know perfectly well what room he's using. But

right now, he's down in the saloon."

Kate headed for the door to the Planters' basement lounge.

"Hey," the clerk called, "ladies aren't allowed in there."

"That's fine, Walter," Kate called back, " 'cause you and I both know I ain't no lady."

She stepped into the saloon, stunned by the opulent surroundings. Velvet curtains, tapestries, crystal chandeliers proclaimed the lush decadence of the place. But her eyes went at once to Hawke, finding him just as she'd found him in the murky Missouri. Was it already four days ago?

He was seated at a round table, a woman in a red silk dress firmly ensconced on his lap. Kate felt her face grow hot with illogical anger. He invites her up to his room and when she doesn't leap at the chance immediately, he merely goes out and finds a substitute.

Seated at the table with Hawke was Frank Blanchard. Kate drew rein on her temper. It wouldn't do to get Hawke angry with her, when she was asking him to accept the job she'd told him flatly he could never have.

"If I'm not interrupting anything too important," she said, furious at the nervousness that seemed all too obvious in her voice, "I'd like to talk to you, Mr. Hawke." Her nervousness turned to anger when Hawke did not look up. The woman on his lap was whispering something in his ear that made him laugh, though Kate detected a certain hollowness to the laughter, as though he really wasn't that amused, or as though he had never really learned how to laugh.

She stepped closer to him, clearing her throat loudly. "I said, I hope I'm not interrupting anything important."

Again she was ignored.

Fuming, she stepped up behind his chair. The woman was nibbling on his ear now.

She tapped the woman on the arm. "I want to talk to him. I'd appreciate it, if you would excuse us for a few minutes."

"Find your own, honey. He's taken."

"He's taken, all right," Kate growled. "The sheriff's in the lobby with a warrant for his arrest. Seems this hombre's been beggin' credit all over town. Come to find out he hasn't got a cent to his name."

The woman stood up, putting her hands on her ample hips. "You're a good lookin' one, honey. But I need payin' customers." She sauntered off.

Hawke glared at her. "You that anxious?"

She balled her hand into a fist at her side. No, she couldn't hit him, she had to get him to work for her! "I'd like to talk to you."

"So talk."

She looked meaningfully at Blanchard. "Alone."

"What you have to say to Mr. Hawke, you can say in front of me, dear. After all, he will very likely soon be in my employ. He does need a job, you know." He raised a forkful of greenish leaves, pointing them in her direction. "A little spinach, my dear? So good for the digestion."

"Choke on it!"

"You have such appalling manners, truly." He reached for the small black bag on the chair beside him. Opening it, he selected three small bottles and sprinkled a little of the contents of each over his spinach. "People should never underestimate the power of plants."

"I'd like to plant you. In about hundred feet of quicksand."

"Get her out of here, Hawke. Even my herbs can't counteract what she does to my digestion."

145

Obviously fighting to control his own temper, Hawke stood up and followed her to an unoccupied table. "You win," she said, without preliminaries. "You've got a job with McCullough Freight."

"Who's to say I still want it?"

She bristled. "Listen, you bastard, just tell me yes or no."

"You have such a charming way of asking, I don't see how I can refuse."

"Then you accept?"

"I didn't say that."

"Then you don't want the job?"

"I didn't say that either."

Kate closed her eyes, her lips compressing in a grim line. He was enjoying this. "Listen you son-of-a-prairie dog, if you think I'm going to beg . . ."

"Beg? You? I couldn't let you demean yourself like that. I'll work for you."

Something in his tone made her more apprehensive than grateful. But she plunged on. "Fine. You'll start tomorrow."

"Not yet."

"Listen, I have a shipment that has to . . ."

"You haven't fulfilled the conditions yet."

"What the hell are you . . ."

"I'll work for you on one condition."

"Which is?" She couldn't stop trembling.

"That night in your bed."

"Of all the cheap, lying bastards." She was livid, more angry than she had ever been in her life. The night in his bed had been agreed to out of mutual lust, now he was putting her on the same level as the woman on his lap. He would make her a whore. A job. Five twenty-dollar gold pieces. What was the difference?

She stood up and drew back her arm, delivering a

146

stinging fist to his jaw, a full right cross. Her hand felt as if she had broken it, but she wouldn't so much as rub it as she turned and stormed toward the door. But before she reached it, she stopped, looking back. He hadn't moved. He was simply staring at her, the look of utter disbelief on his face almost comical. "I'll let you know if I accept your terms," she said quietly. Then she walked out, leaving behind a thoroughly baffled Travis Hawke.

Chapter Twelve

Only after Kate McCullough left the saloon did Hawke raise his left hand to rub his jaw. The woman packed one helluva punch. He would have grinned, but suspected it would hurt too much.

Damn, what had made her so mad anyway? He was only pushing what they both wanted. Instead she was acting like some kind of frightened virgin. But that was ridiculous. Kate was a passionate woman, a woman who knew what she wanted. No virgin could . . .

So long ago, so long. Another time, another place, another woman . . . He'd thought of that night often, though not lately, the warmth, the yielding—and how strangely it had ended.

Cursing, he headed toward Blanchard's table. He was being a fool. Kate would be back. They would spend the night together and be done with it. It was part of the job, nothing more.

"Why did you make her angry?" Blanchard demanded as Hawke took the chair beside him. "I want you working for her."

"Do you want her suspicious?"

Blanchard steadied. "You're so much smarter than I

148

would have expected for a gunfighter. Ed Reno must have sent his best."

"I'm still alive, aren't I? Now when are you and I going to discuss money?"

"You get control of McCullough Freight and you'll get all the money you want. They've got a shipment going out to Fort Laramie in the next couple of days. That one doesn't make it, and they're finished. I'll collect the company as payment on my note. And I wouldn't mind a bit if Kate had an accident."

Hawke considered the venom in Blanchard's voice. There was more to all of this than control of a freight company. Why did Blanchard seem as bent on destroying McCullough Freight as Hawke was on destroying Blanchard? Why so much hate?

Such thoughts only forced him to examine his own motives. Hate. The strongest human emotion. Stronger even, he decided, than love. Hate was safer too. In his hate he felt in control. Those rare times in his life he'd allowed himself to love . . . He stood abruptly. "You don't need me here tonight. If I'm going to work for McCullough I'd best not be seen with you."

"Whatever you say. I'll get word to you when I need something."

Hawke downed the remainder of his drink, flipped a couple of coins on the table and left the bar.

Back in his room, he shifted restlessly on the bed, unable to sleep. The gash in his head still throbbed dully, but what kept him awake was his continuing preoccupation with Kate McCullough. He was confused and angry. He'd always prided himself on being in control. Yet that control was lost each time she came near him.

He recalled the fury in her eyes when she'd all but floored him downstairs. She wasn't a person to meekly

149

accept what life handed out. She met everything head on, daring the world to try and stop her.

As much as he sought to deny it, she sparked the embers of a long dormant fire, a fire he would have sworn was dead.

Angrily, he shook his head, trying to shake off the thoughts. He couldn't be distracted by Kate. This mission was too important.

He'd been on Blanchard's trail for over two years, ever since he'd gotten the letter from Dan Parker, Anne's father. Dan had been Hawke's superior at Wells Fargo and his daughter's death had become an all-consuming obsession. Dan had to know every detail of how and why she died. It was Dan who made the connection between Blanchard and Anne. But it was Hawke who would make the kill.

It had taken all of those two years to bring Hawke this close. Blanchard moved in and out of the most exclusive social circles in the world with the ease of sand shifting in a desert wind. He was the personal confidante of more than one head of state. Knowing where the man was and being able to get to him were two separate realities. Besides, Hawke had long ago decided that just killing him wasn't enough. He wanted to bring Blanchard's empire down with him. And it had taken twenty-six months of exhaustive investigation to compile the evidence they would need to do just that.

Now, for whatever reason, Blanchard had forsaken the company of powerful friends to come to Leavenworth, Kansas, to acquire a freight company that when compared to his international holdings meant no more than would a speck of gold dust to Fort Knox. A Wells Fargo informant had intercepted Blanchard's letter to Ed Reno, setting up the perfect opportunity for Hawke's cover.

But Dan had balked. He did not want Hawke taking the assignment. Hawke could still remember the scene in Dan's San Francisco office four months ago.

"Damnit, Travis," he shouted, "you can't be in on this one. You're in no position to be objective. You'll compromise the whole department, the whole case. Everything we've got on Blanchard will fall apart. What do you think I'm staying out of it for? He killed my daughter, for God's sake!"

Hawke tried to dismiss the feelings of pity that stabbed at him as he watched this man who had once been one of the few people he could call friend. Anne had been dead for over five years now. Five years that had wrought changes in both men. Hawke had gone off to join the War Between the States, returning to San Francisco only when he'd received Dan's letter. He'd come back because he had ghosts to bury.

In that same time Dan Parker had become an old man. His boisterous, easygoing demeanor was gone, replaced by a hard-drinking belligerence — a man driven to despair by the death of his only child.

"You know I'm the best man for the job, Dan," Hawke said quietly. "I'm going."

"I'm still your boss, you'll do what I say, or you're fired."

"If you fire me, there's no way you can stop me from going." He sat down on the corner of Dan's desk. "So I might as well be working for Wells Fargo. Maybe then I won't put a bullet between Blanchard's eyes."

Dan sank into the slat-backed chair behind his desk, burying his head in his hands. "Oh, God, Travis, I miss her every day of my life. How could he? How could Blanchard kill my baby? Why would he? I don't understand."

Hawke didn't answer. He never answered when Dan brought up the subject of Anne's death. Dan could never know the full and awful truth of that night. The only thing that kept the man going was the sweet, untainted memory of his beautiful daughter. Knowing the truth had almost destroyed Hawke.

"All right, Travis," Dan said, "you go after Blanchard. You go after him for both of us. But be damned careful. If that devil ever finds out who you are . . ." His voice broke. "You're like a son to me, Travis. I can't lose you too."

Hawke stood up and crossed to the door, hating himself because parts of him had become so twisted he couldn't comfort his best friend. Yet he embraced the coldness, because nothing and no one was ever going to hurt him again. "I'll get him, Dan," he promised. "For both of us."

Two weeks later he'd been in Texas, where he'd acquired an instant reputation with a gun. A man he'd once arrested for bank robbery had drawn down on him in a saloon. Hawke's shot had been faster, his aim truer, and the escaped convict had died before he had a chance to tell anyone Hawke was a lawman. After that Hawke quickly located Ed Reno and arranged for the gunfighter to disappear for awhile. It was Hawke himself who'd penned the response to Blanchard's letter, naming himself as the hired gun Blanchard would be expecting.

Encountering Kate McCullough in Columbia had been a stroke of luck — though he had yet to decide if it was good or bad. He needed to know everything he could about the company Blanchard wanted him to destroy. But Kate, by her very nature, was certain to complicate things, complicate them in ways he had yet to fully consider.

Besides, meeting Blanchard face-to-face had presented more of a challenge than he could have predicted. He had to resist the urge to end his five year nightmare with a single well-placed bullet. It was more important that he ferret out Blanchard's accomplices before he put the man out of business. Blanchard was getting inside information about too many things — railroad mergers, bank loans, even indiscreet affairs by high ranking government officials, the perfect fodder with which to glean even more sensitive information.

As hard as it was, Hawke knew he had to be patient. If not, he ran the risk of opening the door to someone else who could take charge of Blanchard's international crime network. He had to put his personal stake in this aside. But Blanchard would pay, oh, God, he would pay.

The memories shifted then, taunting him, as they collided with that last night, the last night Anne was alive. He remembered finding her, remembered the blood, remembered the words. Slamming his head against the mattress, he slammed his mind against the past. If he remembered too much, he would never be able to finish the investigation. He would kill Blanchard where he stood.

Instead he thought again of Kate. What was it about her that broke through his carefully nurtured disinterest? He'd allowed no woman access to his feelings for so long, he was almost surprised to discover that he still had any. But why Kate?

He pictured her as he'd seen her in the woods struggling with her stays, pictured her again proud and wet after she'd fished him out of the Missouri, pictured her in her buckskins. Damn, but he wanted that woman.

Kate — with a raw, untamed beauty that fascinated him. Not the beauty of decorous parlors and sitting rooms, tea cakes and samplers, but a raw, untamed beauty akin to this wild land itself. Yes, he wanted her. But he would take it no further than that. He would appease his lust and it would end there. She was an exciting woman, likely very practiced in bed. As long as he had to be around her anyway, why not take the extra benefits? At least she wasn't being coy about it. She wanted him too.

He stood up and crossed to the washstand where he poured himself a glass of the whiskey he'd brought to the room. This was a night haunted by memories and if the whiskey helped him sleep, helped him toward oblivion, he would welcome it.

He gulped down the contents of the glass, his eyes watering as the fiery liquid burned all the way down to his stomach. He refilled the glass and repeated the process.

Why couldn't he forget? Why couldn't he forget any of it?

He raised a third shot to his reflection in the mirror. "To Travis Hawke," he said, his words slurring, his voice laced with sarcasm. "To whoever and whatever he is that people would rather die than be near him." The laughter that followed was hollow, rimmed with pain.

He straightened, hurling the glass at the mirror. The impact shattered both. Still he caught his reflection in the larger shards. Staggering back to the bed, he collapsed face down on the mattress. He dragged the pillow over his head, shutting out the world, but unable to shut out his own tortured thoughts.

The aching void in his life had begun when he was four years old, when both of his parents drowned in a flashflood that destroyed their small farm in Illinois. Neighbors found a terrified Travis clinging to the branch of an oak tree a hundred yards from where the house had stood.

"I won't come down, I won't," he shrieked, his fingers bloody and hurting from his deathgrip on the rough bark. "My ma and pa told me to stay in this tree until they came back. And I'm stayin'!" He'd said the words over and over but no one listened. They'd dragged him from the tree and taken him to a local home for orphaned and abandoned children.

"Mama will never find me here," he pleaded. "Mama will never find me."

"Shut up, boy," a hard voice snarled, a hand reaching out to grab him by the shirt collar.

Travis twisted around to stare up at a gaunt, bearded giant of a man with bushy dark eyebrows and several missing teeth. The man's Adam's apple bounced up and down in his scrawny neck as he railed at the men who had brought Travis to his door.

"I already got too many mouths to feed," he said. "Got thirty brats from babe to fourteen-year-old. The flood brought in five others besides this 'un. You'll have to take him somewheres else."

"Ain't no place else to take him, Liam," said gray-haired farmer Bill Lacey, a man Travis remembered as a good friend to his father. "He's got no other kin. It's your duty."

Liam Jeffers shot a wad of spittle across his front porch, barely missing Lacey's left boot. "The only *duty* I got," he said, "is to make a livin'. What the county pays me for these snivelin' kids don't barely make ends meet."

"You make more than your share, Liam," Lacey said, and even four-year-old Travis could discern the disgust in the man's voice. "You work these kids like slaves . . ."

"I give 'em a roof over their heads, which I don't hear the likes o' you offerin'."

"I got a family of my own."

"Make your excuses, but leave me and mine be. If'n you're leavin' the brat, leave him. And get out."

Lacey turned and tromped down the wooden steps.

155

"Mister Lacey," Travis called after him, "take me to my mama, please." He bit his lip, trying hard not to cry. His pa told him big boys didn't cry. But he wanted so badly to just let the tears come.

"Mr. Jeffers will take care of you now, Travis lad," Lacey said gently. "You mind what he says and you'll be all right."

"Where's my ma, Mr. Lacey? Where's my pa?"

"You mind Mr. Jeffers." Lacey mounted his horse and rode down the narrow road that led away from Jeffers's isolated two story frame house. The nearest town was twenty miles away. Travis looked up at Liam Jeffers and for the last time in his life, he cried.

Jeffers caught a fistful of hair and twisted. "Git in the house and be grateful I don't tie a rock around your neck and toss you in the river. You shoulda drowned with your folks. I got plenty your size already. Don't need no more."

Those were the kindest words Liam Jeffers said to Travis over the next eight years.

Day in and day out any child over three was rousted out of bed before dawn. Most were set to work in the sheds behind the house mending harness, work Liam Jeffers accepted on consignment, all of the money going into his own pocket. Or they were put to work in the fields, tending the crops that put the food in their stomachs and more money in Jeffers's pockets.

Travis settled into a routine of sorts, learning quickly to stay out of Jeffers's way. He did what he was told, finding out the hard way that to refuse was to invite punishment, swift and often cruel. But there were times when his natural recklessness won out over his common sense.

"I want to be adopted," he announced to Jeffers one morning after his seventh birthday. "Others get adopted out, why don't I?"

"Because you're too stupid," the man spat. "Who would want such a stupid boy?"

"Jake was stupid and he got adopted!"

"Maybe it's because you're stupid *and* sassy!" Jeffers arced his hand toward him but Travis jumped back to avoid the brunt of the blow. "You shouldn't have done that, boy." The man's eyes were squinted and mean, his black brows like buzzards' wings.

Travis swallowed hard. He knew what was coming and would do anything to avoid it. "I'm sorry, Mr. Jeffers. I didn't mean to sass you. Go ahead and hit me."

"Shut up! It's too late for sorry, boy." He stepped over to the door of a tiny closet beneath the stairs. He swung it open. "Get in."

"Please, Mr. Jeffers, I'll never ask about being adopted again." Travis was trembling violently. It would be the third time he'd had to spend time in that tiny hole. Each time had been worse than the one before.

Jeffers gripped him by the elbow and shoved him through the small opening, slamming and locking the door behind him. "Be sure to watch out for the werewolves now, hear? They eat little boys like you." Jeffers's cruel laughter lingered long after the sound of his retreating footsteps.

"There ain't no werewolves," he told himself firmly, though his lower lip trembled. "My pa told me so. No monsters, no monsters." Yet even his own voice sounded foreign and frightening confined to the three-by-three foot space. In the wall opposite the door there was a hole, too small for Travis, but big enough for . . . ?

The first time, Jeffers had left him in the box-like enclosure for nearly a day, giving him neither food nor water. The second time, it had been two days. Every few hours the man had walked by telling him he would never let him out. Then had come the sound, the warning rattle of a snake. Travis screamed, pounding on the door, but no one came. The rattle grew louder, nearer. Travis sat absolutely still. When Jeffers opened the door hours later, Travis remained motionless.

"Get out here, boy," he'd said.

"Snake," Travis whispered, his lips barely moving.

The rattle came right at him, so did Jeffers's demonic laughter. The man held the snakeless rattle in his hand, waving it in Travis's terror-rigid face.

"Next time I'll sic the werewolves on ya," he cackled, then walked away.

Now Travis sat in the total darkness of the tiny closet for the third time. The sounds began almost at once — hissing, snarling, scratching. Some real beast at home in the blackness, or Jeffers's madness? Hours would pass when the only sounds he heard were those of the household around him. A couple of the other boys risked Jeffers's wrath by sneaking over to the door and whispering words of encouragement to him.

A day? Two? Three? He didn't know. There was no light to mark the time. The snarling grew louder, angrier.

"It's just you, Mr. Jeffers," Travis told the darkness. "You're not going to fool me this time."

All he had to do was reach out with his left hand, prove to himself there was nothing there in the tiny opening. Just reach out. His hand shook, the noises seemed all around him now.

"There's nothing there. There's nothing there. There's nothing there." He stuck his hand in the opening.

He woke in his own bed, screaming.

"He's coming around, I think he'll be all right now."

He heard the voice, but could connect no name to it. He tried to sit up. His arm was on fire.

"Take it easy, son." The voice. Kind. A hand smoothing his forehead. "You've been bit by some kind of animal, rat maybe, a whole nest of 'em. But you'll be all right. Just scared you a little."

He remembered now. He'd put his arm through the hole. And something had seemed to try and rip it from his body. The pain, the terror. He screamed and didn't stop screaming until Jeffers had opened the door. Even that, he only remembered vaguely. His arm. His arm had been a torn and bloody mess. He'd stared at it, then remembered nothing else until this moment.

"Guess you won't be givin' me no sass any more, boy," Jeffers said. "Won't want to tangle with another werewolf."

He was seven years old, and he wished Liam Jeffers dead. But he never again asked the man why others were adopted and he was not, even though the question gnawed at him as more and more children came and went, and still he stayed. He couldn't even run away. If he was caught, he knew only too well what Jeffers would do to him. He couldn't risk the darkness. Not again. Somehow he had to get himself adopted.

Whenever prospective parents arrived, Travis went out of his way to be especially polite and helpful. That is, on those rare occasions that Jeffers allowed him to get anywhere near prospective parents. Most of the time he was shunted to one of the sheds when a couple arrived. But no matter what he did, each time another child was selected.

Travis had learned early on that Jeffers didn't just give the children to adoptive couples. He sold them. For awhile Travis worked on a system to keep a percentage of the money for the harness mending. Jeffers had gotten to the point where he often let Travis do the dealing with the customers. Once he saved enough money, perhaps he could bribe someone into adopting him.

Unfortunately, Jeffers discovered the scheme, when a woman took the money Travis had given her and told Jeffers all about what she termed "the boy's wild tale." Travis had to be grateful the man simply beat him instead of putting him in the hole. He gave up the idea of asking anyone else for help. If he was to get away from Jeffers he would do it on his own. No matter how long it took.

"I'm gonna get adopted," he said. "I've never given up, and I never will."

The frail looking youth who was sitting across from him in the harness shed looked up from his work. "I don't think you will, Travis."

"Why not?" Travis demanded. Adam had become his best friend since coming to Jeffers eighteen months ago. "I've been here seven years. Nobody else has been here half that long. It's bound to happen. I'm strong. Some farmer will want help with his crops."

Adam tugged at the harness in front of him, unable to meet Travis's gaze. His thin fingers seemed pathetically overmatched, but he continued to fight the tough leather.

"You know something, don't you?" Travis prodded. "I thought you were my friend! Why won't you tell me?" He kept his voice low, lest Jeffers overhear. No one ever knew when he would pop into the shed to check on the work being done.

Adam said nothing but Travis had seen the guilty look on his friend's face and he wasn't going to stop until he had the truth. That night in the bed they shared because there were more boys than beds, he badgered Adam until finally his friend could take it no longer.

"It's your own dumb fault you're still here," Adam said, his voice a croaking whisper.

"What are you talking about? I want out of here more than anything in the world."

"But you're too good at what you do."

"What?"

"I heard Mr. Jeffers talking to some lady who said she wanted to adopt you. He said you cussed a blue streak, hated to do any kind of work, and your parents were put in a crazy house."

"He's lyin' . . ."

"Let me finish," Adam said. "After the lady left, I heard him talkin' to Mr. Olson."

Travis recognized the name of the man to whom Jeffers sold most of the repaired harness. "What'd he say?"

"Mr. Jeffers says you'll never be adopted, 'cause you're the best worker he's got! You know all the jobs, Travis. And you know 'em best."

"That ain't enough reason to keep me here. Jeffers hates me."

"He *knows* you hate it here. He likes people to be unhappy."

"But there's somethin' else, ain't there, Adam? Something you're holding back. If you're my friend, you'll tell me."

Adam rolled over. "Go to sleep."

"Tell me. Or I'll let you mend your own harness from now on."

Adam quivered. "All right, I'll tell you. He did say somethin' else, but I don't exactly know what it means."

"What was it?"

"That you . . . that you were going to be a good lookin' one. That he couldn't wait 'til you . . . 'til you were ripe!" Adam's eyes were wide in his pale face, the moonglow making him wraithlike. "What's that mean, Travis? It makes you sound like a danged apple!"

Travis went rigid. He couldn't know precisely what Jeffers meant, but he remembered the one time he had accidentally opened the door to Jeffers's bedroom when the man was supposedly out in the field. He'd been in bed, naked, with one of the older boys, a six-teen-year-old. Travis didn't know that much about that sort of thing, but he knew what he saw made him sick. He'd closed the door before either of the two saw him, certain that if they did he would have been in the crawlspace for a year.

"Do you know what he means, Travis?"

"I'm getting out of here. I'm getting out of here to-night."

"Travis, don't be crazy! He'd have the dogs after you in five minutes. Nobody's ever gotten away from this place. You told me that yourself."

"All right, all right. Go to sleep. I have to think." By morning he was willing to risk the crawlspace if it meant getting himself a chance to get out of Jeffers's house. He'd come up with a plan. If it didn't work, he was almost twelve years old, he would have to chance running away.

"I'll trade jobs with you, Eric," he said, coming up on one of the new arrivals whose assigned chore was shoring up the harness shed's roof.

Eric eyed him suspiciously. "Mr. Jeffers told me to do this. I don't want him beatin' me again."

"He won't. I should know. I've been here long enough, haven't I? I know how he is. Let me do the roof, and you can feed the chickens for me."

Eric happily accepted the exchange, turning over his hammer and ladder to Travis. Eagerly, Travis climbed to the roof of the shed. Four years ago a boy had fallen off, landing on his head. The boy had never been right again. Jeffers couldn't tolerate the burden the boy had become. He'd actually paid somebody to take the boy off his hands.

It was Travis's intention to have the same accident, only he would be faking the results. He gulped hard, staring at the packed earth some twenty feet below him. At least he hoped he would be faking it. But even dying would be better than what he had here.

He waited until a cluster of boys crossed the yard. He wanted plenty of witnesses. Then he let out his practiced shriek and tumbled off the roof. The air slammed out of his body, a screaming agony ripping through his back. But somehow he had kept himself relaxed, feigning unconsciousness when the boys got to him.

The doctor had had to take twelve stitches in his lower back, where the jagged edge of a piece of an old, broken crock had gouged a hole in him the length of his fist, leaving him with a lifelong souvenir of his fall. But he hadn't even allowed himself to so much as groan. He just stared straight ahead, day and night. Within two weeks he was considered so feeble-minded he was barely allowed to feed himself.

"I don't want your kind around here," Jeffers said. "It gives the place a bad name." He shoved Travis up to his room. "Stay in your bed from now on. I'll do some lyin' about ya and get some fools to take ya off my hands." He tipped Travis's chin upward. "Such a shame. You would've been a good one. Strong, powerful. I would've trained you well to please me." Then he was gone.

When three weeks later, a farmer expressed interest in adopting a boy to help out on his farm, Jeffers shoved Travis at him.

"Travis is one strong worker," Jeffers assured him.

The tall, blond man with the weathered features looked dubious. Travis wanted to do somersaults for the man, but dared not seem too alert in front of Jeffers.

"Boy seems a bit slow," the farmer hedged.

"But strong as a bull," Jeffers said, poking Travis from behind to get him to move closer to the man.

The farmer hunched down in front of Travis, gripping his small hands in his large ones. "You got strong hands for such a young boy," he said. "Strong hands like my Lars."

Everything Travis was, everything he hoped to be, he put into his eyes at that moment. The farmer's eyes narrowed, puzzled, then widened slightly, a small frown tugging the corner of a generous mouth. "I'll take this boy."

Travis's heart nearly leaped out of his chest. But he said nothing, showed nothing. He watched as the farmer gave Jeffers several gold coins, then the man came back over to Travis.

"My name is Nels Svenson. You will live with me on my farm. You will earn your keep, young Travis Hawke. Come." Svenson loaded him into the back of his wagon right next to the goods he'd bought in town.

They were three miles from Jeffers's house, well out of sight of it, when Svenson pulled his team to a halt. He came around to the back of the wagon.

"Now, young Travis, you will ride in the front with me. And you will tell Nels why you pretend to be simple when I see such intelligence in those blue eyes."

"You won't take me back?" Travis almost choked on the terror he felt.

"Jeffers was unkind?"

The story poured out of him, like a bursting dam— the death of his parents, Jeffers's beatings, the crawl-space, his "accident." Nels Svenson held him against his broad chest. "So much pain in such a young life. It will not be so any more."

Travis climbed into the driver's seat beside Svenson.

"Who is Lars?" He wished he hadn't asked, when he saw the look of unspeakable pain come into Svenson's pale blue eyes. "You said my hands were like his," he prompted unsteadily.

"Lars was my son. He's dead."

And now I'll be your son, Travis promised silently. He would make certain Nels Svenson never regretted inviting him to share his home.

For six years Travis worked, sweated, gave everything he had to Svenson's farm. They worked together, laughed together, drank together — Travis's first hard liquor coming from some of Nels's home brew. He'd gotten drunk on his butt. At last he felt he had a home with this strong, hard-working Swede, who was free with his praise, fair with his anger.

"You've become a fine man, Travis Hawke," Nels said.

"Whatever I am, I owe to you." Travis skinned off his sweat-drenched shirt, flinging it onto a small cot in a corner of kitchen. His chest heaved with exertion. He'd just finished another wood chopping contest with Lars, which he'd lost as usual.

"You are your own man, Travis. But I am pleased you are happy here." He pulled a piece of paper from a desk drawer. "Here, for you. Happy birthday."

Travis stared at him. He had forgotten the date.

"Eighteen. A man. A man's present."

He opened the envelope. "A deed?"

"Ya. The deed to the Pritchard farm."

The Pritchard farm was adjacent to Nels's. "I knew he wanted to sell, but . . . Nels, I can't let you do this."

"I did it. Of course, when I die, you will have this farm and then have twice the land."

"Don't say that. You're not going to die."

"We all die, Travis."

He thought of his parents. He couldn't bear to think

165

of Nels . . . "Just don't talk like that." He picked up a towel and ran it across his chest. "You're still an ox."

He sat in a chair fingering the deed. He loved helping Nels keep the farm going, but he'd never thought about it beyond that, about having a farm of his own. But he would say nothing to dim Nels's pleasure at giving it to him. There was plenty of time for that kind of decision. The two of them would work the two farms for now.

"I'll start dinner," Travis said.

"Did I tell you the news? I heard in town this morning, Liam Jeffers is dead."

Travis didn't stop the smile that touched his lips. "Died of meanness, I suppose."

"Actually," Nels looked steadily at Travis, "something bit him."

Travis paled. "The crawlspace."

"Whatever it was had rabies. Ugly death, I hear."

"Ugly man. What'll happen to the kids?"

"I understand a young couple will take over. I know them. Very kind. They've got two children of their own."

Travis finished making supper, remembering his own terror in that closet. He still couldn't tolerate any kind of closed-in space and wondered if he ever would.

He set a plate in front of Lars, who was rubbing his hand across his shirtfront. "You're getting better with the axe. One day soon you will beat me."

"That'll be the . . ." He stopped, his eyes narrowing. "Are you all right, Nels?"

"Ya, of cour—." He sucked in his breath, then collapsed sideways upsetting his chair.

"Nels!" Travis helped him to his feet and got him into bed. "I'm going for a doctor!"

He rode the plow horse like the demons of hell were after him, but it hadn't made any difference. The doc-

166

tor came out of Nels's room, shaking his head. Nothing could be done.

Travis went into the room and knelt beside the bed, holding the strong, gnarled hand that had taught him the power of gentleness. "I love you . . . Pa."

Nels opened his eyes. "I love you, boy. We've had a good life, ya."

He was delirious then, calling out to his dead wife.

"Ya." Travis blinked back tears.

"You're the best son a man ever had." He took a deep, agonized breath, squeezing Travis's hand. "I love you . . . Lars." And then he was gone.

Travis stared at him, his own chest aching. He knew Nels hadn't meant to call him by his dead son's name, knew in his heart the man cared. But still it hurt.

For three years he tried to run the farm alone, but finally he gave up. His heart wasn't in it. He wasn't a farmer. Besides, he admitted, he was still trying to please Nels.

He wandered west, hitting California in 1858. By then he was lightning with a gun. Dan Parker was impressed and directed him toward the prospering Wells Fargo and Company. Travis was cold and hard, the defensive barriers already firmly in place. But for some reason Anne Parker was taken with him. She made it her business to have him.

Some deep, empty part of him decided to try one more time. He married Anne, at long last giving him a family of his own. When he found out Anne was pregnant, it was like the last piece to make him whole.

He'd spent a lifetime trying to fill the void in his life. But that ended with Anne. She cured him of trying. No more caring. Never again. The price was too high.

He twisted on the bed, flinging the pillow to the floor. Was he forever destined to be a fool? When would he learn that his life wasn't meant to be shared with anyone? He was in this alone.

Then why his rash proclamation to Kate that she sleep with him before he would work for her? Hell, he'd have to work for her anyway to get at Blanchard. But she didn't know that. His loins tightened. He wished she were here right now to take his mind off the miasma of pain that was his life — to feel her body beneath his own, her breasts filling his hands, her own hands touching him. As long as she never knew what he was, it would be all right.

Why? Why was she special when so many women had meant nothing? When only one other had ever come close . . .

He recalled that bittersweet night. His virgin whore. He'd all but spilled his guts to that bewitching innocent. She hadn't even hated him for what he'd done, taking part of the blame onto herself, for believing him to be a dream.

That night had been a mistake. It should never have happened. But he had acknowledged years ago that given the chance to relive it, he would have changed nothing, going again to the wrong room, to Katherine.

Leaving the money with her had been cruel, but necessary. Her very warmth, her compassion had made it so. Somehow she had sensed his pain. "Tell me what hurts, and I'll make it better." He'd taken something precious from her that night, but he would take no chance that he would leave that room taking even more. The money had been his way of making certain Katherine would harbor no misguided romantic notions about her first lover.

When he'd left the San Francisco hotel that night, he'd gone over to the registration desk in the lobby. He'd been going to look up the occupant of room five-sixteen. But he'd changed his mind at the last instant. He didn't want to know. Within two weeks he'd joined

168

Lee's forces in the war, because that was the side he'd run into first.

He'd rarely allowed himself to dwell on that night since, but somehow Kate intruded on the memory, prodded him to think of his shadowy lover. Not that Kate with her brash tongue and fiery temper could ever be like the sweet, gentle girl of San Francisco who had possessed an empathy of spirit well beyond her years. But still Kate reached him, just a little. And he would have her. Because she wasn't going to make him wait long. She wanted him as much as he wanted her. It made no sense for either of them, but the passion was there. Then once Blanchard was stopped, he would leave her. She wouldn't do to him what Anne had done.

Anne—the blood, the words. The rage burned through him, consuming him, obliterating his interest in Kate, his memories of San Francisco. Blanchard would pay because Anne was dead and she couldn't pay. But he lay there in the descending darkness and wondered who he hated more—Frank Blanchard or Anne.

Chapter Thirteen

To take her mind off Hawke and his outrageous demand that she share his bed before he'd work for her, Kate decided it was time to probe more fully into the details of her father's death. One person, she was certain, who knew more than he was saying was Leavenworth's former sheriff, Jim Collier. The problem would be getting past Lydia to talk to him. The woman had become extremely protective — or was it possessive? — where Jim was concerned.

"I'm not going to tire him, Lydia," Kate said evenly, as she waited in the parlor for Jim's arrival. "I'm just going to ask him a few questions." If anyone was tired, Kate thought, it was Lydia. The woman looked positively haggard. She was driving herself too hard taking care of Jim. "I have a right to know everything I can about my father's murder."

"It was an accident," Lydia said, her voice shrill, "an accident! Why can't you just accept that, Kate?"

The creak of wood behind her announced Jim's entry into the room.

"Jim, please," Lydia said, hurrying over to his side, "you mustn't . . ."

"It's all right, Lydia. I can talk to Kate. I'm fine.

That is, as fine as I'll ever be."

Kate flinched, but was immediately angry that she did so. It was all too obvious Jim was using his wheelchair to garner sympathy. "I want to talk to him alone, Lydia." Forcing herself, she added, "Please."

Lydia hesitated, but when Jim nodded she left the room.

His first words caught Kate off guard. "Don't mind Lydia, Kate. She means nothing to me. I mean, I'm grateful, of course. But it was you I always cared about. You know that. If I wasn't in this chair . . ."

"I . . . that isn't what I want to talk to you about. We had some pleasant times together, but that's all they were." She was decidedly uncomfortable now. He had seized the advantage, put her off balance. "You never gave me the impression you wanted any more than that."

"Your father wouldn't let me." He laughed. "He was like a wolf on a kill when it came to keeping men away from you."

"Dusty told me my father . . . was a little overprotective. But I still think if a man was truly interested . . ." She stopped. She didn't want to have this conversation with Jim Collier. She had never thought of him that way. If her father had asked Jim to keep things casual between them, she was glad of it. Even without the wheelchair there could never have been anything between them.

"I'm sorry, Jim. I had no idea my father went so far to keep men . . . I mean . . ." She blew out an exasperated breath. "This is not what I want to talk about . . ."

"I'm well aware what you want to talk about." He wheeled the chair over to her and lifted her hand into his. "And I know what I want to talk about." He pressed the palm of her hand to his lips. "I want you to know that being in this wheelchair doesn't mean that . . ." he studied her face, "that I'm not a man."

She felt her face heat. "Please, Jim, don't do this." Had it been Hawke . . . Just thinking his name made her skin tingle. A night in his bed. A night . . . in his arms.

"I see you're not totally unaffected," he murmured. "Perhaps . . ."

Now she'd really done it. Quickly she extricated her hand from his, crossing over to the window. "Lydia seems to be in love with you."

"No, Lydia just needs someone to take care of her. I do what I can for her because, like I said, I'm grateful."

And I'm grateful to you, she thought. *For escorting me about town on occasion, when it was nice to have those snooty women in the sewing circle see me with a man on my arm. But that's all I feel. Gratitude.* "Really, Jim, I think we'd best talk about something else. My father . . ."

"I won't be in this chair forever, Kate. Give it some time. Don't say no. Not yet."

She faced him squarely. "Tell me exactly what you know about my father's death."

He sighed. "All right, but don't think I'm giving up that easily. You're a special lady, Kate."

"You never thought I was a lady at all," she grimaced. Then she could have kicked herself for giving him the perfect opportunity to put off her question about her father once again.

"I knew eventually you'd grow tired of roping steers and hauling freight. Besides, I was worried about you. It's dangerous to ride those trails. Indians, dust storms, God knows what—I care about you, Kate."

She fingered the fringe of her buckskins. "I'll never grow tired of it. And the danger is part of the excitement. I wish I could make you understand." She raised her eyes heavenward. No, she didn't want to make him understand. She didn't give a damn if Jim Collier understood why she lived the life she did. What was the matter with her? Then she knew. She felt sorry for him. And she wasn't very proud of the thought.

With a very deliberate motion she paced across the room and gripped a small wooden chair by the slats in its back. She picked it up and carried it over to Jim. Thumping the chair down in front of him, she sat down and glared balefully at him. "No more sidetracking. Tell me what you know about my father. Now."

He chuckled. "That's another thing I always liked about you, Kate. You could always make me laugh."

"Yeah, just your seeing me in my buckskins would . . . Oh, no you don't. My father. Now."

"There's nothing more to tell. Blue Boy killed him."

"You saw the wound."

"I told you that."

"It couldn't have been staged?"

"Staged? What are you talking about?"

"Someone could have shot him, then used a steer horn to . . ." She swallowed hard. "You know what I'm saying."

"There were two witnesses, Kate."

"I want their names."

"I've got them with my things . . . in the bedroom." He looked meaningfully at her.

"I'll wait.

"Spoilsport." He wheeled out of the room, but before the door closed Lydia stormed back in. It was obvious she had been listening

"You're wearing him down. He's not well."

"He seems fine to me. It's his legs, Lydia, not his mind."

"Don't you talk to me about it. Don't you dare! If it wasn't for you . . ."

Kate's eyes narrowed. She'd never seen Lydia so upset. "What are you saying?"

"Nothing, I . . ."

"Lydia . . ."

"All right, you want to hear it? You spoiled little . . . Bryce is dead because of you! Jim is crippled because of you! Because they both loved you, because . . ." Sobbing, she ran from the room.

Kate stared after her, stunned. The woman couldn't be right. She couldn't be. But when Jim came back with the names, she was too upset to speak. She grabbed the paper from his hand and bolted out of the house.

She walked aimlessly for nearly an hour, her mind constantly going back to Lydia's condemning pronouncement. That she was responsible for her father's death, for Jim being in a wheelchair. No, she wouldn't accept that. She wouldn't. Lydia was either mistaken or lying. Kate shivered. She had to be. Kate couldn't bear it otherwise.

Finally she looked at the names Jim had given her. Neither meant anything to her. She would have to find out if they still worked for McCullough. She frowned ruefully. That shouldn't be too hard to check, very few men still did.

She crumpled the paper in disgust. So many things on her mind at once. Finding her father's murderer, getting the freight through, paying off the notes, and the man who seemed forever in her thoughts—Travis Hawke. Could he help her with any of this? Would she ask? He would have already been working for her if she had followed him to his room last night, instead of . . . Oh, why had she hit him so hard? She rubbed her knuckles. They would hurt for a week.

She came to an abrupt halt, surprised to find that her steps had taken her to the McCullough Livery. So often she had come here with her father before big shipments. She'd help him write up the bill of lading, accounting for every bit of cargo. Then would come the roundup, getting the stock ready. Hundreds of oxen to pull hundreds of wagons. She climbed up on one of the stalls. This was the one Blue Boy had been given. Spoiled as a damned pup. Damn, she simply could not believe . . .

"Yo, Katie! That you?"

She grinned at the barrel chested teamster coming toward her at an awkward trot. Rafe Yates's bow legs would make any gait seem awkward. He was the only man who'd ever fought for the south, whom Dusty seemed able to forgive and forget. She jumped down from the stall and ran over to him. "Rafe, you old piece of buzzard bait, where the hell you been? I've been in town four days!"

"Still the same old flower-tongued Kate!" he roared. "Damn, you make this old man's heart go flutterin'."

"Go on with ya!" She swatted his arm. "Your heart would flutter over any female under a century old that came within fifty yards of you." She gave him the best hug she could manage, her arms not quite reaching to the middle of his back. "You're going to work for me when I take the load out to Ft. Laramie, aren't you?"

He looked at the dirt. "Can't do that, Kate."

"And why the hell not?" she demanded, taking a step back.

"Can't work for no woman."

"Never hurt you before."

"Bryce was alive then. If Bryce got kilt, what can a strip of a gal like you do? I mean . . . well, I'm sorry, Katie. I just can't do it."

She shook her head, sighing. "It's okay, Rafe. I understand." More and more it looked like she would have to take Hawke up on his offer. If only he hadn't connected the night in his bed to the job. The fool jackass ought to know she would have spent the night with him anyway.

Cursing, she grabbed up a pitchfork and set to work, taking out her angers and frustrations on the hay in the stable. She worked for hours, sweating, cursing, until finally she felt like she could cope with her life again.

"Been thinking about your job offer." The voice was low, husky, right behind her.

"Have you now?" She did not turn around.

"I think the terms are right."

"They're your terms."

"You'd change something?"

She shivered. "Maybe you shouldn't ask when I've got a pitchfork in my hands."

His laughter was low and throaty, making her blood surge faster through her veins.

"And maybe I should get something in writing. You might change your mind after . . ."

"You don't need anything in writing, Kate."

She let go of the pitchfork, turning to look at him. His dark jeans were slung low on his lean hips, the buttons of his shirt lay open almost to his navel. "Then you'll . . ."

"Captain Hawke!"

Kate's brows furrowed, as she watched Rafe striding toward Hawke.

"That's you, ain't it, Captain Hawke?" Rafe demanded.

Hawke frowned. "Corporal Yates?"

"Right, captain! Damned, if you ain't a sight for sore eyes. Last time I seen you, you were near dead with them four bullets . . ."

"The war's over, Rafe."

"Right, captain."

"The name's Travis."

"Yes, sir. I mean . . ." He looked at Kate. "You know the cap . . . uh, Travis, Katie?"

Before she could answer, he rushed on. "Hell, he damned near took out a whole Yank regiment at Chancellorsville. Never seen the like. A real hero."

Kate looked at Hawke. He was trying very hard to seem indifferent, but there was a subtle change in him from the arrogant bastard who strode into the barn. Her initial reaction to Rafe's announcement that Hawke might have killed dozens of men had been shock. Now she had to grip the post of the stall to keep from going to him, holding him, feeling the core-deep pain she was now certain lay buried inside him.

But she wondered if anyone else looking at him right now would notice anything amiss in the nonchalant way he continued to talk with Rafe. How could it be that she felt his pain? Surely, she was just imagining things. Yet it was as though he were calling out to her for help without even realizing he was doing so.

She gripped the post tighter; just looking at him made her heart soar. It went well past the need of the dream. She was in love with this man about whom she knew nothing. And the hopelessness of that love left her so terribly vulnerable to him that she wanted to run out of the barn and never look back. But she didn't move. Somehow, someway she would fight through the armor he had braced around his heart. She would make him love her back.

Love her back. The thought brought a curse from her lips. She could well imagine what she looked like right now, after a day of cleaning out stalls and pitching hay. He'd love her all right, but only after every other female on earth had dropped dead.

"What are you swearing about now?" Hawke asked, throwing her a sidelong glance that nearly buckled her knees. What a fool she would be if she dared let him

177

discover that she loved him. She harbored no illusions that he would let her down gently. He would give her the same kind of pain that someone had once given him.

As steadily as she could manage, she answered, "I was just thinking about that wagonmaster position I have open."

"You want me?"

She flushed at the double meaning to his words. Moving out of earshot of Rafe, she looked him in the eye. "I need a wagonmaster, Mr. Hawke. Yes . . . I want you."

He cradled either side of her head in his hands. "You agree to my terms?"

Her flesh grew hot under his touch. "Your room or mine?" she asked huskily.

For long minutes his lips moved over hers, then he raised his head. "Mine." He slipped his hand in hers and led her out of the barn.

Chapter Fourteen

"Hey, Katie," Rafe called after her, as she and Hawke headed away from the barn, "you get Captain Hawke as wagonmaster and I'll bet half the crew signs back on. He's a good man."

"Well, that's one person who thinks so," she grumbled, determined to maintain her normal tone with him. She was on her way to the man's bedroom. She would be lost if he even suspected she loved him.

To her relief he chuckled. "This should be an interesting experience."

She stopped dead. "I beg your pardon?"

"I mean working for you, of course."

"Of course."

She didn't speak again on the long walk to the hotel.

"Don't be so nervous," he said, as they entered the lobby. "I'm not hard to please."

She wanted to hit him. Of all the slimy . . . He had her pegged as experienced in the bedroom, but obviously not especially skilled at what she did there. Well, she would show him.

She cringed when she heard someone call out her name. "Kate, what are you doing here?

She gave the desk clerk a weak smile. "Hello again,

Walter."

He sat behind his registration book, shoving his spectacles into place as though he could not believe his eyes. "And why are you with him?" He eyed Hawke with a mixture of fear and contempt.

"Walter," Kate said, then faltered.

"I work for the lady," Hawke said. "She and I have some business to discuss. And we would appreciate it if we were not disturbed."

"You couldn't be a little more obvious, could you?" Kate gritted.

"Walter a good friend of yours, is he?"

"I've lived in this town since the day they laid the first brick twelve years ago," she snapped. "I know people."

"Is it going to bother you that he knows you're in my room?"

She studied his face, trying to decide if he was asking to be insulting or out of a genuine concern for her reputation.

"I assure you that what I do is none of Walter's business. Nor anyone else's but my own."

"Now that sounds like the Kate McCullough I know." He took her elbow and steered her toward the stairs. "Shall we?"

She would have to brazen her way through this. As imperiously as she could manage, she strode in front of the gape-jawed Walter and headed up the stairs with Hawke. When she reached the door to his room, she unconsciously clutched the front of her shirt together, then gasped, looking down at her clothes. She had completely forgotten how horrid she looked . . . and smelled! She had spent the entire day cleaning out stables. "I . . . maybe we'd better wait. I mean tomorrow would be . . . I can't . . .

"You want to get the wagons loaded up tomorrow.

You're set to move out the day after. There's no other time, Kate." He pushed the door open in front of her and guided her into the room, shoving the door shut with his foot.

"We . . . we could do it . . . ah, I mean . . . on the trail."

"Change your mind?" His voice was unreadable, and she could not look at him.

"No, I mean . . ." In San Francisco she hadn't smelled like an ox.

"Then what?"

"I'm no Queen of Sheba," she stammered, "but I do usually dress a little more formally for . . . for . . ." She looked at him helplessly. "All right," she said, "I stink."

He grinned, and the effect on her was devastating. It transformed his whole face. So damned handsome. Beautiful. "I'll have a bath brought in. For both of us."

She averted her eyes, lest he see her blush. How could she blush about bathing with the man, when she was going to . . .? Would she ever be rational again?

Stepping further into the room, she heard something crunch beneath her boots. Shifting her foot she discovered what was left of a shard of glass. She looked at him, puzzled.

"An accident with the mirror," he said. "They replaced it, but they must have missed a piece." He left then to see about the bath.

Kate couldn't resist sitting on his bed. She turned down the coverlet, caressing the pillow, the pillow where his head would lie when he . . .

The door opened, and she jumped up guiltily. She was grateful when he made no comment. Trailing behind him came a burly man carrying a large porcelain tub. He settled it in the middle of the room. "Finest there is," he said. "You folks enjoy yourselves now." He

181

gave Hawke a leering wink and left the room.

Kate wanted to cry. Why did people have to reduce what she longed for with Hawke to something smirking and sordid? She didn't have time to dwell on it as the maid came in carrying the first of many buckets of water. At least she'd never seen the man and woman before.

"Your bath awaits, madame." Hawke waved a hand toward the steaming tub of water.

"And what are you going to be doing?" she demanded clutching the collar of her shirt.

"Watching. What else?" He stretched out on the bed, his back propped up on pillows, his arms behind his head. His eyes, oh, god, those eyes, had already undressed her.

Watching! How in heaven's name was she going to take a bath in front of this man? Her fingers shook violently as she started to unfasten her shirt. She took a deep breath. *Stop it, Kate,* she told herself fiercely. *You have to do this. You need him to get the freight through.* She took another breath. *You need him period.*

She finished undoing the buttons, but did not remove the shirt. She stood in the center of the room next to the tub trying to decide how best to proceed. He was lounging on the bed with such ill-concealed conceit, as if what she were doing were somehow his due, that she could feel the stirrings of temper dissipating her nervousness.

She fingered the ankle-length nightrail the maid had brought along with the towels. How thoughtful. A slow smile spread across her face. Swiftly she pulled the garment over her head and shimmied it down the length of her body. She did not put her arms through the sleeves.

"What the hell?" Hawke grumbled. "I thought you were going to take a bath."

182

"I am," she said sweetly. With a flurry of movement under the nightrail she removed her jacket, shirt and pants and scrunched them to the floor. She was now cocooned in the nightrail. She smiled demurely at Hawke.

He glared at her. "Take that damned thing off."

"I intend to," she said, lifting the garment up to her knees. She almost weakened at the heated gaze that was directed at her legs, but somehow she managed to step over the side of the tub and into the water without compromising any more of her body. As she lowered herself into the sudsy water, she raised the nightrail. She lifted it above her shoulders, only after her body was fully immersed in the water. Grinning triumphantly, she flung the nightrail aside.

"Think you're pretty clever, don't you?" he said.

"Very clever as a matter of fact."

"Clever enough to reach those towels when you're finished?" His gaze travelled over to the washstand, several feet distant from the tub.

Kate swallowed. She would worry about that later. Groping in the bottom of the tub, she found the bar of soap and began to scrub away the day's grime. She found the sensation so pleasant that she began to relax, almost forgetting that she had an audience.

"Want me to do your back?" came the throaty question.

She started, imagining his hands on her wet, naked flesh. "I . . . I can manage, thank you."

"You're a strange woman, Kate."

"Why do you say that?" She stared straight at him, running the soap along the length of her arms.

"You're a passionate woman. You know what you want. Yet right now, you seem almost . . ." He paused.

"Almost what?"

"I don't know. Frightened. Do you think I'm going

183

to hurt you?"

"Of course not," she snapped. "How absurd. I would hardly be bathing in your room if I thought . . ." What did she think? Not that he would hurt her. Not physically, the way he meant it. But he had the power to hurt her, that much she knew. "I'm just a little nervous, that's all. It's been awhile."

"I beg your pardon?"

"I . . . uh, I've been east, you know. In a girl's school. It's been a while since . . . since I've . . . done this." She ran the soap across her breasts beneath the surface of the water, she hoped unobtrusively, but knew by the darkening of his gaze that he was aware of her every movement. Her nipples puckered shamelessly, as though he, not she, had touched them.

"Then you should be eager for the night," he said.

"Are you?"

"Yes."

He surprised her by admitting it, the huskiness of his voice igniting her body's own passion almost beyond enduring. As she fumbled with the tresses of her hair, she tried to think of something, anything, to change the subject, or she would never be able to finish this bath. "Rafe . . . Rafe said you were a rebel captain."

"Don't."

"Can't I know anything about you? I mean, I have to wash my hair and . . ." My, didn't that sound ridiculous.

"What do you want to know?"

Why you're so defensive and hurt and angry all the time, she thought, but said, "You don't have a southern accent."

"Nope."

"Illinois?"

"You have a good ear."

"Family?"

184

"None."

She ducked her head under the water to give her hair a good soaking, then began to wash it in earnest. "Why did you fight for the south? Do you believe in slavery?"

"I don't believe in anything."

She studied him through dripping strands of hair, blinking the soap out of her eyes. "Then why did you fight?"

He hesitated, but only slightly. "I didn't join to fight. I joined to die."

The words so disconcerted her that she couldn't speak for several minutes. He had said it in San Francisco, and now all these years later he had said it again.

"Do you still feel that way?"

"I don't feel anything."

Her heart was hammering in her throat. It was there and she knew it, felt it. His pain. It wasn't that he didn't feel, but that he felt too much. "You're still a liar, Travis Hawke."

Silence.

She finished washing her hair, then asked quietly, "Would you mind pouring that bucket of clean water over my hair to rinse it?"

He stood up and crossed to the bucket, hefting it and bringing it over to the tub. All the while his eyes never left her face. She gave him a shy smile. "You'll enjoy dumping that on my head, won't you?"

He nodded, then upended the bucket.

She sputtered, cursing, as she caught most of the water square in the face. He strode back to the bed and lay down.

"Oh, you are a bastard!"

"And you've spent enough time in that bath to clean a herd of elephants."

She threw the sponge at him. He caught it, but it splattered water all over his shirt, all over the bed. He jerked the coverlet to the floor, swearing.

"Watch your language," she said primly. "You're in the presence of a lady."

"Oh," he growled, peeling off his shirt, "someone else came into the room?"

She giggled. "I might enjoy this night after all."

He sent her an affronted glare.

"Well, you said you're not hard to please," she reminded him. "But I am."

He looked away at once, making an elaborate display of hanging his shirt over a chair to dry. Now what in the world was she supposed to make of that? He couldn't possibly think that he might *not* please her? All he had to do was be there. She'd dreamed about this night for five years. Of course he didn't know that. She studied the corded muscles of his back, so smooth and supple, such strength lying coiled beneath the flesh. She so wanted to touch him.

"Hawke," she ventured, "what are you thinking? About tonight? About me?"

"Don't turn this into something it isn't, Kate." He sat on the edge of the bed, his arms resting on his knees.

"You must feel something. Or else . . . or else you couldn't . . ."

"All right. I feel lust. When I look at you, I want you. And that's lust."

"That's all."

"What else do you want me to say?"

"I . . . I don't know." Why had she started this? "If . . . if it's just lust, well then, I mean, you could have paid that floozy downstairs who was on your lap last night."

"Who says I haven't?"

Her eyes burned. She had so wanted him to say the

186

things he had that night in San Francisco, when he had been open and vulnerable, because they were strangers and it was dark. But that was long ago. She couldn't expect . . . "Would you hand me a towel?"

He looked at the towels, then at her. Rising to his feet he picked one up and tossed it to her. She caught it above her head, feeling her breasts rise briefly above the waterline. A sardonic smile twisted his lips. "You almost made it."

Her lips compressing with fury, she scrubbed her hair dry, then began to towel her shoulders and lower, holding the towel in front of her as she progressed downward. She stepped out of the tub, her toes dripping water onto the carpet.

"Very nice," he drawled.

She followed his gaze behind her, horrified to see her exposed derriere in the mirror. She wrapped the towel fully around her, so angry she couldn't even think of words foul enough to call him.

"Take it easy. After all, now it's your turn to watch." He undid the buttons of his fly and for an instant she couldn't take her eyes off his hands. Then she realized what he'd said, what he intended to do, that he was going to take a bath. Skirting quickly around him, she scooped up the nightrail and yanked it over her still damp body.

Feeling secure in the nightgown, she relaxed a little, trying to seem nonchalant as she heard his boots thud to the floor behind her, followed by the soft chinking of his pants. He must have a pocket full of coins.

Coins! She picked up the leather pouch hooked to her belt. Five twenty-dollar gold pieces slid into her hand. She had always been going to pay Hawke back for his services. Just as he had paid her.

Her heart pounded. Dare she risk telling him who she was? The money would most certainly convince

187

him. It was also likely to infuriate him.

She slipped the money back into the pouch. If things went well tonight, perhaps she wouldn't need the money to prove her identity. Perhaps he would know . . .

She lay down on the bed, the depression made by his body still warm beneath her. She shut her eyes tight, tucking the money pouch under the mattress. There was another reason she didn't want to throw the money at him any more. She no longer wanted to hurt him.

"Aren't you even going to take a peek?" he said, his voice conveying mock disappointment.

She heard one foot make contact with the water. "I want it to be a surprise," she mumbled.

He laughed. "Kate, you are a marvel."

At least he wasn't being grim any more. And as she heard him settling his tall body into the bathtub that seemed much smaller now with him in it, she did manage to open her eyes just a little. "Very nice," she murmured, amazed by her audacity. And she was again rewarded with the warm sound of his laughter.

She lay there, watching him lather up his broad, hair-roughened chest, imagining her fingers trailing through the warm suds. Her mouth grew dry, her heart pounding. Was she out her mind? In a few minutes he would finish his bath, and then he would come naked to this bed. This man, who thought she was some kind of experienced lover, who expected more than she knew how to give. Just as he had that night five years ago.

Almost desperately, she called on her every memory of that night. She wanted so much to please him. He would not turn away from her this time.

She heard the water sloshing. She looked to see him rising out of the tub, not caring a whit what the towel covered or didn't cover. Instinctively, she closed her eyes, but opened them at once. How was he going to believe her wildly experienced if she fainted at the sight of his . . .? Oh, my, he was most certainly male. She had never seen it in the light before. But she had seen statues in museums in Boston — gods that would be put to shame by the perfection of this man's body. She stared at him now, unashamed, her desire flaming to new heights in her trembling body.

He smiled, settling the towel around his hips. "I trust you can restrain yourself for a few more minutes." He rubbed his hand along his jaw. "I think I'd better shave."

"I'll manage," she croaked, using the respite to climb out of the bed and cross to the windows. It would be dark soon. Even the dim lantern light in the room would make it all too easy to see in. She closed the heavy draperies.

"Don't!"

She started at the harshness in his voice. A second ago he had been teasing her, now he seemed furious. "All I'm doing is closing . . ."

It only took three of his long strides to reach the window. He yanked the cord that opened the curtain. "I like fresh air."

He had said that, too, in San Francisco. It seemed almost ludicrous to have him staring down at her with half of his face shaved, the other half still covered with soapy lather. He kept a firm grip on the towel with his left hand.

"I wasn't closing the window, just . . ." She stopped, studying him closely. Why did she know that if she touched him, his heart would be racing and the sweat on his chest would be cold? "I like fresh air, too."

A breeze stirred the still damp strands of her hair, ruffled the nightrail, tightening it across the firm swell

189

of her breasts. His free hand reached toward her, but fell away without touching her.

He crossed abruptly to the washstand and finished shaving, toweling the excess lather from his face. "Drink?"

"What?"

He poured the whiskey and held it out to her. "Drink?"

She stepped over to him, studying the way the dark hair on his chest arrowed down past his navel to disappear into the low-slung towel. She accepted the glass. "Thank you."

He poured himself a shot, then raised the glass. "To a good night."

Nervously, she clinked her glass to his, watching half the contents spill over the rim. "Sorry."

He refilled the glass. "No problem."

"A good night," she said in a small voice, gulping down the drink in one swallow. "Smooth," she said, blinking rapidly.

His eyes were wide, incredulous. "Another?"

"Yes, please," She did the same with the second drink.

"Thirsty?"

"I . . . no, I'm sorry." She was no stranger to hard liquor, but neither was she used to the effects of what she had just done. Already she was feeling decidedly woozy. Very carefully, she made her way over to the bed. "I'm . . . just a little nervous, I guess."

"I guess." He swallowed his own whiskey and poured himself another. This one he did not drink, bringing the glass over to set on the night table beside the bed. "I didn't mean to snap at you about the curtains."

His apology surprised her. "It's all right."

He twirled a finger around a stray tendril of her damp hair, his eyes locking on hers. She came into his

190

arms as if she'd always been there, surrendering to the warmth, the odd security of his embrace. He tilted her head back and brought his mouth to hers. She clung to him, time suspended, her body pressed full length against him. Then he was pressing her downward, urging her toward the bed.

She allowed him to guide her, settling back onto the mattress, waiting.

He studied her, a peculiar intensity in his midnight eyes. "Anxious?"

She felt the heat in her face, and it was not solely because of the alcohol. "Not especially," she lied. "It's just that it's not often I do this . . . this sort of thing to get a man to work for me. It's usually just . . ." she swallowed, "lust."

He snorted. "You don't even bother to act the part, do you?"

"What part?"

"The shy little coquette. Normally, I'd be expecting things like 'I don't usually do this, but . . .'"

"Cynical bastard, aren't you?"

Her bluntness brought him up short. "If I am?"

"If you are, so what? If was just an observation." She had to be careful. She didn't want to give away anything that would lead him to suspect their previous night together. Not yet. She wouldn't risk his putting an abrupt end to the evening.

Somewhere inside him he held the key to the secrets bottled up inside him, but he guarded it jealously. He would rather be a son-of-a-bitch than risk letting her get close to him. She wondered how many times he'd been kicked before he threw up the barriers. When this had become his way—to hurt first and fast.

"Shall we get on with this?" she murmured, trying unconsciously to primp her still damp hair. "I really do need a wagonmaster."

191

He swigged down the glass of whiskey. "Whatever you say."

His eyes burned her, scorched her flesh, as he sat down on the edge of the bed. She lay perfectly still, the high neck of the nightrail seeming now to choke her. She had to go through with this. She had to. To save her father's business, but more than that, to find out once and for all if San Francisco was merely a memory wildly exaggerated by time and romantic nonsense.

She reached up a trembling hand to gently trace the outline of his lips. "You have a beautiful mouth," she whispered.

He groaned and gathered her to him, his mouth coming down hard against her own. She felt his weight shift on the mattress, as he moved to lie beside her. It would happen. The dream. The dream that was Travis Hawke.

And suddenly it was another hotel, another bed. San Francisco five years ago.

"It's going to be a long night, Kate," he said softly. "A very long night."

She felt the heat of his breath on each word. She swallowed, her own breathing shallow. She prayed her eyes didn't betray the anxiety that coursed through her body as fiercely as her passion.

His fingers deftly worked the ribbon at the top of her nightrail. His palms were like brands as he eased the material aside. But the vee was too shallow and did not allow him access to her breasts. He sat up, the towel still draped, annoyingly to her now, around his middle. Reaching down, he lifted the hem of the nightrail tugging the garment upward. When he reached her hips, she had to lift her body off the bed to allow him to pull it up further. To do so would leave her naked, but he must have sensed her unease, because he kept his eyes on her face until he pulled the gown over her head.

She shivered, though she was excessively warm, her arms instinctively covering her breasts. Then she drew them away. What had stopped him in San Francisco was her innocence. It would not stop him tonight.

He would use her as long as he thought she was using him.

He could not know that she loved him, loved him in spite of whatever secrets he had locked inside him. But she was very careful not to say the words aloud. She couldn't bear to relive the disappointment she felt in the copse by the stagecoach.

"Ah, Kate, you're beautiful," he said hoarsely, circling her wrists with his hands. His eyes fastened on her coral tipped breasts. "I want you, Kate. God in heaven, I want you so much."

He captured a breast with each hand, caressing the firm swells, sculpting the nipples with the tips of his fingers. Kate closed her eyes, immersing herself in the exquisite sensations he was evoking in her body. In some magical way his touching her breasts sparked a searing response along every inch of her flesh.

It was his gentleness that surprised her most. She would not have expected gentleness from Hawke. He was harder, more bitter now than he had been the first time.

She did not realize it, but it was her own gentle caressing of his body that slowed him, kept him from taking her swiftly and perfunctorily as he had at first thought to do. He was mesmerized by the feel of her hands on him. She touched him, petted him, stroked him, as though she had spent a thousand nights in his arms. She praised him when he pleased her, urged him to show her how to please him.

Her fingernails trailed lightly down his arms, across his shoulders. "It's like you can't help yourself," she

193

sighed, revelling in the play of his muscles, rippling to the touch of her hands. As he grew more quiescent, she grew bolder. He was hers. For tonight, he was hers.

Her mouth found his, possessed it, demanded of it. Her tongue parried with his. Then she trailed her attention to his ear, tugging at the lobe until she heard him groan. She held it prisoner, felt his hand jump to her breast, capturing the taut crest. Standoff. She released the lobe, smiling against his cheek.

"Bastard."

"Bitch."

"Take me."

"Count on it." His hand traced circles, lower ever lower, spiraling downward to the quivering core of her. His hand closed over the velvet mound, staking his claim. But when his finger probed the satiny sheath, she denied him entry, suddenly, unexpectedly shy.

He took her resistance as coyness and bowed to her wishes, his hand moving across her hips and down to curve under her buttocks.

She felt the thickness against her thigh, as he moved above her. She wanted him, needed him, but not yet, not yet.

Again he acceded to her wishes, allowing her to press him onto his back. She kissed his chest, his nipples, her tongue trailing past his navel. Closing her eyes, she dared to touch the prickly hair nested between his legs, circling that part of him that fascinated her most. He had not finished what he'd begun that night. Tonight he would.

Her hand closed around it. She felt the hardness jerk in her hand, his groan of throaty pleasure. She trailed tiny circles around it, felt his whole body twitch. She opened her eyes to see his fists clenched at his sides, his eyes closed tight.

"Kate, ah, Kate, damn that feels good. Too good."

"Too good?"

He eased her hand away from him. "Keep touching me like that, and we're both going to regret it."

She was puzzled, but dared not display her ignorance by asking questions.

He twisted away, easing her onto her back in one graceful motion. He settled his knee between her legs, urging them apart, though they seemed to part with no thought of her own. Her head twisted from side to side, her body aching, needing. She had dreamed it so long, wanted it so long, needed it now with a desperation that frightened her.

"Don't stop. Hawke, please, don't stop."

"What would I be stopping for now, woman?" he groaned. "This is the best part." He straddled her. Ready, so ready. "Oh, Kate, I knew you would be good. You know how to drive a man mad."

She felt the heat of him probing at the entrance to her womanhood. Her breathing grew erratic. It would happen now. It would happen. And he would whisper the words. He would love her. For tonight he would love her.

He held himself above her. When she wrapped her legs around him, he could hold back no longer. He was shaking, aching, ready for release.

"Now," Kate cried. "Hawke, please . . ."

He thrust himself inside her, her pleading cry dragging a long, shuddering moan from his throat. He was part of her, his whole being throbbing with the awesome pleasure he found in her arms.

He cried her name, feeling whole and safe, even as he tried hard not to. Kate. She made him feel, made him care. He matched his rhythm to hers, forcing himself to wait, wanting suddenly to please her, more than be pleased himself. How could she know him so

195

well? How? She touched him, stroked him, moved under him, as though she had known no other lovers, as though he were her only lover, as though she had been in his bed a thousand times.

Together they rode the crest, two waves crashing on sun-kissed sands, exploding, shattering, surrendering each to the other.

Long minutes later, Kate opened her eyes to gaze lovingly at the strong, handsome face nuzzled against her shoulder. "Hawke?" she whispered. He didn't move.

Smiling, she trailed a finger along his jaw. "In all the dreams I've ever dreamed since that night, none of them came close to what you just did to me." She kissed his forehead. "None of them came close."

He opened his eyes, shifting groggily. "What night?"

She bit her lip. "I thought you were asleep."

"What night?" He was fully alert now, propped up on one elbow, his eyes searching hers.

"Just go back to sleep." Why had she said anything? Why? He would find out, and it would spoil everything.

"What night, Kate? You made it sound as if we'd . . ." He sat up, the bedsheet sliding to his waist. "No. Oh, my God . . ." A dozen emotions surfaced, skated across his features. For the briefest instant she could have sworn one of them was joy, but then she saw more clearly confusion, then rage.

"You knew," he gritted. "You knew from the first. What was this?" He made a sweeping gesture over the bed with his hand. "Some kind of sick revenge? Do you have the sheriff outside the door to arrest me for rape?"

"Rape? What are you talking about? Hawke, please, I didn't mean for you to find out like this. I . . ." She struggled to sit up, clutching the sheet against her breasts. "Don't be angry. Please." She wanted to add,

196

"Don't spoil it, not again." But she didn't.

"How did you arrange this? How?"

"How did I?" she asked. "How did *I*?" Her temper fired. "You're the one who demanded I spend the night in your bed! How dare you say . . ."

He flung back the sheet, pulling on his pants. "Don't say any more. Just get out."

She put a hand on his shoulder, caressing the taut, sweating muscles. "Don't do this."

He jerked away, standing up and buttoning his fly. He shoved into his shirt, but left it open. "Five years ago I raped a girl in a hotel room because I went to her room by mistake. Now that girl is a woman and I told her to sleep with me or I wouldn't work for her. I told her that, knowing she was desperate enough to do anything to save her father's company."

She came around the bed, holding the sheet against her. "You could never have made me come here tonight if I didn't want to be here. It wasn't the job. I wanted to be in your bed. Since that first day in Columbia. Don't do this to yourself. To both of us. We could talk about that night . . ."

"Get out." He was trembling. "Please."

"Hawke . . ."

"Goddamnit, get out!"

She dressed quickly, feeling thoroughly miserable. She would try again tomorrow to get him to listen. Now that he knew, they would have to talk it out. Somehow, some way they would have to.

On impulse she reached under the mattress for her leather pouch. She dumped the coins onto the bed. "I saved them for you. I wanted to throw them in your face."

"Feel free."

"I wanted to, until I met you again. Now I can't. You've never raped me, Travis Hawke. Not in San

Francisco. Not here. What you did to me, I let you do, because I wanted it as much as you did."

She stepped close to him, running her hand down the front of his chest. "I didn't want tonight to end this way. I'm sorry. Please don't hate me." She kissed his cheek. "And don't hate yourself either." She opened the door and was gone.

He had kept his arms locked rigidly at his sides. If he raised them, he feared what he might do to her. She couldn't know the emotions she had loosed in him tonight. Couldn't know that whatever foolish game she had played with him, he was playing a far more deadly one with her.

And in all of it was the spectre of Anne — the blood, the words. Dead. Both dead. All dead.

With Kate tonight it was only going to be lust. But she'd done it again, just as she had in San Francisco. Some part of him must have known who she was. He had carried that night buried in his gut for five years, never allowing himself to fully examine its impact on his life. Nor would he allow it now.

He slammed a fist against the door.

He wanted fury, anger, disgust, but the only thing that bore through him was an overwhelming despair.

Chapter Fifteen

Kate awoke the next morning, feeling more acutely embarrassed than she ever had in her life. Instead of rousing at once, as was her habit, she burrowed more deeply into the muslin sheets, hugging her pillow tight against her breasts. The dream was gone. In its place was reality, and all she wanted to do was cry.

Vainly, she tried to concentrate on that part of last night that had been wondrous—the taste of Hawke's mouth, the touch of his hands, the weight of his strong, lean body on hers. But the memory that rose to haunt her again and again was the fury in those midnight eyes when she'd been foolish enough to mention San Francisco.

How was she ever going to face the man again? Worse, work with him. Especially when in her own mind what had happened between them last night had been beautiful and right. When every fiber of her being wished for it to happen yet again. But it was all too obvious he wanted no commitments, no emotion, only sex.

"That's why you were angry, isn't it?" she whispered. "Because I wanted you to give a damn, and you didn't."

Yet even his anger had not changed her feelings. Before last night she had thought it. Now she was certain of it. She loved him. The man. Not the illusion.

Sighing, she pushed the pillow away. Lying in bed wasn't going to change what had happened. Nor would it make today go away. It was time to make ready for the trip to Ft. Laramie, time to deal with McCullough Freight's new wagonmaster.

She had just finished pulling on her boots when Lydia pushed open the door and walked into the room, carrying her ubiquitous cup of tea. Kate watched as the woman moved unsteadily across the room.

"Are you all right, Lydia?"

"Jim had a terrible night. I was up quite late."

"Is he better? Is there something I could do?"

"You could come home at a decent hour."

Kate straightened. "Oh. So that's what this is about."

"Where were you until three this morning?"

"I'm twenty-two years old. I'm wherever I choose to be."

"Don't talk to me like that." The cup rattled nervously against the saucer as she settled it on the dressing table.

"Lydia, my father is dead. You don't need to pretend to be concerned about me any more."

The woman paled. She sank into the straight-backed chair, taking a quick sip of her tea. "Dusty stopped by last night. He was looking for you. He said you were taking out a shipment tomorrow. That he found out what it is, and it's very dangerous. Kate, don't do it."

"I'll do whatever I have to do to save the company."

"I think Dusty was afraid."

Kate knotted her bandanna around her neck. "I'll be at the wagon yard most of the day. Probably sleep there tonight. We'll be pulling out at first light."

"Do you really think you can do it?"

"Don't worry, Lydia," Kate said, "I was going through some of Pa's papers the other day. He left the house to you. You won't have to move out, even if I lose the company."

"That wasn't why I was asking." Her voice seemed unnaturally subdued, and Kate felt her conscience nudge her. Lydia had never overtly tried to hurt her. They just never seemed to hit it off.

"I'm sorry. You didn't deserve that. I'm glad Pa left you the house. You made him happy."

Tears slipped down her pale face. "Thank you for that, Kate." She took another sip of tea. "You were with that Travis Hawke last night, weren't you?"

"If I was?"

"Just be careful. A man like that can break a woman's heart."

"I can take care of myself." She picked up her saddlebags and headed toward the door. "Say good-bye to Jim for me, will you?"

"He asked that you stop by to see him before you go."

"I don't think that's a very good idea."

"He loves you."

"No, he's just doing too much thinking about me, because he's stuck in that chair right now. But he'll get better, you'll see. Then he can . . ."

"He loves you, Kate. Please, stop and see him."

Kate fingered the catch on her saddlebags. "Why are you doing this? I've seen the way you look at him."

The woman looked startled. Evidently, she thought she had been doing an effective job of masking her feelings. "You're with him all the time," Kate said softly. "Take advantage of it." *Like I intend to take advantage of this trip to Ft. Laramie with Hawke*, came the unbidden thought.

With that she was out the door. As she strode toward

the freight yard, she tried to shake off Lydia's warning about Hawke. She scarcely needed to have it put into words anyway. She already knew Hawke's power over her heart.

"The battle isn't lost yet," she said aloud. "I love you, Travis Hawke. Whether you like it or not. And I've never given up without a fight for anything I wanted in my life."

She only wished her mood matched the confidence of her words. She'd battled dust storms and blizzards, recalcitrant mules and hungry cougars, but never had she engaged in a battle of the heart. But then never had she loved anyone the way she loved Hawke.

She picked up her pace, forcing her mind to other things. The shipment was due to be loaded up today. If she got it through to Ft. Laramie on time, there was at least a decent chance she could salvage McCullough Freight. Miss the deadline, and she lost everything.

Thirty men, twenty-five wagons. Nothing to it, she assured herself. She'd hauled freight with her father where the first wagon had started out at four in the morning, and the last wagon in the same train hadn't left the yard until four in the afternoon. Hundreds of wagons, thousands of oxen. She could do this one with her eyes shut, and still it would succeed. It had to.

"Mornin', Rafe," she called, as she strode into the barn near the livestock pens. The oxen for the trip had been herded together and settled in two huge corrals. When it came time to harness up tomorrow morning, everything would be ready.

"Anxious to get started?" she asked the burly bull-whacker.

"*Get* started?" Rafe snorted. "We've been wonderin' if you were ever going to get here afore all the work was done!"

"What are you talking about? It's barely past . . ."

She sensed his presence before she saw him. Turning, she studied him framed in the wide doors of the barn, the rising sun behind him casting his features in shadow. His shirt was already sweat-stained, the buttons unfastened to expose the taut muscles beneath.

"A bit early, aren't you?" she asked quietly.

"Someone hires me, I work." He signalled to Rafe and the two of them walked toward the two dozen wagons lined up along the outside of the barn. Kate could only stare at the crew of men hard at work loading barrels, crates, and sacks of grain in the back of each wagon.

When Hawke left Rafe and headed back toward her, she briefly considered running out the other side of the barn, but decided there was little sense postponing the inevitable.

"*Your* room tonight?" His voice was edged with sarcasm. He didn't waste any time.

"You mean last night wasn't a total disappointment for you?" She strove to match his acid tone, but her heart missed a beat as she waited for his answer.

"Not a total disappointment, no. I made a hundred dollars. Maybe I'll make a little more on the trip."

"Damn you!" She had to resist the urge to put her fist in his face again. "You're just not happy unless you're being a jackass, are you?" She was grateful for the anger, because it kept the pain of his words at bay. He couldn't possibly think she was going to pay him for . . .

Her brows furrowed, as she caught the brief astonishment in his blue eyes, as though her anger were not at all the reaction he had expected to his outrageous words. What *had* he expected? Hoped for? That she would dissolve in tears and run home, refusing to go along on the trip?

The spark of hope was so tiny, so fleeting, she could

almost have dismissed it. But what if it were true? That he didn't want her to go on the trip. Not because he didn't want her in his bed, but because he did?

Stop it, Kate, she warned herself sternly. There were a hundred other reasons he might not want her along, chief among them Frank Blanchard. If Hawke really did have a connection with the man, her staying behind would play right into their hands. Hawke would have complete charge of the shipment.

Much as her heart would like to believe he were fighting off an unwanted attraction for her, she had to be sensible. "You're not going to get away with it," she snapped. "I'm going with these wagons every ox's hoofprint of the way to Ft. Laramie, whether you like it or not."

"Who's stopping you?"

"I know what you're up to, and it won't work."

"I thought we were talking about last night."

"You just keep bringing that up, don't you? Well, I'm not going to cry, or scream, or rant, or," she glared at him, "stay home."

He gripped her arm, shoving her toward a corner of the barn. "I don't care what you do. Just keep your voice down. Do you want the whole world to know . . ."

"Why? Are you that ashamed of it?" If he said yes, she would have no defense against the pain.

"Ashamed of forcing you . . ."

Her explosive epithet interrupted him. "You have never forced me. Never! Get that through your head! If anything, last night I forced you."

Now it was his turn to swear.

"All right," she said, clamping her hand over his mouth, "you win." His eyes grew smug, until she quickly added, "You swear better than I do."

She felt his lips twitch beneath her palm, though he

204

was trying hard to keep them still. But he lost that battle too. And suddenly he was laughing, laughing until she was certain she saw tears in his eyes. But by then, she was laughing so hard herself, she wasn't sure the tears were his or her own. They collapsed together onto a pile of clean hay.

"You are the damndest woman I have ever met!"

"I'm glad you're finally starting to figure that out." She picked up a piece of the fresh smelling hay and trailed it down the side of his head and over to his lips, where she allowed it to linger. All the while she watched his eyes, watched the amusement subside, the passion fire. She leaned toward him, her own lips parted, eager.

And just that quickly he shut it all down. He turned away, climbing to his feet, slapping the hay from his clothes. "I've got work to do."

Was she losing her mind? The passion had been there! Hadn't it? "You *are* a jackass!" she hissed, as he started toward the door of the barn.

"Why? Because I won't have sex with you in a haystack in an open barn with three dozen men hanging around?"

"Because you don't just lie to me about how you feel. You lie to yourself!"

He turned slowly, facing her. "What I feel about anything is none of your business."

She dusted the hay off her jacket. "Whatever you say, Hawke. You're right, we've got work to do."

Instead of leaving, he continued to stand there, staring at her.

"So get to work," she said. "We have a deadline, remember?" She was sorely missing that kiss she hadn't gotten from him, yet growing strangely nervous as his intense scrutiny continued.

"What the hell was last night all about, Kate?"

205

"No, you don't," she said. "I don't want to fight any more. At least not today, all right?"

"Then tell me why you came to my room last night."

Why was he doing this? He had been right earlier. The barn was no place to hold an intimate discussion. "Can we talk about this later?"

He drew up to his full height, slapping his hat against his thigh. "You tell me I don't feel anything. Now I'm trying to find out how you feel, and you're . . . ah, hell, never mind." He turned and tromped out of the barn.

"Good going, Kate," she murmured. "He was finally going to talk to you like a human being, and you went and became the jackass."

Last night was bothering him far past not recognizing her. It went deeper than that. And she had to accept a large part of the blame for what he was going through. She had taken what she wanted out of last night, never giving full consideration to what he wanted. She had dared assume him cynical, eager for a night of passion with a willing woman, any woman, even the virgin he had bedded by mistake in San Francisco, when it had been his right not to resurrect ghosts from his past.

Sighing, she followed him out of the barn. He strode away from her, making certain he kept very busy and very much out of her way the rest of the morning. By noon, Kate had exhausted herself loading crates that were twice her size, just to work off the energy it took not to go to him. Finally, when he ordered the men to break for lunch, she could take it no longer.

He was standing over the water trough, levering clean water from the pump over his upper body. He straightened, shaking his head. Tiny drops of water from his hair sprayed her cheeks.

"Now I won't have to take a bath," she said quietly.

206

He jerked around, swiping at the water on his own face. He had not been aware of her approach. "We're one wagon short," he said, keeping his tone ever so businesslike. "We've got twenty-four. The shipment calls for twenty-five."

"Dusty is over at the fort talking to the quartermaster." Her heart was thudding, and she could not match his professional indifference. "He'll be here later to tell us about the last wagon."

"Something special about it?"

"Something dangerous."

"Like what?"

"Like you," she murmured, then caught herself. "I mean, I don't know exactly what the cargo is."

He raked his fingers through his wet hair to get it out of his face. "Did I hurt you last night?"

She bit her lip, unable to take her eyes off the sleek muscles of his chest. "When you told me to get out, you hurt me."

"Why, Kate? Why with me?"

"I . . . I wanted to . . ."

"Why?"

She pressed her hands against his chest, trailing her fingers through the damp hair. "Do you ever think about that night in San Francisco?" She raised a finger to her lips and tasted the salty wetness, water mingled with his sweat. His heart surged against the fingertips of her other hand. "Do you?"

His arms swept around her crushing her to him. "Yes, damn you, yes. I've thought about it. Thought about how I ruined a young girl's life." His lips claimed hers. Damn! How had she twisted this to her advantage? Last night he had been so furious he wanted to throttle her. His anger had hardly cooled when he'd seen her this morning. Now he found not only his anger dissipating, but the fierce passion he'd felt for her rekindling. What was happening to him? What was she doing to him? Whatever it was, he'd best put an end to it and quickly.

He forced her away from him, holding her at arms' length. "We've got a lot of work left to do." His hands dropped away. He balled his fists at his sides to keep from touching her again.

"You didn't ruin my life."

"Fine, but I want you to understand that last night was a mistake, just as San Francisco was a mistake. It's not going to happen again."

Now what had she done? She thought they'd been making some kind of progress. Her pride asserted itself. "You can be certain it won't happen again."

"As long as we understand each other."

"Of course," she said, falling into step beside him as he stomped toward the wagons. *The hell we understand each other,* she thought bleakly. *You want me. You don't want me. And I love you.*

Most of the wagons had already been loaded, but Kate checked each and every one thoroughly. Whether or not the cargo was loaded properly could make the difference between freight that shifted and wagons that broke down on the trail. She slammed a hand against the high wood sides. Each wagon was constructed of the finest osage orange and white oak, well-seasoned to prevent shrinkage by the heat of arid country, but there was no harm in being extra careful, considering what was riding on this shipment.

Besides it kept her away from Hawke. She would give him today. And perhaps the better part of tomorrow morning as they prepared to leave. But last night had been no mistake. Not for her. And she full well intended to repeat it. She smiled. He wasn't as unaffected as he pretended, or he wouldn't always get so blasted defensive. It would be six weeks to Ft. Laramie. Six weeks with nowhere for him to be but near her.

The sun was beginning to dip below the horizon when at last she finished. Slipping the bandanna off her neck, she mopped the sweat and grime from her brow. She was exhausted, but content. It felt good to be working again. She hopped out of the last wagon, ready even to do battle with Hawke.

Which, she grimaced, wouldn't be long in coming, as she noticed him striding toward her.

"We're just using oxen on this trip, right?" he asked, assuming his role as her employee once again. "No mules."

She nodded. "They're slower, but they can forage on the trail. Mules need extra grain. I don't want to use up the space for it in the wagons. Besides the oxen are easier to work with. And if worse comes to worse, they're a helluva lot more edible, too."

He grinned. "I've had mule meat. I couldn't agree more. Like eating tree bark. But I thought you wanted to make fast time on this trip. Mules might make twenty-five miles a day. The oxen fifteen."

She was grudgingly impressed by his knowledge. "I just think the oxen are more dependable over a long haul. They'll make up for the mileage with their endurance." She was also ridiculously pleased that they had been speaking for almost a whole minute and neither had said something nasty to the other.

"When are we going to find out about that twenty-fifth wagon?"

"Dusty should have been here by now."

"Is he going to be able to take orders from me?"

"The company's as much his as it is mine."

"Will he take orders from me?"

She kicked at the dirt. "I don't know. He's pretty much unreasonable when it comes to rebs."

"What do you think about rebs?"

Her eyes widened. Was he actually asking her a personal question? "I think the war's over."

"Never be over to me," came the oddly accented voice behind her.

"Dusty!" She planted her hands on her hips. "How long have you been standing there?"

He ignored the question. "I found out about the cargo. Came by the house last night to tell ye." His look drilled Hawke, though he continued to speak to Kate. "You weren't home."

She couldn't stop the blush that heated her face and was grateful when Hawke distracted him.

"What's the cargo, Lafferty?"

"You'll know tomorrow morning. That's soon enough."

"I'm wagonmaster. I want to know now."

Kate looked at Hawke, then at Dusty. She knew Dusty was waiting for her to back him up, but she couldn't do it. Not this time. "He's right, Dusty. He needs to know, if he's to do the best job he can for us."

The look Dusty gave her nearly broke her heart. He had taken her response as choosing sides.

"All right, Kate. It's your outfit." He directed them over to a quiet corner inside the barn, away from the loading activity, away from other people. "It's some new stuff. Just invented by some foreigner."

"What is it?" Kate asked. She'd never seen Dusty nervous before.

"They call it dynamite."

Kate shrugged. "Never heard of it." She looked at Hawke, whose brows had furrowed with obvious concern. "You know what it is?"

"Rumors. It's an explosive. Made with nitroglycerin. Has to be handled with extreme care. Though it's not quite as unstable as nitro."

Kate staggered. "Dusty! What was Pa thinking of?"

"He was likely thinking of saving the company. We get that through, we got our reputation back. And the money we need to keep running."

"And if we don't, we're dead! Literally!" She sank down onto a bale of hay. "I can't risk the lives of these men. Not like that!"

"The quartermaster told me Bryce planned to keep the wagon away from the others."

"How far away?"

"A couple hundred yards ought to do it."

Kate's mind was spinning. Dynamite. An explosive. She'd freighted guns, gunpowder, even live rattlesnakes for an eccentric in Santa Fe, but never anything as inherently dangerous as Hawke made this stuff sound.

"I'll drive the dynamite wagon," Kate said. "I can't risk anyone else's life."

"The hell you will!" Hawke snapped. "I'll handle it myself."

"You're wagonmaster," Dusty put in. "You lead up the whole outfit. You can't be off with one wagon. I'll take it. And no arguments." To make certain there were none, he tromped away. Kate knew he was hurt, but there was no help for it.

"He'll get over it."

She looked at Hawke. Was he attempting to make her feel better? "How dangerous is this stuff?"

"Very. We'll have to keep it cool. If it sweats it gets more dangerous. It can explode if you touch it."

"Or a wagon wheel drops in a rut?"

"Exactly."

"Great. I was wondering why the payment for this shipment was so high." It was fully dusk now. "I guess there's nothing we can do about it until morning."

"You'll be going home now."

"I'm sleeping here."

"In the barn? What for?"

She thought of Lydia and her pronouncement that Jim Collier was in love with her. She didn't feel like facing either one of them right now. Tomorrow she would be on the trail and Lydia would have Jim all to herself for seven weeks. Maybe it would work to the advantage of everyone concerned.

She grabbed up a blanket lying in the supply wagon. "I've been sleeping in beds long enough. It's time I got used to life on the trail again."

"I was planning to stay here tonight myself."

She shot him a quick glance. "You don't like beds either?"

"I like beds just fine."

She flushed.

"But I want to watch out for the wagons now that they're loaded."

"That seems sensible." She laid out the blanket on a pile of straw, aware that he was watching her every move. "Where are you going to sleep?" she asked unsteadily.

"Out here. By the wagons."

She swallowed her disappointment. "Wake me if anything happens."

"Get some sleep."

She lay down, but did not sleep, listening to the nightsounds she loved—a symphony of crickets, the occasional lowing of oxen, braying of mules. Tomorrow would be the start of the most important journey of her life, and now with the activity of the day behind her, she found herself thinking of just what it would mean to her.

She wanted McCullough Freight to survive. But she now admitted it was for more than the sake of her father's memory. She wanted it for herself. To prove that she could do it, when every manjack on this trip, Dusty included, believed that she could not.

"What do you think, Hawke?" she wondered. She felt her blood heat just thinking about him, in spite of her resolve to ignore the fact that he was lying outside barely fifty feet from her. Was he asleep? Or was he tossing as fitfully as she was?

Rising to her feet, she crept to the open door and looked out. Hawke was sitting beside a wagon wheel, head back, watching the moon, his face bathed in its soft light. She smiled, getting a crazy enjoyment just watching him.

He shifted as though he heard something. Then she noticed the shadowy figure approaching him. She thought about calling a warning, but as she studied the scene more closely she could see that he was fully aware of his visitor's arrival.

The figure stooped down beside him, his back to Kate. She could make out no distinguishing features, except that the man was well dressed. Then he turned, the moonglow catching him. Kate gasped. Frank Blanchard!

Kate sat back on her heels, stunned. No! What was he doing here? In the dark. Meeting with Hawke. Again she recalled Kerns's cryptic comment on the dock. That Blanchard would be upset to have to find a replacement. Replacement for what? Was Hawke working for Blanchard, even as he worked for her? Her stomach churned. Had he slept with her to solidify his position, only to have it backfire because of a bizarre twist of fate?

She scooted back into the shadows, her thoughts reeling. It was too late to get someone else. The men trusted Hawke, respected him. They would desert her if she fired him. She would just have to keep an eye on him, make certain she foiled whatever foul scheme

213

Blanchard was hatching.

Besides, she couldn't send him away. If he was working for Blanchard, perhaps she could get him to switch his loyalty to her. And maybe, just maybe, he was just leading Blanchard on, even taking his money, but with no intention of following the man's orders.

She sighed, her back resting on the barn wall. This trip wasn't getting any easier. She had expected trouble from Blanchard, but not from within her own ranks. And, dear God, not with Hawke.

She scrambled to her feet as she heard the hay rustling to her left. If Blanchard was coming in here . . .

"I was just checking on you," Hawke said.

Checking to see if I saw Blanchard, Kate fumed inwardly, but said only, "I'm fine. Just a little restless." She eyed him warily. Could Blanchard have sent him in here? How far would Hawke go for money?

"You seem more than restless," he said. "Is something wrong?"

"What could be wrong?" She cursed the nervousness of her voice. "I . . . I guess I am a little worried about that dynamite."

He blew out a long breath, and Kate knew he had accepted her explanation. "I'm a little nervous about that stuff myself. But you really ought to get some sleep."

"So should you."

He turned to leave, but paused to slant a glance back at her. "This shipment means a lot to you, doesn't it?"

Her heart was in her throat. "It means the survival of McCullough Freight."

"What happens to you if things don't work out?"

"They will work out."

"But what if . . ." He stopped. "Good-night, Kate."

She watched him until he spread out a blanket near

214

one of the wagons and lay down. How much doubt could she have now? Hawke was working for Blanchard.

All the more reason to keep an eye on him, she decided resolutely. And one way to do that was to work on whatever tiny bit of attraction he had for her. If he had a conscience she was going to find it. Grabbing up her blanket, she stalked outside.

"What the hell are you doing?" he demanded, as she spread the blanket out beside him.

"It was getting a little stuffy in the barn," she said, faking a sweet smile.

"I told you, we're not repeating past mistakes."

"Oh, I couldn't agree more," she said. "I'm going to try very hard not to make any more mistakes where you're concerned, Mr. Hawke."

She lay down, stretching her limbs in a way she prayed was at least remotely provocative. She smiled as he cursed and rolled over so that he was not looking at her. "Sleep well," she murmured.

It was going to be a long six weeks—Blanchard, dynamite, and Travis Hawke.

Chapter Sixteen

Kate tried to move, but couldn't. Something was holding her down. Alarmed, she opened her eyes. She relaxed at once, smiling languorously. Hawke had wrapped himself around her in his sleep. She lay still, watching him.

His dark lashes dusted his cheek which lay pillowed against her shoulder. Impulsively, she pressed her lips against his forehead. She could imagine him opening his eyes, his mouth curving seductively, as he gazed at her. His arms tightening, as he pulled her closer.

Instead, he shifted restlessly away from her, still asleep. Frowning, she rubbed her arms in the pre-dawn chill, robbed of the enveloping warmth of his body.

And she remembered what she wanted so much to forget, that Frank Blanchard had been Hawke's night visitor. That the men had spoken together for nearly half an hour. That Hawke had said nothing of the meeting when he came into the barn afterwards.

It could still have been nothing, she told herself desperately. Nothing that Blanchard should seek out Hawke in the middle of the night, bare hours before she was to take out the most important freight of her life? Nothing that Blanchard was the one man who wanted to take over her company, perhaps even end her life?

Still, she reasoned, it was better the freight leave with Hawke's loyalty in doubt, than not leave at all. She stayed her hand from reaching out to stroke his jawline. In spite of how deeply she now suspected his betrayal, she couldn't stop herself from loving him.

Before she did something completely foolish she rose to her feet, stretching her aching muscles. It had been a long time since she'd slept on the ground. She grimaced to think how dependent she had become on the creature comforts of a bed.

She gave Hawke a nudge in the rump with her foot. "Come on, wagonmaster. It's time to get this outfit on the road."

He jerked awake, for an instant it seemed, unaware of his surroundings, as though in a dream he were somewhere else. Wherever the somewhere else was, it had not been pleasant. He visibly relaxed when he saw her. "Sorry." He was on his feet at once, rousting the men to get them started rounding up the livestock. Getting even a small caravan of twenty-five wagons on the road was going to be a monumental task.

Most of the teamsters had worked for McCullough in the past and needed no help getting the oxen paired up, making six pair per wagon the general rule. The two strongest and heaviest, the wheelers, were hitched directly in front of the wagon. Just ahead of them came the pointers, who helped with the brunt of the pulling. The next three pair, called swingers, were often younger and more fractious, their function to help turn or swing the wagon. Ahead of the swing bulls came the last pair, the pointers, who set the pace.

Blue Boy had been a pointer. Kate couldn't help thinking of the big longhorn who had been blamed for her father's death. The animal had been hand broke almost from birth. As longhorns went, he was a highly intelligent beast, often rubbing his nose along her father's buckskinned thigh, seeking to have his ears scratched like a danged pup. Never had he threatened her father or anyone else with his awesome horns, an eight foot spread from tip to tip.

She shook herself out of her melancholy. Dusty was calling to her. It was time to load the dynamite wagon.

"How much of this stuff are we carrying?" she asked, hurrying over to him.

" 'Bout two tons."

Hawke joined them. "I want each crate loaded separately," he said, directing his attention to Dusty. "Then I want some of those cotton bales we've got in the other wagons brought over to buffer each crate."

"Real good at givin' orders, ain't ye?" Dusty grumbled.

"Just doin' my job, Lafferty."

"Like you was doin' your job killin' union soldiers in the war?"

Hawke stiffened, but let it pass. Anyone looking at him, Kate was certain, would have detected only anger in his stance. But she sensed the fierce hurt in him as well. She remembered his softly spoken pronouncement, that he had joined the war to die. He hadn't wanted to kill anyone. He had wanted to be killed.

Vainly, she tried to defuse the situation between the two men. "Come on, Dusty, I want to go over the bill of lading one last time before we leave."

"You can do that by yourself, lass. Me and the captain," he said the word derisively, "are going to finish loadin' up the dynamite."

Leaving the two of them together could prove more explosive than their experimental cargo. She walked over to one of the crates and opened the lid.

"Leave that stuff alone," Hawke snapped, coming up beside her.

"I like to know all about the cargo I ship." Very gingerly she hefted one of the brown paper wrapped cylindrical objects. "How does it work?"

Hawke lifted it away from her, replacing it with extreme care back into the crate. "You stick a fuse in the top, light it, throw it and duck." He pulled her by the arm. "Now, will you leave it the hell alone?"

"Of course," she murmured. "I'm sorry. I just wanted to get you away from Dusty." She looked over at her bullwhacking uncle, pleased to see that he and Rafe had moved off to discuss the route that lay ahead of them.

"He could make this trip pretty rough on you," he said. "Maybe you should stay home."

"He's my uncle," she snapped, "and I love him. I don't give a damn how rough he makes things. And you can just stop trying to leave me behind. The only way I don't finish this trip is if I'm dead."

She watched his eyes when she said that, but his expression was unreadable. She sighed. "We'd better get rolling. I've got a deadline to meet."

Within the hour twenty-five wagons were ready to pull out of Leavenworth. Hawke mounted his chestnut gelding and rode over to Dusty, who was standing to the left of the last wagon. "When we get about a quarter mile out of town, make sure you keep this thing a good hundred yards behind the rest of the outfit."

Dusty grunted a reply. He would do it, but not because Hawke told him to.

"If you have any trouble, you holler, hear?" Kate said, giving Dusty a swift hug before she mounted her bay mare. "I still don't like you handling this stuff alone."

"I took teams through droughts, blizzards, floods.

219

I'll manage a little dynamite."

"Dusty . . ." She longed to ease the hurt in his griz-zled features. He was still stung by her seeming to side again and again with Hawke. But he stared at the dirt, and she finally nudged the mare into a trot, heading toward the front of the wagon train.

Twenty-five bullwhackers stood beside twenty-five loaded wagons, ready for the march to Ft. Laramie. Because freight wagons had no driver's seat, the men directed their teams with whips and words from just to the rear of the left wheel ox. She watched as each man unwound their often custom-made twenty-foot leather whips.

"Wagons! Ho!"

Hawke's shout sent a shiver of pride and exhilara-tion coursing along her spine. Damn, the man said it like he was born to it. She watched him, sitting straight in the saddle, heading up the small caravan of wagons, and for just that moment she could forget about Frank Blanchard, bank notes, and dynamite.

Rafe set the caravan into motion. Commanding the first wagon in line, he sent his whip snaking out over the heads of his pointer bulls. The lumbering beasts lurched immediately into a steady, plodding gait. Only rarely was an animal struck by a whip. It was the re-sounding crack that inspired the beasts to do the bull-whacker's bidding.

She let out a shuddering sigh, swiping at the sudden moisture in her eyes. This would be her first trip with-out her father. Yet it was as though she felt him there, nearby, watching. And she knew there would be pride in his sky blue eyes. She gigged her horse over to Hawke.

"Whatever happens, I want to thank you," she said quickly, lest she change her mind. "This wouldn't be happening if not for you. At least now I have a chance to save my father's company."

He was about to say something when the sound of a too familiar male voice calling her name diverted her attention. She grimaced, as she turned to see Lydia wheeling Jim Collier toward the wagons.

"Kate, wait!" Jim called again.

She reined her horse over to the pair. "What are you doing here?"

"We've come to see you off, of course," Jim said, grabbing her hand when she dismounted. "And wish you good luck." His gray eyes studied her earnestly. "Lydia must have forgotten to give you my message. I asked you to stop by before you left."

"Lydia told me," Kate said, freeing her hand. "But I've been very busy."

"Of course," he demurred. "But I just wanted to tell you to be careful. And to remind you that I'm not going to be in this chair forever. You know how your father liked us being together, Kate."

"I remember," she said. But that didn't change her feelings. Why did life have to be so mixed up? Jim loved her. She loved Hawke. Hawke loved no one.

"You were always so different from the other women I escorted," Jim went on, much to Kate's embarrassment.

"I know how different I was," she said ruefully, even as her mind worked to think of a way to put an end to this conversation. She could feel Hawke's eyes on her. She didn't need him listening to Jim rattle on about her. But Leavenworth's former sheriff was showing no signs of letting up on his string of superlatives.

"I just wished you could have stopped by, Kate. So we could have had a real talk before you go. Maybe you're a little eccentric in your clothing, but you have the heart of a real lady. None of that carnal behavior so common in women nowadays."

She scarcely dared imagine what Jim's reaction would be to her behavior two nights ago in Hawke's bedroom.

"I really enjoyed your letters from Boston."

I only wrote them because I felt obliged to respond to yours, she thought guiltily. "I'm glad you did," she said, "but I really have to be going now."

"I'll miss you, Kate."

She nodded. "That's nice, Jim." Hawke was still staring at her. Damn him, the wagons were moving out. Couldn't he go do some wagonmastering or something? And then she had an idea.

No, she admonished herself, she couldn't do such a despicable thing. Jim was being so sweet but she could never reciprocate his feelings. Still, if she could make Hawke just a tiny bit jealous . . .

Hating herself, she did it anyway. She leaned over and planted a kiss on Jim Collier's mouth. "I'll miss you too, Jim," she whispered.

Jim's eyes glittered warmly. Damn, why had she done such a stupid thing? She dared a glance at Hawke, only to find that he had indeed ridden off to head up the caravan. Now she had given Jim the wrong impression and gained absolutely nothing for her disgraceful behavior.

She patted Jim's shoulder. "I shouldn't have kissed you. I'm sorry."

"No, no, don't be, Kate. I love you." He smiled, pulling her hand to his mouth.

Now she'd really done it. Jerking her hand back, she climbed aboard her mare. She looked helplessly at Lydia who was looking at her in despair. She longed to tell the older woman she hadn't meant to make a mess of everything for her. That Hawke's presence as always had made her put her worst foot forward. But trying to explain, she suspected, would only make things worse.

She urged her mare into a gallop, wanting only to put distance between herself and Jim Collier.

She caught up with Hawke, telling herself she had to keep him in sight as much as possible, just in case he was plotting something with Blanchard. The train was making slow but steady progress.

"You really like this, don't you?" Hawke asked.

"I love the open, if that's what you mean."

"So do I."

There he went again, being pleasant. She was all but convinced he played these games with her just to keep her off guard.

"We'll have plenty of water most of the way," he said. "Only problems will be the unpredictables."

Like Frank Blanchard, she thought, almost shocked off her horse when he said the same.

"I beg your pardon?" she said. "You . . . ah, you think Blanchard will try something?"

"I don't know. He might not have to. He doesn't think you can make the deadline. And he knows about the dynamite. He thinks you're going to blow yourself up."

"How do you know so much what he thinks?" She could barely breathe waiting for his answer.

"He told me."

She jerked her horse to a halt. "Come again?"

"Blanchard came to see me last night."

Her heart pounded crazily. "Last night?"

"While I was out by the wagons. He offered me a helluva lot of money to see to it that you don't make it back from Ft. Laramie on time."

"And you're telling me?"

"I work for you."

"Yeah, I don't suppose you could sleep with Blanchard." The words were out and she could have bitten off her tongue at the fury in his blue eyes.

"Son-of-a-bitch, Kate! I don't know why I even try. I don't know why." He slammed his heels into his horse's sides, pounding away from her.

She stared at his retreating back. Great work, Kate. He had told her, *told her*, about Blanchard. And she had insulted him for his trouble. Still, she couldn't prevent the unbidden thought — did Hawke know she had seen Blanchard last night? Was he telling her about it to throw her off guard? She grimaced. Even if he was, she had been totally out of line to say such an outrageous thing to him about sleeping with Blanchard. When she watched him rein to a halt in front of Rafe's wagon, she galloped over to him.

"I may spend this whole trip apologizing to you," she said. "But I am sorry."

"Forget it."

"I don't know what it is about you. I mean, I say the wrong thing when I'm mad sometimes, but with you, it seems that's all I say is the wrong thing."

"I said forget it."

Sighing bleakly, she turned her horse away from him. "I'll check on Dusty."

"You stay away from that wagon."

"I will not. He's the only family I've got."

"Stay away from that dynamite, or I'll tie you up and throw you in the back of the supply wagon."

She glared at him. After she had swallowed her pride and apologized to him, the least he could do is be civil. "You're the boss," she muttered.

"You just make sure you remember that."

She waited until he rode out, scouting the terrain ahead. Then she kicked her horse into a trot and headed back toward Dusty.

Hawke studied the mile long caravan of freight wagons from his position on the ridge. Dusty Lafferty was doing a good job keeping the last wagon well to the rear of the others. Hawke straightened as a rider approached that last wagon. Kate.

He cursed, slamming back the impulse to go tearing down after her. She didn't have the sense God gave a jackrabbit. Or more rightly, she was just too damned stubborn to use it.

That waspish tongue of hers was another of her charms that was going to drive him to distraction. Her sarcastic suggestion that he sleep with Blanchard had scratched the memory of Liam Jeffers and what would have been his fate had Nels Svenson not entered his life. The woman was forever pushing him to the edge of his temper, but his own behavior toward her was hardly better.

Yet just watching her set his blood racing. No matter how much anger she aroused in him, she aroused his desire more. And more than that, she fired feelings he swore would never touch his life again.

In San Francisco he had gone to a darkened hotel room seeking out a prostitute to appease the needs of his sex. The prostitute had been eager, willing, surprising him with a passion beyond what he would have expected in a woman jaded by a life of sex with strangers. But it was her capacity for listening, for caring that had reached him when nothing had for so very long. At the time he had credited the dark, anonymous room. Later, much later, he had credited his mysterious Katherine. But even so, he had never wanted to see her again in his life.

Damn that night. Why had it ever happened? It had been the first time he'd been sober since Anne's death three months before. He'd convinced himself a night with a whore would be the perfect way to spend his last hours before he went east to join the war. Like the tides to the moon he had been drawn to Katherine from the first moment he touched her, spoke to her.

"Love me, Katherine. Love me. One night in my life I need someone to love me." The words had come from the depths of his despair—over Anne, over everything. But now just outside Leavenworth, Kansas, he shifted uncomfortably in the saddle as he remembered them and prayed Kate did not.

She'd played the game well. "I love you," she'd said. And he believed it. For that tiny space of time, he believed it. Wanted it. Needed it. And then he discovered his prostitute to be a virgin, a girl-woman who had accepted him into her bed because she thought she was having a most peculiar dream.

Neither of them had been dreaming. He'd felt like a damned rapist, yet finding out she was not a prostitute had unnerved him for more reasons than stealing her virginity. Being open and vulnerable to a nameless woman who serviced hundreds of nameless men was somehow far different than baring his soul to a seventeen year old girl named Katherine, who might learn his identity and know things about him he wanted no one ever to know. And so he had thrown a hundred dollars on the bed to make sure she hated him enough to never want to learn his name.

Through some cruel twist of fate, Frank Blanchard and Anne had brought him back to Katherine. Ever since he'd found out who she was he'd been haunted by how much of that night she actually remembered. And through it all he'd been damned to find out that he was as drawn to her in the light of day, as he had been that moonlit night in San Francisco. Kate. Oh, God, Kate.

It couldn't happen, wouldn't happen. Everyone he had ever loved in his life was dead. Even if he was capable of loving Kate, which he believed he was not, he could never take the chance. He couldn't risk having her die too.

But he was having a hell of time keeping his mind on his mission. Blanchard had to be brought down, but it had become vitally important to him that Kate not be hurt in the process. And she most certainly wasn't going to be hurt any more by him, at least not if he could help it. Which meant he was going to stay away from her at night. If he wasn't careful, she would start thinking something serious could come of the relationship. In spite of her bluster, he sensed Kate did not take giving herself to a man lightly. And he was not going to have her make the fatal mistake of thinking she loved him. People he loved died. People who loved him died.

He swore, kneeing the chestnut into a ground-eating trot. It was time to concentrate on the job at hand. He rode ahead, checking the conditions of what would be their first camp—Cold Spring, fifteen miles out of Leavenworth. Just off the road ran a deep ravine with plenty of wood, water and grass. It would a good night.

A good night, he grimaced, if he stayed away from Kate.

He rode back to the wagons, reining in beside Rafe Yates. Dismounting, he fell into step beside the burly teamster. "Camp looks good ahead."

"It's gonna be a good trip, cap'n, uh, Travis. Oh, hell, why don't you just let me call you cap'n? Seems natural. You saved my bacon at Chancellorsville, you know."

"From you, Rafe, I won't mind being 'captain'." He kicked at a loose stone on the dirt road, studying the deep parallel ruts ahead made by countless wagons before them. "Can I ask you something?"

"Anything, cap'n."

"Why does Dusty Lafferty accept the fact that you

227

fought for the confederacy, yet hate my guts for the same reason?"

Rafe lifted his coonskin cap from his head, scratching thoughtfully at his balding pate. "Dusty's a good sort. But a mite peculiar, like most men that came out west forty years ago, when the only ones here was Injuns and wild animals. Him and me met up by the Wind Rivers in the Rockies, oh, 'bout the winter of '31, I reckon."

Hawke took a quick glance around him, assuring himself all was running smoothly on the train, assuring himself further that he was not looking for Kate. But he did not return his attention to Rafe until he saw her talking to one of the bullwhackers farther down the line. At least she had gotten away from the dynamite.

"I found Dusty near froze to death," Rafe went on. "Got laid up by a busted leg just before a blizzard hit. Like to died if I hadn't happened on him. But we hit it off real good. Trapped beaver together for ten years after that. Then he got the itch again and headed on. We met up again in '56 just after him and Bryce and Kate started up freightin'. They hired me on, and I been 'round pert near ever since. 'Cept for the war." Rafe rubbed his shaggy beard. "Reckon the only reason he forgive me for bein' a reb was 'cause him and me goes back a long ways. McCullough run a lot o' freight durin' the war, lost a lot o' good men to the likes of Quantrill."

"Quantrill wasn't regular army. He was a murderer using a war as a excuse to kill."

"Don't cut no ice with Dusty. He hates rebs. I'm real sorry 'bout that, cap'n. I can talk to him for ya, if you want."

"No. No, I think that would just make a bad situation worse."

"You don't want Dusty comin' between you and

228

Kate, huh, cap'n?"

Hawke shot an astonished look at Rafe. "There's nothing to come between. What the hell are you . . ." He stopped. Damn, did the whole outfit share Rafe's view of his relationship with Kate?

"Sorry, cap'n," Rafe said, looking sheepish. "I didn't mean no harm. I seen the way she looked at ya, and well, I guess I just sorta thought, well, hell, cap'n, you couldn't do no better than Kate. Not anywhere. She's a helluva little gal."

A muscle in his jaw flexed. It was going to be an even longer trip to Laramie than he thought. "I'd better check on the other wagons."

"Right, cap'n. It sure is good to have ya along."

Hawke mounted and rode at an easy canter along the line of wagons, completely ignoring Kate when he rode past her. He hoped she hadn't heard any of Rafe's rumors. More than ever, he recognized the need to stay away from her if things weren't going to get even more complicated between them.

Toward that end, as he rode, he considered the routine he would establish for the remainder of their journey. On good weather days like this, they should be able to put in seventeen hours on the trail. They would break camp in the morning by seven, then travel maybe five hours, stopping for a noonover. The men would eat, the animals would be watered and rested. Toward evening the wagons would circle for the night and the oxen be unhitched to graze. Most of the men, and hopefully Kate as well, would be dead tired by then. An evening meal, a little conversation, then sleep, in order to be up and rolling again the next day by seven.

He twisted in the saddle to look at her, averting his gaze at once when he found her looking at him. His pulse quickened, his loins tightening, in spite of his ef-

229

forts to force his mind elsewhere. Kate wasn't the only one who'd better be dead tired tonight. He'd better get to work on exhausting himself or he would never keep the promise he'd made to them both, that their "mistake" would not be repeated.

Mistake. Mistake to recapture the peace he'd found only with her? Damn. He kicked his horse in the sides, the startled animal lunging forward in a hard gallop. But no matter how far or how fast he rode, he knew he was never going to make it to Ft. Laramie without spending a night in Kate McCullough's arms.

Chapter Seventeen

Kate slammed her hand against the iron rim of the wheel on Dusty's wagon, then cursed feelingly at the nasty scrape her tantrum had produced.

"You want to set off the dynamite, lass?" Dusty demanded, though there was more amusement than anger in his voice. "What the hell you attackin' that wheel for anyway?"

"Just a bad day, Dusty," she grimaced.

"Well, you'd do your hand a whole lot of good if you'd at least wait 'til the wheel ain't movin'. We'll be pullin' up for supper in another hour."

"I'll think about it," she grinned.

She dare not tell Dusty what had really sent her temper past its limited borders. Who else but Travis Hawke? The son-of-a-coyote had managed for the seventeenth day in a row to say no more than two dozen words to her, all of which had to do with the damned freight, the damned freight wagons, the damned dynamite, or the damned livestock. She had had it up to her eye sockets with his infuriating self-control.

"Maybe you'd best get on up with Rafe or one of the others," Dusty said. "Hawke don't like you by the dynamite. And neither do I."

She looked at her uncle and grew even more annoyed. Hawke had done more talking to Dusty these past two weeks than to her. Their conversations had been stilted, but civil. Well, almost civil. Dusty had called Hawke a few choice names when Hawke had noticed one of the crates coming loose in the wagon. But then when Dusty had checked it and discovered it was, in fact, shifting, he had come within a whisker of actually apologizing to him.

Dusty's having more of his attention than she did was the final straw. It was time to get serious. She smiled. Hawke didn't stand a chance.

"Got a chew, Dusty?"

He laughed. "That was one habit your father pure turned green over. You want him hauntin' me?"

"Please?"

He rummaged in his trail-stained pockets and came up with a gritty looking chaw of tobacco. She grinned, biting off a chunk and setting to work on it. "Thanks, Dusty," she mumbled. "I'll see you later."

She mounted and gigged her mare into an easy lope. Except for Hawke, she couldn't believe how smoothly the drive had been going. The weather had been exceptional, water plentiful. Tonight they'd camp near Elm Creek, a full third of their trek behind them. Hawke had already deigned to tell her that the grass looked good at the creek with plenty of good holes to water the stock.

She studied the terrain as she rode. The rolling hills outside of Leavenworth had given way to the monotony of the plains. The soil here was less rich and streaked with alkali. Water ahead might not be so easily had. Too much alkali could make streams unfit for man or beast. But she would worry about that when she had to. Right now, she was worried only about Hawke.

At first, she thought he truly was fighting his desire for her. He seemed to be driving himself to the point of collapse every night. But lately she had begun to wonder if his interest in her had existed only in her imagination. He didn't seem tired at all, nor did she ever catch him watching her anymore.

Unconsciously, she poked at her hair, limp and lifeless in the afternoon sun. The dust stirred up by plodding hooves had done nothing to enhance its luster. Tonight at the creek, she would most certainly indulge her sweating body with a bath.

She continued to work the tobacco, letting fly with a mouthful of juice just off her mare's right front hoof. She frowned. She was definitely out of practice. In fact, she was not particularly enjoying the harsh taste of Dusty's private poke. She was coddling herself too much lately, getting soft.

Soft in the head, she thought, as she caught sight of Hawke. He was checking the hooves of one of the bulls on the third wagon.

She reined over and dismounted. "Something wrong?"

He looked up, his dark eyes bland, disinterested. She tried to tell herself he'd heard her approach and had pasted the look on his face deliberately, but her self-image where Hawke was concerned crumbled a little more.

"He'll be lame if something isn't done soon," Hawke said.

The bullwhacker, Andy Jenkins, was bent over his beast, checking Hawke's assessment. "I can make him up some moccasins out of rawhide, Kate."

"Sounds good," she said.

"But in the meantime, get a fresh animal from the calf yard," Hawke told him, referring to the small herd of extra animals being herded to the rear of the train.

"Will do, Mr. Hawke," Andy said.

As the bullwhacker tended to his animal, Hawke headed back to his horse and prepared to mount. Already he's running to get away from me, Kate fumed. Straightening her shoulders, she marched toward him. His left foot was in the stirrup, his right on the ground. She let fly with a wad of juice that barely missed his grounded boot. "I want to talk to you, *Mister* Hawke."

He lowered his left foot, studying the brown blob in the dirt by his feet. Maybe now she could find out the truth. That he stayed away from her because she most certainly did not measure up to his ideal of a genteel young lady.

"Got any more of that?" he asked.

She could have sworn she saw a trace of amusement lurking in the depths of those midnight eyes. "As a matter of fact," she said, extracting the chaw from her pocket, "I do." She handed it to him.

He bit off a large chunk and began to chew slowly. "Not the best I've ever had." He worked up a sizable mouthful of juice. The glint in his eyes was practically mischievous now, and Kate thought surely her eyesight was failing. He was eyeing her boots.

"Oh, no, you don't," she said, but he continued to study her boots and work on his tobacco.

She took a step back. "I *missed* your boots, remember?"

He took aim.

"Don't you dare! Damnit, Hawke." She backed away, but he matched her step for step. She practically stumbled over a small rock, but he kept coming. Suddenly, she let out a shriek, pointing, "Hawke, behind you! A rattler!"

He jumped sideways, reflexively drawing his gun. There was nothing there.

But the sudden movement had done the job Kate intended. Hawke swallowed his chaw. She could tell by the way his eyes crossed as he turned to try and glare at her. But by then she was rolling on the ground, laughing.

"You'll pay for that, woman," he said quietly, but she was relieved to note there was no menace in his voice, only a softly spoken promise.

"It's nice to have you talking to me again," she said sweetly, spitting out the remains of her own chaw.

"I was never not talking to you." He put a hand on his stomach, obviously beginning to feel just a trace queasy from his recent "meal."

"Bull dung!" she grumped. Her brows furrowed in concern as he doubled over. His groan sent her bolting to his side. "Are you all right?"

His arms snaked around her with lightning swiftness. He didn't let go as he dragged her over to a small boulder and hauled her over his knee. "You behave like a child, you get treated like a child."

"You lay a hand on me, and I'll kill you!"

The train came to a halt, as several of the men noticed the commotion and ambled over. "Looks like you caught yourself some kind of wild animal there, cap'n," said Rafe. "Could you use a little help?"

"Rafe Yates," Kate shrieked, "you make this beast let go of me, or so help me you're fired."

"Now, Kate," Rafe said, "I seen what you done to the cap'n. I think he's lettin' you off kinda easy myself."

She squirmed violently, trying to push off Hawke's lap with one hand and protect her flank position with the other. "All of you are fired! Every damn one of you! And that includes you, Travis Hawke."

The men were chuckling. Hawke had yet to lay a hand on her, but just being seen in such a grossly humiliating position was enough to make her want to crawl under a rock for the rest of her natural life.

"Accept your punishment like a man, Kate," Hawke drawled. "Sentence has been duly passed. Why fight it?"

"I'll kill you! I swear to God, I'll kill you!" She shifted her hands, trying for better leverage. That was a mistake.

He delivered a swift smack to her derriere. She screamed her outrage, even as he released her and stood up. "I think we're even again, Kate."

She rubbed her rear end, skewering him with every curse known to humankind.

He chuckled and headed back toward his horse.

She turned on the bullwhackers. "You're all still fired! Don't think you're not!"

"You gonna drive all our wagons, Kate?" Rafe asked, trying very hard not to laugh.

She sputtered helplessly, slapping her hat against her knee. "All right. You're hired back. But as soon as we get to the fort, I'm killing all of you too."

They all laughed. "Oh, Katie," Rafe said, "give it up. You got what you deserved, makin' him swallow that chaw. Shame on ya. And you being so moon-eyed over him. Why don't you just try bein' nice to him for a change?"

The men began to head back to their wagons, but Rafe came over and slung his beefy arm around her shoulders. "The cap'n's a good man, Kate."

"Don't talk to me about that son-of-a-wolverine."

"But you're in love with him, ain't you?"

"Love that beast? What do you think I am? Touched in the head?"

"Touched with Cupid's arrow for sure."

She swiped at an errant tear. "I hate him."

"And I'm Robert E. Lee."

"He hates me."

236

"I'll tell you a little secret about the cap'n, Kate. That is, if you swear never to tell 'im where you heard it."

She halted, studying Rafe intently. Learn one of Hawke's secrets? One of the hurts he carried inside him? "Tell me."

Rafe unfurled his whip as they reached his wagon. He cracked it over the head of his pointers, setting the wagon in motion. Kate gathered up the reins of her horse, pulling it behind her, falling into step beside Rafe.

"I run into Cap'n Hawke at Chancellorsville," the burly bullwhacker began. "We rebs really give them yanks hell at that one. I was a private in the infantry, but the unit I was in got cut off, pinned down by union artillery. They were cuttin' us to pieces. Men dyin' left and right of me. We were done for sure. Nowhere to go. Ammunition gone.

"Then Cap'n Hawke comes swoopin' in on this big black horse, givin' out with the most bloodcurdlin' rebel yell I ever heard. It was like somethin' straight outa hell. Woulda scared me to death if'n he hadn't had a reb uniform on."

Kate pictured Hawke astride a black stallion. She found the image anything but frightening. But her fantasy would not take place in a war. She listened as Rafe continued.

"He rode right through that yank artillery. Right through it. Yellin', shootin'. Never seen nothin' like it afore or since. Them yanks turned and run, the ones that was still alive that is. We ended up capturin' their artillery and turnin' it on 'em."

"What happened to Hawke?"

"He took four bullets. Four of 'em. But I had to drag him off that horse. He was ready to go chargin' after more artillery."

Joined to die. Kate shuddered. Four bullets.

"I got 'im to a field hospital. The doctors didn't even want to look at him. Said they wanted to work on patients that had a chance of living. But I made 'em take care of him. I made 'em."

Kate mouthed a silent prayer of thanks.

"They dug the bullets out of him, but said they wasted their time. He was going to die. I couldn't stay with him. I had to rejoin my unit. But I come back in a couple of days and he was still hanging on. One of the doctors said he stayed alive because of some woman that musta meant a lot to him. Kept talkin' about lovin' her. I heard him mumbling her name myself. Name of Katherine."

Kate gasped.

"Now, don't be gettin' jealous," Rafe chided, misunderstanding her no doubt ashen face. "Katherine was some woman from his past. She's got nothing to do with you. But whoever she was, I'm glad he cared enough about her to stay alive for her. It was the darnedest thing though."

"What was?" Kate asked, still in a state of shock at Rafe's unwitting revelation.

"When the cap'n came around about three weeks later, I got to see him. I asked him who Katherine was. He got kinda mad and wouldn't tell me. But he couldn't remember anything about dreamin' of her all those weeks." Rafe settled his arm across her shoulders again, giving her a quick hug. "He's a good man, Kate. You could do a lot worse."

"I think he thinks he could do a lot better."

"But that's what I've been tryin' to tell ya, girl. Cap'n Hawke is a real hard man. He don't smile much. And he sure don't play. But he was doin' both them things with you and your chaw, Kate. He was smilin'. He was playin'. With you. I never woulda believed in a million years I'd see him swing you over his knee and take a swat at your behind."

"I'd hardly call that playing," Kate said.

"Then you didn't look at his eyes. He didn't beat ya, girl. He give you one swat, and that didn't even raise the dust on them buckskins."

She supposed there could be a grain of truth in what Rafe was saying. Heaven knew, her pride had suffered more damage than her rear end. And she hadn't done his pride any favors making him swallow that chaw. Maybe they were even again.

"He still hates me," she pouted.

"Ain't you been listening to me? When he was bad sick with them bullet wounds, I seen the look in his eyes when he went on about this Katherine."

"So?"

"So, it's the same one he has when he looks at you."

Kate stopped so abruptly her mare practically walked over her. "I wish you were right, Rafe. I really do. But . . ."

"Like I said. Try bein' nice to him for a change."

Nice. Be nice to Hawke. She rubbed her chin thoughtfully. She supposed she could try anything once. "All right, I'll do it."

"Good for you," Rafe said, giving her a sly wink. "Between you and me the cap'n don't stand a chance. I always told your pa it'd have to be one helluva man to catch your fancy."

"The way I hear it, Pa didn't want any man catchin' my fancy."

"Not the likes of Billy Langley, no. That's why he fired the little ferret, once he seen 'im on the inside."

"More the likes of Jim Collier," Kate grimaced.

"Yeah, your pa saw Jim as a real steady man, hard worker. Ambitious, too. He was thinking about being in politics before he got shot. While you were at school your pa would meet with Jim a lot. I think they were lookin' into that polecat Blanchard."

"Got Pa killed and Jim crippled."

"Blanchard will slip up one day. Somebody will get the proof to put him behind bars for good."

"Proof to hang him," Kate countered.

"Well, we can't worry about that now. We're gonna save McCullough Freight." He eyed her squarely. "I'll tell you the truth, Kate. Just before you came home, I wouldn't have given ten cents that this company would survive. Now, my money's on you. And Hawke."

She gave him a fierce hug. "Thank you." But she couldn't stop the thoughts. She kept seeing Hawke and Blanchard in their clandestine meeting. Hawke had finally told her about it, but that didn't lessen her suspicions.

"You go on and start bein' nice to Cap'n Hawke," Rafe said. "The two of ya stop fightin' what's gotta be."

She smiled, wishing her confidence matched Rafe's. Nice or not nice, she had to keep an eye on him anyway. Just as she'd been doing since the journey's outset. If Hawke had a connection with Blanchard, she was going to know about it. Before it cost her her company. Before it cost her her life.

No, Hawke would not harm her. Not physically. That she would never believe.

She smiled, mounting her mare, urging her into a gallop. She would beat the rest of the wagons to Elm Creek, and she would take a long and thorough bath.

And then she would spend the entire night being nice to Travis Hawke. Very nice indeed.

Chapter Eighteen

Kate stripped off her jacket, eyeing the swift flowing creek dubiously. If she was lucky, it might reach up to her ankles. Tying off the mare, she dug through her saddlebags, extracting her bar of lye soap. She would reconnoiter upstream. Surely she could find a sinkhole somewhere along the creekbed.

A half hour later, she was still walking, still looking, her only discoveries a rattler sunning himself on a rock and a small cave in the stream's south bank. She was just about to give up, when she rounded a bend and discovered a calm, fifty foot stretch of water. The depth in midstream approached four feet. Quickly she peeled off the rest of her clothes. Then on the dead run, she took a flying leap and cannonballed into the creek.

She surfaced, sputtering and laughing, feeling more than the grit and grime of the trail washing away, but much of the melancholy that shrouded her since her father's death. Gripping her soap bar, she worked up a healthy lather. She would get herself clean, and then she would have some real fun in the water. She giggled as a fish brushed by her leg.

A twig snapped.

Kate stilled, listening. The only sound she heard was the creek rushing, tumbling further downstream. But the feeling was there. She was no longer alone.

"Hawke?" she called, her voice tentative. "Is that you?" She shivered slightly. If it was Hawke, she would know it, feel it. It was not Hawke.

Calmly, rationally, she judged the distance to her clothes, her gun. She would never make it. But nothing could stop her from trying. As nonchalantly as she could manage, she started toward the creek's edge.

"Don't bother, little lady," said a rasping male voice.

She ducked quickly under the water, only her head above the surface. "You get the hell out of here right now, mister." Damn, even her voice was shivering.

She took an involuntary step backward as the man moved toward the creek's edge. Squinting, she studied him against the backdrop of the lowering afternoon sun. Dark clothes, dark hat, dark mustache in a swarthy face. She had never seen him before in her life, yet it didn't take a whole lot of insight to figure out what he did for a living. Tied down pistols weighted both of his thighs. An ammunition belt was slung over his shoulder, and a rifle lay nestled in his arm.

"Sure you got enough firepower?" Kate rasped. "I can always wait 'til you get back with the cannon."

"Boss told me you'd have a smart mouth. But don't you worry now. He didn't send me to kill you, only convince you to ride along with me. Unless, of course, you get real stupid."

"Your boss named Frank Blanchard?"

"I'm afraid he asked me not to say."

"Yeah, I'll just bet he did. Well you can just tell your boss that I wasn't the least bit interested in going anywhere with you." She started to back toward the opposite side of the creek, but halted as the bore of his rifle raised slightly.

242

"Don't try anything dumb, ma'am. Just come on out of the water."

"I'm naked!"

His mouth split in a leering grin. "I know. I'm sure the boss won't mind if I get me a bonus."

"You'd best start shooting then. I'm not coming out."

The gunman seated himself on the sloping bank, near a saddle-sized boulder. "I can wait."

Fifteen minutes passed.

Kate's whole body was trembling, the numbing chill of the water seeping into her bones as she was forced to remain motionless. The gunman took off his hat and mopped the sweat from his brow.

"Gonna be sunset in a few hours, little lady. Them wagons you're with will be here by then. If you're still in the water, I'll kill you." His voice was matter-of-fact. "And, maybe, just maybe, I'll have to kill a few of them bullwhackers, too."

"Damn you!" Her shoulders slumped. What choice did she have? Moving awkwardly because she was so cold, Kate stumbled toward shore. As her body cleared the water, she did her best to cover herself, but knew it was a futile gesture.

"Don't bother to get dressed," the gunman said.

Kate picked up her pants, holding them against her, shivering so badly she could barely stand. "You go to hell!"

He cocked his rifle. "Get over here. Now."

Kate stared at her pistol, its barrel peeking out from under her shirt. If she dove for it and rolled . . .

"Drop the rifle," came Hawke's hard-edged command.

Kate almost collapsed with relief. Hawke stood on the small rise just above the embankment, his Colt levelled at the gunfighter.

"You shoot me, I shoot her," the gunman snarled.

"Drop the rifle," Hawke repeated.

The gunfighter shifted his gaze to Hawke, and in that instant Kate dove headlong into the creek. She counted two shots before she resurfaced. Giving no thought to her own safety, she scanned the shore, desperate to know that Hawke was all right.

Her heart only started beating again when she saw him walking toward her. Behind him, the gunman lay sprawled facedown on the ground. "You all right?" he asked.

She nodded, staggering out of the water. Her knees would have buckled if he hadn't caught her. Brushing her wet hair away from her face, he regarded her intently. "Did he hurt you?"

"He didn't . . . he didn't have time, thanks to you." And then she guessed what he was so anxious about. "He never touched me."

A long shudder coursed through him. "Thank God."

She was in his arms, and he was holding her, crushing her to him. Her flesh, wet and naked, pressed hard against his sweat-stained shirt. For long minutes he kissed her, his lips bruising, his possession savage. And then just as abruptly as it had begun, he broke the contact, setting her away from him. "Just what the hell were you doing here all alone anyway?"

"Taking a bath," she snapped, "if that's any of your business." She was annoyed and more than a little hurt that he had ended the kiss.

"Pardon me. I thought I was dealing with the somewhat *intelligent* daughter of a experienced freight hauler. A woman I would have credited with enough sense to know that she doesn't take a bath in this country without someone standing guard."

She let the sarcasm pass, knowing it was justified. "I just felt like being alone."

"I don't give a damn what you felt like . . ."

They both jerked at the sound. The gunfighter was on his hands and knees, his .45 wobbly but deadly in his right hand. Hawke swore, shoving Kate behind him as he sought to drag his own weapon free of its holster.

The gunfighter's shot was wild, made so by the blood oozing from the gaping hole in his chest. He crawled forward, steadying himself against a boulder.

"Drop it!" Hawke ordered, ready to squeeze off a shot to the man's head.

"Hawke," the man wheezed. "The boss told me about you. Told me to . . . to . . ." The gun shook, his eyes glazing. He tried one last time to raise his gun. A blur of motion caught him in the side of the throat. He screamed and pitched forward. He did not move again. The rattlesnake glided silently away.

Holding her jacket against her, Kate followed Hawke over to the fallen gunman. "You should have made sure he was dead before!"

Hawke grimaced. "You're welcome." He checked through the man's pockets but found no identification, then retrieved the .45 from lifeless fingers. "Initials on the butt. J.B."

"For jackass bastard," Kate spat. "And what the hell did he mean about his boss telling him something about you?" She almost asked if Blanchard was sending him messages, but managed to hold her tongue just in time.

"I wouldn't know," Hawke said. "I've never seen him before. But the way he was pointing that gun at me, I had the impression his boss wanted me dead."

"And what does that tell you?"

He shrugged. "I've only had my life threatened by one person recently." He looked at her meaningfully.

She planted her hands on her hips, remembering with mortifying clarity how he had thrown her over his knee. "That's right, I did promise to kill you, didn't I?"

"You mean threaten."

"I mean promise." She grabbed the gun away from him, pointing it at his gut. "Unlike you, Mister Hawke, I am not a liar. Any last words?"

"How about a last request?"

"Maybe. What is it?"

"A kiss."

She straightened, clutching the jacket tighter against her, his dark eyes telling her that she was doing a lousy job protecting her modesty. "All right," she said. "I guess I could manage that."

He stepped close to her, but made no attempt to take the gun away. Leaning down, his arms at his sides, he took his mouth to hers, his lips soft, tender, caressing. He kissed her like that for what seemed like forever. Then he stepped back, his eyes locked on her face. "Thank you. You can shoot me now."

The gun wavered, her eyes travelling the length of him. He didn't really think she was going to . . . Her gaze halted at the stretched taut denim of his crotch, the beguiling bulge seeming to demand to be investigated. "It . . . it would be a shame to let that go to waste," she whispered.

The gun slipped from her fingers. She let go of the jacket.

He sucked in a breath through clenched teeth. "No. I didn't mean for it to get this far. We can't do this. Please. We can't."

"I'm not pretty enough, am I?"

He closed his eyes. "You're beautiful."

Her heart soared. He was not a man to give compliments lightly. Maybe she had some hope after all. Hope that one day he could sort through the pain he carried with him and allow her into his life. Dare she say the words? Her heart answered the question.

"Love me, Hawke. For now. For tonight, love me. You asked it of me once, and now I'm asking you."

Part of him winced that she had remembered, part of him rejoiced. "Kate. I . . . oh, damn." He opened his arms and she flew to him, burrowing against his chest. Her hand sought out his rigid flesh, stroking the taut fabric with the tips of her fingers. He moved more fully against her palm, his body offering wordless encouragement to be bolder still. She caressed him sensually, rhythmically, as her other hand began to unfasten the buttons of his shirt.

His throaty groan met her whimper, his hips rocking instinctively to match her motion. His tongue sought out the warm recesses of her mouth, giving, taking, needing. "Kate, sweet, Kate."

He scooped her into his arms, carrying her downstream along the creek's edge. "What are you doing?" she asked languorously. "I want to . . ."

"So do I," he assured her, "but I've got about six inches of dust on me." When he reached another deep pool of water, he put her down and began to strip off his clothes.

"Let me do that," she said, sliding her hands along his arms, his chest.

He dropped his arms to his sides.

Kate tugged open the remaining buttons of his shirt, sliding it past his shoulders, then smoothing it down his arms. "You are so beautiful," she murmured. She placed one kiss just above his navel. His stomach tightened.

Then she was working his belt, his fly, lowering his jeans to his knees. Smiling lustily, she studied his mid-thigh length drawers. She sat him down, tugging off his boots. Then she settled her hands along the underside of his calves, guiding the pants free of his body, memorizing the muscled texture of his legs.

Only his underwear separated their flesh. Kneeling beside him, she ran her hand over the cotton peak. He lay back, lips parted, eyes closed.

She undid the drawstring that held his drawers flush to his waist. Tucking her trembling fingers under the waistband, she eased the garment downward until it freed his heated hardness to her eager hands.

She explored the swollen length of him, skating the very tips of her fingers all along the turgid staff, amazed at how passively he submitted to her scandalous survey. And then she remembered the magic he had loosed in her that night in San Francisco when his mouth had done the exploring. Dare she? She leaned closer, but stopped on sight of the thin film of alkali dust he had complained of earlier. She smiled. It would most certainly give her something to look forward to after his bath.

His bath! Oh, what fun she could have with that. Jumping to her feet, she ran back to her clothes. Gathering them quickly, along with her soap, she scurried back to Hawke. "Into the water," she said, poking his naked thigh with her toe. "Time to remove the Nebraska soil from your person, unless you're planning to put in crops come spring."

He stood up, grumbling. "Couldn't you just go back to what you were doing?"

"Later."

"Promise?"

She giggled. "Threat."

She linked her hand to his and led him to the creek, her heart savoring every minute of their wondrous idyll. Why he had decided to stop ignoring her didn't matter. It only mattered that he did.

Standing in midstream, the water that teased the underside of her breasts, swirled just below Hawke's navel. "That's not fair," she groused, slapping at the water in front of him. "It hides the good parts."

He laughed, ducking swiftly under the water to wet his entire body. When he surfaced, he shook his head, sending water spraying in all direction. "There are two very good parts of your body the water has been kind enough not to hide." His heated gaze warmed her breasts. "Sometimes I think you can't possibly be real, Kate. That you're only a dream." His hands followed through on the promise in his eyes, kneading the pliant flesh, teasing the nipples into stiff erection. "That one day I'm going to reach for you, and there'll be nothing there. And I'm going to wish to God I was still asleep."

"That's what you were to me," she whispered, arching to his touch. "A dream."

He sighed, letting her go. "A dream I turned into a nightmare."

"No." She turned the soap in her hands, running the lather across his chest. "You didn't."

He gathered her in his arms, even as his mind told him to thrust her away, to get on his horse and ride, never stopping. She was a witch, casting some kind of spell over him. He swore he wanted no part of her. Yet he couldn't stay away. He had come back to the creek after exploring it this morning because he knew—knew—she was in some kind of terrible danger.

When he'd seen her standing there all but naked in front of that outlaw, he had come damned close to emptying his gun into the man. Only the fact that a dead outlaw could tell him nothing had kept him from pulling the trigger. That the man had forced his hand mattered little. He was glad the bastard was dead, even though it left him with dangerous questions unanswered.

The man had not named his boss. But who else could it have been but Blanchard? And if it was Blanchard, why had Hawke sensed the man was there to kill him? Had his cover been blown? Did Blanchard now know he worked for Wells Fargo? Or . . .

He sucked in his breath, gripping her to him, as she dared trail the soapy lather beneath the surface of the water. Her hands fondled him, stroked him, bringing him back to ramrod stiffness, even against the ennervating effects of the chilly water. He thrust toward her instinctively, seeking, seeking . . .

"Kate, Kate." He wanted to say so many things, but all he could manage was her name, as her brazen fingers destroyed all coherent thought.

She pressed him toward shore, urging him without words to lie down at the water's edge. Her whole body was on fire, and only he was fuel to her flame. Her hands never left him, her every instinct telling her that what she wanted to do was right and good because it would please this man she loved, Travis Hawke.

The tips of her breasts grazed his thigh as she moved over him. And then her mouth was on him, licking, tasting, loving.

An animal cry escaped his throat, his fingers slicing through the coarse sand that lay beneath him. Wetness, not of the water, stung his eyes. "Kate. Oh, God, Kate." His voice was a rasping mockery of its normal tone. The fierce intensity of the pleasure she gave him was almost too much to bear.

Finally, it was too much. Such rapture had to be shared to be borne. Gripping her shoulders, he lifted her away from him, bearing her down into the sand, as he rose above her. He prayed she was ready, because he was beyond waiting.

Swift and hard, he drove himself inside her, burying himself in the silken sweetness. She arched her hips, crying out her welcome. Her legs twined round him, holding him prisoner in a rapturous snare from which he wanted no escape.

"Love me, love me," she whimpered. She tried to hold back the rest of the words, but her body, her heart demanded they be said. "I love you, Travis. I love you." In that final instant before the shattering oblivion of his release, some minute part of him still capable of reason, recognized that for the first time in her life she had called him Travis. And then he knew no more.

Kate came awake by degrees, aware first of being cold, then warm, then immeasurably content. She stretched her arms and discovered quickly why she was cold. The left side of her body was being brushed by the constant current of the creek. Her right side on the other hand was cocooned in the body heat of Travis Hawke. Hawke with whom she was immeasurably content.

Surely he could not make love to her like that and not love her. But the niggling doubts began almost at once, and she wished she had not been so caught up in the whirlwind of her emotions. That she had not blurted out that she loved him.

She smoothed his hair with her left hand, unable to retrieve her right, because on it he had cradled his head. She should rouse him at once. The wagons were probably no more than an hour off. And from the looks of the sky, there was one helluva storm brewing to meet them.

But to wake Hawke would be to face his reaction to what had just passed between them. It was that unknown factor that kept her still.

How do you do it to me, Hawke, she wondered. *How do you keep me so completely off balance? One minute I can believe you could love me. Me! Kate McCullough, buckskinned bull- whacker. And the next I see you with Blanchard, and I remem-*

ber how cold your voice can be when you're angry, and I can almost believe that for the right price you could kill me.

Had the dead gunfighter been paid the right price? She remembered his words. He hadn't been sent to kill her, only take her with him. What sense did that make?

She shifted restlessly. What sense did anything make these days? With unceremonious abruptness she dragged her arm from under Hawke's head. He grunted, coming roughly awake.

"What did you do that for?" he demanded.

"Felt like it."

He sat up, eyeing her warily. He had just had the most incredible sex of his life with this woman. So why was she acting like he'd just kicked her puppy? Perhaps the sheer intensity of their lovemaking had embarrassed her. He was more than a little uncomfortable himself, now that he was fully awake.

He remembered she'd cried out she loved him. But he dismissed that at once as a normal reaction to the powerful emotions they'd somehow loosed in each other. He didn't believe she loved him, any more than he . . .

He climbed swiftly to his feet, reaching for his clothes. "We'd better get dressed. The wagons will be here soon. And there's a storm coming."

She pulled on her pants and shirt. "Hawke, we've got to talk."

"It's back to 'Hawke,' is it?"

She wrinkled her nose. "What are you talking about?"

"Never mind." He relaxed a little. She didn't even remember telling him she loved him.

"I mean it. We have to talk."

"What we've got to do is find a few trees to get under, unless you want to get wet with your clothes *on*."

"No, I don't want to get wet," she said. "Not if I don't have to. But there aren't that many trees around here. And I'll be damned if I'll get under one tall one. There's going to be lightning with that storm. Hail, too, I'll wager."

She scanned the creek banks upstream and down, then remembered the tiny cave she had scouted out earlier. "Come on, I know where we can go."

The words weren't out of her mouth before the deluge struck. Grabbing Hawke's hand she raced upstream, one hand shading her eyes as the rain fell in a near perfect sheet of wet.

She paused once to catch her breath, laughing. "I think my clothes have gotten a bit damp!"

He gripped her arm. "They'll get a helluva lot damper if you stand here like a ninny."

"A ninny!" She laughed all the harder. "I've been called a lot of things, Travis Hawke. But never ever a ninny!"

"Maybe you're never been one before," he replied, dragging her along the bank. "Where the hell are we going anyway?"

The hail hit without warning. Not tiny bits of ice, but huge gravel-sized chunks slamming down with bruising velocity. Kate cried out as one struck her cheek and drew blood. Hawke cursed.

"We've got to get out of this." He was nearly shouting to be heard above the roar of the storm, the hail racketing the ground like a fusillade. Shrugging out of his shirt, he wadded it up and shoved it on her head. "Hold it there. It'll protect you a little anyway."

"But your back!"

"Go!" he yelled.

Kate sloshed along the shore, the going made even more difficult by the added weight of her wet buckskins. Where was that damned cave? At last, through

253

the driving rain, she spied the black hole beckoning from the creek bank. "Come on, there it is!" she called, "Hurry!"

Kate hunched down and crawled into the small space, huddling against a wall about three feet back from the entrance. Half a minute passed and Hawke had not joined her. He'd been right behind her. Where was he? Creeping forward, she peered out into the still hammering storm.

He was standing next to the entrance, his arms over his head, staring off at nothing.

"Get in here!" she shouted. "That hail's getting worse. It'll tear your back to ribbons."

He didn't look at her. "I'm fine. I'm going to go check and see if the wagons are coming."

"Don't be crazy! They're big boys. They can handle whatever comes. Get in here!" She grabbed at his wrist, but he jerked away, stalking off along the creek.

"Damnit, Hawke!" she hissed, scrambling after him. "Get back here!" She slogged through the mud and sand, catching up to him only when he turned to glare at her.

"Get back inside, Kate."

"Not until you come too."

He gripped her elbow, all but dragging her back to the cave. "I said get back inside."

"And I said not without you."

He didn't move.

She crossed her arms in front of her, compressing her lips defiantly. "If you can stand it, I can stand it." She blinked back the still fearsome rain, flinching when another piece of hail grazed her cheek.

He swore, pushing her into the hole and ducking in behind her.

Kate quickly scrunched down against the back wall. But when she turned around it was to discover that

Hawke had not moved from the entrance. His body was barely a quarter of the way into the cave. He was still being pummeled by the rain.

"Move back in here."

He didn't respond.

A flash of lightning cast eerie shadows through the tiny gash in the earth. For the first time she saw the dozen streaks of diluted red trailing down his back. "Damnit, Hawke, you're hurt." She reached out to touch one of the nastier cuts. He didn't flinch. He didn't move.

"Hawke? Are you all right?"

Nothing.

She touched him again, noticing for the first time how oddly rigid he was holding himself in his hunched position. "Hawke, answer me."

Still nothing.

Moving awkwardly in the closed in space, she managed to crawl forward far enough to draw even with his left side. "What is the matter with you? Why didn't you answer me?"

She curved a hand over his shoulder, gently caressing the taut flesh. It was then she felt her hand shaking. No, her hand wasn't shaking. Hawke's body was shaking. He was trembling violently.

She shoved past him, looking him square in the eye. "Are you going to tell me what . . ." The words snagged in her throat.

He was staring straight ahead. And if she hadn't seen it, she wouldn't have believed it. Travis Hawke's face was rigid with terror.

"Hawke, for God's sake, what is it?"

Nothing she said, nothing she did got through to him. But when she tried to get him to move farther back into the cave, he slammed her away from him.

"Leave me alone!"

"I will not. Not until you tell me what's wrong."

He was staring straight ahead again, shivering, but not from the cold.

Kate hunkered down at the mouth of the cave. If he wouldn't go inside, she would sit with him here. Very gently, she pulled his still rigid body against her, cradling his head against her breasts. She stroked his hair, speaking soothingly, caressingly, tears mingling with the rain streaking her face. At least the hail had stopped.

Long, long minutes passed. The rain subsided, ceased. And while she could have sat there forever, holding him, she knew it would be best if she got him away from the cave. Fighting her soaking wet clothing, she got to her feet, then stooped to urge Hawke to do the same.

Dazed, he followed her for several yards, then stopped. He shook his head, as if to clear it, looking first at her, then back at the cave. He straightened, a chilling awareness in his midnight eyes. And then his face was rigid with a different emotion—embarrassment.

"I'm sorry."

"It's all right."

"I . . . I don't know what happened. I . . ."

He was lying again, but she didn't care. She only cared that he now seemed to be himself again. "I said it's all right."

Almost distractedly, he reached up to touch the scratch on her cheek. "Looks clean anyway."

"I ran water on it."

He tried to smile, but failed. "I . . . I've never liked small spaces. I . . ."

"You don't have to tell me anything you don't want to."

His eyes seared her. "Damn, what are you doing

256

to me, woman?" He crushed her to him, kissing her with a need so fierce it stole the breath from her body.

I'm loving you, she thought. *I'm just loving you, Hawke.*

He broke off the kiss, gripping her hand. Together they walked along the saturated bank. For Kate those precious minutes of companionable silence meant almost as much as the blazing power of his lovemaking. But the need to know, truly know, this man she loved prompted her to risk losing the fragile link that seemed finally to have sprung up between them.

"Who are you, Travis Hawke?" she whispered, not daring to look at him but sensing somehow that the door to the secrets buried inside him was for the moment at least unguarded, if not unlocked. Whether or not he would allow her through it depended, she knew, on how gently she pushed.

"I'm your wagonmaster."

He wasn't going to make it easy. "Who were you before that?"

"I was a soldier in the war."

So far he'd told her nothing she didn't already know. "What did you do before the war?"

He stopped. "I spent two hours in the wrong room of a San Francisco hotel."

"Wrong for you, maybe. Not for me."

"Kate . . ."

"No. Now we're getting to the important part. The part before San Francisco. What brought you to that hotel that night?"

"Sex."

"Liar."

He let go of her hand, striding off to stand beside the withered stump of some long dead tree.

She wrapped her arms around his middle, pressing her face into his back, loosening her hold only when he winced as she caught one of his cuts the wrong way. "Please."

He turned in her arms, capturing her head in his hands. In his dark eyes hovered a pain so raw it hurt her to look at him.

And just that quickly, he shuttered it away, replacing it with cold fury. His hands circled her wrists like steel talons. She had pushed too far, laying open the wound, old, festering, filled with poison. And to cover the hurt he would hurt back.

"What brought me to your room that night, Kate? My wife brought me. Or drove me. Or . . ."

"Wife?" No, it couldn't be. Couldn't. "You're married?" She didn't recognize her own voice.

"No, not married. Not any more. She's dead."

The pain was back, terrible in its intensity. God, how he must have loved her. She remembered the words. *Joined the war to die.* He'd loved her so much, he didn't want to go on living without her.

"I'm sorry."

"Don't be." His hands circled her neck, his thumbs caressing her skin just above her collarbone. "Don't be." His eyes were focused on her throat, an unnatural glint in their blue depths, his thumbs shifting higher, stroking, stroking. "I'm not sorry."

Kate started. What kind of thing was that to say? She would have asked him, but she was suddenly terrified of the answer. The caressing motion ceased, the pressure of his thumbs growing uncomfortable.

"Hawke!" she rasped. "Hawke, what are you doing?"

"You shouldn't have done it, Annie. You shouldn't have done it." His hands tightened. His eyes were black slits, his lips curved in a feral snarl.

258

This wasn't happening. This wasn't happening. He'd made love to her. She'd sat in the cave in the driving rain and held him, because he needed her. He couldn't, couldn't . . .

With a sudden jerk, he dropped his hands away.

She sank to her knees, trying to tell herself that none of this last minute had happened. Knowing full well that it had.

"Are you all right? Kate, for God's sake, are you all right?"

He reached down as if to help her to her feet, but she pulled away. "Don't touch me! You heard the wagons, didn't you? That's why you stopped?"

"What are you . . ."

"The wagons. I hear them. That's why you stopped. You were going to kill me."

"My God, Kate, you can't believe that."

"Don't lie to me! You're working for Blanchard. He hired you to kill me!"

His eyes widened briefly and her heart broke. It was true. Dear God, it was true. "Get on your horse and get out of here. I never want to see you again in my life."

"Kate, I was not . . ."

Reflexively, she touched her throat. "Get out! Get out!" She couldn't hold back the tears.

For a moment, he seemed determined to stay, to get her to listen. Then he turned and headed toward his gelding, tied off to a cottonwood some fifty yards away.

The first of the freight wagons rumbled in, just as Hawke mounted and rode out. Vaguely, she heard Rafe shouting her name. And then he was at her side.

"Katie, what happened to you, gal?"

She wiped at her tears with the back of her hand,

refusing to give way to the wracking sobs bearing inside her. "Not a thing, Rafe," she said. "Not a damn thing. Did the wagons make it through the storm all right?"

"Just fine," he said, watching her with growing concern. "Where's Cap'n Hawke?"

"Hawke?" She gave him a pathetic mockery of a smile. "Hawke's in hell." Her lips quivered. "I should know. He just put me there with him."

Chapter Nineteen

Kate was dead. Hawke stared at her body, refusing to believe it. Not Kate. Not Kate too. He knelt beside her, lifting her, cradling her against him. How? Why?

He smoothed her russet hair away from her face. Her face, oh God. What had happened to her face? Her warm brown eyes were glassy, lifeless, bulging from their sockets. Her lips, lips that had fired white hot heat through his body, were tinged a hideous blue.

He gripped her, shook her. "No, you're not dead, Kate. Damn you, don't be dead."

Her head lolled back, exposing the sun-browned flesh of her throat. Her throat, twisted at an impossible angle marred by fingerlike marks—raw, red.

His hands were around her throat and he was squeezing, squeezing.

He sat straight up, eyes wide, straining to focus. Everything was shadowed, black. Sweat dripped from every pore of his body. He shivered, a night breeze sifting over damp flesh.

"Kate! Oh, God, Kate . . ." Now he remembered. A dream, it was only a dream. But that didn't change the reality of what had happened at Elm Creek five days ago.

They had been talking and though he felt nervous and uncomfortable, he was determined to answer whatever question she asked. But as the questions probed nearer to Anne, it was as if for just an instant he was back there in the house that final night.

He'd wanted to kill Anne, wanted to break her beautiful neck.

"Son-of-a-bitch!" He slammed a fist against the hard ground. Kate had gotten in the way of anger unresolved for five years. She was the last person on earth he would hurt. He cared about that woman. He didn't want to, but he did. It was only her fear of Blanchard that had read so much into their last minute by the creek. How could she ever believe he could kill her, after what they had shared less than an hour before? Never had he felt so whole, so complete, so willing to give, rather than take, than when he had made love to her by the water.

And when the cave had sent him hurtling back into Liam Jeffers's crawlspace, it was almost as though she understood. He closed his eyes. Five days. Damn, but he missed her. Missed being near her. Missed talking to her. He'd been married to Anne over three years, yet he'd felt closer to Kate in the darkness of San Francisco three minutes after he met her, than he ever had to Anne.

"I'd never deliberately hurt you, Kate. Never."

But she wasn't there. She was with the freight wagons five miles north. He'd kept pace with the train since that night, but had made no contact with anyone.

He'd watched her, watched her head up the wagons. She'd taken on the task of wagonmaster herself. And done a helluva job from what he could discern from his position, never closer than five hundred yards away. The men seemed to accept her, and there had been no major trail problems since he'd been gone.

He'd watched her, too, three days ago, when she had stopped alone near a tiny creek, stripping off her clothes and settling herself in midstream. If he hadn't known better, he could have sworn she knew he was watching, the way she'd allowed the soapy lather to linger on her breasts. She'd played with her nipples, touched her . . .

He swore. He didn't need to think any further about that. Kate played heavily enough on his mind without complicating it with his physical desire for her.

Threading a hand through his dark hair, he studied the pinkening sky in the east. The teamsters would already be up, breaking camp. He had decided last night that he would rejoin them today, though he was not looking forward to Kate's reaction to his return.

Considering her temper, she might put a bullet in his head before she let him offer so much as a word of explanation or apology. Yet he would welcome her anger. It would keep the barriers in place between them. He would bring her life nothing but grief. It would be best if she hated him.

He lay back in his blankets. He would give the bullwhackers time to be well underway. Then he would ride in to face Kate McCullough's wrath.

Damn. Things could have been so different with Kate, if he had never met Anne.

Anne. . . .

"I don't want to meet your daughter, Dan," Hawke said, slouching down in a leather chair in Dan Parker's Wells Fargo office.

"Well, she wants to meet you." Dan's green eyes sparked with amusement. "Ever since I hired you two weeks ago, she's done nothing but badger me about bringing you home to dinner."

"Why me?" Hawke had been in San Francisco for only a month. He'd come to the city for no other reason than he'd never been there before. He'd given up trying to farm Nels Svenson's land nearly two years ago and had been drifting ever since.

Two weeks ago three men had tried to rob the safe in this very office, just as Hawke had been happening by across the street. He didn't know why he'd gotten involved, but he had. When Dan came out of his office shouting about a holdup, Hawke had drawn down on the three men.

One of the outlaws took a shot at Hawke and missed. Hawke's return fire took the man in the shoulder. The outlaw dropped his gun, his two compatriots doing the same. And suddenly Hawke was some kind of hero.

Dan had gushed over him for an hour, insisting that he buy him the best steak dinner in town. Over that dinner, Dan had convinced Hawke that he'd never want anything more out of life than to work for Wells Fargo.

So far, he liked the job just fine. Dan was teaching him all of the finer points of investigative work. He found he liked sifting through clues, building a case, searching for the one piece of evidence that might make the difference between conviction and acquittal. But now Dan was shifting things to a more personal level. Hawke felt his defenses rise.

"Annie's a great cook, really," Dan was saying. "Pot roast being one of her specialties. So don't start making up excuses again, Travis. She'll have my neck. This is the third time I've promised her I'd talk you into dinner."

"She's never even met me. Why should she . . ."

"Last week, when you were headin' out to the Jacobs' ranch, she came by the office. You had just mounted up. She saw you."

"So?"

"So she asked about you, and I told her you were the new man I hired."

Hawke grimaced. "Does she invite every new man you hire to dinner?"

"Of course not!" Dan scolded, taking a mild offense at Hawke's inference. "But I guess you ain't looked at yourself in the mirror lately."

"If you're making any sense, it slipped by me."

"She comes into the office, see," Dan said, coming around his desk in a sweeping motion that Hawke took as a ludicrous imitation of what could only be a flirtatious saunter. "She was all but in a swoon. 'Oh, daddy,' she said," Dan's voice rising to a falsetto, " 'who was that absolutely gorgeous man who just stepped out of your office.' " He slumped down on the corner of his desk. "Well, I was foolish enough to tell her who you were, and she has been on my back ever since to get you over to the house."

"Sounds dangerous," Hawke mused, though part of him was responding to Dan's outrageous humor and his daughter's none-too-subtle interest.

"She's a woman who gets what she wants, if that's what you mean," Dan laughed. "Has ever since her ma died when she just a babe. She's all I got, so I guess I spoil her."

Hawke rapped his fingers on the arm of the chair. "I'll probably live to regret this. But you can tell Miss Parker I'll be by for dinner at seven."

Dan grinned, coming over to give Hawke a hearty slap on the back. "You won't regret a thing. Like I said, she's a damn fine cook."

Standing outside Dan Parker's door at precisely seven o'clock, Hawke fidgeted nervously with his string tie. Why in the hell had he agreed to this? When he had need of a woman, he found a well-practiced one for an hour or two in a room above a saloon. Actually having a conversation with one was as foreign to him as silk sheets to an Apache.

But he decided to remedy that oversight the instant Anne Parker opened the door. To say that her beauty was breathtaking would have done her a severe injustice. She was quite simply the most lovely woman he had ever seen in his life. Her blond hair was done up in a delicate twist accented by dozens of tiny ringlets. Her face was a perfect oval, her creamy complexion flawless. The blue of her eyes was the color God used to make the world's most beautiful lakes. And her lips, full and pouting, seemed to demand a kiss or she would bar him entry.

He quashed the last thought at once as Dan strode into the parlor to plant a swift kiss of his own on his daughter's cheek. "Glad you could make it, Travis," he drawled, extending his right hand.

Hawke accepted the handshake, but his eyes never left Anne's.

He supposed the dinner was good that night, though he could never remember what it was he'd eaten. He came by the house often after that, taking Anne for buggy rides, to dances, to the theatre.

On a lazy Sunday afternoon in June they went on their first picnic together. "Oh, Travis," she said, watching him lay the gray homespun blanket under a huge maple, "I'm so glad you decided to come today."

He gripped her arms, pulling her down beside him. "I have yet to refuse you anything," he said huskily. "You have the same effect on me that you have on your father."

She giggled. "I declare, that is all the two of you ever do is tell me how dreadfully spoiled I am."

266

"Well, aren't you?"

"Perhaps," she allowed, primping her golden chignon, "but only a little." She kissed her finger, then brought it to his lips. "You're not going to go out on that awful two month assignment daddy's offered you, are you?"

"It's my job, Anne. If it takes me to Oregon, that's where I have to go." He took her finger into his mouth, his tongue teasing its tip.

She yanked her hand back, clasping them both in front of her, flicking imaginary dust from the pale green silk dress she wore. Hawke's eyes had not missed its daring decolletage, travelling again and again to the deep vee of her high, firm breasts. He shifted uncomfortably, drawing rein on the tightening in his loins.

If he ever made love to her, his respect for Dan would demand that he do the honorable thing and marry her. He just wasn't certain that was what he wanted to do. He cared about Anne very much. She could be delightful company, stirring him out of his frequently glum moods. But she was also an uncontrollable flirt, both with him and with any other man who stepped into her range of vision.

At first he hadn't minded her teasing him with other men, taking it as silly attempts to make him jealous. But the flirting had not stopped long after he had assured her that he was indeed jealous, that he didn't want it to continue. If and when he married a woman, she would be his only woman, and he had damned well better be her only man.

Anne was also growing increasingly demanding of his time, often insisting that he choose between her and his work. Dan dismissed it as natural to a young woman in love, but Hawke wasn't so sure. She was intractable when it came to having her own way. When she didn't get it, the price was usually paid in emotional blackmail.

He munched absently on the chicken leg she gave him, remembering the night he'd had to cancel their dinner engagement to be in on a stake-out with another agent. She hadn't spoken to him for three days. It had taken a bouquet of roses and a note of apology, as well as intercession by her father before she would deign to be in his company again. Strangely, it was after he'd gone through all of the machinations to get back into her good graces that his interest in her began to wane.

He didn't like being made to dance at the end of a string like some damned puppet. If she didn't make at least some effort to change, their relationship was headed for a rocky ending.

"I thought we discussed how important my job was to me," he said, his voice mild though his temper nudged him.

"I know," she pouted. "But I just miss you so much when you're gone." She scooted closer to him, careful not to wrinkle her dress. "I get all, I don't know, tingly, when I'm near you. I . . . I don't know what it means, Travis."

He wiped his greasy fingers on one of the linen napkins she'd brought along, telling himself she had just broached very dangerous ground and he would be wise to change the subject. But it wasn't a day for being wise. His gaze lingered on her breasts, seeming to strain to be free of the fabric that confined them. He reached up a hand, lazily trailing a finger from her neck to the vee of her dress.

"Travis!" she gasped, sitting back primly. "What are you doing?"

"I'm being a fool," he said quietly, then pulled her down on top of him, weeks of abstinence adding tinder to the flame of his kiss.

They were both shaking when he broke it off. "I shouldn't have done that," he said, working hard to keep from going beyond the kiss. "I'm sorry."

"No, don't be sorry," she said, her blue eyes dancing. "That was wonderful! Truly! I . . . I've never been kissed like that before." She'd lowered her eyes demurely, and like the fool he'd named himself, he'd believed her.

She was a passionate woman, and even in her professed innocence he sensed the potential of what they could have together. He was twenty-six years old, it was time he started thinking about putting down roots. A wife, children . . . they could give him what he'd never had, not since he lost his parents twenty-two years ago. A family, a home, someone to love, someone to love him.

Nels Svenson had been good to him, and they had cared about each other. But a wife and children could fill the void in him as nothing else could.

Perhaps that need was why he ignored the warning signals until it was too late.

He and Anne went on many more picnics. And she really did seem to make an effort to be more understanding about his job.

"Travis," she murmured, as they snuggled together under their favorite maple tree, "you've been my only escort for nearly five months now."

"Uh huh," he said, nuzzling her throat, inhaling the jasmine scent of her perfume. His desire for her had long passed the settling for kisses stage, but he had managed to exercise rigid self-control.

"Well, a girl starts to get ideas, you know. When a man calls on her so often. Even when you are out of town half the time."

"What kind of ideas?" he grinned, kissing the delicate line of her jaw.

"I'm not getting any younger," she pouted, though it was a pretty pout.

"Nineteen isn't exactly fodder for the graveyard, Annie."

"Oh, how you do talk!" She sat up, slapping at the bits of grass that clung to the front of her voluminous taffeta skirts. Then she giggled, leaning forward to give him a passionate kiss on the mouth.

"Sometimes I wonder how you learned to kiss so well," he said.

"You taught me, of course." But she had her back to him as she reached for the bottle of wine in their picnic basket, and he wondered just a little. She had made it patently clear that she was a virgin, and that she was saving herself for marriage. But sometimes the things she did to him, while still managing to maintain her virginity, he found to be amazingly advanced for someone of little or no experience in the bedroom.

What bothered him was that her virginity didn't matter, but her lie would. Still, as he kissed her, held her, touched her, he convinced himself that there was no lie. That he was the first man to be allowed even this much liberty with her, that he would be the first to . . .

He shook his head. "We'd best get back. I've got that trip to Los Angeles to make."

She put her hand on his chest. "I want you to marry me, Travis."

His eyes widened. "I beg your pardon?"

"You heard me."

"Women don't ask men to marry them."

"This woman does, when the man just keeps taking up a lady's time without any sort of understanding." She undid the first two buttons of his shirt.

"Why would you want to marry me?" He sucked in his breath when her hand moved over his chest.

"What girl wouldn't want to marry you? You're so handsome. All of my girlfriends just turn positively green whenever they see me with you."

"That doesn't sound like much of a reason to get married."

"Oh, well, of course, you're nice and everything. And," she trailed a long blade of grass over his lips, "you're a wonderful kisser."

"But do you love me?"

"Of course, silly. I would hardly have asked you to marry me if I didn't. Would I?"

He wondered, but the feel of her lips on his drove the thought from his mind. He so wanted to belong, to have roots. If she loved him, maybe, maybe . . .

She made no objection as he undid the fastenings of her dress. He groaned, taking his mouth to her breasts, the need in his loins blinding him to anything else. "I want you, Annie. Here. Now. I want you." He stripped off her clothes, then quickly peeled off his own.

She was naked in his arms, her hands roving his body, eager, wanton. But when he was ready for the joining, she twisted away. "No, no, Travis, we mustn't." She covered her breasts, her eyes swimming with tears.

"Annie, don't do this. You want it. I want it."

"No, my wedding night, please . . ." Her voice broke, her words jumbled.

He cursed, then apologized for doing so. He gathered her against him, holding her, stroking her. "Do you really love me, Annie?"

Her lower lip trembled. "Oh, yes, Travis, yes."

To belong, to belong . . . "Then maybe we should get married."

Her eyes brightened, the tears disappearing with amazing swiftness. Throwing her arms around his neck, she giggled, "Oh, that would be simply marvel-ous. Marvelous!"

His hands trailed along her body to claim the downy softness between her legs, but again she pushed away. "Not now, Travis. You've waited this long, you can wait a little longer. After all, I'm going to be your wife." In just minutes she was dressed and ready to head home.

Three weeks later they were married. And on his wedding night, he discovered the first of her many lies.

He lay awake in the darkness, long after they had made love. He'd said nothing to her, though she had continued the act, even to crying out in pain. But she had not been a virgin. He told himself it didn't matter. That she loved him. That they would build a good life together. But it was damned difficult to forget how of-ten she had aroused him almost past enduring, only to put him off with her pleading cry of innocence.

The next morning at the office Dan congratulated him for what must have been the thousandth time. "Anne seems real happy, Travis."

"I hope so," Hawke said and meant it.

For the first time in his life he settled into a con-tented routine. Anne raised no objections to the fre-quent Wells Fargo assignments that took him out of the city. And when he returned home, she was always there, ready and eager to share his bed.

"You're a good lover, Travis," she told him one night, after a particularly frenzied lovemaking session. It was an off-handed comment, but something in her tone made him wonder if she was making comparisons. Re-cent comparisons.

"Did you talk to the doctor?" he asked, telling him-self he was just imagining things.

Her voice grew hostile. "I told you there's nothing to talk to him about."

"We've been married over a year. As often as we've made love, it doesn't seem right that there's no baby."

"I had an aunt who was married ten years before she had one."

He pulled her close, not wanting the topic to lead to yet another argument. "I guess we'll just have to keep trying." He smiled against her ear, but she stiffened and turned away.

"I don't know why you want a baby so much," she said. "I'm the one who'll have to do all the work."

"I just feel like it'll make us a family. Maybe that's wrong, maybe it's because of my own life, I don't know."

"Don't tell me about your being an orphan. You know I don't want to hear that sort of depressing thing." She twisted toward him. "Oh, Travis, can't we be happy? Just the two of us."

"Sure we can."

"Then have you been thinking about what I asked you? About going to London? To Paris? It would be so exciting. Please, can't we?"

"It's going to take me some time to save that kind of money."

"Money! That's all you ever say."

"Annie, you knew what I was when you married me."

"I didn't think you'd want to work for that dull, old Wells Fargo forever!" She kissed him long and hard, then drew back to eye him strangely. Her voice had a quality in it he'd never heard before—almost melancholy. "I think sometimes we're two of a kind, Travis. We both want more than we're willing to give. You want to be a family, yet the only thing I know about you from before I met you is that you're an orphan. Nothing else of twenty-seven years. Nothing.

"And for me, I want parties, I want to travel, I want

273

beautiful clothes and a handsome man at my side. And so far, all I've gotten is the handsome man." She urged him on top of her. "We're going to destroy each other, Travis. And there isn't a damn thing we can do to stop it."

He took her then, quickly, because she wanted it that way. But afterward, he lay awake for a long time. Her words hurt. Hurt because they were true. Their whole relationship was dinner parties, and his work. She never asked him what he cared about; he never asked her.

In spite of her protests that she didn't know him, it was because she had chosen not to. The few times the subject of his childhood had come up, she had shut him off, unwilling even to listen to the better times, the years he had lived with Nels. And then there was the afternoon he'd gone down to the root cellar, a feat in itself for him in the dank, closed-in space. He'd left the door wide open, so that the afternoon sun could angle in. But as he rummaged around for the apple preserves, the door had slammed shut, burying him in darkness.

Giggling hysterically, Anne opened it a minute later and came bounding down the stairs. "Did I scare you?" she laughed.

He'd scared *her.* It had taken her nearly half an hour to coax him up the steps and out of the cellar. It was Liam Jeffers and his werewolf all over again. No matter how much he cursed himself for being a fool, each encounter with a small dark place grew worse than the one before.

Anne had never let him forget the cellar incident. He supposed it was her own fear at seeing him like that, but anytime they had an argument, she knew exactly where to stab the knife. She would threaten to tell her father what she had seen. "He thinks you're the

274

bravest man on earth," she'd sniff. "What would he think if he saw you cowering in the dark like a baby?"

Yet the times when they weren't fighting, he could believe their marriage really had a chance. That having a child would be a stabilizing influence, a reason for Anne herself to give up many of her childlike ways and become a woman. So much of her life centered around wanting *things*, expensive clothing, trips to exotic places, jewelry. Things he well knew he would never be able to give her.

But as their marriage continued through its second and third year, his belief that she would change faded and finally died. No longer did she discourage him from accepting assignments that would take him away from home for weeks on end. His suspicions about why that was so ate away at his insides.

"Who is he?" he demanded, as he stuffed his clothes in his saddlebags, readying to leave on a mission that would keep him gone for two months.

"Who?"

"Your lover. Who is he? Anyone I know?"

She crossed over to the stove and stirred the stew she was making for supper. "I don't know what you're talking about."

"Why don't you look me in the face and say that?"

She set the spoon down. "Maybe you should leave tonight, instead of waiting 'til morning."

"Why? Did you tell him to come early? Do you do it in our bed, Anne? Our bed?"

"Don't you judge me! I told you what I wanted out of life. I told you."

"Yeah," he snorted derisively, "London. Paris."

"That's right!" she shrieked, crossing over to him. "And what's so wrong with that?"

"What's wrong with it is that you married *me*, knowing full well that I liked being a Wells Fargo agent.

Like your father."

"My father! My father! All he ever talks about is you! He loves you like a son. You can't do anything wrong. I even told him about the cellar and . . ."

His eyes narrowed to slits. "You did what?"

"Don't worry. He made excuses for you. Both of you, satisfied to live your dingy little lives going nowhere, doing nothing."

He sank into the chair by the kitchen table. "Then maybe it's time we end this farce we call our marriage," he said, his voice now gentle. "Get on with our separate lives. We're not doing each other any good at all this way."

"You'd like that, wouldn't you? Disgracing me with a divorce."

"Why did you ever ask me to marry you?"

She wiped the tears from her eyes. "My friends were so jealous. You are a handsome man, Travis."

He stepped over to her, lifting her chin with his hand. "It's time we put an end to a three year mistake, Annie."

"But what would I do?"

"I'm sure your father . . ."

"My father. My God, he'd side with you. I would be the failure. He'd never forgive me." She threw her arms around him. "I'm sorry, Travis. Please, let's try again. Please?"

Her hands caressed him, stroked him, made him forget, for the night at least, that nothing had changed.

"It'll be all right, Travis," she said, kissing him good-bye that morning. "You'll see."

His Wells Fargo assignment kept him away from San Francisco far longer than he had intended. A series of robberies back east had all the earmarks of an inside job. It took him three months to uncover the

276

thief and his network of informants.

During that time he'd written frequently to Anne, though he'd gotten few responses. He attributed it to her usual complaint that she didn't have anything to do. But he found out differently when he arrived home.

Dan greeted him with a whoop of welcome at the office. "Boy, am I glad to see you. I was beginning to think Annie would have the baby before you ever . . ."

"The what?" he shouted, grabbing Dan by the shoulders. "The what?"

"She made me promise not to tell you in my letters," Dan laughed, "but she didn't say anything about not telling you to your face. Ah, I'm so happy, Travis."

"Why didn't she tell me?"

"Didn't want to worry you when you were so far away, I suppose. Well, go on with you. Get home and see your wife! Say hello to her for me. Just got back in town myself today. Haven't seen her for over a week."

Pregnant. He couldn't believe it. All of the past animosities between them faded, disappeared. He was going to be a father, have a real family.

He swung open the door, tearing from room to room, looking for her, calling her name. He found her in bed.

"Annie, your father told me about . . ." He stopped, staring at her. Her eyes were glazed, dull. "What the hell?"

"Hello, Travis." Her words slurred.

He stooped down beside the bed, lifting the empty whiskey bottle, waving it in front of her face. "Drunk? Why? Does your father know about this?"

"Of course not," she mumbled. "I only did it this morning."

"Why?"

"I'm going to have a baby."

"I know that." He sat down beside her, his temper under tight rein. "Why are you drunk?"

"I knew you'd be home today."

"That's not an answer."

"It is for me." Tears flooded her blue eyes. "Look at me! Look at me!" She slapped the slight swell of her abdomen. "Look what you've done to me. I'm hideous."

"You're pregnant." He reached for her, but she pushed his hand away.

"Don't touch me. Don't ever touch me again."

"Annie, it's going to be all right. We'll have a beautiful baby."

"Get out of here. Just get out."

He didn't move.

"It must have been that last night," she said. "I was always so careful. But that last night, you threatened to divorce me and I couldn't let you disgrace me like that."

She wasn't making any sense. Scarcely believing what he'd come home to, he stood up and tried to put some order back into the bedroom. Clothes were strewn about as though she had torn them from the bureaus in a rage. As he worked his way through the layers, he found two more empty whiskey bottles. A muscle in his jaw jumped. But the anger was as much for himself as for her. He should have been here for her.

When he'd finished cleaning up, he heated some soup and tried to get her to eat a little.

"I'm sorry, Travis," she whimpered. "You were right. You shouldn't have married me."

He set the soup on the table and gathered her to him. "It's all right. Everything will be all right. I'm home now. And I'm going to stay home until you have the baby."

He got her settled, got her to sleep, then slumped into a kitchen chair to think. A baby. What had she said? That last night? The last night he was home? He counted back. It could well have been that night that produced their child.

A boy or a girl? he mused, getting used to the idea very quickly. A dull thump from their bedroom caught his attention. Frowning, he walked quietly to the door, not wanting to disturb her if she was still asleep. He nudged it open a tiny slit and peered inside.

She was leaning out of the bed, trying to get something out of the drawer of the nightstand. A small packet of brown paper. He stared, disbelieving as she ripped open the paper and emptied the packet's contents into her mouth.

"What the hell is that?" he demanded, shoving the door open and storming inside.

She crumpled it into her fist, trying to keep it from him, but he unwrapped her hand and inspected the paper. A trace of a pale powdery substance remained. He wet his finger, touched the paper, then touched his finger to his tongue. He breathed a shuddering sigh of relief. It was not what he had at first feared. It was not opium.

"What the hell is this stuff?"

"It doesn't matter."

"It does matter. What is this? How do you know it won't hurt you or the baby?"

"He said it wouldn't."

"Who said?"

"Fr . . . nobody."

His jaw clenched. "All right, at least tell me what you're taking it for. Is it some sort of medicine?"

"It's too late." Tears trickled down her pale cheeks. "I didn't take it that last night you were home. I didn't take it. I forgot."

He gripped her arms savagely, his battle with his temper lost. "You tell me what the hell you're talking about. And tell me now."

She laughed, a strange sick laugh that sent a chill clear through him. "Don't you see?" She struck her stomach with her fist. "Just look at me. My beautiful body is ruined forever."

"Your beautiful body will be back after the baby is born. In fact, I think you're even more beautiful now."

"Of course you'd say that, with your brat inside me."

He stiffened. "Be careful, Anne."

"I already wasn't careful," she hissed. "Can't you see that? He told me I had to take it every day or it wouldn't work."

"The powder?"

She nodded.

"Just what was it supposed to do?" He heard himself asking, though he knew he didn't want to know the answer.

"It was supposed to prevent *this*!" She pushed at her middle. "This brat!"

"You were taking something to keep from getting pregnant? What kind of . . . ?"

"He knows herbs. He knows their magic."

"Who? Damn you, who?"

She was still too drunk, still rambling. "I didn't take it that night. Didn't take it. How can I go to parties looking like this? How can I go to Paris?"

He took a long breath. Whatever had been happening, it wasn't going to happen any more. He was going to be home, keeping an eye on her night and day. He gathered up all the liquor, tore the house apart searching for any more of that powder, then threw all of it out.

The first three days were hard. She spent a lot of time screaming and being sick to her stomach. He'd had to make certain Dan didn't come near the house. After that, she improved steadily, even to seeming to accept being a mother.

"I'm such a burden, Travis," she murmured, as he changed the bedsheets for the third time in a day.

"It's all right, Annie. You're a lot better than you were. You'll be fine. The baby will be fine."

"Why don't you just go on to work today?"

"Your father is very pleased with how well I'm taking care of you. He assures me my job is secure until after the baby is born."

"Really, Travis," she said, affecting that lovely pout he knew so well, "you've been positively wearing yourself out with me. I want you to go to work. And, to be honest, I'd like some time alone. I have some reading to do, some sewing. I'll be fine."

"You're sure?"

"Positive."

He'd left her alone, but only for an hour, coming back to find her contentedly finishing a sampler she'd started some weeks before. "I told you I'd be fine," she smiled.

He smiled too, beginning to feel that everything was going to work out after all. She was getting on so well, in fact, that he even accepted an assignment to ride shotgun on a stage. He would be gone for four days. She had insisted he go and not worry.

"But your father's in Tucson, I don't like . . ."

"I'll be all right. Please. It's time I started accepting a little responsibility for this child."

It was well past dark when he started toward home that final night. He was a day early. He would surprise her with the gold necklace he'd bought from a jewelry salesman he'd met on the stage.

With only a mile to go, he jerked the horse to a halt. Apprehension washed over him like a death shroud.

281

Something was terribly wrong. Spurring the horse into a reckless gallop, he raced down the darkened streets.

He slammed through the door. "Annie! Annie!"

Silence.

He took the stairs two at a time. "Annie!" He burst into the bedroom. The bed was empty. He turned to leave, but a barely audible moan stopped him. Bolting around the bed, he found her, huddled on the floor in a pool of spreading blood.

He winced at the pathetic whimper that greeted him, as he lifted her and laid her gently on the bed. Her face was as pale as the sheets beneath her. Over and over he cursed himself. He never should have left her. Never.

He eased off nightgown, pulling the blankets . . . He stared at her belly. It was no longer distended. The blood on the floor. No. No. He forced himself to look.

In all of his life he would never forget the naked little figure curled on the floor at the foot of the bed. My God, he could have stepped on . . . Gently, he turned the baby, the umbilical cord and placenta still attached to its tiny blue body. All no bigger than his fist. A girl. His daughter. His hands shook, his eyes blurring. The body was cold and stiff.

Anne's cry brought him back to the needs of the living. He would grieve later. "It's all right, Annie," he soothed, stroking her forehead. "It's all right." He swiped the wetness from his eyes.

Quickly he left the room, returning with clean cloths and cold water. He bathed Anne's body, pressing a cold, wet cloth between her thighs to try and stem the awful bleeding. He knew little of these things, but knew the amount of blood on the floor and now on the bed was dangerously excessive. When he had her settled, he bundled the tiny body of his child into a small yellow blanket knitted by a thoughtful neighbor.

He cleaned himself up, then lay down on the bed beside his wife. She was so cold, so pale. He held her gently, trying to give her the warmth of his own body. He'd caught the attention of one of his neighbor's youngsters, and sent the boy for the doctor. The man should be here soon.

"We'll have other babies. We will." His voice was choked, but he kissed her tenderly, hoping to encourage her to get well, to not let what had happened rob her of her will to live. God, he should have been here. She must have been scared to death, enduring a miscarriage all alone.

Her breathing grew more shallow, rasping. He bolted out of bed at the sound of a knock on the door downstairs.

"Hurry, doctor!" He practically dragged the man up the stairs to the bedroom. But the medical man made him stay outside, pacing the hallway, while he examined Anne.

He stepped out, his weathered face grim. "I'm sorry, Mr. Hawke. There's nothing . . ."

"No!" He grabbed the man by the lapels of his jacket and shook him violently. "No! You're lying."

"Please, Mr. Hawke. You'll only make things worse by . . ."

Hawke released the man, hurrying back into the bedroom to be with Anne. She couldn't die. She couldn't. Everyone he'd ever loved. Everyone who'd ever loved him had died.

He was on his knees beside the bed. He lifted her hand, holding it against his cheek. It already seemed unnaturally cold.

The doctor stepped into the room. "I'll be leaving, Mr. Hawke. There's nothing more I can do here." He crossed to the bed. "It's just nature's way sometimes."

Hawke trembled. "Thank you for your help."

"I'm very sorry."

Hawke did not see the man out. He remained at Anne's bedside. "At least open your eyes so we can say good-bye to each other," he whispered.

Her breathing grew even more difficult. She gripped her stomach, moaning feebly. Her eyes fluttered open. "Travis?"

"Right here."

"The baby?"

"Just try to rest, Annie. Try . . ."

She was mumbling, incoherent. He had to lean close to hear, to understand. The words. He stood straight up, his heart turning to stone.

He left the house, sending a neighbor to stay with her until she died three hours later. He wasn't there. He was in a saloon, getting drunk. He stayed that way for three months.

He flung back his blankets, climbing to his feet. That was all he needed, to remember those final minutes with Anne. Damn her to hell anyway! How could she? How?

Dan had been devastated by her death. But he'd never learned the truth of it. Hawke had had to carry that alone.

But when Dan had made a connection between Anne and Frank Blanchard, Hawke couldn't chance Dan going after the man and learning the truth. So Hawke had agreed to do it for him. Blanchard would pay for that night, just as Anne had unwittingly paid.

Right now, though, his main concern had to be getting Kate to trust him again. And that, he knew, was not going to be easy. But it had to be done. The net was closing on Blanchard. McCullough Freight Company was going to play a big part in his downfall.

In the end, he supposed, that would make Kate happy, though she would never forgive him for using her, not telling her.

He saddled his horse, thinking of Kate, thinking of how she would hate him. Hate him.

He would be free then. Free to lead the emotionless life he had set for himself since Anne died. Free.

He kneed the horse into a ground-eating trot. Free.

Then why did he feel suddenly, as though he'd just locked the door to his own prison and thrown away the key?

Chapter Twenty

Kate studied the ribbon of wagons from her perch high atop the bluff. They were all rolling along smoothly, from Rafe's lead wagon to Dusty's trailing explosives wagon. Smoothly, so damned smoothly. She grimaced. Couldn't a wheel fall off one of them? Except Dusty's of course. Or a dust storm blow up? She'd settle for a stampede. Anything to keep her busy, anything to keep her from thinking about Travis Hawke.

The bastard!

He'd been in her thoughts constantly since he'd ridden away from Elm Creek almost a week ago. In her mind she was convinced he'd halted his plan to strangle her only because he had heard the approaching wagons. In her heart . . . well, as usual, where Hawke was concerned, that was another matter altogether.

It was insane. But still she loved him. Even if she couldn't trust him. She didn't want to believe he could hurt her, ruin her company for Frank Blanchard. But neither could she forget the clandestine conversation the two men had shared. And Hawke himself would never open up to her, not completely. He shared bits and pieces of his life, more often by accident than not, then he would shut her out.

Furious, she slapped her hand on the pommel, the action so startling her mare that the animal shied violently. Kate brought the horse under control, cursing in earnest. "Damn you, Hawke. Even when you're not here, you are."

She scanned the rocky countryside. It was almost as if she could feel him watching her.

Shrugging off the ridiculous notion, she gigged the horse down the steep embankment, reaching the bottom just as Dusty's wagon lumbered past.

"You all right, Katie? You been keepin' to yourself fer near a week now."

"I'm fine. Just getting used to being a wagonmaster."

"I knew the damned reb would desert ye. Just like a . . ."

"How's the dynamite?" she interrupted, not wanting to get into a discussion about Hawke.

"Ain't blowed me to kingdom come yet."

She heard the dull roar from somewhere above and behind her.

"Katie, get out of the way!"

She dove for cover, just as a massive pile of rocks thundered past her. From behind a boulder she covered her ears, waiting for the explosion that would end her life. None came. When she dared start breathing again, she peered over the rock to see that the slide had missed the rear of Dusty's wagon by less than eight feet.

The second miracle was that the oxen had not spooked. They maintained their plodding pace, even as Dusty scrambled over the rocks to get to her.

"You all right?" he shouted.

"I'm fine." She slapped the dirt from her buckskins. "How about you?"

"I'm counting my arms and legs to be sure."

More rocks, smaller than those in the slide, rained

down from the bluff. Kate whirled, casting a glance up the steep slope. A horseman was urging his chestnut gelding down the embankment at a dangerous speed. Hawke.

"What the hell happened?" he demanded, leaping from the horse's back and striding over to her.

Kate looked at him, then looked at the direction from which he'd come — the same direction from which the rockslide had come. "Why don't *you* tell *me*?"

"What's that supposed to mean?"

"It means you were trying again, you low lying son-of-a-snake!"

"I'm real glad to see you too, Kate," he said, his voice husky.

"I don't know why you come back, reb," Dusty put in, "but you can see Kate don't want you around. So why don't you do everybody a favor and get back on your horse and ride out of here."

"Kate and I have something to talk about first." He stepped closer to her, casting a hard glance at Dusty. "Alone."

"I don't want to be alone with you," she said. "I like living."

"Kate," he interrupted evenly, "if I wanted you dead, you'd be dead. Like yesterday, when you stopped by the stream to water your horse. Or three days ago, when you took that bath in the creek. That was especially interesting, the way you . . ."

"Maybe you'd best go, Dusty," she said quickly. When her uncle looked doubtful, she added, "Please?"

Grumbling, he went back to his wagon, heading it up to continue after the others.

Katie turned on Hawke. "You saw me at the creek! You dared do that! You . . ." She threw a punch at him, but he saw it coming and ducked out of the way.

She swung wildly again, and he gripped her around

288

the waist from behind. "You beast! You pervert! You peeping tom!" In spite of her words, her skin tingled just to think that he had been watching. Had she even somehow known he was there? She remembered how she'd allowed the soap to linger on her breasts, circling her nipples. Damn, oh, damn him.

"You behave," he gritted against her ear, "and I'll let you go. You don't, and I may be tempted to take you over my knee again."

"You do, and my hand to God, I'll take you over mine!"

He chuckled. "Does that mean you're going to calm down and let me talk to you?"

She let herself go limp. His arms remained tense around her for several more seconds, then he must have decided to trust her. He loosened his grip.

She whirled, arcing her fist toward his face, but stopped the blow before it landed. He had made no move to defend himself this time, and she was suddenly loathe to break his jaw. Not that she intended to let him know that. Rubbing her hand, she glared at him. "I wouldn't want to hurt myself on that ugly face of yours."

He grinned. "So now we can talk?"

"I didn't say that. We've got nothing to say to each other."

"Kate, I did not try to kill you by Elm Creek."

"Oh? Then whose hands were those around my neck? Frank Blanchard's?"

"I was not trying to choke you, damnit. I was just . . . thinking about something I shouldn't have."

"Oh, please! Do you think I was born under a buffalo chip?"

He tried very hard, but the image was simply too absurd. He burst out laughing.

"Don't you laugh at me."

289

"I could do a lot of things with you, Kate," he said, still highly amused, "but I could never laugh at you."

She crossed her arms in front of her. "Why did you come back here?"

"I told you. To talk to you."

"Fine. You've talked. Now leave."

He stepped up to her, lifting her chin with his hand. "I did not try to kill you. I . . . ," he paused, groping, she sensed, for words that were intensely difficult for him to say, "I've never known anyone like you. Damnit, I like you."

She raised the back of her hand to her forehead. "I feel positively faint. Travis Hawke likes me." Her eyes turned heavenward. "You can take me now, Lord," she cried. "My life is complete. Travis Hawke likes me."

His lips drew into a grim line. "I said I'd never laugh at you. But I can see that hasn't stopped you from laughing at me."

She blew out a long breath. "I'm not laughing at you, Hawke. That is, if I am, I don't mean to. I know it wasn't easy for you to admit you like me. Though heaven knows, I don't see how could help yourself. I am, after all, a truly wonderful person." She batted her eyelashes at him. "Feminine, dainty, refined . . ."

"Nauseating." He pulled her into his arms, planting a hard kiss on her mouth.

Oh, how she had missed him. If she hadn't known it before, she knew it now. She opened her mouth, giving him free access, loving him just as she'd done five years ago. He hadn't tried to kill her. He hadn't. He couldn't. Nothing was so right in her life as when she was in this man's arms.

He stroked her hair, holding her against him. "Am I still your wagonmaster?"

"Do I have to sleep with you again if you are?"

"You have to sleep with me again, whether I am or

not." Damn, she was a sorceress. What else but a spell could make him do what he had sworn never to do again? To care. Care, yes, he assured himself, but not love. He dared not love her. She would die if he did, just as all the others . . .

A gunshot sent them scrambling for cover. Kate stuck her head up over the rock long enough to see a band of half dozen men swarming down toward the wagons.

"They'll pick off the drivers one by one!" she shouted.

"Stay down!" Hawke growled.

"Those men are my friends." She jerked away from him, running toward her horse. But he caught up with her, spinning her around.

"Let me handle it. This is part of what you hired me for."

"All right, all right. Do something!"

He leaped into the saddle and thundered toward the outlaws, who had launched their assault on the middle of the train. The bullwhackers were driving the wagons into a circular defense, but two drivers were already down.

"Dusty," Kate murmured, watching her adopted uncle maneuver his wagon away from the others. He would not risk the lives of his fellow bullwhackers, even if it cost him his own. If any of those bullets hit the dynamite . . .

She swung into the saddle and slammed her heels into the mare's sides, heading toward him. "Dusty, come on!" she shouted, holding out a hand, urging him to jump up behind her. "I'll get you over to the other wagons."

"Can't leave this one, lass!"

She reined in, jumping down beside him. "The hell with the wagon! One bullet and we're the biggest buffalo wallow this side of the Missouri."

"Lose this wagon, we lose McCullough Freight." He grabbed Kate and dragged her under the wagon with him as a bullet zinged too close to home.

"Better the company than you," she said. Most of the outlaws were attacking the main body of wagons, now circled and waiting. But one of their number had spied Dusty's lone wagon and was heading toward it at a full gallop. His rifle kicked up dirt to the right and left of where she lay. Fuming, she yanked her pistol from its holster and took aim. She squeezed off a shot, just as the rifle seemed pointed straight for her head.

The gunman's arm went slack as he tumbled from the saddle. His horse skidded to a halt near the wagon.

"Come on," Kate urged. "Get his horse. We've got to help the others."

"I ain't leavin' this wagon."

"You stubborn old coot, don't you go gettin' addle-brained on me now. What sense does it make to stay here?"

"Don't you call me names, Miss Smart Britches. This is my wagon, I'm stayin' with it."

"Then I'm staying, too." She lay flat out on her stomach, shoving her gun through the spokes of the rear wheel. The sounds of gunfire near the other wagons was sporadic now. The outlaws had abandoned their horses, settling in behind various boulders for a long siege. Kate could only stare in horror as another teamster fell.

"Damn, Dusty, there's nothing we can do here."

"Nothin' we can do there either. At least from here we can make it two more guns comin' at 'em from a different direction."

Two more guns. Two more guns. Kate slammed a hand on the dirt. "It's going to be a helluva lot more than two more guns, Dusty Lafferty. A helluva lot

292

more."

She crawled her way toward the rear end of the wagon, then climbed to her feet, careful to keep her head down. Jerking loose the tie-down rope, she threw back the tarpaulin that covered the cargo. With extreme care she opened one of the crates, extracting several brown cylindrical objects.

"Kate, you ain't thinking what I think you're thinking?" Dusty grinned.

"You bet I am, Dusty. Those jackasses are about to be part of an army experiment. They're going to eat dynamite!"

Chapter Twenty-one

Kate stuffed six sticks of dynamite into the waistband of her pants. She was adding the fuses to her pockets when she heard Dusty's shout.

"That danged reb's gonna get hisself kilt comin' over here."

Kate peered around the wagon's right side to see Hawke pounding toward them. He rode low in the saddle, but the outlaws' bullets whizzed dangerously close. If one of them didn't kill him outright, she could envision one taking down the horse, catapulting Hawke forward and breaking his fool neck.

She held her breath, helpless to do anything but watch. Miraculously, no bullet touched Hawke or his mount. Instead, he nearly set his gelding on its haunches as he reined in behind the wagon. Leaping from the animal's back, he strode straight toward Kate.

"What the hell are you doing by this death trap? We've been waiting to lay down a cover fire for . . ." He stopped dead, staring at the dynamite tucked into her pants. "Now I know you're crazy," he said softly.

"Name a faster way to get those outlaws running back to wherever they came from."

"Give me that stuff. I'll take care of the outlaws."

"No. It's my company, my problem."

"You hired me. That makes it my problem."

She turned her back on him, never more torn in her life. What if it was all a lie? Those were Blanchard's men in the rocks, she was certain of it. Hawke could be in on this whole thing. If she gave up the dynamite to him, she could be giving up McCullough Freight.

"Dusty, what should I do? What would Pa have done?"

"I can't answer that, lass." The grizzled teamster retied the tarp on the wagon. "You been doin' a fine job, but you know how I feel about the reb."

"Damnit, Dusty, this is no time for . . ." She clamped her jaw shut. This was no time for yelling at Dusty. She turned back to Hawke. "All right, what do we do?"

"Not we. Me."

"I go with you or you don't go."

He swore, lifting his hat to run a hand through his dark hair. "You win. We haven't got time to argue."

She waited as Hawke grabbed up a half dozen sticks of dynamite, then followed him to his gelding. He inserted a fuse in each stick.

"I'll get mounted," he said, "then pull you up behind me."

"You ride out of here without me," she hissed, drawing her pistol, "and I'll be on my mare faster than the bullet that'll be heading for your butt."

"Damn, but you are a subtle woman." He vaulted into the saddle, then leaned over and hauled her up behind him. "Promise me you won't get yourself killed," he said.

"Oh, I won't. You and I still have too much to talk about. Like Frank Blanchard and your connection to him, that sort of thing."

"You're riding with me? When you still think I'm working for the man who wants to take over your company?"

"Maybe I'm about to find out for certain."

She wrapped her arms around his waist, as he gigged the horse forward. He headed the gelding along a trail that would skirt the rocks, and hopefully bring them up on the outlaws from behind.

In spite of the very real danger they faced, Kate felt herself grow warm as she pressed her face against Hawke's back. If it weren't for the danger to the teamsters, she wouldn't have minded at all if he reined the horse over behind a tree and made love to her again.

A bullet gouged a furrow in the dirt just ahead of them. "Looks like they've spotted us," Hawke said. He spurred the horse faster, rounding the base of the hill.

Kate breathed a relieved sigh into Hawke's shirt. They were out of the line of fire, at least for the moment.

Hawke jerked the horse to a halt. Kate slid off over the horse's rump, running for cover behind a huge boulder. Hawke let the reins trail on the gelding, then followed her.

"They're not firing at the wagons so much now," she noted.

"This whole attack doesn't make any sense."

"What do you mean? Blanchard wants my company, so he's trying to make sure I don't fulfill my contract with the army."

"But Blanchard would want . . ."

A bullet slammed into the front of the boulder.

Hawke cursed, shoving her head down.

"I can take care of myself," she snapped, tugging one of the sticks of dynamite free of her pants and inserting a fuse. "It's time I gave these boys a real sendoff."

"I am going to tie you to a tree, woman, if you don't

296

let me handle this." He jerked the dynamite away from her.

"Keep slamming that around, and neither one of us will have to worry about who's handling what."

"Why can't you be like other women?" He groped in his pocket for a match. "Docile . . . obedient . . ."

She bristled. "You make women sound like lap dogs. Next you'll be wantin' me to lie down and roll over."

His eyes gleamed wickedly, as he studied her womanly curves. "I may have to see if I can teach you a few tricks at that."

She slapped at his arm, then reflexively grabbed for the dynamite as the movement jostled it free of his grip. She collapsed back against the rock, horrified at what had almost happened. "I think you and I had better postpone our disagreements until after we dispose of these outlaws. Or we're going to end up disposing of ourselves."

"Agreed, now stay here." Giving her no time to argue, he hunched low and hurried forward toward a boulder some twenty yards away.

Kate gasped as bullets ripped by all around him. But he made it to the other rock untouched by any of them. The next boulder was thirty yards away. From that one he should be able to toss the dynamite near enough to the outlaws to cause some real damage. She tried hard to do as he asked. To stay behind and wait. But when she saw him edge around the second boulder heading for the third, she used the distraction to get herself to the second boulder.

She held her hand to her chest, breathing hard. No bullets had been fired at her. Either the outlaws in concentrating on Hawke hadn't noticed her, or had viewed her as no threat. She frowned, the latter thought incensing her, then she peered around the side of the rock to see how Hawke was doing.

297

"Be careful," she whispered, watching him touch a lighted match to a fuse. She was about to find out what this dynamite stuff was all about.

The fuse caught, fire sparking along its length at what Kate considered an alarming speed. Still Hawke had not released it. "Throw it," she hissed, even knowing he couldn't hear her.

He watched the fuse until she could have sworn it was barely an inch from burning into the dynamite. "Hawke, please . . ." she whispered.

He stood up, arcing it high up the hillside, then ducking instantly back behind the boulder. Three seconds later a deafening roar sent dirt and chunks of rock raining over a hundred square foot area. Kate covered her head, but still managed to peek out to see that the dynamite had disposed of two of the remaining five outlaws. She grinned to see her teamsters hooting and hollering down in their circle of wagons. The tide had definitely just been turned.

Hawke was lighting another fuse. One of the outlaws bolted for his horse, evidently having had enough of this particular battle. Kate cocked her pistol, but the man was beyond the range of the small gun. "Probably running to tell Blanchard he's been outmatched."

She smiled. Hawke could not possibly be working for the man and throwing dynamite at his men at the same time.

The last two outlaws were not as eager to leave. One was pumping bullets in the direction of the wagons, the other at Hawke. The gunmen stood no chance now.

"Give it up," Hawke called. "Throw down your guns."

Their answer was more bullets.

Kate shook her head. She had to give Blanchard credit. He sure found himself a loyal bunch of hardcases. He must be paying them a fortune.

Hawke lit the fuse on a second stick of dynamite. Again Kate's heart pounded as he let it burn down. She guessed that if he threw it too soon, the outlaws might have a chance to pick it up and throw it back. More seconds passed, until at last he leaned away from the rock, ready to hurl the deadly cylinder up the hill.

In that instant, the outlaw whom Kate had thought had made a run for it, came over the hill to her left, firing at Hawke's back. Out of the corner of her eye Kate saw Hawke fall, even as her own bullet ripped through the outlaw's chest. He collapsed forward, dead, but Kate didn't notice. She was tearing toward Hawke, the lighted stick of dynamite six inches from his unmoving hand.

Chapter Twenty-two

Bullets whipped past Kate as she plunged toward Hawke. All she knew, all she cared about was getting her hands on that dynamite. If it went off he would die.

The thought that he might already be dead did not enter her head.

As she ran the bullwhackers began to lay down a deadly cover fire, keeping the outlaws at bay. The dynamite. It was her only thought.

Somewhere her mind gauged what was left of the fuse as she lifted it off the ground. A heartbeat. It would go off in the space of a heartbeat. Using every ounce of strength she possessed she heaved it up the hillside, then dropped her body on top of Hawke's.

The dynamite must have exploded in mid-air. The force of the concussion drove the breath from her lungs. She was aware of nothing else until she felt several pairs of hands lifting her away from Hawke.

"No, I have to see to him," she mumbled.

"It's all right, Katie." Rafe's voice.

"Take it easy, lass." Dusty.

She struggled to sit up, trying to rub away the throbbing knot in the back of her head. "Hawke . . ."

"Just take it easy," Dusty soothed, holding a canteen of water to her lips. She drank greedily, then looked around. Most of the bullwhackers were there. She caught the fragments of several sentences, none of which made too much sense to her groggy mind.

"Never seen the like . . ."

"Kate and that dynamite . . ."

"Too bad about . . ."

"Bury him by the . . ."

She shook her head, ignoring the pain, striving desperately to collect her senses. "Rafe . . . Rafe . . ."

He hunkered down beside her. "Right here, Kate."

"Hawke. Please, tell me, he's all right."

Instead he said nothing, taking her hand and leading her toward a huge boulder. He pointed over to the side of it.

Forcing her legs to move, she walked toward it.

"I'll let him tell you himself," Rafe grinned, then left.

Kate broke into a run, careening around the side of the rock. She skidded to a halt, hardly daring to believe what her eyes assured her was the truth. Hawke was sitting up, his back propped against the rock, holding a bloody cloth against the side of his head.

Before she could move, Rafe was back at her side with a bottle of whiskey and some clean cloths. "I think he could use these."

She accepted them gratefully. "You and Dusty can take care of things for awhile, can't you?"

"Take as long as you like," Rafe said gently.

She knelt beside Hawke. "Are you all right?" she asked shakily.

He nodded, studying her with that odd scrutiny that could so unsettle her. "Thanks to you. Again."

She shrugged, feeling self-conscious all at once. "Can I help you with that?" She gestured toward the wound.

He let the bloody make-shift bandage fall to his lap. "I'm all yours."

I wish, Kate thought, but said, "It doesn't look too bad. Kind of a deep gash, but it should be all right." Why did he keep looking at her like that? Nervously, she uncorked the whiskey bottle, turning a little of its amber contents onto one of the cloths Rafe had brought her. Then she spilled more of it onto her lap. Grimacing, she slapped the cork back in and set the bottle down. "Hold still."

"You're not going to . . ." He sucked in a lungful of air as the alcohol came in contact with his raw, bleeding flesh. For several seconds he sat rigidly still, breathing through clenched teeth. "Damnit," he hissed at last, "you did that on purpose."

"It's not my fault you used your head to stop a bullet," she snapped, glad to get things back to normal between them. The look in his eyes had positively made her quiver. For a minute there she had almost been able to believe that he felt something for her, something more than physical desire.

"Damn, you are an exasperating woman."

"And you're a son-of-a-bitch."

"When are you going to clean up that mouth of yours?"

She reached into her pocket and extracted her chaw of tobacco. She bit off a chunk. "Clean enough for you?"

He chuckled. "Just keep in mind that I'm not going to kiss you as long as you have a mouthful of that stuff."

"And who asked you to kiss me?" She spat a mouthful of juice just inches from his boot.

"I'll remember you said that."

"Yeah, and I remember something you said." She watched his eyes as she spoke. "You said this attack

302

these outlaws made on my wagons didn't make any sense. Why?"

"You figure it was Blanchard's men, right?"

"Who else?"

"Exactly. But it just seems more reasonable to me that he would wait until your return trip to Leavenworth before he makes his move."

"Now why the hell would he have to wait?"

"He doesn't *have* to. It just makes more sense." He winced as he shifted to sit up a little straighter. Kate felt as if the pain lanced through her own body, but she found her doubts about his loyalty returning. How would he know what made more sense to Frank Blanchard?

"He takes over McCullough Freight if I don't make this shipment on time."

"That's one way," Hawke agreed. "But he also takes over if you don't pay your note on time."

"So?"

"So why not let you make the shipment, get paid for it, and then rob you of the money on the way back to Leavenworth? You don't make the note, which gives Blanchard the company. But you have fulfilled the army contract, which gives Blanchard control of all McCullough Freight's agreements with the military."

She sat there digesting what Hawke had said. It all made perfect sense. "Too bad Frank's not as smart as you."

His brows furrowed.

"He did attack the wagons."

"But only with six men. Maybe he meant it more as a nuisance raid than to really put you out of business here and now."

"Or put me off guard, thinking we'd beaten him off." She spat out her tobacco, wiping her mouth with her handkerchief. "I'm really getting so I don't like that

303

stuff too much any more."

He grinned. "Better watch it. You might turn into a lady."

She took a swig of whiskey, swishing it through her mouth to rinse out the last of the tobacco. Then she spit out the whiskey. "Not if I can help it." She leaned over him, checking the wound. "Bleeding's stopped. But don't make any sudden moves, or it'll start right up again."

"Then I guess I'd better not grab you and give you that kiss you said you didn't want earlier."

She put her hand on his cheek, brushing her fingertips over the prickly dark stubble. "Why do you know Frank Blanchard?"

He shifted his gaze to the hillside. "Why did it take you so long to ask?"

"I guess I was afraid of the answer."

"You're not any more?"

"Not after you threw dynamite on his hired thugs today."

She scarcely noticed the rumblings of the wagons getting underway as she waited for Hawke's answer. He wasn't ready to travel yet anyway. They could catch up with the train tomorrow. Or the next day. She watched those midnight eyes grow dark with desire. Or maybe even the next. Her hand glided under his shirt. "Tell me how you know Blanchard."

His heart pounded beneath her palm. She prayed he wasn't going to lie, not again. But his words made her wish that he had.

"He killed my wife."

Her mouth fell open. "He did what?"

"You asked. I told you. I don't want to talk about it."

"You can't tell me something like that and then say you don't want to talk about it."

"I can, and I did. So drop it."

"Hawke . . ."

He climbed to his feet, swaying slightly before he righted himself. "I'll tell you this much. I want Blanchard as much or more than you do. Don't ask me any more than that, Kate. Not now."

She stood up and wrapped her arms around him, understanding at last some part of his pain. "Make love to me, Hawke."

He held her to him, kissing her hair. "I think it'd be best if we didn't."

"Please?"

He groaned and cursed at the same time. "Kate, you don't know anything about me."

"You keep telling me that. But I know more than you think." Her lips brushed his. Her hands moved over him, touching him, arousing him.

"Damn you."

"Love me, Hawke. Love me." She lay down behind the rock, pulling him down beside her. "Love me."

"I can't love you. I can't love anyone. Don't you understand?" But he made only a half-hearted attempt to pull away from her.

She urged him to lie back, allowing her to take the lead. She undressed him, slowly, sensually, caressing every part of him until he was tense and hard and ready to take her.

"Damn you, Kate," he rasped, pulling her on top of him. "I don't want to hurt you."

"Then don't."

"You don't know . . . you don't know . . ."

She silenced him with a kiss. And then nothing mattered but the having, the touching, the knowing.

He would hurt her. Yes, he would hurt her. Because one day he would leave her. But for now, for this moment, he was hers.

* * *

Perhaps the openness of the plains contributed to the new openness he displayed toward her in the days that followed. Rafe had said Hawke was playing with her when he'd hauled her over his knee. She had had her doubts. But now, watching him stride toward her, silhouetted against the rose-tinted horizon of descending dusk, she had reason to reconsider.

The grin he gave her disarmed her utterly, replete as it was with its usual casual arrogance, along with a new quality, a boyish uncertainty that snared her heart. Her gaze settled on his right arm, which was visible only from shoulder to elbow. From elbow to fingertip he held the arm locked behind his back.

"What are you hiding?" she demanded.

He shrugged. "A rattler?"

She toed the dirt in front of her, feigning a total lack of interest. But he read her mind and sidestepped quickly to his left as she lunged toward him, grabbed at his arm and missed. She planted her hands on her hips. "All right, don't show me. I couldn't care less."

He slowly drew his right hand out in front of him. "I guess I'll have to give these to Rafe then."

Kate stared at the most profuse bouquet of buttercups she had ever seen, bright splashes of yellow and white dappled against feathery green leaves. "For me?" she whispered.

"You don't seem to want . . ."

She scooped them from his hand, holding them against her breasts. No one had ever given her flowers before. "They're wonderful."

"The yellow ones look like sunshine. They reminded me of you."

His gaze met hers and she could feel her cheeks flushing. She headed away from the trail, wading through knee-deep grass, stopping only when she'd put over three hundred yards between her and the nearest wagon. She grew warmer still, knowing that Hawke had followed. Turning, she faced him. "Why is it so hard for you to admit you care about me, just a little?" She prayed he didn't notice how hard she was trembling.

He surprised her by not ducking the question. "In the orphanage where I grew up, I learned early on not to say what I thought."

Holding on to her flowers with one hand, she gripped his wrist with the other and urged him to settle himself beside her on the ground. "There's no orphanage here, Hawke. And I very much want to know what you think of me."

"What I think doesn't matter. There's no future . . ."

It was his usual speech about why their relationship was doomed to failure, and she ignored it completely. Instead she arranged the buttercups stem to flower until they formed a circle of sunshine in the matted down grasses around them both. She held one back, stripping its leaves and poking the stem through the open buttonhole at the top of Hawke's shirt. Then she sat back on her heels, admiring her handiwork.

"Perfect," she murmured, unfastening the buttons of her own shirt. "A beautiful sunset, beautiful flowers and a beautiful man. What more could a woman want?" She turned in the direction of a delicate evening breeze, allowing it to tug at the open sides of her shirtfront. The material skated free, exposing her left breast to the burning hunger now achingly apparent in those midnight eyes.

"Damn, Kate, this is crazy." But his hand was already closing over the soft mound, urging the nipple to stiff erection. His mouth captured its twin, as he bore her down into the yielding grasses of the plains. "You could get pregnant," he rasped, desperate for logic to regain control of his lust, his need for this woman. He

307

watched her eyes as his words rippled through to her, unaware that he held his breath. But instead of the shock and fear, even disgust, he had expected, she only smiled. Her words sent a surging fire to his loins.

"Would you want me to have your baby, Hawke?" She tore at his belt buckle, shoving his pants past his hips. Her eyes wide and eager, she gripped the rock hard answer to her question. She tickled him, stroked him, then guided him to her welcoming softness, thoughts of babies, thoughts of anything but the awesome power of his possession gone from her mind.

She woke only once during the night, burrowing more deeply into the sheltering warmth of his arms. A baby? She'd never even allowed herself to think about the consequences of their lovemaking before. And though she was being a fool, she wasn't going to start now. Anyway, she had a feeling Hawke would do enough thinking for both of them. That he had at last found the excuse he needed to put an end to their relationship once and for all.

Chapter Twenty-three

Kate watched from the back of her mare as Dusty's wagon was floated across the Platte. The wide, muddy river was the last to be forded before the freighters reached Fort Laramie. Hawke had found them the perfect place to cross, avoiding the deadly, shifting sands on so much of the Platte's bottom.

The low banks on each side had made going in and coming out easier on man and beast than on any previous trip Kate could remember. She studied the river upstream and down, with its pygmy islands, sand bars, and sentinel trees rooted long distances apart on opposite sides. She could almost hear her father's booming voice. "The Platte's always the same, Katie—different."

Here and there along the banks she noticed the shattered wrecks of furniture, lost by pioneers moving west, when the current fought their wagons and won. Clawfoot tables, bureaus, even a once gleaming pianoforte lay rotting in the scorching sun. Bleaching bones of oxen, lost to the vagaries of the same current testified to crossings where the price to reach the Platte's opposite bank was death.

She straightened in the saddle as she caught sight of

Hawke riding toward her. Would there ever come a day when her heart didn't race just at the sight of him?

"Fit to cross today," he said, reining in beside her, "but never fit to drink."

Kate grinned. The men had spent the better part of an hour last night boiling Platte water and removing the scum from its surface, before they dared drink it. And that was after sifting out the minnows and tadpoles. Even then, Kate held her nose while quenching her thirst.

"We should be at Fort Laramie before dusk," he said. "How does it feel to have made it?"

"I'll let you know when I give the bill of lading to Lieutenant Parsons."

His gaze darkened, and she could only attribute its cause to her mentioning Parsons. She smiled inwardly, wondering if he could be jealous? But the look in his eyes dispelled her pleasure. Something was wrong. Whatever it was, she hoped it wouldn't spoil the warmth that had grown steadily between them ever since the outlaws had attacked the wagons two weeks ago.

Two weeks that had been the most wondrous of her life. Try as he might to end any but their professional relationship, on only one night of the last fourteen had they not made love. And that was because they had both been exhausted after a day-long battle with a dust storm. Even then she had fallen asleep cocooned in the warmth of his arms.

With a patience as foreign to her as lilac bath water to a hide hunter, she had gently coaxed from him bits of his life. The death of his parents, his long time later adoption by Nels Svenson, his year of drifting, though nothing of what he'd said had given her any particular insight into why he was so determined to be alone. When she had broached the subject of his wife, he had shut out her with tight-lipped fury. But if he allowed her enough time, she was certain she could fit the pieces together. When she understood why he lived the life he did, maybe, just maybe, she could find a way to share it with him.

"I suppose you're looking forward to seeing Parsons again," he said, as they reined their mounts into step just ahead of the lead wagon.

"You can say that after what we've had these last two weeks?"

Even so remote a bit of civilization as Fort Laramie was a threat to him. He could let the barriers down, however slightly, on the open trail, but get near other people and they were right back up again. Her anxiety increased as he continued.

"What we've had, Kate, has been a mistake on both our parts. You know it. I know it." He raised his hand as she made to interrupt. "Let me finish," he said, gripping her reins, halting both horses. He was obviously ill-at-ease, looking at the ground not at her, and though her heart seemed suddenly to have lodged in her throat, she let him continue.

"I'm not saying I'm sorry for what's happened, only that it shouldn't have happened. You've given me two weeks where for the first time in my life, I can say I was happy."

Kate felt the tears sting her eyes, but she blinked them away. She knew he was not finished, and now he did look at her.

"What I'm saying is it's over, Kate. It ends here."

"No!"

"I'm sorry."

"Sorry? Sorry! Damn you, you can't just . . ."

"It's done." He slammed his heels into the gelding's sides and rode away at a gallop, leaving her to stare after him in aching bewilderment. Why? Why? Everything had been going so well. He had not even resurrected the subject of her getting pregnant, though she suspected he often worried about it.

"Damn you, Travis Hawke," she called after him. "You're not going to get away with this." To herself, she repeated, "You're not."

But he stayed away from her even as they reached the fork of the North Platte and Laramie Rivers and approached the fort itself. She was left to invent her own reasons as to why he would try and end it. Time and again she came back to the one subject he would not discuss, not even a little. His dead wife. Did he still grieve for her? Or, she cringed as she remembered his chilling words when he told her she was dead. *I'm not sorry.* Was there some more sinister reason he wouldn't speak of her?

Whatever the reason, she would not allow herself to give up. He cared about her. He did. And some day, if she wore him down enough, she was going to get him to cave in and admit it.

For now she concentrated on the final few hundred feet to the fort. The timbered gates had been swung open and Rafe's wagon had already been guided inside. She gigged her horse up behind the burly bullwhacker and dismounted.

"Looks good after six weeks on the trail, don't it, Kate?"

"That it does," she said, allowing her gaze to travel along the many buildings housed within the fifteen foot adobe walls. Facing on the inner court were shops and sheds, as well as officers' row and the barracks for the enlisted men.

She hitch-tied her horse, noticing the uniformed figure hurrying across the parade grounds to greet her. All she wanted in the world was to be alone, to have a good cry over Hawke. Instead she forced a smile.

"Wade! It's good to see you!" She didn't have to turn to know that Hawke had come up behind her. When Parsons lifted her hand to his lips, she upgraded her smile to disarming.

"Ah, Kate," Parsons said, bowing low, "journeys end in lovers meeting. Every wise man's son doth know."

Kate kept her smile in place while she tried to decipher what in the world Parsons was talking about. Lovers? Sweet heaven. She wanted Hawke to be jealous, not ready to kill her.

She retrieved her hand, reaching into her pockets to extract the bill of lading. "Everything should be in order," she said. "Except that we're missing a couple of sticks of dynamite."

"I'm most pleased to hear that, Kate. I assured my commanding officer he'd have nothing to worry about with McCullough Freight handling the shipment." He paused. "You didn't have any trouble, did you?"

"None worth mentioning."

Hawke cleared his throat behind her.

"I'm not sure you remember my wagonmaster, Wade. Travis Hawke."

"Of course," Parsons said, extending his right hand, his manner suddenly cold if not hostile.

Hawke hesitated before shaking Parsons's hand, his gaze shifting between Kate and Parsons. "You'll see that Miss McCullough is paid at once, of course. We'll be starting back tomorrow morning."

"Tomorrow?" Kate blurted. "We've got three weeks to be back in Leavenworth to pay off Blanchard's note. On horseback we could make it in seventeen days if we had to."

Hawke stiffened, and she knew he was angry that she'd questioned him in front of Parsons. But she really didn't see the need to be back on the trail tomorrow. A day or two's rest would be most welcome to her bone-weary body.

"You most certainly cannot go tomorrow," Parsons put in. "For one thing you would miss the dance we're having tomorrow night. I would be honored, Kate, if you would allow me to escort you."

"Dance?" How could she tell him she didn't know how to dance? Worse, tell him in front of Hawke. She could feel him waiting for her to turn Parsons down. Damn, why should she, after he had decreed he was putting an end to what they had shared these past weeks. Maybe what he needed was a little dose of seeing her in the company of another man.

"I'd love to go to the dance with you, Wade," she said.

Looking directly at Hawke, Parsons raised his right hand in an exaggerated gesture toward Kate. "She's beautiful, and therefore to be wooed. She is a woman, therefore to be won."

Kate grinned. He'd actually called her beautiful. Maybe the dance wouldn't be a total disaster. Especially if Hawke happened to be there, wearing the same furious look on his face that was stamped there now.

Parsons excused himself, kissing her hand once again. "Welcome ever smiles, And farewell goes out sighing."

"Whatever you say, Wade," Kate said, watching him stride across the parade grounds toward the commanding officer's quarters.

"Pompous jackass," Hawke muttered.

"Jealous?" she sniffed.

"If you're fool enough to fall for that line of horse manure, you deserve what you get."

"You are jealous!"

He straightened. "It won't work, Kate. I told you.

314

It's over between us."

She would not let the hurt she so fiercely felt show on her face.

"I just think you can do a helluva lot better than that Shakespeare-spouting popinjay!"

The helluva lot better I want is you, she thought miserably, but her pride would not allow her to say the words. "I think Wade is a very attractive man, a gentleman."

"Are you saying he knows a lady when he sees one?"

Her hand balled into a fist. "I ought to . . . Damn, you're the jackass, Travis Hawke." She stomped away from him, hurrying over to help Rafe unload his wagon. "Have you seen Dusty?" she asked him, anxious to get her mind off Hawke.

"They're unloading the dynamite over in the southeast corner of the fort. Thank God, we got that stuff through with everybody in one piece."

"Amen."

Rafe eyed her critically. "You all right, Katie? You look a mite down in the mouth."

"I'm fine."

"Cap'n Hawke, right?"

"Don't mention that bastard's name to me."

"Damn! I thought you two were getting along real good. I seen the cap'n grinning and laughing these past two weeks, I thought sure you two . . ."

"I don't want to talk about it, Rafe. The man's impossible."

He stepped close to her, his meaty hand capturing her chin. "Don't give up on him, girl. He's worth whatever it costs ya. I guarantee it."

Her shoulders slumped. "He doesn't want me, Rafe. How can I fight that?"

"If he says he don't want ya, he's a liar."

"I know he's a liar. But not about that."

"Kate, I *seen* him lookin' at ya."

315

There's a difference between lust and love, she thought, but she could scarcely say that to Rafe. "Do you think a *lady*," she sneered the word, "could get a cold beer in this fort?"

"You can get anything you damned well want, Kate. You have all your life. Don't give up just because what you want is a man with a gutload of hurt in him."

She sighed. "Right now, I'll settle for the beer."

She left Rafe and the other men to the task of unloading the wagons. Hawke was nowhere in sight as she walked toward the rustic building on the northern edge of the fort's enclosure. The small hotel was for visitors, travellers passing through. She was looking forward to the beer, cold or otherwise.

Inside the lobby she grimaced to see Hawke in the small dining area. He was having a drink at the bar with a man she had never seen before. It was obvious the two were of long acquaintance. She slipped into a shadowed corner of the lobby, just out of Hawke's line of sight.

As unobtrusively as she could, she observed the two men. Hawke's voice was low, angry, but somehow cajoling. The other man with brown hair graying at the temples and a look of a seasoned drunk about him seemed highly agitated about something.

Finally Hawke tossed a coin on the bar and turned to leave. Kate ducked quickly out the door and around the side of the building. She watched Hawke stride back toward the parade grounds, his purposeful steps belying the frustration she sensed in him. Making certain he did not notice her, she hurried back into the hotel. She breathed a sigh of relief to find the man still at the bar.

She sidled up beside him. "Nice day, huh, mister."

"Bit dry," the man mumbled.

Kate took the hint and signalled for the bartender to

bring the man a bottle. "My name's Kate McCullough."

"Dan Parker."

The name meant nothing to her, but she decided to brass it out. "I saw my wagonmaster leaving. Travis Hawke. He a friend of yours?"

For just an instant there was a look of studied wariness in the man's eyes, as though he were well-practiced at being suspicious of people. But she must have seemed no threat. He was also quite drunk.

"Travis is like a son to me."

Her heart pounded. She felt as though she were somehow going behind Hawke's back, but the opportunity to find out whatever she could about him was simply too much to resist.

"How do you know him?"

"He was married to my daughter."

Kate poured the man another drink, her hand shaking so much she spilled more onto the bar than into the glass. My God, what had she stumbled onto? Had Hawke arranged to meet Parker here? "Your daughter is dead?"

"Annie, oh, Annie." His eyes glistened. "I miss her. I still miss her."

"How . . ." Kate swallowed, "how did she die?"

He laid his head on the bar, rocking from side to side. "Annie, Annie, why did you do it? Why?"

"Mr. Parker? Mr. Parker, maybe you should sit down at one of the tables." Kate didn't wait for an answer. She hooked an arm under him and helped him stagger over to a chair, bringing the bottle of whiskey with her.

He made a grab for the bottle, but she jerked it away. "Please, tell me about Hawke, ah, Travis, Mr. Parker."

"He's like my son."

"Yes, I know that. But what about Travis and Anne?"

"They never should have gotten married." He shook his head, almost falling off the chair.

Kate righted him, digesting what she was certain was whiskey-born honesty. "Why shouldn't they have been married?"

Parker shook his head again, and he spoke as though she weren't even there. "Annie was spoiled, you know. It was my fault. I wanted her to have everything, after her ma died. She was my whole world."

Kate hated herself for listening, eavesdropping on this man's soul, but to find out what might be keeping Hawke from her she would do anything.

"We got drunk one night, Travis and me," Parker said, staring off at nowhere, seeming oddly sober all at once, though he most definitely was not. "He told me about being an orphan, about the son-of-a-bitch that ran the place. How he'd lock Travis in a hole no bigger than a whiskey barrel, leave him there for days with rats and bugs and . . ."

Kate stood up. Now she really did feel as though she were reading Hawke's diary, or worse. But Parker gripped her wrist, forcing her to sit back down. "You asked me," he said, "and I'm going to tell you."

Kate nodded, closing her eyes, mouthing a silent "Hawke, forgive me."

"Annie told me Travis acted real strange one night, when she shut the door to the root cellar. She was just teasing, but . . . I know she never let him forget it. It frightened her, I think, to see a man like Travis scared of anything."

He reached for the bottle. Kate didn't stop him this time, nor did she stop the tears that slid down her cheeks as she remembered Hawke's reaction to the cave at Elm Creek. She thought of a little boy boxed in

318

with rats in the dark.

Parker kept talking, oblivious to her, to everything. "He got adopted by some farmer when he was twelve, but the old man died six years later. I think Travis felt like a substitute for the man's dead son, like he just never fit in anywhere his whole life. But he thought he could with Annie. But then Annie died having the baby."

"Baby?" Kate murmured.

"Travis was so happy. But . . . but I don't think Annie was." The man wiped at a tear with the back of his hand. "She always wanted everyone to tell her how pretty she was. Having a baby made her feel . . . not so pretty." He looked at Kate, his eyes begging her to understand. "She was a good girl. She was. Just a little spoiled, you know. She would have been a good mother."

"She died in childbirth?" Then why had Hawke said Frank Blanchard killed her?

Parker was reading her mind. "That damned Blanchard."

"How?"

"The baby died. Anne died."

No wonder Hawke hated the man. Not only had he killed his wife. He'd killed his child. "How . . . how did Blanchard kill them, Mr. Parker?"

He slumped forward on the table, saliva dribbling from one corner of his mouth. Kate shook him. "Mr. Parker?" She sighed. He was out cold.

As she walked toward officers' row, her emotions were in a turmoil. She wanted to go to Hawke, ask him about the things Parker had told her. She suspected—or was it hoped?—they had a great deal to do with his reluctance to risk a relationship with her. But there was no way she could tell him she knew about Anne's death without exposing her unforgivable behavior with Parker.

She was so upset that she was actually thankful when Lt. Parsons stepped out of his quarters to greet her. "Kate, I'm glad I found you. Some of the officers' wives are waiting for you at Captain Harding's residence." He gave her a conspiratorial wink. "I took the liberty of telling them that you may not have brought along a suitable dress for the dance tomorrow night."

Kate resisted telling him that she had a perfectly suitable cotton dress in the supply wagon, feeling all at once as though Parsons wouldn't have found the dress suitable at all. Hiding her embarrassment, she said, "Can it wait until tomorrow? I'm very tired. It's been a long day for me."

"Of course. I'm certain they'll understand."

"Thank you." She turned to leave. "Good night."

He caught her wrist. "Good night! Good night! Parting is such sweet sorrow!"

Kate rolled her eyes, careful not to let Parsons see. "Good night, Wade." She hurried toward the wagons, pleased to note they'd all been unloaded. Tomorrow she would have the money she needed to save McCullough Freight.

She yanked a couple of blankets from the nearly barren bottom of the supply wagon and spread them out on the ground beside the rear wheel.

"You're not sleeping in a bed tonight?" came the familiar husky voice.

"Nope," she murmured, her heart pounding like the hail at Elm Creek. "And you?"

"Never choose a roof when I can have the sky."

A melancholy smile touched her lips. "Me either." Now she understood his reasons for keeping windows open, staying out of caves. She longed to tell him she understood, thinking that somehow it would help ease his contempt of his own fear. But now wasn't the time.

320

She pretended to ignore him as she lay down, though she was aware of his every movement as he spread his blankets out just behind hers. She listened as he too lay down. "Good night, Hawke."

" 'Night, Kate."

She lay awake, praying he would reach for her, pull her close, kiss her until she couldn't breathe for wanting him. But the night sounds soon mingled with the sound of his deep, even breathing. She twisted around to look, her lips compressing in abject frustration. The son-of-a-gila monster had fallen asleep.

No doubt he'd done it just to prove she no longer had any kind of physical effect on him.

"That's what you think, Hawke," she muttered, staring at his slumbering form. "Just wait until that dance tomorrow night. You'll be sorry. You'll see."

Those officers' wives wanted to gussy her up? Well, for once, she would let it happen. She was going to have Travis Hawke's eyes popping out of his stubborn head even if it meant wearing godawful stays! And then she'd watch him try to keep his distance. End their relationship? Tomorrow night, she vowed, Travis Hawke would be back in her bed.

Chapter Twenty-four

Hawke was up and gone when she awoke the next morning. Disappointed, she climbed stiffly to her feet and shook out her blankets. She would just see what his attitude was tonight.

Wasting no time, she hurried over to Captain Harding's residence. Her knock on the door was answered by a plump, middle-aged woman with a room-brightening smile.

"Mrs. Harding?"

"You must be Kate. Come in, dear. Come in." The woman caught Kate's arm and ushered her into the small spare living room. "Lieutenant Parsons told us you wouldn't be coming by last night."

"I'm sorry. I was just so tired. And I really don't want to put you to any trouble."

"Bosh and nonsense! Nothing to be sorry about, dear. And this is no trouble at all. I enjoy it! It's so seldom we get a single young lady at the fort." She bustled into another room and came back carrying the loveliest gown Kate had ever seen—a floor-length mauve silk with a gathered waist and deeply cut bodice. She blushed just to think of wearing it, then smiled, thinking of Hawke's dark eyes settling on the decolletage.

"I couldn't wear such a lovely thing," Kate stammered. "I, really, I couldn't." What if she spilled something on it?

"You're wearing it! No arguments. Lieutenant Parsons was very specific. He's intending to show you off tonight, you know." The woman gave her a mischievous wink.

"Lieutenant Parsons certainly is an interesting man," Kate managed.

"Such a poetic heart, truly," Mrs. Harding sighed, and Kate had the impression the woman wouldn't have minded being twenty years younger and unmarried. "He's quite the playwright himself, you know."

"We had dinner in Leavenworth once," Kate said, as she allowed Mrs. Harding to shoo her into the kitchen. A tubful of tepid water sat in the middle of the room. On the stove sat a huge pot of boiling water. "Wade told me he had written several plays."

"And they're just wonderful, really." Mrs. Harding wrapped a towel around the handle of the pot and carried it over to the bath water. She upended the pot, then tested the water with the back of her hand, obviously finding the temperature to her liking. "We've put on a couple of his plays here at the fort, and let me tell you, they were well received."

Kate tried to imagine anything to relieve the tedium of life at a military post not being well received.

"Well, climb in, honey," the woman said. "We might as well get started on your transformation."

"Transformation?"

Mrs. Hardy looked a little embarrassed. "Well, the lieutenant did say you might need a little sprucing up for the dance. But don't you worry a thing about it dear, you'll be the envy of everyone there. I'll bet under those filthy old buckskins lurks the body of a lovely

323

young woman."

So Wade said she might need some sprucing up, eh? Her temper flared. It was a good thing she had decided to go through all of this to see what impression it would make on Hawke or she would have turned right around and walked out Mrs. Harding's front door.

Thankfully, the woman left Kate alone with her bath. The warm water felt positively heavenly after a six week long accumulation of grit that never seemed completely washed away by creek water. She inhaled the lilac scented soap Mrs. Harding had left for her, then set to work scrubbing her body clean with it. She didn't stop until her skin fairly glowed, seeming to absorb the faint, sweet fragrance of lilac.

She spent the day at Mrs. Harding's, as the woman and several of the other officers' wives stopped by to fuss over her hair, her fingernails, her figure. Several hours were spent teaching her how to dance at least passably well. It was indeed a transformation wrought over the hours by these determined women. Kate could scarcely believe the reflection that stared back at her in the mirror.

"You look positively radiant, dear," Mrs. Harding chirped, tugging at the lacings in the back of the dress, "Lieutenant Parsons will be so pleased."

Kate pirouetted around the room, caring only if one man was pleased by the way she looked. She touched the delicate curls Mrs. Harding had created in her hair, then trailed her hand down to the daring cut of the gown. In a few minutes she would know what Hawke thought of the dress.

"Isn't she just lovely?" Kate heard Mrs. Harding say. Kate turned to see a short, bearded man in his early fifties step into the room. She introduced him at once as her husband, Captain Glenn Harding.

"My lieutenant has spoken of nothing but you since

he returned from Leavenworth weeks ago," the captain said. "Now I can most certainly see why."

"Thank you," Kate said, her nervousness escalating. What if Hawke didn't come to the dance?

Captain and Mrs. Harding escorted her to the building where the dance would be held. "Lieutenant Parsons asked that we bring you along, dear," the woman said. "He was composing a poem he'd written especially for you and wanted to finish it before he arrived at the dance."

Wonderful, Kate thought bleakly, but managed an understanding smile.

Kate stepped into the gaily decorated hall. Red, white and blue bunting adorned the balcony rails above the main floor. Long tables, laden with trays of food and lemonade-filled punchbowls, lined two of the walls. But her eyes slid past everything, as she scanned the room for Hawke. Her spirits plummeted. He wasn't there.

"Kate, darling!" Wade Parsons's voice sent her spirits skidding even lower. But she smiled as he slipped his arm around her waist. There was always the chance Hawke could stop by. Somehow playing along with Parsons didn't make her feel nearly as guilty as doing almost the same thing with Jim Collier back in Leavenworth. Probably because Parsons didn't seem to be in love with her as much as he was with himself.

As the night wore on, she found herself relaxing, even enjoying his unrelenting attention, as he danced with her again and again.

"My fellow officers," he announced, after a particularly exhilarating polka that had Kate giggling and holding onto him for support, "I have something important to say to you all this evening. But first, I have a poem I must share with you."

Some of the less sophisticated officers among them

didn't bother to suppress groans. But Parsons silenced them with a wave of his hand. "Now, gentlemen and ladies, we all know what it is to be in love."

Kate stiffened, but there was no way she could pull away from the man in front of a roomful of friends. What was he up to?

"I'm going to tell you what my love means to me." He gathered Kate to him, though she kept her hands pressed against his chest to maintain a little distance at least. She swallowed hard, as he stared into her eyes.

"Sunshine is bright,
But not at night,
Hark, the wolf howls at the moon,
Kate, what a sight!
She is my life's light,
Oh, she doth make my heart swoon!"

"How sweet," Kate murmured, looking for a discreet place to be sick. "Could you let go of me now?"

He went on as though she hadn't spoken. "Tonight, I tell the world of my love. Tonight, in this room I ask you, Kate McCullough, to be my wife!"

She might have swooned herself, if his arm weren't firmly ensconced around her waist. How dare he pull such a theatrical stunt on her? She had a good mind to turn him down in front of one and all. But then she saw him out of the corner of one eye. Hawke. He was lounging against the side wall, evidently there long enough to witness Parsons's entire performance.

Kate stepped back from Parsons, fully aware of the absolute stillness in the room. Everyone was awaiting her response. Including Hawke? She shot a glance at him. His eyes were smoky, unreadable. Damn him. He wasn't going to spoil this night for her. She had had

326

fun in spite of his absence. Wade had been absolutely charming up until this little thunderbolt. She would show Hawke she damned well knew how to be a lady if the mood so suited her. Hooking her arm through Parsons's, she led him toward the door, her voice loud enough to carry through the room and as sultry as she could make it, "I think we'd do best to discuss this outside, Wade dear. Privately, if you know what I mean."

Parsons grinned and eagerly led her out the door. Several of the officers gave him a congratulatory handshake before they reached the porch. The self-satisfied way he accepted each and every one had Kate seething by the time they reached the dark of the parade grounds.

"Just what the hell did you think you were doing in there?" she snapped, jerking herself away from him. "How dare you ask me to marry you in front of a room full of people! It would have served you right if I said no right then and there."

"Said no? You're going to say no?"

"Of course, I'm going to say no. I'm not in love with you, Wade. We went out to dinner once. You've very nice, but you can't tell me you're in love with me either."

"What does love have to do with anything? It would be a good match, Kate, don't you see? The money from McCullough Freight could finance my plays. We'll both be rich."

"Of all the arrogant . . ." The door to the dance hall opened and she watched Hawke step outside. He headed across the parade grounds on a line that would intercept them. Likely hadn't noticed them standing in the shadows. "Kiss me, Wade," she said, suddenly, urgently. "Now."

She threw her arms around him, giving him a resounding kiss on the mouth. The lieutenant needed no further persuasion. His arms hooked around her, pulling her to him. Kate moaned softly, deliberately.

She heard the crunch of Hawke's boots coming toward them, come to an abrupt halt for several seconds, then pick up again, faster, more pronounced, heading in the opposite direction.

"Thank you, Wade," she said, pushing him away. "That will be quite enough."

He was looking at her with searching eyes. "My God, I never had a woman kiss me like that before."

"And don't expect to again! Good-night."

"Wait, Kate, about the money . . ."

"I am not going to finance your plays."

"No, I mean the money for delivering the freight, the dynamite."

"What about it?" she demanded, suddenly uneasy. "Don't tell me there's going to be any kind of delay. I need that money tomorrow. I'm heading back to Leavenworth."

"That's just it. You're heading back there with me."

"I beg your pardon?"

"I'm taking a couple of troopers and escorting you back. Hawke was telling me you might be expecting trouble. A robbery attempt, perhaps."

"Hawke told you that?"

"You sound surprised. The man works for you, doesn't he? I admit he's a bit uncouth, but he seems to know his business."

Kate mumbled a reply, then bid Parsons good-night, not allowing him to escort her back to her wagon. Hawke had arranged for Parsons to escort them? That he'd done it without consulting her rankled a little. But that he'd done it at all sent a curious warmth gliding over her.

She was surprised to find Hawke at the wagon, expecting him to be anywhere than where she might be.

"Congratulations," he said, his voice hard.

"For what?" she snapped, in no mood for his games.

"Your engagement."

"Oh, that. Yes, well, Wade certainly is full of surprises."

"When's the wedding?"

"What would you care?"

"Just making polite conversation with the woman who sleeps under the same wagon I do."

She swore.

"Tsk, tsk," he chided, "Wade isn't going to care for that language in an officer's wife."

"I told you once you were a jackass, Travis Hawke," she hissed. "I was wrong. And I apologize to jackasses everywhere for the insult to their good name."

Even in the dim moonlight she could see the muscle in his jaw flex. But he said only, "You didn't set a wedding date?"

She crossed to the back of the wagon, smiling a trifle smugly. He kept coming back to the subject of the wedding. For a man who wanted to end his relationship with her, he seemed inordinately concerned about her relationship with another man.

"Do I understand by your interest, Hawke, that you would like an invitation to the wedding?"

Now he swore, then grabbed up his blankets and slapped them down on the ground several feet distant from her.

She hugged her own blankets against her, watching him shift restlessly, trying to get comfortable, finally settling on his right side. She waited until he was still. Then she knelt down beside him, stroking the back of her hand against his cheek. He stiffened. "Don't."

"You never said what you thought of my being all gussied up in this dress."

"I didn't notice." He'd always thought her beautiful.

But tonight he'd been stunned by just how beautiful.

"I think it does wonders for my breasts," she murmured, trailing a finger along the deep neckline. "What do you think?"

"I'm tired. I'm going to sleep."

"Damn, why are you doing this? You're hurting us both."

"You've got Parsons."

"I've got nothing if I don't have you."

He shifted to his back. "I told you. It's over."

"You didn't tell me why."

"There doesn't need to be a reason."

"I need one."

"You won't want to hear it."

Her hand curled over his. "I love you, Hawke. You must know that. I only kissed Wade to make you jealous."

She hadn't meant for the words to come out, but she'd held them in too long. She wished she could see his face now, but the shadows of the wagon hid it from her. For several seconds he just lay there, and she could have sworn she felt his body heat beneath her hand. But then he climbed to his feet and stalked away from her, and when he spoke she not only wished she hadn't bared her heart to him, but that she had never met him in her life.

"Kate, I want to explain something to you about me." He stood with his back to her, facing off toward the parade grounds. "I've probably had a hundred women in my life. And I'll have hundred more."

"Shut up!"

"At first everything is good between us, but then, things get a little stale. You know what I mean."

"You're lying! You've never had what you've had with me!"

"No? What have I had with you besides sex?"

"Friendship."

He seemed taken aback by her answer and did not at first dispute it.

"I'm in love with you," she repeated.

He walked back to her, settling his hands on her waist, then stroking upward, teasing her nipples beneath the smooth silk of her dress. "It's not love, Kate. Do you feel it?" His mouth nuzzled her throat. "You're so ready for me, Kate. So ready." His own body was not immune. His loins tightened. His mouth devoured hers. He would have her. This one last time before he ended it completely, he would have her. But he would be certain she hated him when it was done.

"Hawke . . . please . . ." Her fingers worked the buttons of his shirt, tugging at the opening of his fly. But there was something wrong with the way his body was moving against hers. She had accepted his lust, wished for his love, but what he was giving her now was neither. It was possession, ownership, control.

He didn't even take his clothes off, pressing her down into her blankets. He shoved up her dress and covered her body with his. His chest was warm against the open bodice of her gown, his hand knotted in her hair.

"Stop it!" she gritted. She didn't want it, not like this.

"Stop? You didn't come here in that dress to ask me to stop." His hand roved cruelly up and down her body.

"Don't do this. Not like this. Hawke, please."

He stood up, fastening his jeans, his voice filled with contempt. "My wife was the most beautiful woman I've ever seen, Kate. I've never had any trouble attracting women. Why would I settle for you?"

She pinched the bodice of her dress together. She would not cry. She would not. But the tears came, and she thought they would never stop.

* * *

Hawke strode across the parade grounds, resisting the urge to find a stiff drink. He was still shaking from what it had cost him to hurt Kate.

"Mr. Hawke?"

He turned in the direction of the voice. "Parsons?"

The lieutenant stepped out of the shadows near his quarters. "You were with my fiancée just now?"

"Where I am and who I'm with is none of your business."

"Just stay away from her. You work for her. That's all. She's mine."

"Did I say I wanted her?"

"Stay away from her."

"That's a little hard to do. I'm going back to Leavenworth with her, remember?"

"And so am I."

"Then we've got nothing more to say to one another, do we?"

"Actually, we do," Parsons said, his voice oddly thoughtful. Then he straightened, "But I think you've gotten too damned personally involved in all this for me to risk it." He seemed to make up his mind about something. "We'll just keep things the way they are for now. Good night, Mr. Hawke."

Hawke brushed past Parsons and headed toward the hotel, unwilling to dwell on Parsons's cryptic comments. He wanted to make certain Dan Parker had gotten to bed all right.

Dan should never have come here. He could ruin everything. He couldn't stay sober for five minutes any more. And when Hawke at last confronted Blanchard, he didn't want Dan finding out the truth about Anne.

Hawke was having a hard time handling the truth himself these days—not about Anne, not anymore, but about Kate and his feelings for her. It tore him apart to hurt her, but it had to be done. He couldn't allow her to care about him. People who cared about him died.

Friendship. That was what she'd said they'd had together besides sex. She'd said it so matter-of-factly, yet he'd never even thought about it before. Friends. He and Kate were friends as much as lovers. He told her things he'd never told anyone. Her reaction to him at the cave had not been contempt, but compassion.

His jaw clenched. All the more reason to end it. There were things even Kate could never know about him.

She would get over him.

It was just that the question that gnawed at his gut more and more every day was would he ever get over her?

Chapter Twenty-five

Kate studied her travelling companions covertly. The return trip to Leavenworth could prove even more dangerous than the trip out. Hawke and Parsons were already at each other's throats, and they hadn't even left the fort yet.

Two enlisted men, Privates Sheridan and Farley, would be part of the escort. Hawke expected Parsons and his troopers to follow his orders. Parsons was having none of it.

Of the bullwhackers only Dusty and Rafe would make the ride back. The others would scatter looking for work elsewhere, or until McCullough Freight sent out the word it was heading up another train. Kate hoped fervently it was the latter.

"Please," Kate said, talking to Parsons, "if you and Mr. Hawke can't settle this, the rest of us are going to leave without you."

Parsons looked at her. "If you would just explain to your wagonmaster that he no longer has wagons to master, then I'll be happy to join you."

Hawke said nothing. He'd told Parsons he was in charge of the outfit, and as far as he was concerned nothing further needed to be said.

"I'm leaving," Kate said. "You boys do what you want. I have a deadline with a skunk."

"The lady has a point," Hawke said.

Kate bristled, just to have him speaking about her in any way at all. She had not forgiven him for what he'd said last night. No matter how she'd tossed and turned trying to convince herself he hadn't meant it, it didn't ease the hurt of the words.

"We'll leave," Parsons said, "when you defer to the military, meaning myself, being in charge of this party."

"West Point man, right?" Hawke said, striding over to the man, so that their voices would no longer be overheard.

Parsons squared his shoulders. "Class of '59."

"And you're here. At Ft. Laramie." Hawke's eyes were mocking.

"A minor indiscretion regarding the wife of my commanding officer in Maryland." Parsons's only obvious regret was being caught. "He's retired now. Soon I'll be back on the east coast where I belong."

Kate nudged her horse over between the two men. "This has gone on long enough." She glared at Hawke. "The army has been most generous to offer this escort. As far as I'm concerned, Wade is in charge."

Hawke stiffened. "Whatever you say, Miss McCullough," he said, swinging into the saddle. "It's your company."

"Then kindly act like it," she snapped. "And do what you're told."

"Yes, ma'am." His voice was openly sarcastic.

Kate reined her horse into step beside Parsons as the party rode out of the fort. Making her voice loud enough for Hawke to hear, she said, "This is really terribly sweet of you, Wade. Providing the escort and all."

"My pleasure," Parsons said, grinning disarmingly.

"It gives the army a chance to provide protection for one of its most efficient suppliers. And," he winked, "it gives me a chance to continue my most honorable pursuit of a lady's hand in marriage."

Kate smiled, though her heart ached to think of Hawke. She allowed her horse to drift away from the others, wanting to be alone. Unfortunately, Dusty and Rafe had other ideas. They rode up on either side of her.

"Rafe's been talkin' my ear off about ye, lass," Dusty said. "Says I'm being a mule-brained fool to not see yer feelin's for the reb."

"I don't want to talk about it."

"Katie," Rafe said, "don't give up on him. Cap'n Hawke liked to bite anybody's head off that come near him this mornin'. You've just got to . . ."

"I said I don't want to talk about!" She slammed her heels against the mare's sides, but didn't miss Dusty's muttered comment, "Even I'm startin' to like that reb."

Liking him, isn't my problem, Dusty, she thought despairingly, *it's loving him.*

She turned at the sound of a rider bearing down on the group at a hard gallop. Squinting, she could just make him out. Dan Parker. Quickly, she jerked her hat brim down lower over her eyes. God forbid Parker should recognize her and tell Hawke that she'd been asking about him.

She shot a glance in Hawke's direction to see that he was watching his former father-in-law's approach with tight-lipped annoyance.

"I saw him, Travis," Parker said, slowing his horse to fall into pace beside him. "Last night. He was in the fort. I saw him."

Kate felt a twinge of embarrassment. The man was already drunk and it was barely past nine.

"Saw whom? Who are you?" Parsons demanded,

eyeing Parker suspiciously. "Wait a minute, I've seen you around the fort. You're a Wells Fargo agent, right?"

Kate started, looking quickly at Hawke. Wells Fargo? Hawke's annoyance had changed to disgust. "You shouldn't have come, Dan."

"It's my right. Besides, I'm telling you," he looked at the others, then leaned over conspiratorially to speak only to Hawke, "I saw him."

"We settled this. You agreed to do it my way."

"She was my daughter."

"Damnit, Dan, keep your mouth shut." He looked at Kate, obviously trying to gauge her reaction to Parker's pronouncement, but she kept her features carefully neutral. He gripped the reins to Parker's bay, leading the horse away from the others.

"What was that all about?" Parsons demanded.

"I wish I knew," Kate said, watching as Hawke continued his heated conversation with Parker out of earshot.

"It's my right to know," Parsons said. "A drunk like that could put all of us in danger if this Frank Blanchard you told me about makes a try for the hundred thousand dollars in my saddlebags. That money is my responsibility."

"And it's my money," she reminded him.

"Ah, Kate, just think of how many of my plays you could put on with money like that."

"That money is going to pay off Frank Blanchard and save McCullough Freight."

"Not if Blanchard has anything to say about it," Hawke said, riding back to join them. "Somewhere between here and Leavenworth he'll make his move to get it."

"That's why I'm here," Parsons said, looking back to check Parker, who was now keeping pace some fifty yards behind them. "But what I don't know is why that old drunk is here."

Hawke kneed his horse against Parsons's mount, the two men stirrup to stirrup facing each other. "You call him that again and you'll be eating soup the rest of your life."

Parsons blanched, then caught himself. "Just remember who's in charge here, mister."

"Just remember what I said."

The small party of riders rode in silence for much of the remainder of the day. But whenever Kate stole a glance at Hawke, it was to catch him gazing at her. He would immediately feign interest elsewhere, but Kate had not missed the burning desire in those midnight eyes. Whatever else he had said last night, he had lied when he told her it was over between them.

In camp that night Hawke volunteered to take the first watch. Parsons, amazingly, offered no objections. Kate lay awake in her blankets for over an hour before she felt certain all of the others had fallen asleep. Quietly, she slipped away, determined to once again confront Hawke.

"That's a good way to get yourself killed," he hissed, reholstering his gun as she stepped up beside him the darkness.

"I want you to tell me about Dan Parker."

"He's none of your business."

"If it has to do with Blanchard, it is my business, and you know it. Did he tell you he saw Blanchard at the fort last night?"

Hawke gave a disgusted snort. "God knows what Dan does or doesn't see in the night," He shook his head. "I'm sorry. I didn't mean that. Dan's a good man."

"He's never accepted his daughter's death, has he?"

"No."

"And neither have you," she added gently.

"That *is* none of your business."

Kate sighed. "All right, but tell me about who Parker saw last night."

"He thinks he saw Blanchard skulking around the stables, around the barracks. But it's just not Blanchard's style. It was dark. Dan was dead drunk. Who knows who or what he saw?"

"You really think Blanchard will attack us sometime before Leavenworth?"

"He wants your company. It's the only thing that makes sense. But I can't see him attacking. He's more subtle than that."

"Then what?"

"I don't know. He poisoned Jeb Kerns."

"He what?"

He told her about the dinner he'd had with Blanchard.

"And you didn't do anything about that? Jeb Kerns was a snake, but you could have put Blanchard in jail."

"There wouldn't have been any proof. You can be sure of that."

For each step she took toward him, he seemed to take two away from her. She gave him an exasperated sigh. "Keep this up, we'll be two miles from camp by morning."

"You've had your say. Go back to sleep."

She caught hold of his belt and tugged him toward her. "You wish you'd never met me, don't you?"

He said nothing, but neither did he pull away.

"You know why?"

"Why?" The hardness in his voice was forced, and she smiled.

"Because I'm too stubborn to take no for an answer. Because even when you say terrible things to me, like last night, I don't believe you, and I come right back to prove you the liar you are." She hooked her arms around his middle. "Because I love you, and you can't stand to be loved."

She felt him tremble before he pulled away, and she knew she had cut to the heart of him with that last one. "Give it up, Hawke. I know I'm not the prettiest thing in the world, but . . ."

"Who says you're not pretty?" he snapped.

"You did, you bastard, last night!"

"I never said that."

"You said your wife was the most beautiful thing in the world or some such rot, so why would you settle for the likes of me?"

"Damn, I didn't mean it that way."

"You didn't?" Her eyes widened with wonder. He didn't?

"I just meant she was genteel, feminine, never took a chaw in her life, that sort of thing." Damn, Kate was doing it again. Scaling the barriers. Never in his life had he talked so easily with anyone. Maybe she would even understand about Liam Jeffers's crawlspace, about Anne.

"So you don't think I'm ugly?" she persisted.

"I never figured you the type who needed false flattery."

"Oh, please, please, heap all the false flattery on me you like. Lie! You do it all the time anyway."

"Damn you, woman! I do not lie, at least not all the time."

"Prove it." She stepped close to him, undoing the buttons of his shirt.

"Don't. I am on guard, you know." He sucked in his breath as she began to knead the crotch of his jeans. "You're going to get us all killed."

"Ah, but what a way to die, don't you think?"

He chuckled in spite of himself, then suddenly he

thrust her away.

"Hawke, what the . . .?"

"Quiet! Did you hear that?"

"Hear what?"

He pressed her down beside a boulder, drawing his pistol. "Stay here."

"Be careful," she whispered, before he was swallowed by the darkness.

When several minutes had passed and still he hadn't returned, she could wait no longer. What if he was in trouble? Hunching low, she hurried in the direction Hawke had gone.

A sound to her right caught her attention. With the new moon she could scarcely make out shapes ten feet in front of her. The campfire some six hundred yards distant now had all but burned itself out. She resisted the urge to call out to Hawke. What if it wasn't him?

Cautiously, she crept forward. She stumbled, nearly falling, but righted herself, groping along the ground ahead of her. She expected to find a rotted log; instead she found a body. Still warm, but definitely dead.

"Oh, God no!" She searched frantically in her pockets for a match. Striking it on her backside, she held it over the corpse. She gasped, experiencing a wave of both relief and horror. Relief that it was not Hawke. Horror that the dead man was Private Sheridan. He was still in his bedroll. He'd been stabbed to death in his sleep.

"Hawke! Parsons!" she cried. "Everybody! Get up! We've had a killer in the camp."

Instantly, Rafe and Dusty were at her side, along with Parsons, Farley, and Parker, all demanding to know what had happened.

When she'd told them what she knew, Parsons asked the question that had been tearing her apart, "Where's Hawke?"

"He heard a noise. He went to investigate." She ran a hand through her hair. "He hasn't come back."

"Hawke!" she called. "Hawke, where are you?"

"I'm right here," he said, striding out of the shadows. "What the hell is all the . . ." He stopped when he spotted the body. "What happened?"

"Maybe you should tell us, *guard*," Parsons said, emphasizing the last word.

"I heard a noise."

"So Kate said. You disappear and my man ends up dead."

"You want to make it plainer, Parsons," Hawke growled.

"Let me see your knife."

"Like hell."

"Just show it to him," Kate snapped. "Then we can get on with finding out what happened."

He stared at her. "You don't think . . ."

"Of course not!"

He unsheathed the knife and handed it to Parsons.

The lieutenant looked skeptical. "You could have cleaned it off."

Hawke gripped Parsons by the shirtfront and drew back his fist. But Kate's shout stopped the blow.

"There's a murderer out there somewhere in case anyone's interested. Maybe we should do something to find him."

"There's nothing we can do in the dark," Hawke said. "Except get somebody else killed. We'll double the guard. The rest of us should try and get some sleep. It looks like we're in for a rough trip."

"You don't give the orders," Parsons put in. "I do. One guard doing his job should be sufficient."

"Lieutenant," Hawke said evenly, "you've got a dead man on your hands. Either someone stole into this camp and killed him, or someone in this camp killed him. That means you need two guards. A guard to guard the camp. And a guard to guard the guard."

Parsons stiffened, knowing Hawke was right but unwilling to admit it. "Private Farley," he barked, "you and one of the bullwhackers take the next watch."

"Yes, sir."

"I'll do it," Dusty said.

"You be careful," Kate told him.

Kate doubted anyone slept too well the rest of the night.

As Hawke saddled up the next morning, she stepped up behind him. "Do you think it was Blanchard?"

He shrugged, not looking at her. "It's subtle enough. I wouldn't put it past him. But it just doesn't feel right." His gaze shifted over to Parsons. "Blanchard gets a lot of inside information in his business dealing and in his thievery, including military shipments — gold, silver, guns."

"You were only in Leavenworth five days, yet you certainly know an awful lot about Blanchard."

"I made it my business to know." He paused. "Before I kill him."

"How did he kill your wife?" The question was out before she could stop it.

He turned, his eyes blazing into hers. "I won't tell you again, Kate. Don't ask me that."

Then I'll ask her father, she thought, though she said nothing to Hawke. She mounted her horse and to avoid Hawke's suspicion kept to herself most of the day. That night, after supper, she waited until Parker wandered off by himself, as was his habit. It was well past dusk.

"How are you feeling?" she asked.

"I need a drink," the man said. Kate knew that Hawke had confiscated the two bottles of whiskey the man had had in his saddlebags.

343

"You shouldn't leave the camp alone, you know. It's dangerous."

"You like Travis, don't you?"

The question surprised her, but she answered it honestly. "I love him."

He nodded approvingly. "You'll be good for him. Better than Anne." His voice grew wistful. "She wanted things he could never give her, things I don't think anyone could ever give her."

She felt it an odd thing for a father to say, but rather than press him, she let him tell her about Anne in his own way.

"I talked to you at the fort, didn't I?"

"I didn't think you remembered."

He smiled. "I get drunk, but not that drunk."

"You didn't tell Hawke?"

He shook his head. "Your secret's safe with me."

"Thank you." She found herself gaining a new respect for this troubled man. He'd lost himself when he'd lost his daughter, but she sensed a core of decency in him that had surely once made him a fine agent for Wells Fargo. "How do you know Hawke? I mean, besides your daughter."

His eyes twinkled. "Travis always was so damned closemouthed about himself. But I'll wager you know more about him than I do."

"I don't know much of anything."

"Oh, but you do. I've watched you, both of you. He's at ease with you, more than I've seen him with anyone. I love him like a son, but except for that time when he was drunk, he never really said much about himself. It's like some part of him is still that little boy clinging to a tree after the flood, waiting for his ma and pa to come get him."

"Goddamn you, old man!" Hawke hissed.

Kate jerked her head toward the sound of his voice,

astonished to find him less than six feet away. She'd been so enthralled by Parker, she'd been oblivious to his approach. "Please, Hawke, it's my fault," she said quickly.

"I know it's your fault," he snarled. "You just won't leave it alone, will you? You have to keep meddling in my life."

"Travis, she's only asking because she cares about . . ."

"Where'd you get the bottle, Dan?" he interrupted. "Or do you spill your guts sober now as well as drunk?"

"I told you it was my fault," Kate said, pleading with him to understand. She could feel Hawke's trust in this man crumbling. "I asked him."

"He didn't have to answer." He glared at Parker. "If you expect me to get Blanchard, you'd best be gone from camp tomorrow."

"That I won't do, Travis. He killed my daughter."

"Your daughter! Your daughter! My God, do you know what that woman did? Do you know?" He stopped. "Damnit, Dan, I'm sorry."

Dan's voice was shaking, agonized. "I know, Travis. I know. But she was still my little girl."

Kate couldn't bear the tortured look in Hawke's eyes. Her heart aching, she ran back to camp alone.

The next morning Dan Parker was dead.

345

Chapter Twenty-six

Kate found Hawke sitting next to Parker's body. He blinked his eyes savagely, and she knew her presence had forever stopped him from crying for his friend. Next to Parker's body was a half empty whiskey bottle.

She knelt beside Hawke. "Knife wound?" she whispered, hating to disturb his grief.

"Poison."

She gasped. "What? How?"

"The whiskey."

Kate looked then at Parker's face. His features were grotesque, distorted. He had died in agony.

Parsons strode up to them, surveying the scene. "Where did he get the whiskey?"

"From my saddlebags," Hawke said. "Damn, I should have broken the bottles."

"Do you often carry poisoned spirits?" Parsons demanded derisively.

"Dan brought them from the fort."

"Sure he did." Parsons motioned to Private Farley. The trooper pulled his gun. "You're under military arrest, Hawke. Don't try anything or you're dead."

"What are you talking about?" Kate cried. "The man was his father-in-law. He wouldn't have killed

346

him."

"Private Sheridan is killed on a night when we have one guard. Hawke. Parker is killed with whiskey obtained from Hawke's saddlebags. Whiskey he knew this souse could never resist."

Hawke launched himself at Parsons, driving himself full length against the man's knees. Parsons stumbled back and went down, Hawke raining blow after blow to his face, his body. Parsons could only hold up his arms in self-defense, unable to escape the bruising punishment.

Dusty and Rafe tried to pull Hawke away, but he fought them off, his eyes fired with fury. Parsons was shrieking for help. Kate did not interfere when Farley clipped Hawke on the back of the head with the butt of his pistol. But as soon as he collapsed, she was at his side.

"Chain the bastard," Parsons snarled. "Now."

"You got what you deserved, Wade," she said. "Leave him alone." She hurried over to her bedroll and picked up her canteen. "His father-in-law is dead. You accuse him of murder. Then you insult Dan Parker's memory. If he hadn't slugged you, I was considering doing it myself."

"Maybe I was a little out of line," Parsons allowed, gingerly testing his jaw, "but he's still under arrest."

"Don't be stupid."

"He is a prime suspect, lass," Dusty said.

"You're just saying that because he fought for the south," she choked. "You'd probably love to see him hang!"

"Kate!" Rafe snapped, "that's not fair. Dusty never said any such thing."

Tears spilled from her eyes. "Oh, Dusty, I'm sorry. I'm sorry." She tilted the canteen onto a clean cloth and dabbed at the knot on the back of Hawke's head. "He's got me crazy."

"It's all right, lass. I have been a mite unreasonable when it comes to rebs. 'Cept Rafe, of course. But Hawke there got me thinkin' maybe I've been wrong. I just meant the lieutenant didn't have no choice in arrestin' him."

"I suppose not," Kate said. Still she shivered as Private Farley locked the manacles on Hawke's wrists and ankles.

Rafe and Dusty buried Parker. With Hawke slung over the back of his chestnut Parsons led out the small band of riders, their number now reduced by two. The barren landscape of the Nebraska plains only added to Kate's mounting feeling of desolation. They were still two weeks out of Leavenworth. She had to wonder if any of them would ever see it again.

By noon Hawke was awake, but groggy. He swore viciously, as soon as he realized what had been done to him.

Kate guided her horse over to Parsons. "He doesn't have to ride like a sack of grain now that's he's conscious."

"I think the position suits him admirably," Parsons said. "He stays that way until nightfall."

Kate grabbed the reins to Hawke's horse, pulling the animal to a halt. "No, he doesn't."

"We'll stop here for the noon meal," Parsons said, salvaging his pride, as Kate helped Hawke to the ground. "Private Farley, see that the prisoner is chained to that juniper over there." He pointed to the twisted tree thirty yards distant. "He's not to be fed."

Kate said nothing. She merely followed Farley and Hawke over to the tree, carrying provisions for both herself and Hawke.

"He won't turn you loose," she said, handing him her canteen. The chain jangled as he tipped it to his mouth. "At least not for awhile."

He handed the water back to her. "Thanks."

"How's your head?"

"Smarts." He caught her wrist. "Dan. Did someone . . ."

"Dusty and Rafe buried him. I said a prayer. I didn't know what else to do."

He nodded. "I appreciate it."

"He loved you."

"Yeah, and now he's dead too."

"Dead because of Blanchard, not you. Don't tell me you hold yourself accountable. Are you responsible for trooper Sheridan, too?"

"Leave it alone, Kate. I know what I am."

"No, you don't, you big . . ." She decided against the choice epithet she had in mind, thinking he was in no mood. "What I'd like to know is how Blanchard can hide out on an open plain like this."

"I've seen Apaches who could hide themselves behind a blade of grass."

"Blanchard doesn't look Apache."

"I know what you mean. This whole thing doesn't smell right. Something . . . something . . . I don't know."

"You think it's one of us?"

"Us? You mean me?"

"I mean any one of us," she said. "Except you, me, Rafe and Dusty."

He smiled. "Well that leaves us with Private Farley and your beloved lieutenant."

"He isn't my beloved anything! Though," she added coyly, "he is very attractive. And he does read to me from his plays every night. He has such a romantic way with words." She batted her eyelashes at Hawke. "He could turn a girl's head."

"Then maybe you should let him turn it."

"I keep telling you to give it up. You're not going to get rid of me."

He stretched out, leaning back against the rough bark of the tree. "Why? Why do you . . . ?"

"Why do I love you?"

He stared off into the distance.

"Because underneath all of that horse dung you throw around to keep people away from you beats the heart of a man I very much want to spend the rest of my life with."

He swallowed hard. She couldn't have chosen a worse way to put it. The rest of her life. With him around that wouldn't be very long. Damn, he couldn't take the chance. Couldn't let her take the chance.

Time and again he pushed her away, said something, did something to hurt her. But she'd come back and she'd find out that he hadn't really meant it, because never could he maintain his facade of anger or indifference when he was near her. God help them both, he loved her.

Chapter Twenty-seven

Kate sat there, puzzling over Hawke's sudden withdrawal. One minute he was talking to her amicably enough, considering he was Travis Hawke, and the next he wouldn't say a damned word to her.

She poked the cork back into her canteen, glaring at him. "I had a mule once that liked to think he was the most stubborn animal ever put on this earth. When he decided he wasn't going to move, you could've set his tail on fire and he wouldn't have budged one inch.

"But you know what? I got that danged beast to come to me whenever I whistled. Whether he was leader on a freight wagon or loose in a corral full of livestock, I whistled — that mule came runnin'. You know why?"

He seemed not to be listening, but she continued anyway.

"Because that mule loved apples. He would have died for an apple. And I always had an apple whenever I whistled for that mule."

He poked at the dirt with a stick, twisting the manacles so that they didn't chafe his wrists.

She leaned over, brushing her fingers along his cheek. "For you, my stubborn, stubborn Travis

Hawke, I will always, always have an apple."

She stood up then and walked back toward the others. She didn't see Hawke tilt his hat down over his eyes and bury his face in his hands.

"Kate," Parsons said, "I do wish you would stay away from vermin."

"You shouldn't talk about yourself that way, Wade," she grated. "You're not that bad." She poured herself a cup of coffee.

"Better drink it fast," Rafe said, "Dusty made it."

"Before it cools?"

"Before it eats through the bottom of the cup!"

Kate laughed. "I don't know what I'd do without the two of you." She hunkered down between her two favorite bullwhackers.

"How's the Cap'n?" Rafe asked.

"There's no captain here!" Parsons grunted.

"Hawke was a cap'n in the confederacy," Rafe said.

"Damned good one," Dusty put in, as Kate's mouth dropped open in stunned amazement.

"He's a bit grouchy," Kate said, "but then, he's always a bit grouchy."

Rafe gave her a playful nudge. "It's you keeps him that way. He don't know which is north or which is south when you're around. Why don't you put him out of his misery and marry him?"

Parsons slammed down his cup, his gaze skewering Kate. "Tell me this man is joking. Not you and that . . . that . . ." he gestured toward Hawke, "that murdering scum!"

"You found me out, Wade," she said, shrugging her shoulders. "I'm really sorry. But when I was a little girl, I promised myself that one day I'd fall in love with a man, but only if he was murdering scum. I wouldn't settle for anything less."

"I must say, I'm very disappointed in you."

"I'll try not to put a gun to my head. But you think about this, lieutenant. Hawke didn't kill anybody. Your keeping him chained only gives the murderer a clearer chance to strike again."

"Ah, Kate, the most unkindest cut of all. I must do my duty, as honor binds me."

"I hope you don't have to say those words over the next grave. That is," she paused meaningfully, "assuming you're not in it."

He straightened. "You have so much money, Kate. I'm afraid I simply must keep forgiving you your viper's tongue."

She had to laugh. "Maybe I will put on one of your plays, Wade. It would be worth it, just to see you speechless."

"See? I'm wearing you down already." He stood up. "If we're going to make another fifteen miles before nightfall, I suggest we get moving."

"You'll take off Hawke's chains?"

"I can't take that chance."

Kate grimaced, but did not waste her breath on further argument. She started toward Hawke as the others prepared to mount. Frowning, she looked around. "Where's Private Farley?"

"He was answering a call of nature behind them rocks yonder," Dusty said, pointing toward a pyramidal arrangement of boulders left in the middle of nowhere by some ages past geologic event.

Hawke ambled toward them, stepping cautiously to avoid tripping on the chain that fettered his ankles.

"Farley!" Rafe yelled. "We're leavin'! Get your pants up and come on!"

"Mr. Yates, there is a lady present!" Parsons fumed.

Kate watched the rocks. There was no sign of Farley. "There's something wrong."

"Stay here," Dusty ordered, drawing his gun. To

Hawke he said, "Watch out for her."

Dusty, Rafe, and Parsons approached the rocks, guns drawn.

"Not again," Kate whispered. "Please, God, not again."

The three men disappeared behind the boulders, Dusty reappearing almost instantly, his gun still ready, as he scanned the empty plains.

"Oh, God," Kate cried. "Oh, God."

Awkwardly, Hawke gripped her shoulders, keeping the manacles from digging into her back.

Dusty lengthened his bow-legged stride, hurrying over to them. "Throat's cut. I can't believe it. I just can't believe it. It's like we're fightin' a ghost."

Parsons came back, looking pale enough to pass for a ghost himself. He slipped a key out of his pocket and handed it to Kate. "You were right. It's not Hawke."

Quickly, Kate unchained him.

Hawke studied Parsons with a grudging admiration. The man might be a pompous jackass, but he could admit to making a mistake.

"Nobody's alone for the rest of the trip back," Hawke said. "Nobody. Not for one minute. It might be our only chance."

Parsons nodded. "We'll bury Farley, then try to find a decent place to defend for a camp tonight."

They settled on a flat stretch of ground Hawke considered virtually impossible to approach undetected. Even so, they built up the campfire and crowded close.

"Why doesn't this maniac just shoot us where we sit?" Parsons asked. "If he can get close enough to kill us one by one, surely he could pick all or most of us off with a rifle."

"I think he's enjoying himself," Hawke said.

Kate snuggled closer to him. For once it was he who insisted she sleep with him.

354

"Rafe 'n me will keep the first watch," Dusty said. "You three try to get some shuteye."

Kate lay down, wrapped in Hawke's arms, but she found sleep impossible. She was shaking like a rabbit cornered by a badger.

"It's all right, Kate," Hawke whispered, kissing the back of her neck. "I'm not going to let anything happen to you."

"It's not just me I'm worried about. It's you and Dusty and Rafe, and even Wade. I'm afraid to go to sleep, because I'm afraid I'll wake up and somebody else will be dead." Her lower lip trembled. "Damn, I hate this. I don't like being afraid. I feel so damned helpless."

He hugged her. "I know, believe me I know."

She twisted around to face him. "The cave?"

She felt the shudder pass through him. "I'm sorry," she murmured, "I didn't mean . . ."

"No, it's all right. It's so stupid, really. I know why I'm afraid, but I can't seem to do anything about it."

"Dan told me about the man at the orphanage."

His eyes narrowed. "Damn."

"And that you were drunk when you told him." She brushed her lips against his forehead. "Why do you shut out the people who care about you?"

"It's safer that way."

She kissed his eyebrows, his eyelids.

He moaned softly. "Damn you, don't get me started. We have an audience, remember?"

"Maybe Wade would have an appropriate quote from Shakespeare to go along with the activities on stage."

His mouth found hers, tasting, devouring. He wanted her. God in heaven, he wanted her so badly. It was all he could do not to tell her how much he loved her. But his fear of small, dark spaces was suddenly

355

nothing compared to his fear of losing Kate.

He held her away from him. "You may not mind an audience, but I do. Go to sleep."

She sighed. "I guess I'll just have to settle for my dreams again."

"It was dreaming that got you in trouble five years ago."

"No," she corrected saucily, "got *you* in trouble. I had a wonderful time."

He wrapped his arms around her waist, pulling her back against the rigid evidence of his need. "I should have known I stumbled into the room of a sorceress. My luck has always been a bit suspect."

"You luck was never better in your life than it was that night." She sighed. "Nor mine."

His hands rode up under her blankets, cupping her breasts. "You'll drive me mad yet, woman."

She giggled. "Always the apple, Hawke. Always the apple."

"Bitch."

"Bastard."

He held her close and, for a few hours at least, they slept.

Dawn shattered the sweet idyll. She sat bolt upright, a mindless terror gripping her heart.

Hawke was gone.

Chapter Twenty-eight

Kate was on her feet, scrambling up to Dusty's side. He was curled up in his blanket, and she breathed again only when she discovered him warm and alive. She did the same for Rafe, then marched toward Parsons, who was seated on the ground, his head lolled forward on his upraised knees.

Fearfully, she nudged him. He came awake with a start, reflexively levelling his pistol at her. "Sorry," he mumbled, stumbling to his feet. "Must have drifted off."

But Kate was no longer paying any attention to the three men. Her gaze scoured the landscape, searching for Hawke. His horse was still there. Surely, it was nothing more than nature. He was not lying dead . . .

"Where's Hawke?" she demanded of Parsons. "Damn you, you were on watch with him! Where is he?"

All three men were fully awake now.

"Take it easy, Katie," Rafe soothed, "Cap'n Hawke can take care of himself."

"Then where is he?"

They fanned out, each keeping the others in sight, walking in an ever-widening circle. Kate bit her lower lip so hard she drew blood. "He's all right, he's all right." She repeated it over and over, but the farther she walked, the less she believed it.

"Yo, Katie!" Rafe called, signalling for her to return to the campfire.

On trembling legs she hurried back to him. "Anything?"

He shook his head. "But that don't mean he's hurt. Don't you go thinkin' the worst now."

"Where is he? Where is he?" She was as close to hysteria as she had ever been in her life.

"We'll find him, Kate. I promise." He cupped his hands around his mouth and shouted to Dusty and Parsons. "Yo! Come on back!"

Parsons started in, but as Kate watched, Dusty seemed to stumble at the top of a small rise, the report of the rifle reaching her ears at the same instant he pitched forward into the dirt.

"Dusty!" she cried, racing toward him. Rafe's thundering strides kept pace behind her.

She collapsed beside her uncle, hauling him over onto his back. Jerking open his weathered buckskin jacket, she half-sobbed at the spreading red stain creeping across his homespun shirt. Her fists clenched in helpless fury. Then she was ripping open the buttons, using her bare hand to staunch the flow of blood. "Get something!" she hissed at Rafe.

He tore back to the camp at once, returning with her saddlebags. He upended the bags, dumping the contents onto the ground. Grabbing a clean shirt, he jammed it against the wound.

Parsons reached them, sinking at once to his knees, dragging air into his lungs in deep, shuddering gasps. "How bad is it?"

"I don't know yet," Kate said. "I think the bleeding's slowed a little."

She looked at Parsons. "Don't worry," he said, holding up a hand, "I'm not going to blame this on Hawke."

"Did you . . . did you see any sign of him?" She packed Dusty's wound as best she could, then bound it with torn strips of a second shirt.

"Nothing. It's like he vanished into the wind."

For the most absurd of instants Kate was grateful that Hawke's disappearance hadn't conjured a quote from the bard. But she would have sat through all of Shakespeare's plays in Swedish if she could have just so much as heard Hawke swear again.

Dusty groaned feebly, his eyes fluttering open.

"Don't move," Kate said, running a moistened cloth across his forehead. "You've been shot."

"Did ya see anything, pard?" Rafe asked, squeezing Dusty's hand in his own.

Dusty's mouth moved, but he winced suddenly, closing his eyes. The spasm seemed to pass. He opened his eyes again, though they were glazed with pain.

"Just take her easy, pard," Rafe said, "and tell us what you seen when you was shot."

A single word, but there was no mistaking it.

Hawke.

"Hawke did not shoot him," Kate seethed, bathing Dusty's fevered forehead, as the afternoon shadows lengthened.

"Then why did he say he did?" Parsons shouted. "I should have realized it all along. The son-of-a-bitch has had an accomplice."

Kate climbed to her feet, her body exhausted, her nerves on the teetering edge of pushing her to commit murder. "First of all, he did not say Hawke shot him. All he said, or seemed to say was that he had, in fact, seen Hawke before someone shot him."

"You'd defend Hawke if you'd seen him pull the trigger yourself."

"No. I wouldn't. If I'd seen Hawke shoot Dusty, Hawke would be a dead man."

"You know what's odd? I believe you."

Kate made Dusty as comfortable as possible. He seemed to be holding his own, but sudden movement could still kill him. "We'll have to stay here for awhile," she said.

"No, you don't, Katie," Rafe said, "you've got to get that money to Blanchard. I'll stay with Dusty."

"I'm not leaving you two alone."

"Miss Katie McCullough," Rafe said, "are you telling me that Dusty and I cannot survive without your protection? Shall I tell you of the winter I met Dusty in '31, the blizzard that . . ."

"I think I remember this one," she said, holding up a hand in self-defense. "You and Dusty can survive anything without me."

"Thank you. Now get that money to Blanchard."

"Blanchard's not in Leavenworth. He's out there right now, watching. I feel it. Besides, I'm not going anywhere until I find out what happened to Hawke."

"Then it looks like it's you and I, Kate," Parsons said.

"I beg your pardon?"

"Rafe will have to stay here with Dusty. So if this Blanchard is to be found, then you and I will have to find him."

"That's your way of saying you still think Hawke did it."

"I tell you what. When we find him, you can ask him."

"Count on it," Kate said. "Count on it."

She made certain Rafe was settled in with Dusty.

"You sure you'll be all right?"

His baleful stare prevented her from asking again. Dusty's fever was high, but she had every confidence in the grizzled old bullwhacker. He'd survived a lot worse.

Parsons brought up her horse as well as his own. She swung aboard. "I expect to see both of you old reprobates back in Leavenworth, Rafe," she said, blinking hard to hold back the tears. "You hear me?"

"I hear," he grinned. "You just make sure you're standin' at the altar ready to hogtie Cap'n Hawke to ya for life when me and Dusty get there."

"It's a deal," she whispered. She and Parsons rode out, heading toward the hollow from which she guessed the bullet had come.

When she reached the farthest range of the best rifle she knew, she dismounted and began to cast for sign.

"What if it was Hawke?" Parsons asked softly.

Kate clenched her fist, but didn't answer. Maybe it was an officer's nature not to trust anyone who'd rather give orders than take them.

"Here!" she called, stooping down to pick up a paper wrapped cartridge. "Sharps .52, I'd wager." She shot him a triumphant glare. "Hawke didn't have a Sharps."

Parsons shrugged. "We'll see."

They walked their mounts for nearly a mile, Kate constantly studying the ground for sign. Why would Hawke have gone off by himself? The question nagged at her, but she could come up with no sensible answer.

When they neared a rise, they tied off their horses. Stealthily, Kate crept to the top and peered over. What she saw sent a wave of fury through her such as she'd never known.

Sitting across from one another in front of a roaring campfire, laughing and drinking as though they were lifelong friends, sat Frank Blanchard and Travis

Hawke.

Her eyes blurring, she staggered back to her horse, yanking her rifle from its scabbard. There was no mistaking what lay on the ground beside Hawke. She had seen them in the hands of too many buffalo hunters.

A Sharps .52.

Chapter Twenty-nine

Hawke had fallen asleep holding Kate hard against him. Even though three men had been murdered, it was the most peaceful sleep he had ever known.

But long before it should have ended, Lt. Wade Parsons jabbed him awake with the tip of his rifle barrel. "Your turn on watch, Hawke. Get to it."

Coming grudgingly awake, Hawke unwound himself from Kate. He kissed her hair, tucking the blankets around her shoulders, then climbed to his feet.

"Yates or Lafferty see anything?" he asked.

"Nothing," Parsons said. "But that doesn't mean we won't."

Hawke grimaced at being told the obvious. "If you hear, or even think you hear something, yell out. No sense being a dead playwright. Shakespeare's already accepted the honor." He grabbed his Springfield and padded to the firelight's perimeter, grinning at Parsons's muffled oath.

He'd stood watch for about two hours when he caught the sound. He listened again. Nothing. But it had been there, he was certain of it, perhaps carried on a vagrant night breeze.

Voices.

He was about to call out to Parsons, when he changed his mind. The lieutenant was not someone he cared to have guarding his backside. If he went back to camp to rouse Rafe or Dusty, there was a good chance the commotion would awaken Kate. She would be on their tails two seconds after they left camp. It would be best if he did his own investigating. Hefting his saddle-bags over his right shoulder, he started walking.

He'd travelled over three miles, though he guessed barely one in a straight line, as he'd crisscrossed his own trail time and again seeking to pick up on the sound of the voices. His pace quickened, when at last he pinpointed their direction. Over that next rise.

At the top of the small hillock he flattened out to peer into the shallow valley below. A Conestoga wagon sat near a thicket. A young Chinese bustled back and forth between the wagon and a man seated on an ostentatious throne-back chair near a well-camouflaged campfire. Scarcely any smoke drifted from the fire and Hawke could detect nothing of what was being cooked over it. Blanchard, it would seem, could manipulate even nature to his whim.

Hawke knew he should return at once to his own camp for help, but the need to take down Blanchard alone was a strong one. Nestling his rifle under his arm, he stood up and walked down the hill.

Chin Li stopped dead with the food-laden tray he carried, his eyes meeting Hawke's. He darted a glance at Blanchard, then away. Bowing, he returned the tray to the wagon.

"Come in, Hawke," Blanchard called, not once turning in his chair to confirm his visitor's identity, "I've been expecting you."

"Because you killed three men?"

"You just won't understand me, will you? I only kill when absolutely necessary. Please," he gestured imperiously with his left hand, "join me in a light repast. I do so enjoy a treat for the palate in the cool embers of night just before dawn."

Hawke gripped the rifle in his fist, skirting Blanchard's chair by several feet.

"So suspicious. How sad for you." Blanchard clapped his hands, and Chin Li returned with the tray. The boy raised the lid of the silver serving dish. Bowing, he handed Blanchard a tiny china plate on which lay a curved, delicate French pastry.

"Croissant, Mr. Hawke?" asked Blanchard.

"No. Thanks just the same."

"Such polite sarcasm. I can arrange for beefsteaks and potatoes, if you like?"

"Nothing. Really." He levelled his rifle at Blanchard, drawing back the hammer. "I think we can stop the games."

Blanchard sighed. "I suppose that's so." He held out the china plate and Chin Li was instantly at his side to retrieve it. Blanchard nodded toward the wagon. "I would have expected you to be a bit more wary. A pity."

"Drop it!" came a hard voice Hawke did not recognize.

"If I don't?"

"I'll kill you," the voice said.

"And I kill Blanchard. Guaranteed."

Blanchard chuckled. "Stalemate. How droll." He took a sip from the cup of tea resting on the arm of his chair. "Surely you recognize your former employer, Mr. Hawke? The man who sent you to me. Mr. Ed Reno."

Hawke straightened, but did not turn. "So that's how you found out."

"Some friends of mine busted me out of jail," came the voice. "I found out what you were up to. I decided to spoil the party."

365

"Doesn't matter," Hawke said. "I've got enough evidence on you, Blanchard, to put you away for six lifetimes. Except that I'm not going to put you away. I'm going to kill you."

"I'm well aware of your intentions," Blanchard said. "But I've yet to uncover just what precisely your motive is for wanting to bring me harm. I will assume it was some sort of personal injustice."

"You might say that," Hawke said. "You killed my wife."

"What?"

The shock in Blanchard's voice was genuine and for just an instant it startled Hawke. "You don't even remember, do you?" he snarled.

"I've never killed a woman in my life. Not even that little snip, Kate McCullough, though I may yet enjoy the pleasure. But those reasons are my own." He studied Hawke intently in the gray light. "I'm certain I did not kill your wife, nor anyone else's. Perhaps, if we could discuss this calmly, we could get to the root of our misunderstanding and become friends after all."

"Go to hell!"

Blanchard's lips compressed, the muscle in his jaw doing somersaults. "I'm sorry you've decided to be unreasonable."

Otis, the hulking gorilla from Blanchard's suite in the Planters Hotel, stepped out of the shadows of the trees.

"He takes another step," Hawke said, "and I'll kill you both."

Blanchard snapped his fingers at Otis, calling Hawke's bluff.

The big man advanced toward Hawke. Hawke raised his rifle to his shoulder, sighting on Blanchard, fully expecting Ed Reno's bullet to slam into his back. But Blanchard only smiled. Hawke settled his finger on the trigger, sweat beading his brow in spite of the morning chill.

"It is no use." Blanchard said. "When you know your enemy, he cannot defeat you. A Wells Fargo agent does not commit murder, Mr. Hawke. You might want to kill me, but you cannot unless I am foolish enough to point a gun at you myself."

Otis stood still, waiting for further signals from Blanchard. Reno had started brewing himself a cup of coffee. Hawke cursed, lowering his rifle. He'd been a fool to confront Blanchard alone. Yet some part of him needed to talk this out. He couldn't have the man dead. Not yet. He had to know the whys he had never found out from Anne.

"Tell me about your wife," Blanchard said, the silken tone of his voice seeming to enhance its underlying malevolence. "I'm most distressed that you could accuse me of killing her when I don't even know who she was."

Hawke said nothing.

"I told you, I kill only when absolutely necessary. Your silence, I'm afraid, is making it necessary." To Reno he said, "Take the Sharps and kill one of the bullwhackers in the camp."

"No." Hawke started toward Blanchard, but Otis stepped in his way. Hawke stopped. For now. "I'll tell you."

Reno returned to his place by the fire and poured himself a cup of coffee. Hefting one of Blanchard's croissants, he dunked it into the brew. "Not much to this little bitty bread loaf," he said. "Like eatin' air."

Blanchard gripped the arm of his chair, sipping pointedly on his tea. "I'm waiting, Mr. Hawke."

"Her name was Anne." His guts churned to be talking about her to the man responsible for her death. But he had to know the whole truth, and he had to protect Kate. He kept his voice deliberately emotion-less, just wanting to get it said. "Six years ago we were living in San Francisco. Anne decided she didn't want to have children. You gave her some kind of powder."

Blanchard laughed derisively. "Do you know how many women I have given those powders to? I can assure you they have absolutely no ill effects when taken in the proper dosage. Now if your wife was foolish enough to . . ."

"She got pregnant. She was scared. She was angry. But mostly, she trusted you and your powders."

"I still fail to see how I killed her," Blanchard said. "I merely gave her what she asked for."

"She came to you again," Hawke gritted, "after she was pregnant." And suddenly it was as though he and Blanchard were the only two people in the world. He could never confront Anne with what she had done, because she had cheated him of the chance by dying. But Blanchard would know what he had done. And he would die for it. Self-defense or not.

Blanchard shook his head. "I was very busy in San Francisco. Buying up railroads, shipping lines, banks. My patients came by in the evening. But most of the ladies, I assure you, did not use their real names."

"Patients!" Hawke snarled. "My God, you make yourself sound like a doctor."

"Oh, much better than any doctor. As I told you, Mr. Hawke, I'm going to live to be one hundred, and be healthy every minute I'm alive. I feel it is my duty to help others who seek good health and long life."

"You're a liar!"

Blanchard lifted a finger toward Otis. The big man stepped forward, backhanding Hawke across the mouth. Hawke reeled, but stayed on his feet. "You killed my wife. You killed my baby. And I'm going to kill you."

Otis hit him again. Hawke tried to right himself, tried to raise a hand to defend against the next blow. He might as well have tried to fend off an enraged bear with a willow branch. Otis landed another crunching blow to his jaw.

Hawke staggered, a blinding pain melding with a blinding light, exploding, shattering inside his head. He tumbled forward into the welcoming arms of oblivion.

Chapter Thirty

Hawke sputtered, turning away from the second bucket of cold water that had just been emptied on his head.

"Come now, Mr. Hawke," Blanchard said, "we haven't got all morning. Our guests will be arriving any moment. We must be ready."

Hawke shook his head, shoving himself up to a sitting position. "You should have killed me while you had the chance."

"You persist in being foolish," Blanchard chided. "It could have been very different between us. I detect a strong sense of loyalty in you. I honor loyalty above all."

"You're about as loyal as a hungry snake."

"Enough of this." He looked toward the top of the hillock, where Otis was hidden away in the trees. "Our guests are almost here." He pointed at the side of the fire, which would put Hawke's back to the hillside. "Sit down there, please, Mr. Hawke."

Hawke didn't move.

"If I say anything else twice, our guests won't be enjoying breakfast with us. They'll be dead."

Hawke's eyes narrowed. "What the hell are you

talking about?"

"More precisely, *who* am I talking about? I believe you've developed quite an affection for the little tart. Kate McCullough. She's just over the hill with some man in uniform."

Hawke stiffened, but Blanchard raised a hand in warning. "One move, and Otis will drop them where they stand. Oh, and if you're wondering where Mr. Reno is, I assure you he's quite nearby, and would be only too happy to accommodate you, should you choose suicide."

"You harm her in any way, any way at all, and I'll take you apart a piece at a time."

"Your threats are growing most tiresome. I assure you I was quite serious when I said I will kill when necessary." Blanchard seated himself across from Hawke in front of the fire. "I'm going to tell you something, and when I finish, I expect you to laugh. I want Miss McCullough to hear you laughing. Just remember that Otis is waiting."

Hawke clenched his fists in impotent fury. He'd been every kind of a fool to come into Blanchard's camp alone, just to satisfy his own damned hate. Now Kate was going to pay the price.

"While you were unconscious," Blanchard said, hefting a Sharps .52 and laying it on Hawke's right side, "Mr. Reno was kind enough to shoot Dusty Lafferty with that gun."

Hawke's features contorted. "You son-of-a-bitch!"

"Laughter, Mr. Hawke. Amusement, remember? Or Kate McCullough only has seconds to live."

Somewhere inside of him, he conjured the sound of laughter, though he thought surely it sounded as sick and hollow as he felt. But sincerity wouldn't matter. All that would matter was Kate seeing him with Blanchard, laughing about anything at all, when four men had been killed.

Blanchard chuckled. "She's seen you now. She's gone back to her horse for her rifle. I wonder which of us she'll shoot first?" He dabbed at the corners of his mouth with his napkin after finishing another croissant.

"When Otis brings her and her companion down here you're to make it absolutely clear to her that you're working for me and always have been."

Hawke laid his hand along the breech of the Sharps, assuring himself of what he'd already known, Blanchard was not stupid enough to give him a loaded gun. In a way, he was about to get his own wish. Kate would hate him. But somehow he no longer welcomed the idea.

He cocked an ear toward the sound of her cursing and swearing behind him. She was giving Otis more than his share. He shook his head, smiling in spite of the circumstances. She was one helluva woman.

Blanchard stood up as Kate approached the campfire. Hawke used the distraction to shift his saddlebags next to his left hip. He tugged open the leather strap, then turned to look at Kate.

"Welcome, my dear," Blanchard was saying. "Might I invite you . . ."

"Shut up, you pig-faced skunk. You think you got away with killing my father, well, let me tell you, you won't get away with the others. With Sheridan and Farley and Parker."

"As usual you're rattling on like a magpie and I haven't the slightest idea what you're talking about. Though had you mentioned Dusty Lafferty's name, I might have been able to shed some light on his misfortune for you." He looked at Hawke.

Kate forced herself to look at him too. His one word was a question. "Dusty?"

She arced her fist back, but let it drop harmlessly to her side. What was the use? "Damn you, Hawke. Damn you to hell."

"What a charming young woman," Blanchard clucked.

"Give me my gun back. You'll see how charming I can be."

"I don't think so, dear."

She picked up her saddlebags, and, under the watchful eye of Otis, tossed them at Blanchard's feet. "There's your money, bastard. Now I want that note. McCullough Freight is mine again. Free and clear."

Blanchard laughed. "Do you really think I care about your silly little freight company? I have millions and millions of dollars. I have no need of you, your freight company, or your money."

"Then just what the hell is all of this about? You killed people, my father, and you don't even give a damn . . ."

"All in good time, my dear. All in good time. Please, join me for breakfast. And have the good manners to introduce me to the lieutenant. You haven't allowed him a word . . ."

"Lt. Wade Parsons," Parsons said. "And you're under arrest, Mr. Blanchard."

Blanchard laughed. "Charming! Charming!"

Kate raked a hand through her hair. How in the hell were they going to get out of this mess? Did she even care? She looked at Hawke, her heart aching. How could he have betrayed her so utterly? All of it a lie. The garbage about Blanchard killing his wife, everything. Just to throw her off. What else could it be?

She reached down and gripped his arm. "You must be so very proud of yourself. Making a complete fool of me. Did you especially enjoy laughing after the day on the creek?"

He shrugged, his voice hard. "There were times I found you interesting, but I was being paid to do a job."

"You said Blanchard killed your wife."

"If he hadn't, I would have killed her myself."

"My God, you're as much a monster as he is."

"If you two are finished with this touching exchange," Blanchard put in, "I'd like to attend to a little business I have with you, Miss McCullough."

"Go to hell!"

Hawke grabbed her wrist. "You do what the boss tells you, and quit smartin' off. He might have Otis break your neck."

She clenched her fist. "Maybe I'll see that yours is broken before the day is out."

"Enough of this!" Blanchard snapped, obviously growing impatient. "Hawke, I want you to tie up Miss McCullough and Lieutenant Parsons. We're going to have a little celebration for her successful shipment to Ft. Laramie."

Hawke took the rope from Otis and stepped over to Kate. She glared at him.

"Put your hands behind your back, Kate."

She did as he said, swearing the whole time he stood behind her. He wrapped the rope around her wrists, careful not to cut off her circulation, wishing there was some way he could tell her this was all a lie. But Reno was on the hill with a rifle, he dare not take the chance. He knotted the rope, then started to step back. In that instant, as Kate continued to harangue Blanchard, she caught Hawke's fingers and squeezed.

Then she whirled, facing him squarely, cussing a blue streak. And winked at him!

He turned abruptly, carrying the rest of the rope

over to Parsons. He couldn't have looked at Kate another second without grinning. She knew! Somehow she knew. With all the evidence stacked against him in this camp, she was telling him that she believed none of it, that she believed in him.

He was not as mindful of Parsons's circulation. "I knew you were murdering scum," the lieutenant muttered. Hawke merely smiled and walked back over to his saddlebags.

"Now, my dear Miss McCullough," Blanchard said, taking a sip of his tea, "I'm going to tell you a little story. You always loved to hear stories around the campfire with your father. Well, this should be an especial favorite, because it's about your father."

"How you killed him!"

"My dear, my dear, no one regretted that abominable bull's timing more than I did. If I had my way, your father would be with us today. Here. Now." He paused, stepping over to grab a fistful of her hair, jerking her head painfully back. "Because I would kill you right in front of his eyes."

"Why? What did my father ever do to you?"

He shoved her away from him. "He took the one thing in my life I ever loved."

"I can't imagine a pig like you loving anything," she spat. If he was going to kill her she was going to make it worth her while.

Blanchard slapped her. Out of the corner of her eye she didn't fail to notice that Hawke hadn't so much as blinked. Damn him! How long was he going to let Blanchard get away with this?

"I never could understand what Jim Collier saw in you, you little bitch," Blanchard said. "A dedicated servant of the law slobbering after you like a moonstruck hound. He would come to my office to post a wanted dodger, and he would never fail to tell me what a pure, chaste young woman you were." He laughed. "At least, he noticed you were a bit eccentric, though he preferred the term unique."

"He should have thrown you in jail, then set a pack of starved wolves in your cell. But you took care of him, too, didn't you? Crippled him."

"You blame me for so many things." Blanchard lifted her chin, shaking his head. "You just don't understand. No one does. There was only one person I wanted dead when I came to Leavenworth. One. But first I wanted him ruined. Then I wanted to kill his daughter. But fate cheated me. A damned ox cheated me."

"You liar! You killed my father!"

"I wanted to, because twenty-two years ago he killed me."

"What are you . . ."

"The only thing I ever loved. Bonnie McDonough."

Kate's mouth fell open. She didn't recognize her own voice. "My mother? You?"

"My name was Jacob Sinclair then. I lived on the same street with the McDonoughs in Boston." Kate watched him, fascinated, as he lost himself in memory. It was the look on his face that stunned her most. The cruel sadist that had slapped her gave way to a gentle, almost placid face, as he spoke of her long dead mother. "I asked Bonnie to marry me every day of my life from the time I was ten and she was eight. I promised her the world, and I meant to give it to her."

As he talked, Kate worked on the ropes that bound her, glancing at Parsons to see that he was doing the same. Hawke seemed to be paying no attention to anything. His eyes were on Otis, and oddly on the hills behind the wagon.

"On the day I bought her a ring, her seventeenth birthday, your damned father came into town, fresh off the boat from Scotland, acting like America was his for the taking. Turned a young woman's head. I don't blame Bonnie. Bryce was full of bluster."

"My mother loved my father."

"No! No!" Blanchard raged. "He'd simply turned her head for awhile. She would have come back to me. She would have. Even after she had his squallin' brat, I knew she would come back." His eyes misted. "But he packed her in a wagon and took into this godforsaken country. He killed her. Killed her as sure as stuck a knife in her breast."

"You're out of your mind. My father loved her. It broke his heart when she died."

"I promised her the world, and I built it for her. The whole Blanchard empire, for my Bonnie. And your son-of-a-bitch father had to go and get himself gored by an ox before I even had the pleasure of telling him who I was and what I was going to do to him."

"He knew," she whispered.

"What did you say?"

"He knew. He must have known. That's why he sent me to that damned school. Because he was afraid for me. Not just because some rival freighter was in town, but because he knew who you were." Her eyes widened. "Sinclair! Of course, Dusty told me Pa was worried about someone named Sinclair, right before he died. But Dusty never knew who he meant."

Blanchard clapped his hands and Chin Li brought him a wicked looking carving knife. "Your father might be dead. But I have the feeling he's here, watching. So I'm going to kill you in front of him, after all."

He raised the knife above her face.

"That's a bit crude for you, isn't it, Frank?" Hawke said softly, easing open his saddlebags.

"A crude death for a crude young woman."

Blanchard was aware of nothing and no one but Kate. It gave Hawke the precious seconds he needed to stuff the fuse into the stick of dynamite he had extracted from his saddlebags.

"If my father's watching," Kate said, "then so is my mother. My mother. The woman you supposedly loved."

He hesitated, then shook his head. "No. You're no daughter to Bonnie. Bonnie was a lady. She would never have been mother to whatever it is you are." He raised the knife higher, readying it for the plunge. "This is for Bonnie."

"No!" Hawke shouted.

Blanchard did not look up. "Kill him, Reno!"

Hawke lit the dynamite and heaved it up the hillside, diving toward Blanchard, as a bullet kicked up dirt behind him. The explosion rocked the entire camp. No more shots came from the hill.

Hawke slammed into Blanchard, driving him sideways and down.

Kate jerked her hands free of the rope, twisting away as Otis lumbered toward her. She shoved Parsons under the wagon ahead of her, working him free of his ropes, just as Otis grabbed hold of her ankle and pulled. "Wade, help me!"

He scrambled for one of the fist-sized rocks that circled the cookfire and slammed it against Otis's bear-paw hand. Kate yowled as the concussion rocked through to her ankle, but at least Otis had let go.

For an instant she feared he would come under the wagon after her, but then to her horror she saw that his attention was now diverted to Hawke. Hawke, who had thrown himself full length against Blanchard, just as the man had been about to . . . She shuddered, unable to take her eyes off the two men grappling just inches away from her at the rear of the wagon.

"Shoot him!" Blanchard shrieked. "Otis, shoot him!"

Hawke was on top of Blanchard, but Blanchard still held the knife. He slashed upward wildly. Otis was picking up her rifle, aiming it at Hawke.

In a hundred years she wouldn't have been able to move Otis. Instead she threw herself at Hawke, waiting for the bullet from her own rifle that would end her life. But Otis had not been told to shoot her, only Hawke. While she clung to Hawke's back, Otis held his fire.

She could feel the muscles of Hawke's back bulge as he bore down on Blanchard's upraised arms. Then suddenly, she crumpled forward, as Hawke's superior leverage broke through Blanchard's only defense. The man's arms collapsed, bringing with them the knife plunging downward in his own hand.

Hawke strove with everything in him to stop the momentum of the knife, but it was impossible. It slid to the hilt into Blanchard's heaving chest.

Exhausted, Hawke couldn't even roll off him, Kate resolutely refusing to remove herself from his back. "Otis will shoot you," she hissed in his ear.

"He could shoot *through* you," he hissed back.

Kate twisted a look behind her. "Drop the gun, Otis."

"Brilliant," Hawke said.

But to her amazement Otis dropped the gun. Apparently, the man followed orders, regardless of who gave them.

She gave Hawke a smug grin. "It was rather brilliant, wasn't it?" Blowing out a shuddering breath, she sagged away from him.

Parsons crawled out from under the wagon. "A most horrifying experience," he said. "It puts me in mind of a little thought from Will out of *Hamlet*. 'I could a tale unfold whose lightest words would harrow up thy soul, freeze thy young blood, make thy two eyes, like stars, start from their spheres . . .'"

"Later, Wade," Kate sighed. "Please. Later."

She was content to lie beside Hawke, who had struggled to sit up and was staring at the uneven rise and fall of Frank Blanchard's chest. The knife still protruded grotesquely from just below his breast bone.

"Don't you die on me, you son-of-a-bitch," he said. "I've waited too long. Don't you dare die."

"Leave him be, Hawke," she said. "It's finished."

"No! No. He has to tell me what Anne said . . . why she . . ."

"Why what?" she asked gently.

He pulled away from her, not answering, then none too subtly changed the subject. "How did you know?"

"Know what?"

"That I wasn't working for Blanchard."

"I told you. I can always tell when you're lying, Travis Hawke. So you might as well give up the habit."

His throat tightened. "I'll think about it."

"So when are you going to admit you love me?"

He looked away. "Nothing's changed, Kate. I want no ties. None."

"Hawke, don't you turn your back on me. Not now."

"Everyone I've ever loved is dead."

"I'm not going to die, at least not 'til I get good and ready."

"I won't risk it, Kate. I won't."

"I'd risk anything for you."

He looked at Blanchard, his chest barely rising now, his face ghostly pale. "The bastard's going to die, and I'll never know . . Damn." He climbed to his feet. He did not look back.

He left Blanchard.

He left Kate.

Not accepting his past.

Turning his back on his future.

Chapter Thirty-one

Kate slammed open the door to her freight office, slammed it shut behind her, stomped over to the waste container beside her desk and kicked it into the wall.

"One more person," she screamed to the empty office, "one more person on this earth tells me to forget about Travis Hawke and a judge is gonna be hangin' me by the neck until I am dead."

Eight months. It had been eight months since she, Rafe, and Parsons had buried Frank Blanchard on the Nebraska plains. Eight months since she'd seen or heard from Travis Hawke. Eight months that had seemed more like eight lifetimes.

"He's out there," she said grimly, "he's out there, and the bastard is as miserable as I am. But he's just too damned jackass stubborn to admit it."

Or so she kept telling herself. What was worse was that lately it was as though she could almost feel him near her. But every time she whirled to look, there was no one there.

She turned at the sound of the door opening, ready to kick the scattered trash under the desk if it happened to be a customer. She grinned. "Hi, Dusty!"

"Havin' a private conniption, or can anybody join

in?"

"Never mind."

"I won't say his name. I learned my lesson three months ago in 'Frisco."

You didn't learn it well enough, Dusty, she thought, *or you wouldn't bring up San Francisco.* She and Dusty had made a late season shipment, and to her eternal regret she had been foolish enough to go to the same hotel she'd been in six years ago with Hawke, even to finagling the same room. It had been a disaster. She'd spent the entire night in tears. And Dusty had made the mistake of commenting on her appearance the next morning, intimating it might have something to do with a certain missing reb.

"It looks like it's going to be a good year," she said, changing the subject.

"McCullough's got the contracts, the reputation. You've done a damned fine job, lass."

"Thanks, Dusty." What else had she had to do? She'd thrown herself into the company lock, stock, and broken heart. She'd solidified the freighting business, while diversifying to railroads, manufacturing, and ranching. She was a wealthy woman, and she was miserable.

"You goin' with the next outfit up to the Humboldt?"

She shook her head.

"You ain't gone out since 'Frisco. And that was the only one since Ft. Laramie last year. Tired o' the trail, lass?"

His voice was gently probing, and she knew he meant well. But unlike Rafe, Dusty had never really accepted the fact that she was in love with Hawke. To Dusty, once Hawke was gone, it was time she got on with her life.

"I just have a lot of bookwork now," she said. "With

the different businesses."

"Uh huh."

She sat down behind the desk and opened one of the mammoth ledgers. Even the entries on the page jumped out to haunt her. A twenty-five thousand dollar loan to one Lt. Wade Parsons, shortly after his transfer to New York in January. He'd written to tell her that two of his plays had already become popular and critical sensations. She was happy for him, but as with everything else the notation on the loan inadvertently twisted the knife on her never-ending memories of Hawke.

After Dusty left, she threw down her pencil, unable to add three figures and get the same number twice. Eight months and not a word. Would she feel any differently in eight years? In eighty? What made her any different than Frank Blanchard, who had carried a lifelong torch, grown twisted and cruel, for a woman who had chosen another man?

Hawke may not have chosen another woman but the results were the same. He'd taken himself out of her life of his own free will. She had not ridden after him and begged him to stay. She had not tried to find him. Not written to any place he might have been. But she ached for him every minute of every day.

San Francisco. God, why had she gone back? A reporter for a San Francisco newspaper, Randall Lloyd, had stopped by her hotel room, collecting facts for a story on the late multi-millionaire, Frank Blanchard. A connecting piece in the reporter's puzzle had been a Wells Fargo agent named Travis Hawke.

Kate had corrected Lloyd, telling him Dan Parker had been the agent. But the reporter had been adamant, both Parker and Hawke had been agents.

The whole thing from the Columbia stage depot to his wanting a job as wagonmaster had been part of an elaborate scheme by Hawke, by Wells Fargo to build a case against Blanchard.

"Why are you digging all of this up now?" Kate had asked.

Lloyd had been like a hound on a hunt, excited, eager. "Rumor has it someone is trying to take over Blanchard's empire. The law wants to make sure the pieces never get put back together. The man was one master criminal—embezzling, robbery, murder, extortion—on an international scale. It's hard to believe he died in a knife fight on a dusty trail to nowhere."

Kate hadn't been able to resist. "You think this Hawke fellow is anything important in the story now?"

"I don't know. Nobody's been able to track him down. Not even Fargo's best." The reporter had given her a conspiratorial wink. "Everything I get on this Hawke says that he's licking his wounds somewhere. Busted up pretty bad over some woman."

Kate had gripped her hands together so tightly her knuckles whitened. "I knew Mr. Hawke fairly well. I find that extremely difficult to believe."

Lloyd had only shrugged and thanked her for her time. Kate had spent the evening in tears in a room that had once brought her magic.

Sighing, she slapped the ledgers shut and put them away. For all the good she was doing here, she might as well go home. She did have a dinner engagement tonight.

Standing in front of the mirror in her bedroom, she stared unconcerned at the drab olive color of her simple cotton dress. Her hair hung limply, and she made no attempt to pin it up in a stylish braid. It hardly mattered if she was wearing a rain barrel and hip boots, Jim Collier would tell her she was the most beautiful woman in the world. And she would feel guilty that she had again succumbed to his wheedling and gone out to dinner with him.

Opening the door to her room, she nearly collided with Lydia.

"You have another evening planned with Jim, I see," the woman said.

Kate nodded. "I know I'm a fool. You don't have to tell me." Kate and Lydia had grown closer over the winter months, their first without having to vie for Bryce McCullough's attention. Still, neither confided in the other. It was just that they didn't exchange harsh words very often any more.

Lydia pulled a lace kerchief from her dress pocket, the cough that she had developed over a month ago seeming only to grow worse, never better. The dark circles under her eyes had become so much a part of her that Kate would have noticed them only by their absence.

"When are you going to see a doctor?"

"They couldn't help me," she said, so quickly that Kate shot her a curious look. "I mean, I'll be all right." She set her teacup down on Kate's bureau. "How much longer do you think you can put off Jim's proposals, Kate?"

"Forever. I'm not marrying him. I've made that clear enough." She gave Lydia a wan smile. "Have you given up on him?"

"You mean about him ever walking again?"

"No, about his getting interested in you instead of me?"

Lydia seemed to pale visibly. "I've never wanted his attentions, Kate."

"That wasn't the impression I got."

"Well, it's the truth."

"Whatever you say." Though Lydia's denial of a romantic interest in Jim left Kate perplexed as to what in the world the woman got out of caring for him twenty-four hours a day, seven days a week.

Kate trudged down the stairs, finding herself hoping that Jim had changed his mind, as he had done several times lately. He'd been very secretive about why he'd cancelled, assuring her that one day she wouldn't mind. Each time Lydia had then taken him for long rides in the country, though she had adamantly refused to say where.

If they did it again, Kate had decided, she was going to follow them. She had grown to detest secrets.

Besides, she could guess where they had gone. The cave. Jim's secret discovery. His favorite place. Jim had taken her there once, long ago. Just before she'd left for Boston. The labyrinth of mazes and darkness had held no fascination for her then, and now it would serve only to remind her of Hawke.

"I love it here," Jim had said. "It's like my own world. Like nothing else exists but you and me."

She shivered, remembering how he had pulled her into one of the tunnels, then laughing had dropped the torch and left her there. She groped about blindly for nearly ten minutes, calling Jim every foul name she'd ever heard in her life before he had come back.

"I was only teasing," he'd said. "Maybe I should keep you here, then you can't go to Boston and leave me." The look in his eyes in the flickering torchlight had for just an instant made Kate wonder if he was going to do just that. But then he had smiled, gripped her hand, and led her back out to the sunshine.

Angrily, Kate pulled herself back from the disturbing thoughts.

"Ready for dinner?" Jim asked, gliding out of the bedroom Kate would forever consider her father's.

"Of course," Kate said, hiding her disappointment.

"You look positively stunning, Kate."

"Thank you, Jim." Next time she'd try the rain

barrel.

Kate took her place behind the wheelchair and guided it out of the house. In all of her time with Jim the fact that he was in the wheelchair had never once entered into her thoughts about why she wanted no serious relationship with him. But a night never passed when he didn't assure her that he wouldn't be in the chair forever. That one day they could be married.

At dinner at the Continental Hotel he pushed things a step further. "I think it's time we set a wedding date, Kate."

The bit of potato she had been about to eat made its way back to her plate. He had chosen the wrong day to test her temper. "Jim," she said evenly, "this is really getting tiresome. I've tried to be kind. I've tried to be firm. Now I'm afraid I'm going to have to try being angry."

"I love you, Kate."

"I do *not* love you. I've told you time and again that I go out with you because I have no other beaux, nor do I have any interest in finding one. And I told you why. I am in love with, and will forever be in love with, a man named Travis Hawke. How much more honest can I be?"

"It'll take time, but you'll learn to love me, Kate."

"I'm going to learn to hate you."

"You were always such a character, Kate. That's why I love you. How about if we're married a week from Saturday?"

"Not a week from Saturday. Not ever."

"I've arranged everything with the preacher, invited the guests . . ."

Kate set her napkin on the table. "Don't ever ask me out to dinner, or anywhere else, ever again, Jim Collier. Ever again. I'm sorry. But I don't think we can even be friends anymore. You simply do not hear anything I say." She stood up and left the restaurant.

Fuming, she tromped up the street, waving away carriages with polite offers for a ride home. She wanted to walk off the storm of emotions that roiled through her.

Jim Collier was her own dumb fault. She'd used him as a cushion, a fence, between herself and men who'd begun to make overtures to a successful business-woman. No longer was she anathema to Leavenworth social circles.

Saying she had a dinner engagement or theatre engagement with Jim often enough had finally discouraged even the most ardent among them. But never, never had she been dishonest with Jim. He was just totally blind to reality. Maybe it was being in the wheelchair, giving him too much time to indulge in fantasies.

"Lydia!" she called, as she strode through the front door. "Lydia, we have to talk!"

The woman hurried into the parlor, looking oddly guilty for a moment, but Kate chalked up the notion to her own overactive imagination. "You're home early, Kate."

"I'm moving out."

"You're what? Kate, what are you talking about?"

"You've been very kind allowing me to stay in the house. It's your house. I'm moving out."

"What happened?"

"The same old thing that always happens with Jim. He talks about when he's going to marry me. I'm just not able to handle it any more. I can live at one of the hotels for awhile, then maybe I'll buy a house of my own."

"He won't let you . . . I mean, you can't leave. It's not right. This was your home."

"My home is out on the prairie. Maybe that's what's

389

wrong with me. Staying behind that damned desk. Just to keep from thinking about that Hawke." She laughed without humor. "That's the absurdity. I think about him behind the desk as much as I would on the trail."

"If you could just forget him. Jim is a very nice . . ."

"Jim is obsessed, crazy! A lunatic! I . . ."

Lydia's stricken face, as she stared at the open front door, told Kate all she needed to know.

Kate's shoulders sagged. "I'm sorry, Jim. I'm just angry. But you . . ." She turned, her eyes widening. Jim Collier was standing on his own two feet, a .44 Colt levelled at her middle.

Chapter Thirty-two

Kate glared first at Jim, then at Lydia. "How long?" she hissed. "How long has he been able to walk?"

"We don't need to discuss that right now, Kate darling," Jim said.

"And what the hell do you think you're doing, pointing a gun at me?"

Jim gave her an apologetic smile. "It's the only way, isn't it? I mean, you wouldn't come with me, if I didn't have it?"

"Come with you?"

"Yes, we're going for a ride, Kate. Right now." He jerked the gun toward the door. "Please, don't make me shoot you. I won't kill you, of course. But it would be quite painful." He thumbed back the hammer.

Kate moved toward the door, raking her hair away from her face. "Why, Lydia?" she asked. "Why are you helping him do this to me?"

"I'm sorry, Kate," the woman choked. "Truly I am."

"Why?"

Jim laughed. "This is why." He held a small vial

of white powder in his hand, waving it tauntingly in Lydia's direction.

Lydia licked her lips. "Please, Jim, give it to me. I was good. I did what you told me. Please?"

"Oh, my God," Kate said. "Opium?" The dark circles, the coughing, the trembling. Damn, she'd been too wrapped up in herself and her own problems to see what had been happening to Lydia for months. Kate grimaced. That damned tea. Lydia was never without it.

Jim tossed the vial to Lydia, who made a pathetic grab for it, but missed. It struck the hardwood floor, shattering, the deadly white powder dappling the broken glass. Lydia dropped to her knees, sobbing. Moistening her fingers, she began to dab at the powder, bringing it to her lips.

Kate rushed over to her. "Lydia, for godsakes, you're going to cut your mouth. There's glass . . ." With surprising strength the older woman shoved Kate away. "I'm sorry, Kate. I'm sorry. But I couldn't help myself. I need it. I've always needed it."

Kate's eyes narrowed. "Not my father . . . ?"

"No, no, Bryce tried to help me stop. I did for awhile, but after he died . . . after he died . . ." Her body trembled. "I'm sorry. I'm sorry."

"We're leaving, Kate darling," Jim said, gesturing toward the door with the gun. "I'm not saying it again."

"You were a lawman. How can you do this?"

"Outside, Kate."

"How . . . long will you be gone?" Lydia whimpered.

"It won't matter," Jim said.

"But who will give me what I need?"

"I'll give you what you've needed for a long time,

Lydia." Before Kate could react, he squeezed the trigger on the Colt.

Lydia screamed, grabbing her stomach, pitching forward onto the floor. Kate tried to go to her, but Jim grabbed her arm. He gave her his most dazzling smile. "Now no one but you and I know about the caves."

Kate gasped. "If you think I'm going with you to those damned tunnels . . ."

He shoved the gun in her face. "You're going wherever I tell you."

Kate jerked away from him and walked out the door. She had to keep her wits about her. The bastard would have to go to sleep sometime.

He already had her mare saddled and ready for her. She swung into the saddle. "You're not going to get away with this."

"It'll be all right, Kate, you'll see. Just like I've always told you. You'll learn to love me." He looped a rope around her mare's neck. "I wouldn't want you to get lost."

Together they rode out of town, Jim keeping to the back streets and alleys. They saw no one. This was a nightmare; it wasn't happening. Jim Collier was whining and obsessive, but he wasn't dangerous. How could she have lived in the same house with him all this time and never seen just how sick he really was? But she knew the answer.

It was the same one she had for poor Lydia. She hadn't cared enough to notice what either one of them did with their lives. They were grasping, dependent people, and rather than be annoyed by them, Kate had chosen to ignore them. Now she was paying the price.

The caves. Oh, God. Jim loved those caves. Jim, a healthy Jim, who had no doubt walked every inch of those black mazes.

A man could lose an army in those caves. He would most certainly have no trouble losing one woman.

Hawke swore, pacing back and forth in his room in the Planters Hotel. He paused only long enough to glare at the neatly mustachioed blond in the impeccably tailored tweed suit. The regional director of Wells Fargo operations on special assignment from New York—Wade Parsons.

"Quit acting like a caged tiger," Wade groused. "You'll get over the shock soon enough."

"They coded me a wire two days ago telling me you were coming. I've been achin' to break your neck ever since. There's no excuse for not telling me. None. I could see not telling Dan." He slammed a hand down on the bureau. "The fact that I should be watching Kate, not meeting with you, isn't helping your chances of living through the night."

"It had to be secret, top to bottom. We had to find out who Blanchard's inside man was. You know it. I know it. You're a professional. Act like it."

"If anything happens to Kate . . ."

"She's been fine for eight months."

"Collier's a powder keg waiting to go off. He thinks he's in love with her, for godsake!"

"Jealous?"

Hawke gripped Parsons by the shirtfront, then thrust him back in disgust. "I wondered why she suddenly had a military escort back to Leavenworth."

"I told her you requested it. Besides, you were too caught up with Kate's charms to pay strict attention

394

to your job."

"You know what getting Blanchard meant to me."

"I heard rumors."

"Then leave Kate out of this." Hawke crossed to the door. "If you're finished?"

"Just about. Any idea yet where Collier's hidden the papers on Blanchard's operation?"

Hawke paled. He'd followed Collier and Lydia out of town on more than one occasion, watching the man climb out of his wheelchair to disappear into an underground cavern. "I've got a pretty good idea," he said quietly. "But someone else will have to get them."

"Fine, just tell us where to look."

"Tomorrow. Right now, I'm going to check on Kate."

"Going to make contact this time?"

"No."

"You're a fool, Hawke. I saw the way she looked at you. I wish to God she'd looked at me that way." He raised his right hand, striking a theatrical pose. " 'And when Love speaks, the voice of all the gods makes heaven drowsy with the harmony.' " He grinned, scratching his chin thoughtfully. "Now that I'm here, if you're really going to be fool enough to leave her fancy free, perhaps . . ."

Hawke slammed the door on his way out.

Stopping at the Continental Hotel, he was surprised to see that Collier and Kate had already gone. He was careful not to be seen by anyone who might recognize him.

As he kneed his gelding toward Kate's house, he fought down a growing sense of unease. Kate could take care of herself. He'd spent much of the last eight months convincing himself of that.

He'd been in Leavenworth, or rather camping on

its outskirts for five months, slowly, methodically, continuing to piece together the ugly puzzle of Frank Blanchard's relationship with Leavenworth's former sheriff, Jim Collier. The more pieces he found, the sicker he got.

The nights he'd sat watch outside her house were the hardest, knowing she was inside asleep in her bed. His whole being ached to be near her. But that could never be. Never. And over these eight months, he had at last accepted that fact.

But because Kate was the innocent caught in Blanchard's web, he had made it his personal business to stay assigned to the case even after Blanchard was dead. He'd had to do some bitter accepting with Blanchard, too. That the man had gone to his grave not even knowing who Anne was, or what he'd done to her, what she'd done to herself.

Sometimes he allowed himself to dwell on how intertwined Kate's life was with his own. Blanchard and her father. Blanchard and Anne. A San Francisco hotel room. A Leavenworth hotel room. Almost as if the fates were trying to tell him something. But always he would shrug it off. Too many ghosts haunted his past. Too many dead people he loved.

He hitched his horse two blocks from Kate's house and approached it with even more caution than was his habit. His unease escalated.

The front door was wide open.

He drew his gun, edging along the side of the house to the door. Ducking low, he peered inside.

Lydia's body lay sprawled on the parlor floor. Keeping the gun at the ready, he eased into the room. He knelt beside her, feeling for a pulse in her neck.

It was there. Very faint. Gently, he shook her.

She moaned softly.

"Lydia, Lydia, can you hear me? Where's Kate? Where's Collier?"

"Shot me. Shot me."

"Where's Kate?" He fought an unfamiliar panic. Collier had played his hand tonight at dinner, and something had gone wrong. Tonight. The one damned night he hadn't been watching her. And now Kate could be in terrible danger. She could be . . .

"Lydia, where's Kate?" His voice was harsh, but he controlled his anger. He knew Lydia's part in all this. But it was a part controlled by weakness, not malice.

Her eyes fluttered open. "Mr. Hawke?" she choked, obviously not believing what she was seeing.

"Where's Kate?"

"She loves you so."

"Where is she?"

"Jim . . . he . . . shot . . . me."

He thought about telling her there was a doctor coming. But no doctor could help her now.

"My . . . medicine . . ." she whispered, reaching for the powder scattered in the broken glass. "I need . . ."

"Where is Kate?" His voice was near despair, the fear that perhaps her body lay somewhere else on the grounds tearing at him.

"Kate . . . yes. Kate." Lydia coughed up blood. "Jim . . . took . . . her . . ."

"Where? Where?"

Lydia's breath caught. She tried to force the word past her lips, tried to help Kate, tried . . . The word was her last. "Cave."

Hawke sat back on his heels, trying to control the

fear that had controlled him since he was seven years old. Trembling, he staggered to his feet. He would tell the sheriff. He would get a posse together.

No. Collier would panic. He might shoot Kate.

The cave.

God in heaven. The cave.

Hawke climbed on his horse, the animal balking at the terror it now sensed in its rider.

Kate was in the cave.

Kate was in the cave with a murderer, a madman.

Kate.

The cave.

Monsters in the dark.

Chapter Thirty-three

Kate woke up screaming. She sat up, eyes wide open, seeing nothing. Rubbing her eyes, she opened them again. She saw nothing but the deepest darkness she had ever known.

She reached out wildly, her hand scraping across the damp wetness of cold stone.

Anger overrode her fear.

"Jim! Jim Collier! You light that torch right now! Damn you!"

"Now, now, Kate darling," Jim murmured from somewhere off to her left. "What have I told you about cursing? No light until you apologize."

His wheedling voice clawed along her spine, making her skin crawl.

"Keep it dark then," she snapped. "That way I don't have to see your ugly face."

She felt him groping toward her. Quickly, she backed away.

A match rasped along the rock wall, the tiny flame dancing satanically across his already dark features. "You shouldn't do that, Kate. You shouldn't try to hide from me. No one can hide from me in these caves. They're mine." He giggled, a strange, high-pitched sound to be coming from a man's throat. "No one else even knows where they are but you and me and Lydia. And we all know what happened to Lydia."

"If you really love me, you'll take me home."

"Oh, I will, Kate darling. I will. But first you have to learn to do what I tell you. You're a very disobedient woman. Very bad. And you've only been here one night."

"I don't have to obey you or anyone else. Now take me home."

"But then, I don't have to obey you either, do I?"

He let the match drop, plunging them into darkness once again. Kate had never realized how utterly black a world without light could be. Even on the cloudiest nights of a new moon, she could always see just a little. But here, there was nothing. Nothing.

She held her hand in front of her face, staring at it, her eyes straining, straining to focus. Absolutely nothing.

Jim had led her through tunnel after tunnel, criss-crossing, backtracking, standing tall, crawling. All without any kind of light at all. Not a torch, not a match. Nothing. Not until he'd stopped here for the night.

She laughed. The night. Would she ever see the sun again?

"Take me home, Jim. Please?"

"That's better. See, I told you, you could learn to love me."

She shivered, glad at least that he had never shown more than the mildest interest in a physical relationship with her. With Jim, when she could understand him at all, he seemed most interested in controlling people, manipulating them to do things his way—his methods most often including whining and self-pity. He had a way of grating on people until they finally

400

did what he wanted, just to get him to shut up and leave them alone.

"How long are you planning to keep me here, Jim?"

"I told you. Until you learn to love me."

Wonderful, she thought grimly. That should be along about the time feathers grew on frogs.

"What if I said I love you now," she whispered, glad of darkness so he couldn't see her face screwing up in disgust.

"Ah, Kate, I'm afraid I wouldn't believe you. I have a schedule all worked out, you know."

"Schedule?" Her breath caught in her throat. "What do you mean? Damn you, Collier, how long are you planning to keep me in this mausoleum?"

"We're going to have so much fun together, so much fun."

"How long, damn you!"

"I think you'll love me just fine in maybe five or six years."

She sank back against the wall. "No."

"You're very bad, Kate. It will take at least that long." He giggled hysterically. "But don't worry, I'll bring us plenty of food and water. There's an underground spring in one of the tunnels. You'll never have to worry. As long as you never make me too angry. Because then I might go back to town for awhile."

His voice lowered to its more natural tone, which somehow chilled her all the more. "And I'll tell you the truth, Kate. You might be able to find your way out of here purely by accident in three hours, if you made every turn, every twist exactly right. But make one wrong turn, make two wrong, make three, and you could crawl through these caves a hundred years and never, ever see the sun again."

Hawke sat in front of the mouth of the cave, trembling so violently it took him three tries to shove his gun back in its holster. It was dark outside, just past midnight. He wasn't afraid out here.

It was dark inside, just past midnight. And he wanted to die just thinking about going into that hole.

Kate was in there. Collier had hidden their tracks well, but no one could cover up everything. She was in there. Alone with a murderer.

"Kate! Kate, forgive me. I can't. I can't." He climbed to his feet, stumbling to his horse. He gripped the pommel, but didn't mount. "Kate."

He led the horse to a small glade and tethered him there. Slinging his saddlebags and canteen over his shoulder, hugging the rifle under his arm, he walked back to the cave.

"One step at a time. One step. One."

He took one step and bolted back two. He leaned his forehead against the outer wall or rock, the coolness of it chilling the sweat that dripped like rain from his body.

"Kate is in there. Find Kate. Kate will hold you. Kate will make it better. Find Kate. Find Kate."

He stepped into the darkness that would have no dawn.

Kate had no idea how much time had passed. She slept fitfully, waking often, her perception of day and night gone. Edging her way along the wall, she found the canteen of water Jim had left for her. She'd become fairly adept at doing things by feel. She opened the canteen and took a drink, then took care to set it back in precisely the same place.

Jim had been gone for hours. Or was it days? She hadn't apologized for calling him a son-of-a-bitch, and so he'd announced he was going to teach her a lesson.

402

If she could get her hands on his gun maybe she could force him to lead her out of this maze. She shook her head. What would the threat of a gun do? He knew she couldn't shoot him. He was her only way out.

She lay back, stretching the muscles of her arms and legs, trying to keep herself as limber as possible. Exercise helped keep her warm as well. The cave's temperature was as constant as its darkness, somewhere around sixty degrees. Jim had taken the blankets as part of her punishment.

There were times when she was certain she would wake up. That all of this was a grotesque nightmare. Jim Collier was not keeping her prisoner in a cave. Jim Collier was a gentleman law officer who occasionally escorted her to dinner, to a play, and only once had asked for a kiss. She had refused, and he had never asked again.

She rubbed her hands along her arms, trying to ward off the hopelessness that more and more settled over her. She was so desperate, she had actually started to imagine Hawke was somewhere nearby. The absurdity of the notion made her wonder if she was going mad.

Not only hadn't she seen Hawke for eight months, but even if he should come for her now, he would never know where to look. And the very last place Travis Hawke would ever look was a cave.

She sighed, allowing her thoughts to drift to more pleasant things. Hawke's lovemaking. She trailed a hand over her shirt-covered breast, tracing a lazy circle around her nipple. What would it be like to make love in this cave, totally sightless, depending fully on touch and taste and scent and sound?

She groaned. "Damn you, Hawke. Even in the bowels of the earth I want you."

"What did you say, dear?" She heard Jim scraping toward her.

"Nothing."

"Did I hear you apologizing?"

"No."

"Do you want me to leave again?"

"Do what you want." At least if he left, she would be free to dream again of Hawke. Her brows furrowed. Now why was she remembering how he had almost drowned that day in the Missouri? She had closed her eyes in the muddy water and sensed where he was, because she loved him.

Sensed where he was.

Because she loved him.

She sat bolt upright.

Hawke was in the caves.

Chapter Thirty-four

Kate tried to shake off the feeling. It was absurd. How could Hawke possibly be in the cave?

But the feeling would not go away.

Hadn't she always been able to sense when he was near her? At the Columbia stage depot. In the murky depths of the Missouri. Always she knew. Yet, she cautioned herself, hadn't she felt that he was watching her in Leavenworth these past months, only to turn and find no one there.

Eight months. It was a long time. She missed him so much. Perhaps she was just imagining . . .

No. He was here. Hawke was here in the cave. Looking for her. She felt something else too. He was scared to death.

She grabbed her canteen. Crazy or not, looking for Hawke made more sense than sitting in a corner like a whipped hound.

A match flared. She blinked her eyes at how blinding the tiny flame seemed after hours of black.

"What are you doing?" Jim demanded, eyeing her suspiciously.

"Getting a drink. What does it look like?" She popped the cork from the canteen and tipped it to her lips.

"Just so you don't get any notions about finding your way out of here. Who knows, you might get yourself so twisted around that even I couldn't find you, until it was too late."

"Dead sounds a helluva lot better than being in this cave with you."

He cocked his pistol. "Does it really, Kate? Or are you just being a bitch again?"

For once she swallowed her pride. If she wasn't insane, Hawke was here. This was no time to get herself killed for the sake of an insult or two to Jim Collier. "I'm sorry," she whispered. "Truly. It's just being in this darkness all the time. It's . . . it's frightening."

He wasn't watching the match. It burned down, singeing his fingers. He dropped it, sucking in his breath sharply, but he quickly struck another. "You be good and I'll take you outside in a day or two. Just for a few minutes, mind you. Would you like that?"

"That would be wonderful. Thank you."

"See how much more pleasant the time can be when you're nice to me?"

"Yes, Jim." To herself she added, "Drop dead, Jim."

He crawled over to her, sitting with his back propped against the wall, and began telling her about his childhood in Ohio. Three brothers, three sisters. The litany droned on. She paid no attention. Why did he have to come back now? She dared not make him angry. If he left the cave, he might stumble onto Hawke. Jim was at home in the caves. Hawke would have no chance.

Something Jim said brought her abruptly back to the here and now.

"What did you say?" she demanded. "What did you say about my father?"

"Don't be angry, Kate."

"I asked you what you said?" She gripped her hands together, to keep from attacking him. She couldn't have heard him right.

His voice had taken on that whining tone that set her teeth on edge. "He came to me. Told me Frank Blanchard was somebody named Jacob Sinclair. That he was a crook, stealing money, killing people. But, you see, I already knew all that. I'd been working for Frank for years, long before Leavenworth. We always kept in touch. I used to run opium for him. That's how I kept Lydia happy."

"You're worse than Blanchard. To use a badge . . ."

"Don't be sanctimonious, Kate. Your father was like that. I didn't like it at all." He let the match wink out, and continued his story in darkness. "Of course, I pretended to investigate Frank."

"Don't," she whispered.

"Bryce had already sent you off to school, because he knew Blanchard would be out to get him. One night he came to me with this plan to set Frank up. He told me he had some top officers at Fort Leavenworth in on the plan. I went along with it, then I told Frank all about it. Only problem was, Bryce hadn't really told anyone about the plan. Except me. He'd set me up, too. When Frank didn't take the fall, Bryce knew who'd warned him."

Tears slid down her cheeks.

"I thought I'd throw him off by getting shot. Only that old bastard Scot actually had me brought to your house to recuperate. One night he drugged my supper and found out there was no bullet hole in my back. He should never have done that."

Kate wished she had a gun.

"He wrote letters to some Wells Fargo people who'd gotten in touch with him. Told them all about me and Frank. Only he never got to mail the letters. He'd even

407

written one to you. Too bad for Bryce I had a man working for me in the post office. He said I was never to see you again. That was the worst of it. He was going to keep me away from you."

His laughter was soft, demonic. "You see, there never were any witnesses to what happened to Bryce. I made up the names of the two teamsters. I shot him. Then I shot that stupid ox. I shoved Bryce's body onto the horn right where the bullet . . ."

Kate threw herself at him, screaming, screaming. She tore at his face with her fingernails, pounded at him with her fists. Her fury was so great that at first she outmatched him in strength. But he recovered from the surprise of the attack, and Kate grew rational enough to realize that she had to get away from him or he would kill her. And then he would never pay for what he had done to her father.

She tried too late to grab for his gun, but managed to grope for and scoop up the matches he had laid beside him. Hands outstretched, she ran blindly forward, wanting only to put distance between herself and Collier.

She longed to call Hawke's name, but to do so would be to warn Jim that Hawke was in the cave. Pausing, she listened but could hear nothing but the sounds of her own labored breathing.

She sank to her knees, Jim's voice echoing and reechoing through the tunnels, until it seemed as though he surrounded her. "You'll never get out, Kate. Never. I'll kill you, Kate. Kill you. Kill you. Kill you."

She closed her mind to the terror, closed her mind to everything but Hawke. He was here. She would find him.

Trembling, she stood up, letting her hand trail along the wall to guide her forward. Forward? Forward where? With all of the tunnels, the crawlspaces, the dropoffs she could be going in an endless circle.

Jim had killed her father. All along it had been Jim. Not Blanchard. Blanchard hadn't lied when he'd told her he'd felt cheated. He'd wanted to kill her father, but Jim had beaten him to it. All these months she'd been living under the same roof with her father's murderer.

She walked, stumbled, crawled for what seemed like hours, finding nothing. Pressing her back against the wall, she sank to the cave floor, trying to hold back the sobs threatening to engulf her. "Hawke, where are you? Hawke, please. I love you." *What if he's not here? What if you're crazy?*

Angrily, she swiped at her tears. "Stop it!" she muttered. "Hawke doesn't take to caves. It isn't going to do him a mule's whiskers worth of good for you to fall apart, Kate McCullough."

Blowing out a deep breath, she sat there, thinking, just thinking, about Hawke.

Then she was on her feet again, moving slowly, but moving. An hour later she stopped, dropping to her knees. He was here. Just ahead. He was here.

"Hawke?" Her voice was no more than a tiny sigh.

No response.

She inched forward, then stopped again. She could hear him breathing. "Hawke?"

Nothing.

Calm down, Kate, she told herself fiercely. *He is breathing. He's all right. Maybe he's asleep. Yeah,* another part of her said, *and maybe he's a grizzly bear. Or Jim. Maybe your stupid senses are off about Hawke after eight months of not seeing him.*

She reached out her hand, unable to stop its trembling. A sob of unimaginable relief tore through her as she encountered an achingly familiar well-muscled arm. "Hawke, oh, God, Hawke."

She wrapped her arms around him, pulling his head against her breasts, crying, crying in a way she never had before in her life. Minutes passed before she could control the sobbing. Only then did she realize that while she was holding him, he was not holding her. He hadn't moved, hadn't spoken, since she'd touched him.

"Hawke?" She traced her palm along the side of his face, gently moving her fingers to his eyes. They were wide open. "Hawke, it's Kate. Hawke, talk to me."

Nothing.

She noticed then how shallow his breathing sounded, recalling his reaction to the much shallower cave at Elm Creek. He'd only come near that one to keep her from being hurt in the hailstorm. He was inside this black pit for the same reason — for her. Damn, how long had he been like this? Groping about, she found his canteen. She tipped some water into her hand, smoothing it onto his face, leaned forward and kissed him on the mouth. He didn't move.

She grimaced. "It worked for Sleeping Beauty." On her knees, she pulled him close, held him, stroked him, loved him. Still, he didn't move.

Trembling, she kissed the top of his head. "You are not going to panic, Kate. You are not going to panic. He'll be all right. He'll be all right."

She sat down beside him, lifting his nearly rigid hand in her own. For long minutes she held it against her cheek. "I love you, Travis. I love you so much." She shifted to snuggle against his chest.

A violent shudder coursed through him. His arms, still tense, closed over her back. The trembling increased, as he tried hard to speak.

She kissed his forehead, his cheeks, his mouth. "I'm right here. I'm right here."

"Kate. Kate."

He held her so tight she couldn't breathe. But she

didn't mind. "It's all right. It's all right."

His mouth found hers. He kissed her, his lips at once tender and savage, building within her the sweetest tension she had ever known. And she thought of her fantasy to make love to him in the darkness, gasping as his hands tore at the fastenings of her dress, until he had freed her breasts to his loving.

His urgency, his need transferred itself to her. She was as desperate, as eager for the joining as he was. She clawed at his clothes, forcing them from his body, revelling in the rippling power of the muscles that danced beneath her fingers.

He pressed her against the rock floor, touching, tasting, his hot breath fanning the flame that already seared through to her soul.

And then he was inside her, and she forced him to hold himself still, as she reached between them to explore the wonder of their mated bodies. She touched him, touched herself, glorying in the animal cry of pleasure ripped from his throat as he quivered above her.

"Kate, let me, let me. I need . . ."

"Yes, yes. Oh, Travis, yes."

He was moving, driving himself against her, her legs locked around his hips. The feel of her, the taste, the scent, the sound. Only Kate. Always Kate. In the darkness, the darkness—the power of her love surrounded him with light.

Afterwards, long afterwards, she nuzzled her face against his neck. "Caves can have their good points," she murmured.

He shivered.

"How long have you been in here?"

"I don't know. Couple of days, I think. I'd be all right for awhile, telling myself I'd find you. And then, there were just times . . ." He spoke with more diffi-

411

culty, and she knew he was fighting a fierce embarrassment, if not outright self-disgust. "Times when I just couldn't . . . couldn't move. Like when you found me." He stroked her hair. "Some knight in shining armor, huh?"

"Don't you ride yourself down in front of me, mister. You're here, aren't you?" She kissed his cheek. "Dan Parker told me about that horrid man at the orphanage."

"Jeffers is dead. There's no such thing as werewolves, and yet, when I get near a place like this . . . I . . ."

"You're here, damnit. You don't have to apologize to anyone. Ever."

He kissed her, feeling more at peace with Kate in the darkness than if he'd been sitting with angels on a sunsoaked field.

Stretching languidly, she murmured, "How did you know Collier was here anyway? In fact," she sat up, "how did you know I was here? And how in the hell did you know about the cave?"

He chuckled. "Which one of those do you want first?"

"All of them." She reached for her dress and tugged it over her head. Without the warmth of Hawke's body even the flimsy material provided some protection against the bone-seeping chill of the cave.

"I know all about Collier," he said, pulling on his pants, "because I've been building a case against him for eight months."

"Wells Fargo?"

"I work for them."

"I know." She told him about the reporter in San Francisco.

"I'm sorry I didn't tell you before."

The full impact of his earlier words slammed home.

"Eight months! You've been building a case against him for eight months! The eight months I haven't seen you? You've been in Leavenworth part of that time, haven't you? Haven't you?" But she gave him no chance to either confirm or deny it. "Damnit, Hawke, you've been letting me go out to dinner with a maniac for eight months!"

"I've been keeping a close eye on you."

"Then what are we doing stuck in this cave?"

He explained his ill-timed meeting with Wade Parsons.

"Wade? An agent? Why that low lying son-of-a-cow pie! He borrowed twenty-five thousand dollars from me for those damned plays of his."

"Oh, the plays are legitimate. He's the most sought after dinner guest in New York."

Another thought struck her, more disturbing than the others. "Did you know Collier killed my father?"

He hesitated. "Not until a couple of months ago."

"And you didn't tell me? Damnit, Hawke . . ."

"If we moved against him too soon, the people he's in this with could get away clear. That's why I was watching out for you." He curled his hand around hers. "Collier killed Farley and Sheridan last year on the trail. He poisoned the whiskey Dan Parker drank. It was Collier Dan saw skulking around at Fort Laramie that night. It was even Collier who sent the gunman to kidnap you at Elm Creek."

She pulled her hand back. "You should have told me."

"Maybe. But I didn't. I can't change that now."

"I love you. How could you stay away from me for eight months? How could? . . ."

"I told you. I want no ties."

"And I'll say it one more time, Travis Hawke. You are one helluva liar."

413

"I am getting very tired . . ." He stopped, groping toward her, shoving his hand over her mouth.

Her one thought. Jim.

When she nodded her understanding, Hawke released her, inching away. Kate hugged the wall, following after him.

In the barest of whispers, Hawke said, "He's up ahead. Close. Real close."

Kate kept her voice equally low. "What are you planning to do?"

"Get you out of here."

"You know the way out? In the dark?"

"I marked the walls, but we'll have to use a torch."

"But if he's out there, we can't . . ."

"We can't stay here." He took a deep breath. "Damn."

"What?"

"Damn, damn, damn." His voice was shaking. Kate touched him. So was he.

Her arms went around him, but he pushed her away, shoving his gun in her hand. "Be ready, Kate." He was trembling violently.

"You're there, Kate, aren't you?" came Jim's high-pitched giggle.

Kate twisted to listen behind her.

"I know you're there, Kate. I'm going to light my torch and then I'm going to shoot you. Unless you've decided to be a good girl."

Kate edged away from Hawke. Jim couldn't know he was here.

"Have you decided to be a good girl, Kate?"

She rounded a bend in the tunnel. If Jim lit the torch now, he would not see Hawke. She stuffed the gun behind her in the waistband of her pants. She was shaking herself, aching to go back to Hawke, but terrified that to do so would bring him a death sentence from Jim. Collier hadn't just killed her father in his insane plot to have her to himself. He had coldly and methodically killed at least three other men, strangers. And he was well aware of her love for Hawke. She had not the slightest doubt that he would take infinite pleasure in killing him.

She started at the sound of a pistol cocking. "I'm not going to ask you again, Kate. I'll just start shooting."

"All right, all right," she snapped.

Quickly, she scurried back to Hawke. He hadn't moved from where she'd left him, lost to his personal hell.

She stroked his hair, leaning close to his ear. "I don't know if you can understand me right now, but I'm going back to Jim. I can't take the chance that he'll find you. He's threatening to shoot his damned gun. The ricochets in here could kill us all." She kissed him. "I love you so much, Travis."

Sidling back down the tunnel, she called out to Jim, "Don't shoot, I'm coming."

"Always giving the orders, Kate." He struck a match, a torch flaring to life. "Come over here."

Shielding her eyes, she walked toward him. "Why don't you give this up and take me out of this maze?" She took an instinctive step to her right as she noted the sheer dropoff to her left. The blackness seemed to fall away forever.

"I told you, when you learn to love me." He kept his gun pointed at her.

She stopped five feet from him. "I'll never love you, Jim."

"I've been thinking about that, Kate." His voice was softer, more chilling than she'd ever heard it. "You were always telling me about this Hawke you loved."

She stiffened. Dear God, he didn't know . . .

"I always thought it was a chaste, pure love, Kate.

415

But the other day when I was gone, I talked to Walter over at the Planters House. He told me you spent the night in Hawke's room. I was very disappointed."

She said nothing.

Jim crossed to a bracket he must have pounded into the stone at some time during his long explorations of the cave. He mounted the torch, facing Kate with his .44. "You weren't chaste at all. You indulged in carnal love. I tried to change you, tried to show you that my love was better. But now, I'm going to prove it to you." He started to unbutton his shirt with his left hand.

"What are you doing?" Kate demanded, trying without success to draw rein on her mounting terror.

"I'm going to show you that carnal love is not the way, Kate." He shrugged off his shirt, then opened the fly of his pants, shoving them down past his hips.

"Touch me, and I'll kill you."

"I have the gun, Kate."

"I'll still kill you."

He stepped out of the last of his clothes, then fondled himself in front of her. "Take your clothes off, Kate darling. I'll teach you things that Travis Hawke could never have shown you."

"Like how to be sick! You're a pig, Jim."

He raised the gun. "Take off your clothes."

"You rape me, Collier, you'll be raping my corpse."

"Whatever you say, Kate," he whispered, aiming the .44 at her head. "Whatever you say."

Somewhere in the dark prison of his irrational terror, Hawke heard the words. "I love you so much, Travis." He clung to them, clawing his way back to the light. Kate. She loved him. Loved him in spite of how he'd failed her. Kate. God, Kate. What else had she said? What? Then it hit him. "I'm going back to Jim."

"No. No." He struggled to sit up, though he could not control the trembling. With stiff fingers, he felt around beside him. Damn, he'd forgotten. Kate had taken the gun. Staggering to his feet, he scraped along the wall toward the flickering light at the end of the tunnel.

What he saw sent a shaft of rage ripping through him, holding at bay his agonizing fear. Collier was naked, his gun levelled at Kate.

Hawke stepped away from the cave wall. "Leave her alone, Collier!"

Jim jerked the gun toward Hawke. His eyes were crazed. "Here!" he shrieked at Kate. "You had him here with you! In my cave!"

Kate lunged at Jim, shoving him back, then leaped for the torch, jerking it from its bracket and tossing it into the abyss, plunging them all in darkness. She didn't have to see Hawke to know where he was. All but running, she threw herself into his arms.

He pulled her close. "Forgive me."

"For what? Saving my life?"

Jim fired his pistol, the single shot seeming to echo and reecho into eternity, the bullet zinging off wall, ceiling and floor.

"Do you still have my gun, Kate?"

She nodded, then realizing how ridiculous the gesture was in the dark, she yanked the Colt out of her pants and settled it in his hand. He hunkered down next to the cave wall, pushing Kate behind him. "Get down the tunnel out of the way."

"I'm not leaving you."

"Damnit, Kate, I've got enough problems in this cave."

Jim's demonic cackle filled the chamber. "There'll be no mercy now, Kate. No mercy. I'm going to kill you and your lover." His voice cracked slightly. "You should have loved me, Kate. You should have loved me."

Hawke cocked the Colt and waited. "When he fires, I'm going to aim for the spark from the barrel. You keep behind me, Kate, or so help me . . ."

She hugged his waist. "I love you."

Jim fired. Hawke's answering shot followed instantly.

Kate let go of Hawke to hold her ears against the sound of the fusillade loosed by the echoes of the cave. When at last the deafening noise subsided, she leaned close to him. "Do you think you hit him?"

"No, you didn't hit him!" Jim shrieked.

Kate gasped, twisting around. He was now behind them. Though she could see nothing.

"I know every crack, every crevice of this cave. Every one! You're dead, both of you! Dead!"

Hawke slammed his body on top of hers as Jim's gun sounded again. Kate screamed as Hawke's body jerked. The gun fired again. And again. Or was it the echoes? She couldn't tell.

Hawke's weight seemed limp against her. Tears streaming down her cheeks, she shifted a hand to his face. She nearly fainted, when he hissed against her cheek, "Hold still!"

"You're alive!" she whispered.

"And shut up!"

"Don't you tell me to shut up."

He kissed her, cocking his Colt and turning toward Jim's last position. She felt him stiffen, sucking in his breath.

"You're hurt!" She ran her hands along his body, searching for the wound.

"I'm all right." He felt in his pocket for a match.

"You're not going to light that?" she cried, guessing his intent. "Jim will kill us both!"

"I don't think so." Hawke struck the match.

Kate stared at Jim's lifeless body sprawled barely two feet from where they sat. A bullet had entered his head behind his left ear.

"Ricochet," Hawke said.

"How did you know?"

"He landed on me when he fell."

"That's why your body jerked?"

"Uh huh."

"Then you're not wounded?"

"Nope."

"But you were acting like . . ."

He grinned, pulling her down into his lap. "You had your hands all over me, didn't you?"

"Damn you, Travis Hawke!" She slapped away his hands, climbing to her feet. "You scared me half to death." She stomped down the tunnel. "I'm leaving."

"Jim's dead. I'm the only one who knows the way out."

She stopped. "I hate you."

He chuckled, getting to his feet beside her. "Still leaving?"

"You lead me out of this cave," she hissed, "so that I can see your ugly face when I kill you."

He continued to bait her, as he struck match after match, following the arrows he had drawn to lead them out of the cave. It was only after they'd passed through a particularly narrow passage that she realized what he was doing. He was shaking, trying with everything in him not to give way to the paralyzing fear of his childhood. The best defense he had come up with was her anger. She smiled. She would be more than happy to accommodate him.

She kept him furious, herself furious, until at last they saw the light of the sun spilling into the tunnel ahead of them. Kate shrieked with delight, streaking toward it. "We made it! Hawke, we made it!"

She hurried back to him, seeing that he was now taking it one step at a time, his eyes wide but determined. "I love you," she sighed, giving him a hug. "You are one helluva man, Travis Hawke." With her arm around his waist, she led him out into the sun.

He sank down in front of the cave's rocky front, shaking his head. "If I never do that again . . ."

She kissed him. "I love you. I love you. I love you."

Trembling, he pulled her against him and kissed her thoroughly, then lay back, allowing his face to drink in the warmth of the golden fire in the sky.

"So, have you given up?" she asked, long, languorous minutes later.

"Given up?"

"On leaving me out of your life."

"Don't start, Kate."

She stood up. "Don't start? Don't start? Travis Hawke, it has been *started* for six years! What you're saying is you want to end it! Still, after all this, you don't want me, you don't love me."

"I love you, Kate."

"Damn, you just can't admit it, can you? You're insufferable. I mean why else would you have gone into that damned cave than if you loved me! But no, you deny it at every turn. You refuse to accept . . ." She stopped. "What did you say?"

"I said I love you, Kate."

She was on her knees beside him. "You do? You admit it at last?" She threw her arms around him. "Oh, Travis, I've waited so long for . . ." She leaned back, eyeing him closely. "Love isn't enough for you, is it?"

He gripped her arms. "No. Admitting I love you isn't enough. Kate, everyone I've ever loved, ever cared about in my life is dead. I can't . . . I can't take that chance with you. I survived the others, but, oh, God, Kate," he pulled her close, "I could never survive losing you."

"Everybody dies, Hawke," she said gently, burrowing her hand beneath his shirt to caress his chest. "It's what goes on between the being born and dying that counts. I know what you're saying about losing someone you care about, because I feel the same about you." She kissed him. "But I'm willing to take the risk. To know the wonder of having you today, I'm willing to chance losing you tomorrow."

"I can't do that, Kate. I can't."

"You went into that damned cave. You can do anything."

"No." He stood up, gripping her hand and pulling her up with him. "Come on, I'll take you home."

"Hawke, this is stupid. If you think . . ."

He put an end to her tirade with a kiss. She threaded her arms around his neck, crushing herself against him, her breasts swelling to his exploring hands. But then abruptly, he put an end to it, setting her away from him. "We're leaving. I've got this Blanchard-Collier case to wrap up."

Her heart lurched. "You're not leaving Leavenworth?"

"I have to."

"For how long?"

"It'll probably take a couple of weeks to take care of the arrests and the paperwork."

"And then you'll be back."

He didn't answer.

"Hawke?"

He walked over and retrieved his horse. Kate stared at the ground. He offered her a hand to help her mount. She ignored it. "If you think I'm going to keep asking," she said quietly, "you're wrong. I'm not going to get old waiting for you to stop being a fool."

He fingered the reins of the horse. "I'll be back,

Kate."

She bit her lip. "Promise?"

"Promise."

"Two weeks?"

"Maybe three."

"And then we can talk about . . . about us?"

He caressed her cheek. "We'll talk. But I can't promise there'll be an 'us.' There're still things you don't know about me."

"I know all I need to. I love you."

He shifted his gaze, as though seeing that love reflected in her eyes were somehow painful to him. But he had promised to come back. And, for once, he was not lying.

He was not lying.

It was what she clung to, when he left her in Leavenworth and once again rode out of her life.

Chapter Thirty-five

Kate stared at the fast flowing waters of Elm Creek. She hadn't cried. Not once in the three months he'd been gone. She wasn't going to start now. Tugging off her boots, she tested the water with her toes. Chilly, but tolerable. Just as it had been . . . Furious, she shook off the thought.

She had the rest of the day and the night. The two-hundred wagon freight outfit she was heading wouldn't be here until late tomorrow. She'd left Rafe and Dusty in charge and ridden ahead. She wanted to be here alone.

Sighing, she undid the buttons of her shirt. What rankled most, she supposed, was that when he'd said he'd be back, she would've staked her life he was telling the truth. Damn.

She shrugged out of the shirt, then fiddled with the lace ribbons of her chemise. She'd taken to wearing the frilly undergarment lately, because it helped camouflage the added fullness of her breasts. One of the ribbons snagged into a knot. Grimacing, she poked at it with a fingernail.

"Can I help?"

She whirled, crossing her arms in front of her, at

once furious and overjoyed. The fury won out. "Get out of here! You had your chance, and you lost. I told you I wasn't going to grow old waiting for you to stop being a fool."

His boots crunched on the sand as he crossed to a boulder and sat down. "Collier had Blanchard's papers in the cave. I, uh, sent someone else in after them." He seemed oblivious to her rage, droning on as though he'd last seen her yesterday instead of three months ago, as though she gave a damn about Collier, about Blanchard, about anyone, now that he was here. "Blanchard kept a record of everything. Billy Langley was only supposed to scare you. The outlaws who attacked the wagons were supposed to do the same, and maybe kill a few bullwhackers in the process."

She stepped closer to him, though she said nothing.

"All the names of his inside men were there in black and white, it took time to coordinate the arrests. This close we didn't want any of them slipping through the net."

Her voice was unnaturally soft. "No, we certainly couldn't have them slipping through the net. And, of course, you certainly couldn't have sent a letter or a telegram."

"You have a right to be angry."

"Angry? Me?" Her hands were curled into fists. "Why on earth would I be angry?"

"It's better this way."

"What's better?" Damn him. She was so shaken by his unexpected arrival that she could hardly think straight.

"That you hate me."

"Hate you?" So that was it. "Oh, no, Hawke. You don't get off that easily. I'm angry, yes. But I don't

424

hate you. I love you. I'll always love you, whether you like it or not." She lifted his hat, brushing her fingers through his hair. "Always."

He gripped her waist, pulling her down onto his lap. "I've thought about nothing but you these past three months. I love you, Kate. But there is just no way we . . ."

"Buffalo chips! You didn't ride all this way to tell me you never wanted to see me again. You could've just never come back."

"I wanted to say it to your face."

"You wanted me to tell you you're a fool and convince you to stay." She caressed the line of his jaw.

"It's over, Kate. I can't chance your dying."

"So you condemn us both to a life of misery." She undid the first button of his shirt.

He stood up, dumping her unceremoniously onto the sand and tromping off upstream. Grimacing, she grabbed up her shirt and jacket and hurried after him. He halted near the small cave on the north bank, hesitating, then crossing over to it. He stooped down at the entrance, peering into the dark interior. She hunkered down beside him. "Are you all right?"

He shook his head. "I came here to end it between us."

"I know."

"Damn it, Kate, I want you to hate me, but all I can think about is how you held me in this cave, how we made love on the sand, how much I can't bear to be apart from you." He gathered her to him, his kisses hungry, desperate. He loved her, loved her with a passion born of lifetime of aching loneliness. But she had to understand why he couldn't stay.

She traced his lips with the tip of a finger. "What is it? It's not just that you're afraid I'm going to die.

What?"

"I can't talk about it."

"Then it must have something to do with Anne."

He stiffened. "What's that supposed to mean?"

"I mean it's the only subject you've ever closed off to me. I remember the day Blanchard died, you said you would have killed her yourself." His heart thudded against her hand. "Why did you say that, Hawke?"

"Damn."

"I'm not going to give it up. You must know that by now. I love you, and I'll fight for you 'til my last breath."

"You won't want me after you know . . ."

"Try me."

His jaw clenched, fighting the memory of that last night. "Maybe I should tell you. Then you can know why it has to end."

She bit her lip, suddenly nervous. For so long she'd wanted this last piece of the puzzle — to know the awful hurt that kept him from her. But what if it destroyed what they had together? What if . . . No! She pushed the thought away. She held him, listening, as slowly, haltingly, he told her about Anne.

"She was three months pregnant. I'd left her alone for a few days, while I was on a Fargo assignment. But I came back early." Unconsciously, his body tensed as though girding himself for a physical attack. "I found her on the bedroom floor." He closed his eyes. "There was so much blood."

Kate tightened her hold on him. "A miscarriage?"

"Blanchard . . . Blanchard . . . had given her some kind of powder to keep her from getting pregnant. But she hadn't taken it the last time we . . . the last time . . ." He stopped. "I'm sorry."

"It's all right. Just tell me."

426

He was staring off at nothing, but she knew he saw everything just as it had been that night. "I put her to bed and sent for the doctor. But he said there was nothing he could do. I sat beside her. I held her hand." He was trembling, trapped by his memories as surely as he had been trapped by the cave. "When she opened her eyes, she looked so scared. I told her everything would be all right. That we would have other babies."

Kate longed to stop him, but she couldn't speak, couldn't move, as he repeated the words she knew must have ripped the heart from his body. Anne's words. "He said the new powder wouldn't hurt me, so I took it. My stomach hurt so bad. But it worked, Travis. It worked. It got rid of the baby."

Tears slid from Kate's eyes at the agony in his voice. An abortion. Anne had had an abortion.

"She was my wife," he said, "not some unmarried wench with no one to care for her or the child. It was my baby, too. Mine. She knew what having a child meant to me." He swallowed hard. "I would've taken care of the baby. I would've . . ."

"You've got to forgive her, Travis. She paid a helluva price."

"She didn't pay nearly enough!" he hissed, jerking away from her. "I hated her, Kate. Hated her! If she hadn't been dying . . ."

"Then maybe it's you you have to forgive. For not loving her. For wanting to kill her." She touched his cheek. "You never loved her, did you?"

He stared at the sky. "I wanted a family. To belong."

"And you never loved her."

He shook his head. "You see, how can you love me, Kate?"

"How can I not?"

"I'm not worth . . ."

She put her hand over his mouth. "You're worth the world to me. I love you."

"It's dangerous to love me."

She sighed, not quite smiling. Would he ever give that up? "You are one arrogant bastard, you know that? Your parents die in a flood, and you're conceited enough to believe you caused it. And Nels Svenson's heart attack. And, of course, you made Anne take Blanchard's concoction. What power you have, Travis Hawke. How many times a day does the Almighty call on you for advice anyway?"

He spoke through clenched teeth. "I spill my guts to you and this is what I . . ."

She was opening the remaining buttons of his shirt, uncinching his belt. "Shut up and love me."

"Kate, damn you. You haven't heard a word I've . . ." He sucked in his breath, as she trailed a hand beneath the waistband of his trousers. "Damn you." He groaned, his hands moving over her, firing the heat of his flesh, firing the heat of his love. "Kate, oh, God, Kate. . ." The fire blazed into an inferno that consumed them both.

Afterwards, she nestled contentedly against him. "You were doomed the minute you walked into my room that night in San Francisco, you know." She feathered a hand over his chest. "And so was I."

His eyes burned. "I don't know how you do it. But with you, I can forget the whole world. Blanchard. Anne. Crawlspaces. You make me see it's not a family that's been missing in my life. It's you. Just you."

She smiled. "It's about time you figured that out." She could tell him now. Now that she was certain he wanted her for herself alone.

"Just don't die on me, Kate."

"Not for at least fifty years. But I'm holding you

to the same half century."

"Deal."

She giggled, nuzzling his throat. "We could snuggle into a cave somewhere when we're old and gray and die doing what we do best."

"Does it have to be a cave?"

She studied his face. "You might have to reassess your opinion. After all, a cave's where we conceived our first child."

He went absolutely still. "Child?"

She touched her stomach. "Little Kate, Jr. Or Travis, Jr."

"And you weren't going to tell me?"

"I just did."

"But you weren't . . ."

"Not if you hadn't come back, no."

"But the baby . . ."

"Would've had a mother who spent all of her days and nights cursing the child's fool of a father. But a mother who loved the child and the father more than life."

His hand slid to her abdomen, caressing it with such tenderness, she had to blink back tears.

"You are one helluva woman, Kate McCullough."

"I had to be to land one helluva man."

"I love you."

"You're damned right." She brought his hand to her breast, her flesh warming to the sweet intimacy. She smiled. "You never could lie to me, remember?"

His midnight eyes darkened, as his desire flamed hot. And then he took her, where only Hawke could. Travis Hawke, her dream. Travis Hawke, her life.

THE BEST IN ROMANCE FROM ZEBRA